ABamber ♡

The Lost Hourglass

Book 1 in The Moonlight, Amber and Time Trilogy

Alice Bamber

Cover lettering: Farjana Bithi
Cover design: Francesco Musiani
Character Portraits: Francesco Musiani

ISBN-10: 9798491152483

Dear Reader,

This world will always be here for you. May it bring excitement and everlasting hope into your life.

Love
Alice

Ghosting

There is magic to be stolen at dawn. Today the skies are vibrant with fiery colours, like the world is just seconds away from igniting. A young wolf prowls in solitude over cool desert lands beyond the city walls, fatigued but leisurely as she returns home after the night's long hunt. Olive trees rustle idly, bearing witness to the breeze as it snatches dreams from the dusty eyelashes of early risers. It snatches ash from the hemline of my cloak, too; a cloak that's far too heavy for this hot, hectic city, but one I must tolerate for the sake of stealth – because although I'm also a wolf cub caught in the dawn chorus, and my eyes are a surprisingly similar shade of amber to the blazing sky overhead, my hunt is far from over.

I pause to perch on the edge of a rooftop, taking in the scene below. This is the moment when life is caught between the serenity of night and the urgent, unapologetic breaking of day. It's wild, magical and dangerous. Know why? Because I *live* to bathe myself in moonlight, and it's all but disappeared now. With no veil of darkness, I'm increasingly at risk of being seen...and that's not something we want.

The solution is to keep moving, so I jump down from my rooftop onto a lower house, feet kicking up grey ash as I land and take off running. In the middle of a washing line strung between two squat, shabby sandstone buildings to my left, a nightingale chirps a sweet but aggressive song. He is loud and persistent, like a petulant child trying to be heard over his arguing older siblings; and he grows even more so as I pass him by. Is he serenading me, or urging me to mind my business and leave him be? Feel like it might be the latter.

The robed figures I'm following through Ioxthel's streets have also lost the safety of night, enough for me to discern a pair of slender ankles beneath the hemline of one of their cloaks. A large hood covers her face, but it's clear my target is a woman – the swinging gait and delicate slope of her shoulders tell me that. I don't know who she is, or the man who strides beside her also garbed in dark fabric, though I have my suspicions about him. His footsteps are light on the sandstone cobbles despite his height and broad frame. The slipstream of his cloak wafts the scent of smoke and arnica to the rooftop, indicating his recent visit to a healer. My nose instantly twitches in irritation, threatening to break the silence, yet sneezing now would be a disaster. I haven't spent my night waiting with bated breath to stalk these two, only to be discovered *right* when things start happening...

Something moves in my periphery. I skid to a halt and settle in a crouch, ready to pounce or flee...but there's no one there. Letting out a breathless laugh, I watch the silhouette of an owl race over the flat rooftop as it flies overhead; and grimace when I realise his form is cast from sunlight, and not my favourite thing ever...besides my best friend and my silver bow, that is.

Not the moon.

It's a warning I should return to the Guild, before the early risers throw open their shutters or the patrols double in number, but I don't heed the caution. I need secrets like the breeze needs dreams, and I'm well on my way to witnessing them.

Members of the Guild – the city of Ioxthel's armed forces – can be fickle and indistinct, like the shadows these two soldiers are trying to keep to. Guilders are usually anything but easy targets, honed into sharp weapons before they've outgrown their childhood years. I would know, because I am one. Fortunately, I'm also better than the shadows these two covet. I'm a ghost...or rather, I'm incredibly good at impersonating one.

My marks are travelling to Alcázar, a sandstone fortress on the Western Peninsula, and home to the monarchy of Astyros - our kingdom. I stalk the rooftops behind them like a wolf cub in silent, bumbling pursuit of her prey, melting into a line of washing when they stop before the fortress's large arched gateway. My foot bumps into an empty fluted urn, no doubt eagerly awaiting a sample of next season's spicy red wines. Doesn't matter if it's hollow or full, though, because it's still rife with potential for me.

Voices drift up from the street, tickling my ears. I wait until the gates swing open before tossing the urn high into the air, launching it over the squat buildings to my left. Muscles tear in my arms at the movement, a reminder that for all my silence, speed and stealth, strength will always be a weakness...but I guess that doesn't matter right now.

Whilst the gate guards freeze and then fumble forwards in confusion towards the shattering terracotta, I jump from my rooftop to the outer walls of Alcázar, grabbing hold of the thick wisteria vines growing there. Loose scree tumbles to the street below, sure to raise suspicion, but within seconds I've scaled the wall to a forgotten water outlet hidden under the vines, cape billowing out behind me.

Squeezing through the small, crumbling hole, I land beneath the battlement in a crouch and halt, reaching overhead to ensure my bow and quiver are still in place. They are - they'd never desert me on a mission like this.

The smell of wisteria from the fortress walls clings to my clothes and fills my surroundings with a heady perfume, sure to linger long after I've disappeared, and that's the thing about ghosts, isn't it? The echo of a wayward soul never tries to hide itself. The warning signs are always there, in the unexplained leap of exhilaration in your heart or the caress of anxiety raising the hairs on the back of your neck...or in the scent of wisteria blooms when there are none.

I set off into the fortress, casting a furtive glance over my shoulder. Sentries stand atop the rampart facing the waking city, but no one looks around, like always.

It doesn't take long to locate the pair of guilders again. A sentry in a blood red sash is leading them through a series of quads and gardens – well watered, unlike everywhere else in the kingdom – to a small, circular courtyard almost entirely devoted to a raised meeting platform.

Nine people sit on a stone bench there; hooded, silent and unmoving. A thin walkway surrounds them, patrolled by a pair of sentries moving in opposite directions, and a tenth figure stands at the entrance, the only participant without a cloak. Even from this distance the pointed angles of her cheekbones and chin are visible. Wisps of dark hair are gelled to her temples to create an intricate pattern of swirls atop caramel skin. Her lips are painted in a bright crimson, her hands stained the same colour...or that's what *I* see. She is immaculately beautiful, and the most powerful person in the Kingdom of Astyros.

Queen Ruby Sabir.

An artfully disguised tyrant, leader of the secret Council meeting here this morning, and an idol to the elitist echelons of Ioxthelian society. The person I haunt most of all.

I stop in the shadows of an adjacent courtyard and peer through the gateway as the two newcomers display their wrists to her, exposing the markings of the Council; something I've yet to see for myself. Ruby smiles to signal their admittance, kohl-ringed eyes bright and astute, and waits until they settle next to their brethren on the bench before addressing the group. Her voice is assured and noble, as you might expect from a monarch whose family have held the throne to Astyros for hundreds of years.

"Welcome, my friends," she greets. "We have much to discuss this morning. I have news which will surprise most of you, and entreat both your patience and understanding in the limits of how much I can disclose on the matter. As you are well aware from these meetings, some secrets are best left veiled to protect their integrity; some truths are best left untold until they're useful to know..."

She allows herself a small, simpering smile after this. I mirror her, then roll my eyes.

"You will recall the blood oath sworn by each of you upon initiation to this Council many moons ago. For one of you, it's time that oath was transacted. The world is growing darker, and we must now put in motion forces to honour the *true* gods and goddesses of this age. For this, I seek the fulfilment of your vows...and a most impressive weapon lost long ago. It will protect the Kingdom of Astyros from its foes, and retain the glory we strive for; though first, I need a map to it...a guide of sorts. I am presently searching for this." She turns to where the group's two new additions sit – the guilders I followed here. "Lieutenant Jensen has already accepted the honour of having his oath fulfilled, and sets an example to you all in doing so. His debt will be collected during the passage rite in the Temple of Poseidon, during the full moon twelve nights hence. And *this* brings me onto yet more news, which the Lieutenant will be talking of in a moment. It concerns the arrival of some very special visitors in the city. Visitors I hope will help us in our endeavours to reclaim the glory of the true gods and goddesses."

She now takes a moment to glance over each of her council members in turn. I use the opportunity to start stashing away every bit of what she's saying into a rather haphazard vault in my mind. The name Lieutenant Jensen means something to me, and also means I was right in those suspicions I told you about earlier. Tonight, we've confirmed who one member of this anonymous council is.

"We also have some unwelcome visitors in the city," Ruby continues, her tone dropping low. "Intruders have breached our walls without our knowing of it. Our greatest enemies now stalk Ioxthel's streets, hidden, waiting to pounce."

One of the hooded council members speaks up in shock; male, with a crisp accent most often associated in Ioxthel with a life of privilege.

"Our greatest enemies? But that would mean—"

"Yes," Ruby nods. "It is as you believe. It is for this reason I search for what is without doubt deemed humankind's greatest weapon. I believe these intruders are within our walls to spy on us, and to plot for another devastating war against our people just like they did those four hundred years ago...and we cannot allow that to happen."

"What is this great weapon?"

It's the same council member speaking up again. Ruby tilts her head to the side, but doesn't deign to glance at him this time. She merely casts her cloak aside to reveal a silver censer hung on a long chain from her waist, and lights it with unhurried reverence.

"Thank you for your interest," she eventually responds, and the sudden cold edge to her voice tells me she doesn't appreciate him speaking out of turn a second time. "I cannot disclose to you what it is, but I *will* tell you that the map to it has been lying beneath our noses for years now, without our knowing."

And the Council's oath? I think, shifting forwards eagerly. *In the Temple of Poseidon, during the next full moon? What does that involve?*

Nothing good, a very familiar voice in my mind responds. *And, Skye? Someone is coming.*

The back of my neck suddenly prickles as the whispering scuff of footsteps reaches me, different to those of the sentries patrolling the perimeter of the meeting platform. These are fast, furtive and filled with purpose.

They're also overhead.

I twist sharply in search of them. A figure sheathed in a cloak of midnight is wending its way over the walls of Alcázar's courtyards, just like I might do if the daylight wasn't meddling with my stealth; and with just as much ease.

My eyes narrow.

I don't like that one bit.

I can hear the council members chanting in prayer now, the censer *ticking* softly as Ruby throws it out, puffing incense over them all...but I daren't look back. My eyes are solely focused on the leaping shadow; on the breadth of their shoulders and their aggressive stride. I hold my breath as they pass over me hiding amongst the foliage, and continue to do so when those confident footsteps falter, as if sensing an unwelcome presence lurking nearby. Sure enough, to my absolute horror, they stop and glance down...and raise a hand in mock salute.

Not good!

I flee from my hiding spot, heart lurching into overdrive - pumping way faster than my little arms do as I streak back through the courtyards to the hidden water outlet beneath the battlement, alive with fear. I've *never* been seen in the fortress during a ghosting mission before...and it gets worse.

I'm almost to the battlement when I hear the same quiet, purposeful scuff of footsteps following me, and a slow *tsk* of displeasure. Or rather, pleasure? Goosebumps spring to life as a shadow strolls out *right* in front of me, so at leisure it's like he's been waiting there for hours; except I know he hasn't because he was *just* following me.

"Morning, Skye."

I jump at least a foot into the air at the sound of my name, then become stiller than the statues in the courtyard to our left. I don't recognise the hushed, humoured voice, or the face to it, and I think that's a *very* bad thing. His hood is down now, revealing dirty blonde hair, a straight but strong nose...and a very obnoxious smirk. One of his hands rests casually on the hilt of the scimitar at his hip, the other fiddles idly with the foliage encroaching on the walkway. The gesture is easy, playful and sadistic.

"Yes," he says conversationally, as if he can see the expression of horror dawning beneath my hood. "I know your name, Skye, though I've a feeling you don't know mine yet. I'd expect Sholto, your pretend foster father, might, and that handsome Lieutenant you throw your fists at in play fight with every day." He snorts out a dark laugh. "Gosh, dear Fjord...he's so very patient, isn't he? Will you tell him Xavier sends his regards? I expect he'll be *thrilled* to hear from me...just like I'm thrilled to find you here today. Simply giddy off anticipation. Makes me want to skip tens of chapters and jump right to the part where I steal your blood as easily as you steal through the night...and the start of the end begins. I want to do that. More than I thought I would."

Goddesses, do you understand what he's saying? Talking of stealing blood? And the start of the end? Obviously I don't, and I don't respond to him...couldn't even if I wanted to. My pulse is going haywire, disbelief and dread like a cold boulder in my belly. No one knows the face that lies beneath my hood or the name given to it except the three people I trust most in life, two of whom he just mentioned - Fjord and Sholto.

Xavier tilts his head to the side, blonde locks falling carelessly over his forehead. He doesn't seem to mind my silence. "Phantoms, ghosts...they intrigue me, Skye. There's a mystery to them. A *seduction.* What happens if I t—"

I don't let him finish his sentence, just draw my dagger and lunge forward in attack. The move is impulsive and reckless, not entirely consciously done...but something in me deems it necessary. I need to leave here right now, like steam from a fiercely boiling kettle.

Xavier's blade flashes up to meet mine. The sound of clashing steel is much too loud in the still morning, our conspicuousness rife – no doubt music to the surrounding sentries' ears. We start duelling. He's far stronger than I am, clearly a very practised swordsman, but then I'm fast when I want to be, sometimes so fast even I don't understand how I do it. Cloak, limb and bow blur together as I strike, feint, dip low and spin, over and over again, until I wonder if it's difficult for him to see where I end and the air begins.

The Ghost of Ioxthel.

That's what I like to think of myself as, sometimes. A phantom vigilante haunting The Queen's footsteps, and those of her gaudy politicians. The shadow who can barely tie her own shoelaces but still tries to safeguard the poor's pitiful prospects with her unquenchable thirst for moonlight and mischief and danger, an—

Focus, Skye! the same internal voice of earlier interrupts, sharply. *You must focus! You must flee!*

I do as she says, refocusing on the fight, and promptly let out a yelp as Xavier lunges forwards and slips past my defences. I dart to the side, but he still manages to nick my upper arm in what's a surprisingly soft swipe for someone who just said he'd steal my blood...which is gross, if you think about it. I mean, I'm a thief, but I don't steal *blood.*

"Careful," he taunts. "Don't hurt yourself, Skye. We've enough time for that, yet."

I stumble away as he thrusts at me parrying the blow with difficulty. Muscles in my shoulders ache from withstanding the hit. I told you speed and stealth are my friends but strength is always a weakness – and so, you should know, is a distracted mind.

I stagger back, trying to put distance between us, trying to figure out how to pass him and escape from here. My thoughts reel with horrible vigour as I do, because how on earth does he know my name? How did he even see me in the thick shadows of the gardens? No one sees me when I ghost unless I want them to, and I *didn't* want him to.

Please focus, Skye! the voice in my head pleads. *There are others coming!*

In my periphery two figures are running towards us. I'm positive it's the guilders from the Council – the ones I followed here. I can hear shouts and running footsteps from the alcázarian guards, too, which means we're about to be rushed.

I surge forwards in another reckless move, narrowly avoiding Xavier's swipe overhead as I fling my own blade out to the side. He twists to avoid a cut to his ribcage, creating an opening for me to breeze past...and you know what he does as I slip away?

He laughs.

A full on belly laugh!

My feet are in tandem with my heart as I pelt over the battlement, running too fast for the stunned sentries on either side of me to react. Cool air pilfers the hair beneath my hood as I jump over the edge, snatching my breath and stinging the shallow cut in my arm. I throw my cape out to slow my fall, but the impact is still jarring. Shockwaves ripple through my bones and teeth as my legs crumple from the impact. I let out a moan, rolling and stumbling to the side, then set off haring beneath white canvas awnings and rooftops littered with open spice vessels. Only when I'm well out of range from any arrow or throwing knife do I turn, heaving in great lungfuls of air sweeter than relief itself.

Framed by one of Alcázar's famous battlement archways, away from the flurry of sentry activity, a figure stands watching me. He raises his hand in mock farewell, just like his mock salute earlier. I think I can even see his obnoxious smirk from this distance, too.

Don't like it.

Don't like him.

I start running again, back towards the Guild. My thoughts race faster than my poor, shocked heart and fatigued limbs; but I'm not just wondering who on *earth* Xavier is and how he knows me, and how he *saw* me. No, in being prematurely chased away from the Council's meeting, I've also missed vital information on the city's visitors Lieutenant Jensen was due to speak about. Who are they? Clearly someone important enough for Ruby to bring up during one of her precious meetings, just like her mention of our "greatest enemy" infiltrating the city.

You should know I'm in no doubt about who they are. Nixen. Guardians. Folk from Elysium on our streets. On *my* streets! Goddesses, if they really are here, it's for the first time in hundreds of years...which means we should be really worried, and really afraid.

Really excited, too.

Fjord

Technically, I'm not supposed to be a guilder. Not just because I'm terrible at being prompt and polishing my leather armour, and even worse at following the rules, but because for the first half of my life I lived orphaned on the streets, sleeping beneath upturned boats in Ioxthel's forgotten harbour and stealing every single morsel of food I ever ate. Stealing every single thing I ever owned. It's just a fact of life that ruffians don't become soldiers, mostly because they spend their life breaking the law with pride, and so they don't *want* to become soldiers.

And I'm not saying *I* was the weird one who wanted to.

That's not true.

I love breaking the law, I love stealing, and I *love* the ruffians – especially their leader, my best friend. I suppose the opportunity for me to become a guilder just came along, and I took it.

I wake up the morning after spying on Alcázar to the sound of the city's bell tower chiming noon...and fly out of bed. I'm late for sparring just like I was yesterday, and the day before that, and I promised him I wouldn't be.

Hurriedly, I wash my face and brush my teeth with stale water from the brass pitcher beside my bed, then shrug into my shirt and breeches and leg it towards the quads. There's a Lieutenant waiting for me in the shade at the base of the barrack steps, gazing pensively into the gardens beyond; and these aren't luscious like those I hid amongst in Alcázar last night. These are dry and scraggly, lacking the vigour rain brings to the natural world because it *doesn't* rain in Ioxthel, and any accessible groundwater here is spared for drinking, washing, or grooming Ruby's stronghold.

The Lieutenant is different to the Council member of last night, too. He's younger, with dark hair and regal features, and surprisingly creamy skin for someone who spends their life under the sun; and he has the posture of a soldier who's really very excellent in a fight, but perhaps in another life would definitely have suited high society – unlike me. His leather armour is buffed, the colour of burnt terracotta, and the shirt beneath it immaculately pressed. Even his breeches are free from creases...which is also so unlike my attire.

This is Fjord. My well-presented and unwaveringly gracious friend, and the boy I pretend is my older brother because he acts like one, and I am so beyond desperate for a family it's sort of...sad.

"Hey," I say breathlessly, rushing to a stop beside him. "Sorry I'm late. I forgot to put on my shoes...then had trouble tying them."

He turns to me with a smile, and immediately offers a bow of greeting. He doesn't address the fact I'm late because he never does, even though every single time I promise him I won't be again.

"Good morning, Skye."

"Morning," I echo.

"How're you? Besides troublesome shoes?"

"Tired."

"Oh?"

We fall into step together, hastening through the gardens towards the dusty sparring quad that, at least during the day, is always occupied with guilders training. Gnarly orange trees laden with white, wilted blossom cast dappled shade over the paved walkways here, and I can just about hear the feeble drip of a nearby fountain.

"I spied on Alcázar last night," I explain as we walk. "Didn't get back until very late, or early, then struggled to fall asleep because my brain was going, you know? Thinking up a storm like it does. It was a cloudy one, lots of rain and wind and problems."

"Ah," Fjord nods in understanding, wholly used to me saying something that sounds so...odd. "Does that mean it was a good ghosting session?"

I nod vigorously. "One of the best, actually, if a little strange."

"Strange?"

"Mhm. I ran into someone in the fortress, and—" I stop abruptly as a pair of guilders walk past us on their way back from sparring, sweat beaded on their skin, hair damp and wispy. That will undoubtedly be me in a few short minutes, except I'll also be redder than those fat tomatoes sat sweltering in the sun...the ones I stole from the markets the other day. "But I'll tell you later," I go on, quieter. "Somewhere less open."

Fjord gives me another nod of understanding, and gestures me through the quad's arched entrance. He, Sholto, and *the* best friend ever – leader of the ruffians – are the only three people that know I often run wild through the city, bathing in the freedom of moonlight and spying on Alcázar. Ghosting, I call it. Fjord always listens to my stories, and in fact *all* the nonsense that comes out of my mouth, with patience and genuine interest...and I love him for that.

"So, you ready?" I ask, as we find an empty spot to practise. "To be bested by my goddesslike fighting prowess?"

"I've a feeling not."

"You never are."

"No."

"You should up your game."

"Yes."

It's a joke, because Fjord is a much better sparrer than me. I watch as he starts taking off his armour, a fond, humoured smile lifting the corners of his mouth. I'm thinking how lucky I am to have found a friend in him for five years, and feeling quite happy that he *always* smiles around me. I love being the one to light up his handsome features.

Then I frown.

His expression is endeared, but it's not reaching his eyes like it usually does, and it's already started to fade. Turns out I'm not the only one who might be tired. Taking a closer look at him, Fjord also appears weary and stressed; with faint bruises under his eyes, and the sharp angles of his face even tauter than usual.

"You ok?" I blurt out. "I forgot to ask you earlier, didn't I? Just started rabbiting on about me...but you look tired, too. Don't tell me you were also ghosting last night?"

His free hand immediately lifts to the tiny hourglass hanging from a long leather cord around his neck; the one I never see him without. He starts fiddling with it reverently before he realises what he's doing, and drops it.

"I'm fine. Thanks, Shye."

"You sure?"

"Yes."

"You *sure?*"

He turns to set his armour down on the ground, I think in a ploy to hide his expression from me. "Yes. I'm fine."

I narrow my eyes on his back, then dart around him so we're facing one another. "Are you absolutely s—"

"Good morning."

I peer quickly over Fjord's shoulder and see Sholto, the man I think of as a foster father but who everyone else thinks is my uncle - even though he's not - nearing us. He's fairly short, with a delicate frame that hides surprising strength, and these fathomless brown eyes that look like they've seen *everything* life can offer. It's like he's hundreds of years old, the way he speaks sometimes; the hallowed wisdom he comes out with.

Now *here's* the reason I'm a guilder even though I shouldn't be - here's the opportunity I seized.

Sholto.

He was the one who took me, the skinny street rat with ravenous eyes and a savage rip in her soul, in off the streets seven years ago and put a roof over my head. The Guild's roof. He did so on the very same day I stole his wallet, and nurtured me as best a middle-aged man with a busy schedule, and a slight superciliousness to his character, can.

I owe him.

He taught me how to read and write, and how to be normal...or as normal as a ruffian turned soldier, but really still a ruffian, can be. Which means I still usually fail at biting my tongue every second of the day, *still* elbow my way through crowds but do throw an incautious apology over my shoulder afterwards.

Still can't read very well.

And, yeah, Sholto can be really stern and indifferent sometimes - too much for my hot, rough ruffian mind and manners to understand - but that doesn't matter, when I think of how generous he's been for the past seven years.

He offers us both a short bow as he arrives. "Lieutenant Winters, and Skye. How are we this morning, besides late? I've been waiting for you on the other side of the quad."

"I'm preparing myself to be bested," Fjord says, as usual quickly diverting the topic of conversation *away* from something that would make me culpable for our tardiness.

Sholto turns to me. "Does this mean you're finally on good form today?"

"Yeah," I lie. "Totally. I'm not tired at all."

"Then let's set to."

That's something else you should know about Sholto, alongside his wisdom. He doesn't dither around.

He takes up his usual coaching stance some metres away, arms folded and weight evenly balanced on his feet, brown gaze considered and unfooled. I shrug myself back from Fjord and start bouncing side to side, limbering up. I'm stiff from leaping off Alcázar's high battlements onto the rooftops, which makes me think for about the fiftieth time already since waking up...who was that Xavier fellow? What was he doing in the fortress at dawn? Why was he smirking so smugly? How did he know my name? How did he know who I spent my time with...the people I'm with right now?

My jigging slows a little at the last question. In front of me, Fjord has taken up sparring stance; and there's no need for him to warm up, because I bet you he's been awake for hours, practising with people who must actually challenge him. I peer through the stringent sunlight, waiting for the faintest tremor of his muscles that might warn me of his impending offence.

His shoulders tense.

Then, in the blink of an eye, he strikes.

I use my forearm to block him and then drop low, sweeping my leg at his ankles. He steps over it easily, and blocks my following strike with his elbow. There's no real force behind the blows from either of us, because this is practise.

I let out a giggle as he lunges for me, dipping beneath his arm and popping up behind him. I like doing that, and I mean to kick him gently in the backside after it, but Fjord is ridiculously fast for someone of his height and build. He's already facing me, knocking my shin aside with a swipe of his forearm and then lunging into my space again. I do the same as before, dipping beneath his arm and popping up on his other side, laughing – except this time I also trip over my own feet in the process, and then I start tripping over my thoughts, too.

This is how sparring tends to go, every single day. I'm late, talk big beforehand, get distracted within minutes or even seconds...and end up losing.

I know it.

Fjord knows it.

And so does Sholto.

"Συγκεντρώνω, Skye," he scolds from the sidelines, his voice low with dissatisfaction. "You were doing well. Don't slip now. Keep focus."

I want to tell him I'm trying, but it's a lie. I *have* started slipping, and now I'm falling fast down a rabbit hole in my weary, wandering mind; a burrow brimming with problems to solve, questions to dream up and storms to think...

Xavier.

The figure cloaked in cloth of midnight.

What *was* he doing in Alcázar? Did his presence have something to do with the weapon Ruby was discussing with her Council? Ioxthel's special visitors? Or perhaps the city's unwelcome Nixen intruders? Is *he* Nixen? With his blonde hair, there's a chance he doesn't hail from Ioxthel, but then I have fair hair - freaky silver hair, to be precise - and I do hail from here.

Or...I think I do.

I can't remember much of my early childhood until just a few years before Sholto found me, but...I guess that's beside the point.

The point is, who is he?

I'm looking forward to bringing this up with Sholto, after sparring. He probably knows the answers to my questions, because he seems to know everything - and it sounded like he and Xavier might have a history together, albeit a sour one.

And if Sholto *doesn't* have the answers, then I'll just have to find them out for myself, which means more ghosting. That won't be so bad, though with Nixen intruders and other more welcome visitors in the city I expect surveillance everywhere will be upped, and not just in Alcázar. Thinking more on it, I'm a little sceptical over who Ruby's guests are and why they're here. Very rarely, if ever, can one say The Queen's intentions are wholly good.

"It is the will of the gods and goddesses."

The monarchy's longstanding claim of divine intention, backed by the gaudy grades of politicians that stay tucked away in their fortress, is a very difficult one to stand against. No one wants to question it and be the one cursed for their impiety by the gods and goddesses, even when their family's measly earnings can only buy enough bread to feed four of their five children because the tax levy was ridiculously heavy one year for *no* apparent reason, or when it's used to justify conscription into the Guild.

That's what I like to think I do, though, in ghosting on Alcázar more nights than not. I like to think that in my own way I'm standing against Ruby, stealing *back* the riches she and the upper echelons of society take from Ioxthel's hard working peasants, because they're greedy, and I don't like greed.

And...I'm a ruffian, so I like stealing.

Love it.

That's not to say I don't revere the gods and goddesses just because I don't believe Ruby and her family are doing their bidding, though.

I do revere them.

I really do.

I think they're all very impressive and mighty...except I don't pray to them very often, and I steal a *lot*, which is a sin, isn't it? I guess I'm impious already. Probably cursed already, too, and I don't like to dwell on that thought, so let's not? That's the virtue of having a mind that thinks up a storm. It's going so fast it's so easy to get lost in the next cloud, the next probl—

Skye?

The very same voice of last night speaks up in my mind; the one that warned me of Xavier's imminent arrival in the courtyards, and later told me to concentrate during my fight with him. It's a voice that's distinct from my thoughts and instincts, a female who doesn't sound like me...but still obviously *is* me. She's in my mind, so she *has* to be me. I call her "my counsel" and I usually listen to her, because she's great at giving advice.

Yeah? I reply. *You ok? Haven't heard from you in a few hours.*

I'm ok, thank you.

What's up?

Nothing's up, she echoes, sounding a little awkward at the phrase. *You just might want to focus...again.*

I blink back to the here and now, and veer away as Fjord easily slips past my pitiful defences, moving in close enough for me to see every mesmerising fleck of green in his hazel eyes. He taps me under the chin and on the sternum, signalling if he were an enemy, he could have easily landed the blows. I stand frozen for a second, then huff out a heavy sigh of defeat. My arms fall limply to my sides, mouth tipping into a sheepish smile – I was slow then, and it's blindingly obvious I wasn't paying attention.

"Disappointing, Skye," Sholto calls from the sidelines. "I told you to focus."

"I tried."

"Did you?"

"Yeah. For a while."

His lips press into a stern line. "Go again."

I raise my arms, widen my feet and lock my thighs, taking up sparring stance. "Ready?" I ask Fjord, hoping he sees the penance in my eyes.

To my surprise, he shakes his head, wiping a wrist over his damp forehead. "I think I'm done actually. You're obviously tired, and the sun is getting to me."

My hopeful smile slips into something filled with regret. "I'm sorry, Fjord. I know I was so bad then, but I promise I'll try harder to focus. And...what do you mean, the su—"

"Finished so soon?" Sholto asks, drifting closer. Obviously he didn't hear him the first time.

Fjord isn't Sholto's student. In fact, as a Lieutenant in the Guild he's actually his senior, but they're still close colleagues and I think they knew each other before I knew either of them. Even though Fjord and I are now firm friends, basically surrogate siblings, I know he's fulfilling Sholto's favour in sparring with me every day. It's unusual for him to quit halfway through a session, though, no matter how mindless our fight is or how distracted I am. Fjord is *the* most patient person I know - so kind, and forgiving.

I examine him closely. He looks as serene and sincere as he always does, but there are definitely shadows of tiredness under his eyes, emphasised by the full sun overhead. He's also holding the hourglass pendant hanging from his neck again, turning it over reverently like I might my silver bow.

Like it's incredibly important to him.

"Same time tomorrow, then," Sholto suggests lightly to him, without questioning further how unusual it is for him to finish early.

"Well actually, it's my day off," I pipe up hopefully. "So..."

21

"So you'll have even longer to spare? Even more energy to focus your mind? That's good news, Skye."

I grimace. "Well, I think I'll have *less* time to spare, Sholto, because Enye and I—"

"Your training sessions are more important than your friends," he interrupts, fixing me with a firm stare down the bridge of his nose. "Today's sorry excuse for one has made that more apparent than ever. I expect you here at the same time tomorrow, please. We go again...for longer than five minutes."

Oh.

Ouch.

To be fair to him, I *did* bring that remark upon myself...but it still hurts to know that's all it's been. Most people spar for over an hour.

"Ok," I sigh. "I'll be here. Midday. On time. So focused. More concentrated than...Ioxthelian olive oil."

"Why don't we let Skye rest, Sholto?" Fjord suggests, bending down to pick up his armour, and giving the older man a slightly pointed look. "I could use the time tomorrow, anyway. Perhaps we both could?"

Sholto raises a brow. "Speak for yourself."

"I am, actually. I could really use the time tomorrow."

They continue observing each other. I watch them, feeling like I'm missing something, then bounce forwards and pick up Fjord's weapons belt when he reaches for it, offering it to him with a smile – an apology, for ruining today's session. He smiles back in a strained manner, returning his attention to Sholto expectantly.

"Alright," the older man finally yields. "You're lucky, Skye. No sparring tomorrow."

"Seriously?!"

"So it would seem."

I look to Fjord and *beam*. The expression soon slips when I see how weary he looks, like there's a great weight preying on his mind.

"I'm really sorry for wasting your time, today," I mumble. "I enjoyed it, whilst it lasted...and even though I wasn't on good form."

He reaches up and touches my cheek briefly, fondly. "You never waste my time, but just make sure you get some rest tonight, please? Maybe give ghosting a miss. Sleep is important for you."

I nod. "I know it is."

"I'll take my leave, now. Goodbye, Sholto."

"I'll stop by your office later."

Fjord nods, and bows to us both. We watch him walk away. Immediately, I feel the need to follow and pester him about why he's tired and stressed, if only to learn how to make him feel better, but that's not an option.

Reluctantly, I turn to face Sholto. I just know he's going to be stern with me, and chide me further. His expression is highly disapproving as we pick our way around the other sparrers towards the garden quads, his lecture imminent...

"Tiredness is selectively felt," he remarks as soon as we hit the path. "All feelings can be mastered, if you wish them to be. Thus I would ask if you strive to be the master of yourself, Skye?"

Mistress of myself, you mean. "Yes," I say, bumbling along beside him with frisky eyes; a guilty wolf cub famished from having missed breakfast, wondering if she can slink away to the mess for lunch. "Who doesn't?"

"From your behaviour today, I'd say yourself. I am really disappointed, Skye. Five minutes is a poor show."

I hide a grimace, then give the same excuse I give after every failed sparring session, "I swear I'll do better next time and be more focused, Sholto. I'm just tired from last night, and thinking up a storm about it. Something happened. Something important that I need to tell you about."

"Indeed, you *are* tired," he continues, ignoring my last remark, "and yet did I not just inform you that that can be selectively felt? You have the ability to instruct yourself unhindered by fatigue, if only you summon the appropriate resolve. Time and again, you do not do this. You're...beyond repair."

Ouch. "I sometimes try really hard to be there and to focus," I reply quietly, trying to hide my offence. "But today I was just too busy in my mind, Sholto. It was too busy in there, like a house full of guests. No chance for peace and quiet, or focus. I'm really sorry about it. I am. But last night was different to when I normally ghost and I heard some really interesting stuff and I just...would like to talk to you about it? Please? Because I have questions, and you know everything, don't you? Being so wise...and clever..."

Sholto spares me a glance at the flattery. His expression is still disapproving, and unfooled, but with a sigh he yields, "Let us walk together then, if you have pressing things to discuss with me. You're on duty in an hour? That should be plenty of time to cover what we need to, knowing how fast you talk. Wash up and meet me back here. We'll take to the streets."

I move to leave, only to twist back immediately. "Will you buy me lunch, please? I'm really hungry. Missed breakfast because of how late I got back here last night, and then had to dash to training with wonky shoelaces..."

Slowly, he nods. There's now maybe just a hint of something softer transforming his stern features. Lunch money – or any money, really – is somewhat of a running joke between us.

The Guild's interior is cool and dim, a welcome reprieve from the scorching, dry heat of the day. I bustle my way through the halls to the barracks and hastily shrug into my leather chest plate and knife harness in my room. Both pieces of uniform need a polish, because Fjord was busy last weekend and couldn't buff them for me...and I'll admit I'm not the *best* at keeping myself well presented. Before I leave, I glance longingly to where my silver bow is stashed within a narrow, self-made alcove in the stone wall beside my bed. Leaving it behind is always like walking away from a piece of myself, but for some reason I don't like wearing it in daylight – too worried someone will steal it, I guess.

Sholto is right where I left him, out in the garden quads. We leave the Guild promptly and stop at a stall selling flatbreads and salted vine leaves. He buys two lunches – both for me – before we start strolling through the streets. They're hectic with merchants peddling their wares, cajoling to passersby. Coffee, spices and the slightly sour smell of sweltering fruit stings my nose, and canvas awnings overhead provide much needed shade as we walk, dodging the children dashing bare feet over the ashy cobbles. In the recesses of a private courtyard shrouded in bougainvillea, someone strums idly on a bouzouki...and though it's not my best friend, the ruffian king, it reminds me of him.

The sensual overload is completely different to the silent streets of last night, but almost as magical; and scenes like it make it easy to miss the suffering in much of Ioxthel.

It's there, though.

In the bowed legs of toddlers and the smudged kohl rings under their parents' fatigued eyes, or on the unnatural winds that whip through the streets, constantly blanketing our city in a layer of dark ash from the volcanic eruptions on the border between Astyros and The Nether. It can even be heard in the call of the desert wolf as she pines for her lost brethren beneath the moonlight...which, you should know, is sort of an analogy for me.

A little wolf cub, mourning the family she never had.

"I'm listening," Sholto says, after minutes of letting me chomp down my lunch undisturbed. "What happened last night that you'd like to tell me about, Skye?"

I swallow a giant ball of spittle and dough, clearing my throat, "The Council held a meeting in their usual manner. Twelve members in Alcázar's smallest courtyard at dawn. They discussed a weapon, a powerful weapon that's been lost for many years, except Ruby didn't mention what it was. She was very cryptic about it, as she can be, and even chided her members for asking about it out of turn...but then she said one of their names, and we *were* right, Sholto. Lieutenant Jensen *is* one of the twelve members. He was due to talk of foreign visitors soon expected in Ioxthel, but I had to leave before he started...and before *that*, Ruby mentioned that our greatest enemies were here intruding in the city. You know? Nixen and Guardians from Elysium, sworn exiles to Astyros for hundreds of years, intruding in the city..!"

Sholto spares me a glance at my growing excitement, blinking quite serenely. Nothing *ever* surprises Sholto. "Could you tell me more of this weapon?"

I take a huge bite of flatbread, chewing vigorously. "It's powerful, and there's apparently a map to it that Ruby is hopeful of finding...a guide that's been hidden in plain sight for many years, right under her nose. Lieutenant Jensen might have discussed it more when he talked of Ioxthel's special visitors, but someone showed up and I had to flee. I'm frustrated, because it was a good meeting. A good ghosting opportunity."

"Who is *someone*, Skye?"

"I don't really know, though he seemed to know you, Sholto, and Fjord. And he knew my name..." I heave in a sudden breath, disliking what those words sound like said out loud for the first time; how real of a problem it is if someone *knows* the face beneath my ghosting

26

hood. "He said to tell you and Fjord that '"Xavier sends his regards"'", and he was pretty obnoxious about it. Really obnoxious. We fought—"

Sholto has stopped walking. "Xavier?"

"Yes. He didn't catch me or see beneath the hood, but like I said he knew my name, and we fought. I managed to run away, but it was a bit strange..." *Or scary.* "He was a very experienced swordsman, Sholto. Blonde. With this massive, smugger than a smuggler smirk."

I stop talking then, unnerved by the way Sholto's expression is shifting, tightening in a way that tells me this news for once *has* surprised him. There's a long bout of silence before he eventually gestures for me to walk on, lips pressed together. "Are you injured?"

"No. I'm fine. Just a little scratch on my arm...although I *did* have to leap from Alcázar's battlements to the rooftops, so my knees feel like I imagine yours might right now. A bit stiff because of your age. Not that you're *old,* Sholto. Not at all..."

I peek sideways at him, worried I've unintentionally insulted him; but in another sign he's unusually taken aback Sholto doesn't appear to have heard me.

"I can see why you'd be especially distracted today," is what he says. "I imagine this has been occupying a large space in your mind."

"Yes," I nod vigorously. "A big space. A big room in the house busy with guests. I was wondering who he is and why it seemed he knew you?"

"Xavier is...someone from my past," Sholto provides stiffly. "And Fjord's, too. Someone inherently obnoxious, as you astutely judged. Now, tell me more of the meeting, please, or was that all you managed to see before you were forced to leave?"

"No," I say, a little hot at the suggestion. "A blood oath taken by the Council during their initiation was also mentioned. Lieutenant

Jensen is expected to be the first to fulfil his, during the next full moon. It's happening in the Temple of Poseidon."

"Any news on what that will entail?"

"No. The conversation surrounding it was pretty cryptic, because that's Ruby, isn't it? Likes to keep everyone in the dark, and in poverty..." I take another big bite of flatbread, chewing fast. "So, Nixen and Guardians, Sholto. Intruders here in the city. What does that mean? And who are Ioxthel's special visitors that Lieutenant Jensen was due to talk about?"

"I believe they might be the royal entourage from the Kingdom of Wivern, expected to arrive here in Ioxthel soon. Alcázar is planning to host them as diplomatic guests for some weeks."

My steps slow in astonishment. "Guest from Wivern?"

"Yes."

"How did I not know about this?!"

"No one does, besides General Marco's immediate juniors. Fjord told me of it yesterday...and it's why you've managed to escape training tomorrow. We *could* use the time to prepare for this."

"Wow," I blink rapidly, really very surprised. "This is a serious thing, isn't it? A wow moment."

"It's an unprecedented situation, yes," Sholto confirms, with much more eloquence than me.

There's a backstory to what we're discussing...a reason why a royal visit from the westerly Kingdom of Wivern is so unusual, and why Nixen are deemed Astyros's greatest enemies. A reason I'm so excited and scared they're here in the city right now with their Guardians.

You see, Nixen are the distant offspring of nymphs, spirits of nature long ago descended from the gods and goddesses. They dwell in the northern Kingdom of Elysium, along with their legendary protectors, The Guardians...who I don't think are Nixen, but couldn't tell you that for sure because we don't know much about them here in Ioxthel. Really nothing much at all - except there *is* something in the history books about tethers and eternal ties, whatever they might be, and how they're insane fighters. Other than that, Guardians are a big mystery to us all...and maybe especially me, the wolf cub who'll *never* be able to tame her curiosity.

Once upon a time, everyone lived together in peace and harmony. Then the Impurity War of four hundred years ago happened, and everything changed. Nixen and Guardians turned on humans, and started fighting against us. Those who now dwell in Wivern fled before the battle commenced, but we Astyrosians stood our ground. Supposedly thousands on both sides died, and the conflict was so ferocious and destructive that the wastelands we call The Nether were created. Eventually Nixen were defeated; exiled to Elysium and forever branded as our undying enemy. As far as I'm aware, none of them have been seen within our borders since the war.

Until now.

The reason why a royal entourage from Wivern is so unprecedented is that our kingdoms aren't on good terms; exchanging only essential trade, and very little political communication. The tension is a relic from the Impurity War, because it's really not good form to desert your allies. In fact, here in Ioxthel, the saying goes that it's far better to be carried home dead on your own shield than to use it protect yourself over the soldier next to you; to use it to help you flee from your brethren still on the battlefield. Perhaps that's why members of Wivern's monarchy are travelling here, to formally apologise for fleeing from the war those four hundred years ago? Or does their visit have something to do with Ruby's weapon?

A weird, cold feeling unsettles the lunch in my stomach at the thought. Her talk of obtaining something with the power to obliterate even the gods and goddesses themselves should be reassuring with news of a Nixen infiltration, but it seems too godly, doesn't it? Mortals wielding a weapon with enough power to destroy a deity just doesn't seem right, especially when The Queen's intentions are never truly good.

No one knows what the Nixen or their lands look like these days, but there's something terribly alluring about The Forbidden Kingdom, at least to me. I'd be lying if I said I didn't yearn to see Elysium for myself. Is it the sun-kissed paradise Astyros fails to live up to? Is it cool and mountainous like Wivern? Or is it fouler than The Nether, the barren wasteland that lies between the kingdoms, whose terrain is permanently charred and pockmarked from the Impurity War? One day, I think I might set off to answer those questions...to hunt those secrets.

Thinking about it now, it's no wonder Fjord looked so tense and tired this morning. With foreign visitors from Wivern expected in Ioxthel, he'll be heavily involved in the practicalities of hosting them; as might Sholto.

"Were you invited to General Marco's meeting?" I ask him. "You usually are, aren't you?"

He nods. "I was invited, but could not attend."

"Why?"

"I'm a busy man, Skye. Unless something is compulsory, I'm usually forced to pick and choose between duties. Like now, I *should* be organising next month's patrol rota with your Staff Sergeant, Yasmine Hajjar, but instead I find myself here, buying you lunch, listening to your stomach gurgle in pleasure."

He spares me a rather stern glance, but...you know what, I think it's a ruse to cover up the fact that Sholto is withholding information from me. There's a slight tip of his chin towards the sky when he faces forwards again, an act I've learnt to read as secrecy from him. I'm sure it has everything to do with why he wasn't at Marco's meeting.

I open my mouth to press him, and probably to aggravate him in the process, but we're already back in the square abutting the Guild. Two sentries posted on either side of the large armillary sundial occupying its centre hail to the bell tower. It chimes 2 pm, signalling the start of my patrol duty...and the fact that we stop *right* outside the Guild's gates in the very same moment they finish ringing doesn't surprise me one bit, because Sholto is an excellent timekeeper.

I'm not.

I'm always trying to find more of it – to steal it back.

"You should do as Fjord suggests and get some good rest tonight and tomorrow, Skye," he advises. "I expect you to be on your best form for our next sparring session given tomorrow's reprieve. No more of this distracted nonsense, please. You're better than that, and *we* have better things to do than waste energy. Yes?"

I nod seriously, even though I bet you any number of stolen silver drachmae, or fat tomatoes, I'll be just as bad at focusing the day after tomorrow as I was today. "Thanks for buying me lunch. It was really good, and I was really hungry. Ravenous. Like a wolf."

"You're welcome. I generally enjoy entertaining novelty in life, especially when I'm not too busy to do so."

I grin immediately, and broadly. Sholto is teasing me, even though he might not sound like it, because *this* is our inside joke. Him buying lunch for me isn't a novelty. Far from it. He's done so ever since he took me in seven years ago, and as such I've never bought food for myself, or anyone else, in my life. When I'm not with him or Fjord, or eating in the Guild's hectic mess hall, I still tend to steal it. Ruffian turned soldier, but *always* really just a ruffian...and I'm gods damn proud of it.

Just minutes after Sholto bids me farewell at the gates, someone nudges me in the ribs. I turn to see my friend and fellow patrol partner, Enye Tsitak, bounce to a stop beside me.

"Drachmae for those thoughts?"

"Not thoughts, just fantasies down rabbit holes. You ready?"

She nods eagerly. We fall into step together, brushing shoulders like we've done ever since we graduated training two years ago; although Enye and I have been friends from the very first day we joined the Guild together in the same cohort, aged twelve. She's kind and diligent, with a sarcastic spark ready to be provoked when her older brother, Fin, is around. He's less ruffian than me, but definitely a little rogue and something *beyond* ridiculously handsome.

You'll meet him very soon.

"So, you excited for our days off?" Enye asks as we walk. "What shall we do?"

"Lie in?"

"Yeah, that's a given."

"Eat. Twelve meals. One for each of the gods and goddesses."

She huffs out a laugh. "I like that idea, although I had to put an extra notch in my knife harness this morning."

"Don't worry. We've all been there."

"Really, Skye? *You've* been there?"

I hum vaguely, returning her dry look with a sly grin. Unlike pretty, plush Enye obviously still growing into her body, I'm short, with jaunty elbows and ribs and tiny, busy feet; and these sharp teeth that are perpetually prepared to snarl or grin goofily, like I'm doing now. All traits are a legacy from my childhood on the streets. I guess I also have too many scars for anyone to call me pretty, which is a bummer but also what it is, right? Can't change it, so I shouldn't wish to. Far more important things to worry about, like stealing secrets on the breeze.

My thoughts return to Wivern and Elysium as Enye and I roam the streets, and stay there until the early hours of the morning when our shift ends. Muscles twinge as I ease myself out of my leather knife harness and breastplate and roll into bed. I'm exhausted, but I bet you somewhere in the Guild, or perhaps in Alcázar itself, Fjord is still awake and preparing for our Wivern visitors. I also bet you Sholto is with him, listening with eager ears for talk of Ruby's great weapon or the map to it – he likes following up on the things I spy on when I ghost.

And what of Xavier?

That obnoxious fellow from their past?

Is he tracking them, smirking from the recesses of his midnight cloak, or hunting a different prey altogether...perhaps the Nixen intruders and their Guardians?

Or is he hunting *me?*

The thought has me springing from bed to the open window, fatigue momentarily forgotten. The quad below is dark and deserted, but I still bolt the panes shut, and I still remove my silver bow from its hiding spot in the wall crevice above my bed and slip it beneath my pillow. It's not the first time I've done that at night. There's something inherently precious and protective about the weapon; and not only because Sholto gave it to me when he first took me in.

There's more to it than that.

I just don't know what.

Amber Eyes

Excitement rushes through me like freezing lemon water on a hot day when a compulsory meeting for all guilders is called the following morning. A full assembly here is rare, especially one at such short notice, and though it takes little imagination for me to know its reason given my walk with Sholto yesterday, everyone else can't stop talking about it.

Enye and I have a late breakfast in the mess hall before joining the bustling crowds walking to the bouleuterion, a tiered semi-circular meeting house my peers and I have barely stepped in besides graduation at sixteen. General Marco, the Guild's leader, is standing in the room's sunken orchestra, with Lieutenant Jensen, his second-in-command and Ruby's favoured council member, if you remember, flanking him. I expect to see Fjord and Sholto seated in the first few rows along with the other lesser Lieutenants, Sergeants and Captains, but neither are here yet. That's quite unlike them.

Enye and I shuffle along a stone bench near the top of the seating area. There's a particularly frenzied hum of conversation and anticipation here amongst the foot soldiers, probably because the newer a recruit you are – i.e. the younger you are – the higher up you sit in the bouleuterion. Enye and I graduated just under two years ago now, which means we're new, but not the *newest* new.

"I wonder how they're covering morning duties," she muses, looking down over the sea of uniforms to the two leaders on the stage. "Everyone in the Guild is here, aren't they? There's no one left to patrol the streets."

"They're probably using alcázarian sentries," I guess. "I doubt they'll return to the Guild for their briefing, and I can't see any here."

The sentries of Alcázar start out as regular soldiers trained in the Guild before specialising as personal guards and watchmen of the monarchy's stronghold. We don't see much of them once they're assigned there...except I guess I do, because I'm a ghost who sneaks into their abode in the fickle depths of night to spy on their queen.

There are two other routes guilders might follow after graduation. Ioxthelian foot soldiers like Enye and I are directed by Lieutenants like Fjord. Our kind supervise the streets on daily patrols, waiting to be drafted into action beyond the city walls...or to recover from it. Then there are the Forces of the Front, who fight in the far reaches of Astyros to protect our borders from the wastelands beyond, The Nether. Their ranks are divided into infantry and cavalry, and I don't ever want to be one of them. I don't want to leave the city or my friends, and besides...cavalry, and me?

No, thanks.

I've never liked horses, and I never will.

Warm, peppery air stirs my hair, and Enye's too. We turn in unison to see her older brother, Fin, slide onto the stone bench behind us. I say slide...but it's really a firm wedge he does, because the area is already packed with soldiers, and he's big and strong. Roguish. Irresistible. *Not* a new recruit like everyone else around us is – and from the way they're staring at him in shock, they know it, too.

"Morning," he chirps, eyes meeting mine briefly before bouncing to his sister. "How goes it?"

Enye's sigh is laboured. "Must you always seek us out during things like this? You belong in the front rows with the other Captains, Fin. Your peers."

He tips his head to the side, flashing her an impish grin. "Is it always friends before family these days, then? Don't tell me you're embarrassed to be seen with me, Enye?"

"No."

She says that quite grumpily, fooling no one. Fin's grin widens as he turns to me, and I tell myself to ignore the way my heart is jumping around like it's never seen a boy before. "What about you, Skye? You embarrassed to be seen with me?"

"No," I echo, less grumpily.

Sea-green eyes twinkle at me, just a *little* bit hooded. "Well, that's good to hear. How're you, today?"

"I think better than the last time you saw me. Definitely better than then."

"The tavern brawl last week? You know I didn't start it."

"You didn't stop it either, Fin! You just sat there, buying people drinks to watch. Offering to buy *me* a drink even though I was on duty, responding to it with your sister!"

"That is true. I'm sad you didn't take me up on that, but I enjoyed watching you swan in with your little feet and daggers to save the day. You're feisty when you want to be, Skye."

I sit up a little straighter. "My daggers aren't little. They're just as big and sharp as yours...as everyone's."

"Mhm. Yeah? You tell yourself that, trouble, whilst I think about the late hours you *also* saved...just for me."

Goddesses. There he goes, talking of midnight happenings between us in front of his sister to provoke a blush. He succeeds, just like he's succeeded for years, before the midnight happenings became something that *weren't* a joke and were sort of...real.

I fancied Fin from the moment I first saw him show up at Enye's thirteenth birthday celebrations; the older brother who'd already graduated training and was so impossibly handsome he didn't seem real. Big, strong and mischievous. Far superior to the boys my age. He was always nice to me as Enye's friend. Polite, gallant...and now over four years on, flirty. And I'm not stupid. I know I'm not very handsome like him. My elbows are still tough, sharpened seemingly forever from the street fights of my childhood, and I have these freaky amber eyes and scars which I'll tell you about soon. I know they make me look weird and definitely *not* someone in Fin's league...and I know he kisses loads of other girls and maybe even guys, but he's also started kissing *me* recently, doing other stuff with *me,* and that's something to blush about, especially in front of his sister.

"Don't know what you're talking about," I reply stiffly to him, even though I do, and so does he...and so does the friend sitting beside me.

"Want me to remind you, trouble?"

"No."

I peek at Enye. She's watching us, a muscle in her cheek twitching – either because she's fighting a smile or a grimace. I'm not *entirely* sure what she thinks about catching me kissing her brother in the gardens a few weeks ago, but she hasn't said anything bad about it, so I'm hoping maybe it's ok? Especially when she says, "Behave, Fin. No one wants to hear, or see, your obscenities at this time of day. At any time of day."

He raises a brow. "I don't want to behave, Enye. I don't know how to, especially in front of so many people. They're all watching me, and the attention is like fuel; lights up this spark inside me that tells me to do reckless things."

"How about you learn fast," Enye quips back. "Or I'll tell Skye the story of that time you did, you know, *that* back home. Twice. Then she'll see *you* blush."

"I don't blush."

This time, Enye does grin. "Want to bet?"

Fin opens his mouth, then shuts it. Eventually he murmurs, "It's always such an interesting welcome from you two."

"Yeah? Maybe you should sit with your own friends and leave us be, then. We don't like seeing you every damn day, Fin."

"Cold, Enye. You wound me, and after I bought *three* rounds of drinks for you and your friends..."

He leans back, eyes meeting mine. Slowly, so damn slowly, one side of his mouth kicks up into a small, private smile, like he's thinking of something funny or flirty or dirty...maybe the last time we saw one another, which wasn't, you should know, the tavern brawl. I feel my cheeks heat again and turn around fast, which I immediately think might be a mistake because I can feel his gaze burning the length of my spine for *minutes* afterwards.

Having more than one sibling enrolled in the Guild is fairly unusual. Ioxthel's law of conscription dictates that any firstborn child within the reaches of the city joins the Guild aged twelve to spend their lives serving Ruby and her kingdom, so it's no wonder any subsequent children are coveted by parents for their own use.

The Tsitaks are an honest family of grape growers with land just beyond the city walls. Though I'm not sure why Enye chose to join the Guild three years after her brother was conscripted, I do know she loves and misses her parents - and their farm life - dearly. Perhaps she loves her brother *more*, though, and that's why she's here...but I've never asked her. If I don't want people to know of my real past on the streets, why on earth would I seek out theirs?

The bouleuterion is almost full now, with perhaps two thousand soldiers seated. I watch General Marco murmur something to his second, Lieutenant Jensen, just as Fjord *finally* enters the meeting place. His eyes sweep over the tiers of stone benches quickly, finding me. He does that a lot - seeks me out and minds how I'm doing, like he really *is* my older brother. It's nice. He's nice. I think I should definitely apologise again for wasting our sparring session yesterday with my distractedness, but now isn't the time to think about that, because General Marco is preparing to address us, moving to the very front of the sunken orchestra.

"Good day, guilders," he begins, voice strong and steady to solicit a hush. Quiet and stillness immediately descends, and then, very gently from behind me, I feel Fin poke my spine.

Twice.

"You might be wondering why this meeting was called today at such short notice," Marco is saying, as my entire body fights a flush. "Seven days from now, for the first time in hundreds of years, Ioxthel is expecting guests from The Cold Kingdom. Guests from Wivern."

Quite predictably, a collective ripple of surprise passes through the bouleuterion. Without taking her eyes off the general, Enye elbows me in the ribs, as if to say, *Are you hearing what I'm hearing?* I nudge her back, even though I expected this. There's another poke in my spine, too, this time a little lower.

Lingering.

"Yes," Marco heeds the room's reaction. "It surprised me when I first heard the news, too. Our kingdoms haven't held discussions like these with one another for nigh on two hundred years...and as you know, those talks started and ended in hostility. The Queen is keen for this meeting to be different. She hopes for a positive outcome, and so must we all. And yet, as guilders, hope is not all we must do. Hope is not enough. We are Ioxthel's safe keepers, and keep safe this city and its citizens we *will*. Patrols will immediately double upon the entourage's arrival in the city. Your seniors are aware of this, and will discuss the new schedules with you in the coming days. Though Wivern's officials will be staying in Alcázar, you should expect to see them on the streets. The Guild will be working closely with its brethren amongst the fortress sentries to remain vigilant of our guests' movements. I will endeavour to keep you informed of anything important in meetings like these, but it goes without saying that these are unprecedented times and your work should be exemplary, guilders. All of Ioxthel is relying on you to keep our streets safe. I hope you understand the gravity of this, and step up to the challenge." He pauses for effect, eyes sweeping over the masses, before ushering his second to the stage. "Lieutenant Jensen will now discuss arrangements for the arrival of the entourage itself, eight mornings hence."

Jensen's broad frame moves forward, dwarfing his boss. He's a gruff looking fellow with a thick beard, heavy brows and strong features, but we already know his feet can be surprisingly light on cobblestone at dawn, if he wants them to be. I'm positive no one but Fjord, Sholto and myself, and his fellow cloaked companion we still haven't unveiled the identity of, know he's involved with Ruby's Council.

He starts talking logistics for the day Wivern will reach Ioxthel, divvying up responsibilities between units. Enye and I are in Delta together, and are expected on the city wall to monitor the guests' arrival. It's a surprisingly good allocation given how lowly we are as young foot soldiers.

I let my mind drift throughout the rest of his address, instead imagining what his oath with the Council might entail. Ruby mentioned a passage rite back at their meeting in Alcázar, so perhaps he's undergoing a transition in his status within the group? It's impossible to know anything really, other than the inescapable debt a blood oath entails; for if it's not fulfilled, if the given word was sworn falsely, you provoke the wrath of Horkos, the God of Perjury. He's known for placing *horrible* curses on people for all eternity if they don't honour their word – curses like throwing the wrongdoer off a cliff, or promising to destroy the wellbeing of every heir or heiress born of their blood thereafter.

I think that's the worst curse I've ever heard of, to be honest. Entire lines of families living in immeasurable suffering just because their great, great, great-something grandmother had a bad day and refused to honour her word helping the village farrier shoe his horses...not that I blame her for that, because horses are dangerous and definitely to be avoided. But it's still a chilling thought, that those types of curses could be waiting for you just around the corner, or indeed placed upon on you without you knowing.

It's not long before General Marco takes to the stage again. "We cannot forget that this is our city, guilders. These guests must abide by our laws. Should you come across a situation where they aren't doing that, use your judgement and your training to inform your actions; and if you have time to, please consult a senior. They can bring the matter before me." He nods to the Captains and Sergeants in the first few rows. "We have a duty to keep our people and their livelihoods safe. I'll be relying on you heavily for this over the next few months, and so will our Queen. Let's do her proud, together."

Excitement erupts after the two men stand to attention, then leave the sunken orchestra quickly, dismissing us. Enye and I file out amidst mayhem, and with so many rows of bodies between us I miss Fjord and Sholto leaving...not that I saw Sholto arrive, thinking on it.

"That is *not* what I expected from this morning," Enye says from beside me as we hit the open air, her eyes wide with surprise, cheeks flushed with excitement. "Did you, Skye?"

"No," I lie.

"I'm glad we have these two days off now before patrols double. We'll be run into the ground for weeks with it. What should we do, today and tomorrow? How should we make the most of them?"

"I thought we figured that out yesterday."

"Eat? Sleep? Repeat?"

"Yep."

She peeks at me. "Ok, but just know I'll probably need to put *another* notch in my dagger belt if we do. I'm expanding like an orange swelling in the sun at the moment...unstoppable, set to burst."

"Well," I grin, "I'll do it for you, if you want? You can just sit still looking pretty, drinking your family's wine...and because I'm awful at sitting still, I'll dote on you. Feed you up, watch you burs—"

"Can I join?"

My heart jumps at the low interruption. I turn quickly, and find him right there looking greatly humoured...

Outside, without the bodies of other juvenile foot soldiers packed around us, it's impossible to miss how Fin's shirt isn't tied properly and his hips are free from daggers, suggesting he woke up *just* before the meeting and isn't on duty yet. There's a day of stubble and a slight pink puffiness to the skin beneath his eyes, like he was in the sun too much yesterday. Knowing him, he fell asleep in it. Fin falls asleep anywhere...with anyone.

I open my mouth to respond to him, to riposte back, but lose the words when I see his gaze is doing *exactly* the same to me as mine is to him – but his is so sultry. Fin has incredibly sooty lashes, a weapon made for wiling people like me to do his will. I've never met anyone so persuasive, or who uses their powers so shamelessly.

Beside me, Enye huffs out a very frustrated sigh, as if she *knows*. "No, Fin. You can't join us. Get a life. Get your own friends."

"I'd like to steal yours, actually."

"You can't."

"Not even for two minutes?" He turns to me, blinking wide, innocent eyes. "Walk with me, Skye? Please? I'd be honoured."

You don't even need to say please. "I was just about to have lunch."

"So I heard. I'll be quick, only a few minutes."

"A few minutes?"

"Yeah, just a few."

I glance at Enye. Her eyes are narrowed on her brother, her arms firmly folded...but there's a very, *very* slight tilt to her lips, as if she's hiding a smile.

She returns my gaze, raising a brow. "What? Don't look at me, Skye. It's your decision."

"Yeah, but we were going to have lunch..?"

"Was that a yes? Great gods, I think it was..." Fin seizes my wrist and tugs me forwards. "I'll have her back with you in two, Enye."

"Sure you will."

He grins at her, then me. Startled, pulse meddling with my ability to walk properly, I let him guide us beneath the stone stoa running the length of the Guild's meeting rooms. It's rapidly clearing of guilders dispersing to their respective duties for the day. Scented air from the surrounding gardens greets us, and although the walkway is completely shaded, I very soon start sweating...because Ioxthel is hot, and so is Fin. And before you condemn me for being quite so guileless, so helpless to his charm...it's only him that makes me like this. No one else. No other boy, or girl, or any of my seniors in the Guild. Fin is just Fin, and he meddles with my ability to think and just *be* like no one else.

"How're you doing?" he asks lightly as we walk, dropping my wrist and draping a lazy arm over my shoulders. Half of me wants to shrug it off, the other half...not so much. "Interesting meeting just now. What do you think of the Wivern entourage?"

I think I'm going to say something even more stupid than I usually do. "I think I'm not sure what to think about it. Building bridges is always good, but it's been a long time since the two kingdoms met like this, hasn't it? Tension is bound to linger...like when you bump into someone on the street who used to be your enemy but you haven't seen in years, so the bad blood between you is sort of over, but it's sort of not, because you've had bad blood in the first place. That's how imagine the lingering tension between the kingdoms will taste...just like really old, bad blood. Grotty. Very grotty. But, uh, what do *you* think?"

"I think you say some hilarious things."

"Mm," I feel my cheeks heat. "Yeah, I sound stupid a lot of the time. Young...even though I'm seventeen." *Or I think I am, but I don't know exactly when my birthday is...or what birthday it would be...and I don't know why I'm reminding you of my age, as if it would matter to you. As if I want you to know I'm not a child.* "I know I sound that way," I repeat. "Especially when I'm nervous."

"You're nervous?'

"No."

He spares me a humoured glance, "I didn't say you sounded stupid or young, Skye. Far from it. I think tension *is* bound to linger...like old, bad blood."

"Yeah?" I clear my throat. "Well, who knows if it really will taste grotty, because I've only ever tasted fresh blood. I suppose most people have only ever tasted fresh blood, right?"

Another humoured glance thrown my way, this time one that's also highly bemused. "What're you talking about?"

It's quite obvious I need to shut up. "Like...when you snick yourself with a dagger during practise or something and have to stop the bleeding somehow. That type of fresh."

Fin brings us both to a stop at the end of the stoa, dropping his arm and tapping me on the nose. "Generally you're supposed to avoid cutting yourself during training, Skye. Why not save that for the beefy fellows in Ioxthel's rowdy taverns who think you're rude getting in the way of their fists, and decide to push you over?" His lips twitch. "You know, you were wrong earlier. I didn't just sit and watch that brawl happen. I only sat and watched *you* start swanning in, and as soon as you hit the deck and Enye hauled you out of there I used my big, sharp daggers and set the world to rights."

"The worlds to right?"

"No, the *world* to rights."

"Oh...what does that mean?"

He taps my nose again. "It means, do you really think I'd let you or my sister get shoved around?"

"I...didn't see you move from that table?"

"Mhm, well I expect you were too busy ducking tankards, but I shouldn't worry. I got the γάιδαρος who threw them at you. Put the drink you declined to good use."

"Really?"

His lips tip up and stay there. "Really, Skye. And I could go on, and tell you I did my mother proud, but I promised Enye I'd have you back with her in two minutes. So...to the point. Guess who I overhead talking together yesterday?"

"Who?"

"Your uncle, and my friend. That handsome fellow you spend most of your time with here, besides my sister..."

"Fjord?" I feel my eyebrows raise, and not just because I still find it odd people believe the fib Sholto and I are actually related. "What were they talking about?"

"Something almost as intriguing as the look in your eyes."

"The look..." I blink rapidly. "What look? What do you mean?"

"I mean, I think you look exquisite today, Skye. Full of life. Lit by a spark...and it makes me want to do something reckless."

My cheeks immediately threaten to turn pink again, and I tell them very sternly *not* to, because I don't think there'll be enough *fresh* blood left in my body to keep me standing if they do, despite how fast my heart is going. I tip my head back to meet his gaze, something fluttering in my belly when I do. Fin isn't so very tall, but

I *am* so very small, and he's looking down at me like he's thinking the same thing...and liking the thought.

"Why're you sweet talking me?" I manage to get out.

"I can't talk sweet to my favourite girl?"

"I'm not a girl, anymore, and I'm most definitely not your favourite."

His lips twitch again. "You're up there."

Hoax. "What're you up to, Fin?"

"Something I hope you'll join me in. Fjord, ever your spectacular sparring partner and my ridiculously gracious friend, said something to your uncle yesterday that piqued my interest. Have they mentioned a meeting at the Medical Syndicate to you?"

I shake my head. "They haven't mentioned a meeting there to me, no. When is it happening?"

"Tonight."

"Who with?"

"Friends, apparently."

"Well, that sounds...unusual."

"You didn't expect an invitation?"

I frown in puzzlement. "Did you?"

"Not exactly, but the Medical Syndicate is a strange place to meet with friends, don't you think? It's also a choice time to do it, just days before the entourage arrives."

I think on that. "Maybe their friends are patients in the Medical Syndicate? Did you think of that?"

"Yes, I did."

"But...?"

His lips purse. "But are you not at all curious who they're meeting, resident there or not?"

"Well, I guess...a little? I managed to get out of sparring with them today, but perhaps they were planning on mentioning it to me then. And...it's not like I know everything they do with their lives, Fin. Far from it."

"Even though you spend all of your time with Fjord?"

"I don't spend *all* my time with him."

"No?"

I shake my head.

Neither of us speaks for a moment. I've a feeling Fin is biting his tongue, choosing his next words carefully, and when he voices them his tone is far less playful than it was.

"I'm on duty from now until dawn, otherwise I'd go to the Medical Syndicate myself to see what they're up to. I know Enye is off today and tomorrow and assumed you were too...and wondered if you'd do the honours instead?"

My eyes widen. "Spy on Fjord and Sholto tonight?"

"Yes."

"Why?"

He reaches up and tugs on the end of my braid, then runs the same hand through his own hair. "Honestly, I don't know. I just have a funny feeling about it. Fjord sounded stressed talking to your uncle, and I guess I enjoy pulling pranks on him. He hates surprises."

"You want me to surprise him there?"

"Sure, if you want to...but not necessarily. I just want to know what he's up to, so I can bring it up over drinks with him. He'll be flustered. Pay for two consecutive rounds because of it. It'll be a win win for me."

I hum a little at that, amused but...confused. Fin's eyes are mercurial, an intense whirlpool of blues and sea-greens that usually manage to tell a story better than words. Right now, their depths are shining with something surprisingly serious, telling me he really wants me to do this...and it's not hard for me to say yes. I want to impress him. I want to do what he asks of me, because I fancy him – a lot.

And I can't deny I am curious as to who Fjord and Sholto are meeting there, and why they haven't mentioned it to me even just in passing.

Besides...spying is what I *do* isn't it? I live to hustle, and to ghost. Live to run wild through the city beneath the silent guile of moonlight, with only my silver bow and my giddy exhilaration for company...

"I'll go, Fin. I'll spy on Fjord and Sholto in the Medical Syndicate tonight and see who they're meeting...but don't be too hopeful, and don't hold it against me if I come back with nothing exciting to report."

"I won't hold it against you, Skye. Pretty sure I wouldn't hold anything against you these days, except myself."

"These days?"

"Mm. These days."

"Except yourself?"

"Mm."

Without warning, he dips his head and drops a kiss to my lips...totally out of nowhere, in broad daylight. I flush redder than those fat, sweltering tomatoes in the markets, heart jumping yet again like I've never seen a boy before, because that's how it goes *these days* with Fin, and I don't know how to stop it. Don't know if I want to.

"You heading to lunch, then?" he asks when he pulls away.

"Yes," I squeak. "Are you?"

"I wish. Unfortunately, I'm on duty soon."

"Oh..." *Why am I so disappointed by that?* "I hope it's a good one, with no tavern brawls that you have to throw tankards in. No grotty bad blood or any other kind of trouble to deal with, either."

"Got enough of that right in front of me, don't I?"

He dips his head again before I can respond. This time, I'm expecting the kiss and meet him. His lips are hot, firm but still soft, unnervingly expert at moving with mine. An elbow hooks around my

48

shoulders and tightens, pulling me in, and then his hand slips to the nape of my neck, holding me there. I hope he can't feel how fast my pulse is going – but then, it's so vigorous he can probably feel *and* hear it. I know I can, racing in my ears...wreaking havoc on my senses.

Gods, I'm nervous. Not only because I'm bursting out of my skin with excitement. What if someone is watching us, watching me, be a sloppy kisser from the surrounding quads? I bet you they are...but I still edge closer, lost in the feel of him. My hands land hesitantly on his waist, wanting to pull him in so our bodies meet but not quite sure if I should, because although we've kissed and done other stuff before, we haven't done it that much – as in once – and he's sort of my first guy.

You know?

"Nice," he murmurs when we slow and then break off, moving to kiss me softly on the cheek.

I swallow tightly. "Nice?"

"Mhm, yes. Maybe more than nice. I'll see you later, Skye. Thanks for doing what you're doing tonight. Let's talk about it tomorrow evening if you're off duty?"

"Yeah, I am. Enye and I have the next few days completely off."

"That's nice for you...hence the plan to eat, sleep, repeat?" His eyes twinkle, and he taps me on the nose for a third time. "So, tomorrow, how about we meet at the library? Want to steal a book together?"

I blink in surprise. A ruffian *always* wants to steal something – not that Fin knows of my past. "Uh, I guess?"

"Want to read it together in my room?"

"I...guess," I say, feeling my cheeks grow hotter. We all know what *that* means. "If you do?"

His lips kick up on one side, the smile roguish and charming. "I do want to, Skye. I'll see you tomorrow after dinner by the library. Looking forward to it."

Me too. Way more than I should.

* * *

Enye and I stay true to the plan for our first day off, eating our weight first in the Guild's mess hall, and then out on the streets, lounging beneath the scorching sun and musing together about the Wivern entourage. It's funny, walking about without our usual armour on, but also nice; especially knowing I'll be back here in just a few short hours, moonlight fuelling my nimble feet, silver bow whistling in my hand as I go.

I bumble back to my room after we exhaust ourselves, feeling warm and sun kissed and...simply kissed, after everything beneath the stoa with Fin. Pattering around, I do nothing except try *not* to think about him, fail at that, and decide to take an early shower. The bathrooms are empty when I do, and I guess I should make use of it. Guess I should tell you about those freaky eyes and scars that make me look so weird...

I strip off and step before an eyelet mirror hanging over the basins. It's polished bronze rim is embossed with a depiction of Eros, God of Desire and a well-known mischief maker in the hearts of humankind. Strange amber eyes stare right back at me, the colour of rich honeycomb set on a summer's day. Many a night I've fallen asleep wondering which of my parents I inherited them from – time wasted, because I'll never find out. I've been orphaned for forever, so the chance of discovering information on my family is nought, and I tell myself that's fine. Tell myself I'm over the hurt - except it's a gods damn lie. A pesky, irremovable ache in my heart has already flared to life just thinking on it.

Where are they, my family?

Who are they?

Why did they leave me?

It troubles me that I don't know, and no matter what people tell you or what I tell myself, unlike other sorrows time does no favours for feelings of abandonment and neglect. Most days...it just gets worse.

With a sigh, I focus back on the beckoning mirror. My amber eyes are bright with emotion, but they're also daring me to do...gods know what. They do that a lot. Burn with determination or pain or excitement. Maybe that's what Fin was talking about earlier, telling me something in my eyes was intriguing? Or maybe that was pure sweet talk to seduce me into accepting his favour in spying on the Medical Syndicate tonight.

It's probably that, isn't it?

I sigh again. I think I'm a bit besotted by him, which is worrying and new, and part of me thinks I should speak to Enye about it. Or not even part of me. I *know* I should speak to her about it, because she's his sister and I'm *her* friend, but I don't really know how to, not least because I don't even know what's going on. All I know is Fin started kissing me, and the other week we went back to his room after drinks out and did stuff. And...I suppose I know he's out of my league, too, because he's older and I look so damn weird.

My hair is an indecisive shade of ash, sometimes white, sometimes silver, sometimes mousy; I suppose always trying to emulate the moonlight I yearn to bathe in every night. It looks funny in Ioxthel, where the majority of individuals have dark hair and black, brown or bronzed skin. Mine is pink over the soft bridge of my nose from days spent patrolling under the sun, but relatively pale, and there are scars on it. Big ones. Markings sprawled over the left side of my face, throat, torso and waist like forks of lightning or river tributaries. They lie under the surface of my skin with no puckering, almost like vein-like bruises, but they're still very obvious.

Still very weird.

I've spent just as much time thinking of my lost family and bizarre amber eyes as I have on how my skin ended up like this. What would cause it? It's like someone took quill and pink ink to me and tried to sketch out the sprawling branches of a tree.

Was I born with them?

I hope not, because a very cruel voice in my mind likes to remind me that if I were, maybe they're why I was orphaned – because I looked so freaky, and my parents didn't like that. I really hope that's not the case. I want the scars to mean something, to signify resilience or survival through hardship. They're obvious and weird, and make me uncomfortable quite a bit, but there's glory in carrying battle wounds, isn't there? They're something to be proud of. And...I *am* a warrior. A phantom warrior. *The* Phantom Warrior. The Ghost of Ioxthel. The Girl with Amber Eyes. The *Ghost* with the Amber Eyes. The best of the b—

One eyebrow suddenly arches high, as if my reflection is laughing at me for my thoughts...mocking me for staring at myself for so long and being a narcissist. Probably rightfully so. With *another* sigh, I turn and step under the cool groundwater pipe, washing away the day and my vanity.

Do they bother you, Skye?

The soft question surprises me. I pause in reaching for the bar of sandalwood soap and contemplate fibbing, but quickly realise that would be foolish. My counsel has an unwavering propensity to know when I'm lying, which would make sense, wouldn't it, given that she's part of my mind.

Yes, I reply lightly. *They bother me, but I guess it bothers me more that I don't know how I got them, or what they're from. Do you think I'll ever find out?*

Yes.

When?

In time, I expect.

"That's so helpful," I say out loud, fingers fiddling with the slippery bar of soap. "Really. Thank you. A thousand drachmas, thank you."

I don't remember ever *not* having these quirky responses in my mind; a good-natured muse with a tendency to give excellent guidance that, as I've told you before, is distinct from the hiss of instinct or my rambling thoughts but very much still an internal voice. From the few times I've quizzed others about their experience of something similar, they've been bemused by what I meant, and I quickly realised it was because they *didn't* have a sage, sentimental voice in their mind.

They don't know about her. No one knows about my counsel, because I'm not about to become *more* of a freak and tell everyone my mind is as weird as my skin and eyes. I suppose I quite like it, too. Quite like that I have a very treasured secret to cherish that no amount of moonlight will ever unveil to others.

Do you know what else I quite like?

The prospect of preying on *other* people's treasured secrets tonight. Fin didn't mention when I might encounter Fjord and Sholto meeting their friends at the Medical Syndicate, but I shouldn't waste time. It's late and the moon is already shining. Pining for me – or me her. I hurry washing myself, then examine my reflection in the eyelet mirror one last time before I leave the bathroom. My cheeks are flushed, lips curved into a wolfish smile, amber eyes bright and fiery.

I admit, I lied before. The shower has done very little to cleanse me of vanity, but I find I don't really care; not now the allure of running wild through the night has taken hold.

Living for the next hustle.

Living to ghost.

That's me.

The Guardian

The Medical Syndicate is south of the city centre, where the buildings are slightly larger and more sophisticated than the box-like, rough and tumble homes characterising the rest of Ioxthel. Two sentries are patrolling the streets when I arrive, but there's little activity within the walls of the complex itself and the only torches lit are those near the infirmary ward.

I jump from my rooftop onto the perimeter wall, skirting the entrance courtyard. The quad is empty – unsurprising given the hour – but beyond it lies a medicinal herb garden. I pause on my way as a strange, soft thrum fills the air. Energy slips over my skin, a cool, pleasant balm against the slight humidity of night – like a caress, inviting me over. This is the moonlight pulling me towards a secret. Maybe several secrets.

I crouch low on the wall, creeping closer. There are four people in the herb garden. Light from the infirmary illuminates the scene poorly, so I can only discern dull impressions of their clothing and faces, but instinctually I know none of them are Fjord or Sholto. Two stand beneath the bows of a large orange tree overhanging the quad's straight pathways, and the other two, both significantly smaller and probably female, sit on a nearby bench.

Something stirs the air by my ankles – a nightingale landing beside me. He hops around a few times before settling to watch the courtyard below, incredibly silent and serene. It seems I'm not the only one drawn to the hum of energy here. A strange desire has seized my heart, stretching like cotton or an ardent moment of nostalgia. I suddenly ache with the need to be closer to the figures below, to see them and be with them, and to...I don't even know what.

Shifting restlessly on the balls of my feet, I tune into their conversation. One of the figures on the bench is speaking, her voice pinched in delighted amusement. She sounds young but very different to an Ioxthelian child – with a light, lyrical accent...

"It was *so* funny, Jay. You should've seen his face. He was petrified, as white as those sails we saw earlier in the harbour, and then when he noticed there was a second snake he took off like his shirt was on fire. Didn't he!?" She elbows the person beside her in the ribs, I think quite sharply. "Didn't he, Wren!?"

"Ow," the other girl, Wren, says. She sounds older, but also not Ioxthelian. "Ember, stop it! Mind your manners."

"Yeah but didn't he?! Idris took off like he was on fire!"

"I would have liked to see that, Ember," replies a deep voice from beneath the orange tree. It's tone is rich, male and heavily accented; and *also* not Ioxthelian. "Was he faster than he is when he runs from my classroom at the end of a tutoring session? I didn't think that would be possible..."

Another new voice pipes up from the orange tree; an older female, clearly displeased...and I don't think I even need to tell you she doesn't sound Ioxthelian, either. "And *I* didn't think it was possible for Idris to be any more irresponsible. A fear like this is exactly what he shouldn't conceal as your Guardian."

Guardian?

"Oh..." Ember shifts uncomfortably, the amusement vanishing from her voice. "Oh, dear me. He's not in trouble, is he? I shouldn't have said anything."

One and then both adults step out of the shadows. The man has a very thin layer of tight, dark curls for hair, and a broad build beneath his dusky lavender cloak. He's tapping out a soft rhythm with his fingers on the side of his hip, seemingly for no reason. The woman looks small and slight beside him, with greying hair shimmering in the moonlight. She also wears a lilac cape, but beneath it I see the glint of metal weapons.

My hand tightens instinctually around my bow. Talking of Guardians with strange accents and having a clandestine meeting under the silent guile of moonlight...? I think these are Nixen, Astyros's sworn enemies from the Kingdom of Elysium, right here within the Medical Syndicate's walls.

"Idris is at fault," the woman is saying, approaching the bench. "You're very right to tell us of this, Ember. I will inform your uncle imminently, and speak to the young Guardian myself. He puts you at risk not disclosing this to us."

The girl grabs a handful of her thick, auburn curls and starts twisting them vigorously. "I didn't *tell* tell you it, Rose. It was meant to be a funny story. I wasn't snitching on him...wasn't doing it to have him told off. That's *my* job, isn't it? Getting told off. Totally my job."

Funny.

I relate to that.

"I shouldn't worry yourself, Ember," the man, Jay as she'd called him, says. "Idris is your Guardian. He's there to take the edge off your troubles, including receiving a reprimand or two for you."

"But I feel *bad*," Ember replies, heaving in a deep breath. "Really bad."

"Worse than how you felt about that stray dog eating your homework yesterday?" Jay offers her an impish smile. "Shan't worry, Ember. Idris is a tough young man."

She doesn't look nearly consoled.

"I wonder where he and the others are, actually," Jay adds, looking around the medical herb garden. "They're late."

My eyes also scour the courtyard. I find nothing out of the ordinary besides the four figures...although it's not like *they're* ordinary, is it?

Nixen.

In Ioxthel!

It seems whoever they're meeting here hasn't arrived yet. No Fjord or Sholto either, who you should know I'll be going *straight* to, to tell them about this. Scrap Fin's plan for me to spy on them. This is *far* more exciting and scary. Huge news. Definitely the biggest secret the moon has ever unveiled to me. And...goddesses, you know I think I was wrong just now. There *is* something else out of the ordinary in the courtyard, a fifth presence I've been very stupid to miss.

Someone leans against the courtyard wall opposite me, where shade from another orange tree provides him with ample camouflage. He's some metres away from the rest of the group, almost lost to the shadows just like me...maybe *more* than me, even though he's wearing a white shirt and no cloak. There's a leather knife harness extending over his shoulders and disappearing under his folded arms, with at least one wickedly sharp blade held there. I know immediately who he is. He's one of Elysium's lethal, legendary protectors in the flesh, no doubt safeguarding the Nixen here in the courtyard.

He's a Guardian.

My heart starts pounding, scattering coherent thought. His expression is blank and shadowed, but somehow still a silent storm of focus, and he's looking *straight* at me; watching me with an intensity that defies the absolute stillness of his body. There's no way he can see my face in the shadowy recesses of my hood, but I suddenly feel very exposed. And fearful. He's eight metres from me, but *all* the legends tell you that Guardians move incredibly fast, their blades faster still. Ghost or not, I think I'll be lucky to disappear before he attacks.

He is so still, frozen to pounce.

I am his prey.

The conversation below is ongoing, both girls on the bench talking to each other – or rather, *over* each other – but I have little hope of hearing them with the rush of blood in my ears and my screaming thoughts. I daren't move. I daren't even take a breath, for fear he will execute me unless I stay as motionless as he is. *No one* sees me when I ghost, except Xavier a few nights ago...and now this Guardian. How long has he been watching me? How long was I unaware of him? How long do I have before he attacks?

Steady, Skye, my counsel murmurs.

It confuses me she'd say that, knowing what we do about the people below, but I try to do as she says; try to stay present. My muscles seize in an effort to keep still, blood coursing through me in hot and heady waves, scouring my veins with an order that is as impossible to ignore as it is to carry out.

Run fast.

Run far.

Yes, I must flee from here like a wolf's prey, but I don't know how to. Not without getting hurt...or killed. Perhaps ten seconds have passed since we locked gazes but it feels like an hour, and I am most definitely on borrowed time. The silver of my bow is slick with sweat in my hands, my lungs burning with the need to breathe. Somewhere far in the distance a fox barks out an abrasive, territorial warning...and is it one I should heed myself? Is that what the Guardian's stare is; a territorial warning, telling me that if I so much as *move* towards his ground and his people, he'll pounce on me?

I don't know.

I don't know what to do.

The air expires in my lungs. My chest heaves in a huge inhale because I couldn't stop myself, and then every sense in my body sharpens in response to the Guardian's muscles tensing, a predator preparing to pounce.

Skye, my counsel urges, sensing the change in me. *Steady, sweet girl.*

To Hades with steady!

I turn and fling myself from the wall, throwing my cloak out behind me to hide the shape of my body and to obscure his sight. My sudden movement startles the nightingale beside me, but I barely heed him fleeing to the skies in terror as I land in the entrance courtyard, palms and feet skidding over the stone paving slabs as I right myself and gain momentum...and then I'm running faster than I've *ever* run in my life. I don't need to look back to know the Guardian is following.

He must be.

I must flee.

Shrines cut into the walls and large terracotta urns filled with scraggy foliage blur as I pelt down the pathway, premature victory fuelling the force behind my little strides when I spot the city's tiered skyline looming through the gates. So close. I'm so close. I know I have every chance of losing him amongst the rooftops, on my terrain and my hunting ground.

I'm so cl—

I let out a harsh, winded yelp as an arm comes out of nowhere, snatching me firmly around the waist and lifting me mid-step from the path. My feet leave the ground as I'm hauled through the air, and then my back hits a very hard, very large body. Fear explodes in me, so potent I lose every single semblance of thought, and instead fall into something of violent instinct; writhing fiercely, bow whistling through the air as my limbs cartwheel all over the place.

Mad.

Drunk on terror.

My head kicks back, meeting thin air. My heels kick back, meeting thin air...and yet I know he's *right there,* his entire front pressed to my back, hold like steel across my belly...

"I won't harm you," he says in a hoarse, quiet voice. "Stop struggling please, so I can put you down."

I don't stop struggling.

Who on all of earth would?

My breath is scorching and frantic, puffing past trembling lips, heart pounding so fast I think I might faint from the pressure inside my veins. Panic grips my gut, like my hands are trying to grip his arm and tear it away from me...fingers fumbling all over the place and bow almost slipping from my slick palm, because I'm sweating and...gods, I'm scared.

I'm so scared this might be *it.*

What will Sholto think when my body is found? And Fjord? He'll be heartbroken. I never apologised to him again for being such an absentminded sparring partner. I never thanked him for buffing my armour at the end of every week or helping to train me when he could have been doing a thousand more important things...never thanked him for being the pretend brother of my dreams. And Fin. Magic and mischief incarnate, who I fancy so damn much. Fin will blame himself for this. I think he'll torture himself for asking me to come here to pull a prank on Fjord and getting *killed* in the process.

And...and *Tristan.*

My dear, dear best friend who I can't wait for you to meet. Will he ever know what happened to me? It's been a week since we saw one another, which is way too long for us. I want to see him. I *need* to see him, and I need you to meet him...except will that even happen now?

I let out a low whimper at the thought, and then a fierce growl, because my best friend needs me in this life just as much as I need him, and goddesses does that ever mean I need to fight.

"It's not my intention to harm you," the Guardian repeats as I wriggle with *everything* in me, knees levering all the way up to my torso to gain momentum to try and throw myself from his grip. It doesn't work. He's impossibly strong, and big, and he's seriously right there; and yet when I throw my head back again, hoping to hit something that will break and hurt, I almost snap my neck meeting nothing. "Stop struggling so I can put you down."

"I'm not going to stop struggling!" I hear myself cry, voice tight with panic and anger. "Let me go!"

"If you stop struggling, I will."

"No!"

Time passes and I'm tiring - inhales harsh, limbs aching from straining away from him. I'm not going to stop fighting. I'll never stop fighting, even if I kill *myself* in doing so...and I think the Guardian might realise this, because his arms give a notch, and then he murmurs supposedly in warning, "I'm going to drop you."

The hold on me disappears. I fall into a hard, ungracious heap on the floor, then scramble to pick myself up and back away *fast*. My fingers shake as they search blindly overhead for my arrows, except they're not there. With horror, I see he's holding my quiver, standing in the middle of the quad's walkway looking totally unfatigued. Grey eyes bounce over my hooded form, quick and efficient, as dim and deadly as the night shadows I wish to turn and flee into...but I won't do that because he's holding my quiver, and that's really damn important to me.

"Give it back," I say, trying to sound firm. "Drop it now. It's mine."

"I would first ask what you were doing overlooking the herb garden, please?"

Please. Who says please during an interrogation? An altercation?! "What were *you* doing there?" I throw back. "In the middle of the night? With children? With...strange accents? Talking of snakes? Highly suspicious. More suspicious than what my dinner looked like earlier this evening..."

Unsurprisingly, he doesn't reply to this. His attention is lingering on the silver bow clutched white-knuckled in my hand, and then with unnerving precision the dark nothingness beneath my hood, like he might actually be able to see something there. You should know there's nothing I'm able to see in his expression; no spark or shine in his grey irises to pick up something of the moonlight. No hint of resolve or focus, or even violence. Everything is just...dull.

Tarnished.

Lifeless.

Long seconds pass before he finally moves, shifting his weight from both feet to one, taking a deeper breath than any of his last. It stretches the shoulder harness across his shoulders; a harness home to just one straight knife, except I couldn't tell you for sure that there aren't more hidden away, because my mind doesn't *work* after what he says next.

"Are you Skye?"

Yep.

There goes my mind, and my lungs...ruined. My heart flips high and then *low* in fear; caustic sweat and adrenaline stinging my armpits, thighs tensing to flee. I have a feeling the Guardian misses none of it, because predators never do.

"No," I deny, the response far too delayed and forceful to be believable. "Who is Skye? What kind of a name is that? Very uninventive. Boring, and ordinary...because the sky is everywhere, isn't it? I'm glad I'm not called that. I don't want to be boring. Not me, thanks."

His mouth open then shuts, eyes drifting again – and *now* I see something fleeting in them for the moonlight to unveil to me, something of intuition and intent. "Forgive me."

Those words ruin my poor, thundering heart too, and I swear to you I don't see him move. One moment there are metres between the two of us, the next he's inches from me – the smell of woodsmoke on his shirt hitting the back of my throat, his warmth stifling, his hand pushing my hood back.

Even though it's not cold, my skin chills as he bares it to the night air, wholly unused to being exposed when ghosting. As in...I *never* lower my hood on missions like this. I've told you before that only three people know the face of Ioxthel's pitifully little known spy, and to have a fourth see it now – a stranger and an enemy who also knows my name – is beyond unnerving.

Beyond bad.

We stare at one another, me in impossibly profound shock and horror, fearful and furious and torn between snatching my quiver back from him or running fast and far, so *far*, from here. The Guardian looks like his suspicions are undoubtedly confirmed by my appearance, taking in the freaky amber eyes, the scars of lightning forking down the left side of my face and disappearing beneath my shirt's collar, the stubborn, stroppy mouth that is so *bad* at lying. Something like regret falls into his features, before the blood pounding in my ears roars and I pounce on him, moving recklessly to steal back what's mine...

"Skye!"

It's no surprise I fumble my offence at the sound and sight of Fjord running through the quad towards us, one hand on the hilt of the sword at his hip, his expression stark with shock.

"Run!" I cry to him, horrified. "Don't come here, Fjord! You need to run away!"

He doesn't. He takes a very quick inventory of me, his gaze moving behind and...he slows. "Silver? Είναι όλα εντάξει? Τι συμβαίνει?"

Is everything ok?

What's going on?

The Guardian immediately murmurs something in a foreign tongue that sounds nothing like I've ever heard before. He steps back, seemingly about to move for Fjord...and I don't stop to think. I lurch into motion and fling myself into his path, standing before him with my arms spread wide and my heart *wild*. "Stay where you are! Don't you dare go near him! If you touch him you'll...you'll regret it. Big time!"

The Guardian halts, strange words loitering unspoken on his lips, his next stride never falling to the walkway. His eyes bounce between Fjord and I, lingering on something behind...and that's when two gentle hands land on my arms, encouraging them down to my sides and rubbing them reassuringly.

"It's ok, Skye," Fjord says quietly. "Levi isn't going to harm us."

Levi? Guardians have names?! "He is, Fjord. He's a Guardian! From Elysium! And he stole my quiver!"

"I see that. I'm sure he'll give it back to you once things settle down. Once we're all on the same page."

"Things aren't going to settle down! He's a Guardian! I saw him in the courtyard with other people I just *know* are the Nixen intruders Ruby was talking about. We need to go! Find Sholto! He'll know what to do, and...he's with you, isn't he?! He's due here tonight, and he's good with things like this. Good with a sword, too. Isn't he?!"

"Sholto is nearby," Fjord confirms levelly.

"Then get him!" I urge, throwing an arm out behind and shoving him back by his stomach. "You go, Fjord! Run! I'll fight! Distract the Guardian. Slice his thighs with his dagger...that I'll have to steal from his shoulder harness..." *Except I won't do that, because I've gone and said it out loud.* "Go, Fjord! Get help!"

"I'm not leaving you, Skye."

He steps before me, giving the Guardian his back. I stare in horror, then reach out frantically to pull him behind me again, because that is *not* what he should be doing. You should never give an opponent your back – it's probably *the* most basic principle in a fight.

"Turn around and get behind me!" I order, locking fierce gazes with the Guardian, expecting him to pounce. "If you touch him I'll end you. Don't come *any* closer. Get behind me, Fjord. Now!"

Fjord doesn't do anything of the sort. He stands there steadily, his expression striving for something reassuring, palms out and raised as if to quieten a frightened animal...and I know that's me, the wild wolf cub losing it, pretending she's big and bad enough to take on the gods damn alpha. "None of us is going to fight, Skye. Levi is a very dear friend of mine. He's not going to hurt you, or anyone else in Ioxthel. The same goes for the Nixen in the courtyard. They're all my friends, and they mean you no harm."

"Your *friends?*"

He nods. "They mean you no harm."

"I..."

I can't finish the sentence, because something *scary* hits me. The Fjord I know doesn't have friends from Elysium. No one here does, because they haven't set foot in the Kingdom of Astyros for hundreds of years...because they're our *enemies.*

"What is going on?" I manage to get out. "Why do you say they're your friends? Folk from Elysium? How do you know them?

And...and why are you still standing there, with your back to him?! Get *behind* me, Fjord. Get somewhere safe."

He doesn't. The soothing hazel eyes bouncing between mine suddenly fill with apprehension, his shoulders locking up like he's tensing to take a hit or preparing for something *bad* to come.

Turns out I should be, too.

"This is not how I expected to tell you this," he confesses, bowing his head in defeat. "I wish there was an easier way. Please know I'm sorry for not telling you it sooner."

My gut swoops. "What? What is it?"

"You're from Elysium, Skye. And you're a demigod."

Playing The Fool

A weird sound bubbles from my throat, withering as soon as it leaves me. I think it's supposed to be a laugh, except it's not that, because this isn't funny.

"What...did you just say?"

"You're from Elysium, and you're a demigod."

Yes. I definitely heard him right, so either I've gone mad or maybe *he* ate something funny for dinner...or maybe the Guardian dropped me on my head, and I'm delirious, or dreaming?

"What're you talking about, Fjord? The Guardian didn't kill me or...or knock me out, did he? I'm not dreaming this?"

"You're not dreaming."

"Is this a joke?"

"No, Skye. This isn't a joke. I can explain everything."

"That would be really very nice," I croak. "Nicer than my dinner, and maybe yours, too. So...please do that? Explain? Because I'm really confused."

Fjord opens his mouth to reply but doesn't speak. His gaze darts over my shoulder, eyes sharpening with vigilance. I hear it seconds later. The sounds of slamming doors and running footsteps...gruff orders voiced in the next courtyard. Unsurprisingly, my scuffle with the Guardian has alerted the Medical Syndicate's guards. It spurs all of us into motion – motion for me that's dogged by disbelief at how tonight is going. This is *not* what Fin asked me to spy on. He'd never have requested I do this if he knew what was waiting for me here...a Guardian with arms of steel who moves impossibly fast, and who Fjord is *friends* with?!

Then he tells me I'm a demigod?!

I jerk my hood up to hide my shocked features, and as soon as I do Fjord seizes my hand, pulling me towards the gates. His grip feels strange, gentle but possessive...like he's nervous I'll run from here.

From *him.*

"Tell the others please, Silver," he throws over his shoulder. "But only bring yourself."

I've no idea what he means by that last point, and I don't have the wherewithal to think on it. Self-preservation is the only reason I let him drag me from the Medical Syndicate and out into the quiet night...the only reason I bite my tongue on the questions and exclamations burning its tip, because ghosts get caught unless they're silent – and even then it's not enough if the pursuer is a Guardian, is it?

The two of us hurry north through the city, to where the houses start climbing on top of one another again and the streets narrow...but we're not heading for the Guild like I think we might be. Instead, Fjord tows me up a flight of outdoor steps to a tiny, nondescript building that I've never seen before, unlocking the worn wooden door there.

"This is our safe house," he murmurs, holding it open for me. "We're safe, here. You're safe."

I watch him as he shuts the door behind us and busies himself with lighting several copper lanterns dotted around the room. We're in a *salóni* of sorts, with very few, if any, personal effects to it. Two wicker chairs and a diphros stool provide the room's only seating. The floor is stone, and a collection of wine amphorae of different sizes are huddled in one corner of the room; a shadowy staircase descending to lower levels in the other. The large unshuttered window opposite me looks west over the rooftops, framing the starry night sky and the dark, menacing mass of Alcázar in the distance. I see three escape routes from my observations, and it frightens me I'm even thinking I might need to use them in Fjord's presence.

"Did you follow me to the Medical Syndicate tonight?" I ask, and my voice sounds weird - pinched with stress, and accusatory. "Or did you go there to meet the Nixen? Your...friends?"

He glances up from lighting a lamp. "I didn't follow you, no. I checked in on you at the Guild but you were gone, so I assumed you were in the harbours with Tristan. It was a very great surprise to find you at the Medical Syndicate instead. I would ask why you were there?"

"Fin told me he overheard a conversation between you and Sholto about meeting friends there tonight. Asked me to spy on it because he thought it was suspicious..."

"Fin?!" Fjord looks worried. "Was he there with you?"

"No. He's on patrol, which is why he asked me to do it instead."

"Uh..."

He rubs his eyes with the heels of his palms, like he's just as exhausted as he was yesterday during sparring. Seconds later two knocks sound on the door - light but purposeful. After giving me what I think is supposed to be a reassuring glance, Fjord opens up.

It's his *friend*, Levi.

The Guardian's eyes bounce over the salóni in a way that looks entirely instinctual, and they linger on me. My pulse starts leaping around, bow slippery in my sweaty palm. He enters but hesitates as he passes by, offering my quiver out to me. I snatch it back and bounce - or maybe fly is a better word - to the other side of the room. I fling the quiver strap over my shoulder, priming it to grab one of the arrows.

Fjord's expression becomes troubled as he locks the door and sees me standing there skittishly. "You're entirely safe with us, Skye.

I swear to you. You're possibly the safest you'll ever be right here and now."

"I don't understand how that can be," I breathe back, because I really don't. It's impossible for me to tell you how torn I feel hearing that from him - hearing the boy I think of as a brother and trust *second* most in the entire world saying I'm *safest* in the presence of someone I've been told my whole life is dangerous. An enemy. The same person who just subdued me effortlessly in the Medical Syndicate.

"Why don't you have a seat?" Fjord suggests, gesturing to one of the wicker chairs as he heads for the other himself.

I watch him go, frozen...and stay that way. I'm not sitting. I couldn't be still or reposed even if I tried. Even if I trusted the fact there's a Guardian just metres from me. My eyes track Levi hungrily as he moves through the room to the window, his knife winking at me from his leather shoulder harness. Goddesses, he looks strong, and we're in such close proximity here. It's a poor shooting landscape for me; small, with dim lighting and a high risk of ricochets. I wait with bated breath as *he* waits for Fjord to take his seat before he thinks of settling himself, folding his arms and resting against the wall...and then he looks at me again.

Those eyes.

Grey and listless.

Unnerving enough for me to question whether I want to look away and never look back again, or do the *opposite* in the name of vigilance. I observe Fjord. He's taking a moment to get comfortable in his wicker chair, running a nervous hand through his hair. He seems to be steeling himself for what's to come...and it turns out I should be doing the same. I should be *seriously* preparing myself for the world to just flip itself over; to plonk its head on the ground and its bottom in the air and leave me, and everything I've ever thought, upside down.

"So...we're here, and this is not how I expected your first meeting to be. I suppose I should introduce you formally, even if you're not entirely new acquaintances." He offers me a strained, hopeful smile. "Skye, this is Levi Silverstone. He's —"

"He's from Elysium!"

"Yes."

"But he's...your friend?!"

"He's my dearest friend. He's also my Guardian."

I blink rapidly. "*Your* Guardian?!"

"Yes, Levi is my Guardian, Skye. I have a Guardian."

"You have a Guardian of Elysium?" I echo dumbly, then look to the person in question. "You're Fjord's Guardian? His...friend?"

Levi nods once, seriously. "I apologise for what happened between us in the Medical Syndicate, Skye. Had I known who you were, I would never have subdued you as I did. I hope I didn't harm you?"

"You attacked me!"

"I merely meant to stop you escaping, and to find out who you were. It was never my intent to fight you, or harm you in any way."

"That's not what it seemed like to me, holding me like that! That felt horrible!"

He nods slowly, as if he can believe it. I stare at him, a little wild in the eyes, then seek explanation from the wicker chairs. Fjord is leaning his elbows over his knees there, expression tight.

"Levi is my dearest friend, Skye," he repeats. "I trust him with my own life more than I trust myself...and with yours, too. I trust him entirely. He means you no harm."

"Has he been here with you the whole time we've known each other?"

"No. Levi recently travelled to Ioxthel with the others, the Nixen at the Medical Syndicate."

"Our enemies?"

"They're not our enemies, Skye. Nixen are not the enemy here...and nor am I."

I blink stupidly, immediately understanding what he's implying but refusing to accept it, even though the logic is *right* there. Friends with Nixen from Elysium, with a Guardian from Elysium...

"Are you Nixen, Fjord?" I ask, voice very quiet. "From Elysium?"

"Yes. My family is of Nereid descent...the oceanic nymphs. I live on the west coast with them."

"You live here, though?"

"For the last five years, yes."

"But not before?"

"No, I'm Nixen. I live in Elysium."

More stupid blinking, and my heart starts to thump fast. So many feelings and instincts rise in me, a storm of shock, disbelief, betrayal and fear.

"You're safe, Skye," Fjord assures me, looking like he sees it all. "I am not your enemy."

"I...don't know about that," I reply weakly. "Don't know which way up the world is anymore."

"Would you like me to start talking? Start explaining everything?"

"Yes, please. I'm listening. With two ears. I'll need two ears for this, won't I? Big explanations. Big...shock."

"Yes," Fjord lets slip a low sigh, preparing himself to turn the world upside down, and leave me and everything I've ever known thoroughly disoriented and lost. "Everything you've been told about Elysium is a lie, Skye. The history books depict false truths, as do most if not all of the rumours that stem from them. Nixen didn't wage a battle on humans four hundred years ago during the Impurity War.

It was The Sabirs, prominent leaders of the lands at the time - now our monarchy - who turned on Nixen, and they gave them a very cruel, very sudden ultimatum. Leave Astyros, or die." Fjord's expression becomes troubled. "We don't know why they did this. Fear, maybe? Or jealousy over our favour with the gods and goddesses...not that we were favoured. Whatever it was, at first it seemed laughable that Scarlett Sabir, head of the family then, felt she had the power to force an entire race of beings much stronger than she was from what is now Astyros. Except it turns out she *did* have the power. A great, godly power, and she used it on Nixen, even though they eventually surrendered to her orders and fled Astyros. Everything in its path was destroyed, creating the wasted leagues that lie between the Kingdoms of Astyros, Wivern and Elysium - what we know today as The Nether. Millions of Nixen simply ceased to exist, Skye, wiped from the edges of the earth as carelessly and crudely as a hand sweeping crumbs to the floor - only their souls never landed on the ground or in the underworld. They just ceased to be. Obliterated. Millions of us just gone. And so *that* was the Impurity War of old. Not a battle waged on humans by Nixen, but instead...the opposite. Centuries of harmony and recovery have since passed, with the mortal Kingdoms of Astyros and Wivern separated from Elysium, but twenty-five years ago that harmony shifted. We started to suffer a slew of assassinations. Thousands died, millions lived in fear...something terrible was afoot. The attacks involved indiscriminate targeting of the twelve Nixen Dynasties, collective rulers of the kingdom; but though everyone was hit hard, only one dynasty suffered a systematic loss of life, and that was *your* lineage, Skye. Your people. It was just before your fifth birthday when you disappeared from Elysium, and those who knew you feared the worst...feared the assassins had killed you. Thank the gods, those fears weren't realised. Instead, you'd fled with your surrogate mother in search of safety. There was just one who knew this...and to this day, excepting him telling a very few trusted friends, he has kept that a secret. No one else in Elysium knows the heiress to your dynasty is alive and well."

Fjord stops then, watching me in readiness of an outburst, and Hades he might just get one. This is...this is something else. The very biggest, strangest of explanations that needs *four* ears to hear it.

A past life of mine in Elysium?

Genocide by The Sabirs?

A surrogate mother?

Nixen dynasties?

Assassins?

Sudden pressure in my lungs advises me to breathe, to be present, but it does little to ease any of my discomfort – nothing ever could. "You expect me to believe you? To believe that this isn't some big, whacky joke?"

His frown is immediate and severe. "It's not a joke, Skye. I would never joke about this. You know me."

"I...thought I did," I say slowly, something cold and permanent settling in my belly; fear that I *don't* know him, and that I never did. "So if I'm from Elysium and a demigod – you said I was one of those back in the Medical Syndicate – then which god or goddess is my parent?" As soon as I voice the question, I let out one of those funny, throaty laughs haunting me tonight, the kind that aren't a laugh at all. "You *have* to be joking, Fjord. I'm not descended from a god or goddess. Look at me. I'm a mess, and I can't even tie my shoelaces. Or read. I can't be a demigod."

"You are," he assures me softly. "In the flesh. Your father is a god...but before you ask who, we don't know."

"My dad is a god...but you don't know who? What of my mother?"

"Saffron was Nixen, and from Elysium. She was a prominent member of the Aeolus Dynasty, beings of the storm winds. So are you."

I become very still. "Saffron? That's my mother's name? You know who she is?"

Fjord hesitates. "I knew of her, Skye, but I never met her."

I open my mouth, then shut it fast. It's suddenly terribly dry. Disappointment and pain rise in me, potent and unwelcome, because Fjord just used *was* and *knew*...the past tense.

Stupidly, I still ask the question. "Is my mother still alive?"

"No, she isn't. I'm sorry, Skye."

"What about my surrogate mother? The one you said fled with me from Elysium? She's not the same person is she?"

"No. And she has since passed, too."

"I don't have any mothers?"

Fjord shakes his head slowly. I suck in a sharp breath that scorches my soul. Goddesses, did I ever lie looking into that mirror earlier, staring at my freaky amber eyes and spieling about my lost family. I haven't given up hope that they're still out there. Part of me has always clung desperately to the possibility that they're waiting for me, if only we pass one another on the street at the right time on the right day, or if only they suddenly wake up from the world's longest sleep and realise they *have* to start searching for their lost baby, regardless of her freaky amber eyes and scarred skin. They'd find me and I'd be part of a family for the first time, and my abandonment would be talked of as a huge mistake and tragedy, but something that wasn't forever. And...maybe it *was* a mistake, and maybe they didn't care what I looked like, maybe even *liked* that I looked so weird and special...but it is forever.

I'm alone.

Without a mother.

"I'm so sorry," Fjord ushers again, watching me with an expression of deep feeling. Tears immediately sting my eyes, and though I'm looking at him, I'm no longer seeing him. I feel so betrayed. Fjord has sparred with me and befriended me for *five* years. He's witnessed how I ache to know of my past, how it scars me not having a family...and now he's saying I'm a street ruffian, demigod *and* leader of a Nixen dynasty, and he's known it all along and never told me? He's known who my mother is, her *name*, and that she's *dead*, and he didn't tell me? Did he not think I deserved to know about the Impurity War, either? Did he not think I had a right, especially with everything I do in ghosting on Ruby Sabir, whose ancestors supposedly committed genocide?

I realise my earlier fear is so damn real. I don't know him, and I never did. Not the real Fjord. Not Fjord the Nereid from Elysium who is friends with a Guardian because he *has* a Guardian.

Swallowing tightly as if he heeds my thoughts – and he probably does with them always splashed so starkly over my face – Fjord glances to Levi by the window, I think for reassurance. His Guardian is watching us silently with nothing in his expression.

"Sholto thought otherwise," Fjord murmurs to him, as if he does see something there and is responding to it. "I regret not disputing that, now. I really regret that."

I blink rapidly. "Sholto? He's part of this? He knew this? About my past? My heritage? The Impurity War?"

"Yes. He's the one who knew your surrogate mother fled the kingdom with you."

This confirmation ruins me.

Completely.

The cruellest feeling of betrayal rises, hollowing my stomach so viscerally it's a wonder my legs don't give out on me. Sholto thinks I'm a demigod? He's friends with people from Elysium? He's known of my past, and of my surrogate mother? Of how I ended up on the streets he took me off?

He lied to me?

Lied *big?*

"He knew?" I ask, tears brewing rapidly and spilling. "He knew who I was? That my mother was dead? For...for seven years? And he didn't tell me? He knew all along? When he first picked me up from the streets?"

Fjord's expression falls into even greater sympathy. "Yes. I'm so sorry, Skye. I know this is so much to learn, and so hard to understand."

"I don't," I say in devastation. "I don't understand. How *could* you, Fjord? Both of you? How *could* you hide this from me?"

He heaves in a breath, remorse and guilt painted on his features, but doesn't get a chance to reply. Soft footfalls have suddenly started echoing through the saloon, a sign that someone, or *two* someones, are stealthily climbing the staircase in the corner of the room. Beyond thought, beyond *everything*, I draw an arrow and prime it against my bowstring, pulling taut and taking aim for the intruders...or rather, for someone's heart.

A Guardian's heart.

You should know I didn't even see Levi move across the room, and yet he's here now, my arrow pressing into the hard flesh of his sternum. Then, in the blink of an eye, he reaches up and snaps the sharp tip from its shaft, breaking the projectile in two.

"I'm not going to hurt you," he says as my bow's snout drifts down in shock and horror, thumping heart rampaging wild. "I just don't want you to hurt them, Skye. Or me."

Them, being the hushed, vaguely recognisable whispers hurrying up the stairs.

"*Ow,* Em. You're stepping on my heels!"

"Go faster!"

"I'm not going to go faster!"

"Go *further*, then."

"They'll see us!"

"Well, we'll never see *them* from here, will we! Go on, Wren. Do it. I dare you. Faster!"

The whine in the young voice is obvious even when quiet, and I think it belongs to the little girl in the herb garden with curly auburn hair. Fjord spares Levi and I a cursory glance, but seems to think *nothing* of his Guardian standing so close to me, or of the feverish fear I know must be lighting up my eyes. He merely gets up from his wicker and drifts towards the stairs...away from me.

"Girls," he calls softly. "We can hear you."

The footsteps stop. A great stillness and silence fills the room...and then a voice squeaks, "No. You can't hear us, Fjord. We're not here."

"You're not?"

"Nope. Not here."

"You sure?"

There's a pause. "No. But also maybe..."

"Oh, for the love of Zeus's lovers, Ember!"

The footsteps start up again, unmuted this time. A girl appears at the top of the stairs, her russet hair wispy, cheeks pink, eyes wide and fingers dancing nervously over two jade bracelets circling her wrist. The copper lanterns paint her to be mid-teens and very pretty, with a sea of freckles covering her face and ankles. She's the second, older girl from the Medical Syndicate.

"Hi," she says sheepishly. "We're sorry. We were just being nosy."

Something stirs the hem of her lilac cloak, and then another portrait of fiery auburn curls and emerald eyes pops into view, peering through the bannisters. Pale little fists clench the bars on either side of her face, and from the way her shoulders are jumping around, she must be on the very limits of her tallest tiptoes.

"Hello," Ember says breathlessly, face shining with excitement and exertion. "Hello everyone."

Fjord might hide a sigh. "Good evening, Ember."

"Good evening," she echoes, grinning impishly, toothily. "We just wanted to see you, and the sky. I wanted to see her. I *really* wanted to see her."

"Where is your tutor?" Fjord asks.

"Somewhere," she replies with so much dignity she sounds indignant, and then she glances to me. Her expression turns to shock, mouth forming a brief perfect o before whispering, "The sky. Breathtaking. I've dreamed about her too many times to count."

Fjord follows her gaze, and I hope he sees the injury in my eyes. I would *never* let someone stand this close to him armed with knives and my arrowhead, snapped with bare hands – especially someone I knew he didn't know or trust, and very definitely feared.

"Είσαι ασφαλής, Skye," he murmurs, looking troubled. "Please believe me. You don't need to be scared."

My inhale shakes. "Who are they?"

"This is Wren and Ember Irving. They're Sylvans, which means they're descended from the wood nymphs...and they're not your enemy. No one here is your enemy."

"How can you *say* that!" I exclaim. "How can you say that with a Guardian so close, holding the arrow he just snapped! Easily! Like...he's very strong!"

"I apologise, Skye," Levi says seriously, like he actually *means* it. He goes to lift the hand holding the broken weapon, maybe to give it back...but maybe to attack. Fear riots through me, heart-stoppingly fierce, igniting instinct. I jerk the splintered arrow shaft from its hasty, halfway position against the bowstring and press its tip beneath his jaw, expecting to receive a brutal retaliation but...but not *thinking* enough to stop myself from provoking it, because I'm scared.

I'm so scared.

Only it seems Levi does mean what he says. He doesn't harm me. He doesn't even move to defend himself, really; just blinks twice, lets out a measured breath...and stands very still.

"Levi is worried you'll lash out," Fjord explains, using that same voice from the Medical Syndicate, like he's talking to a wild little wolf cub *losing* it. "He's just worried. He won't hurt you. I promise you, Skye, no one here will hurt you."

"I don't believe you," I breathe, pressing the splintered bolt into the flesh of Levi's neck. I can smell bronze residue from the broken tip, and still that woodsmoke on his shirt. *I* must smell of nothing but panic and fear, and deep, irreversible hurt. "Step back or I'll cut you, Levi..." *Except I've only ever cut myself accidentally during training. Never someone else. Even beefy men in tavern brawls, and least of all Guardians.* "Hurt you really badly. Step back."

"He won't retreat until he's sure you won't lash out with your bow at the girls, Skye. Why don't you drop it?"

"I'm not dropping my bow, Fjord! They're Nixen! *You're* Nixen! He's a Guardian!"

"I know," he says with quiet emphasis. "But please trust me when I say you're safe here, safer than you could possibly i—"

"Trust?!" I interrupt incredulously. "Με δουλεύεις, Fjord! I'll never trust you again! Never! Friends from Elysium? A past life you *kept* from me? Knowing of my dead mother?" My voice splinters more completely than my arrow. "What you've done is unforgivable! You're...you're a bad person who I thought I knew but didn't! You're so bad!"

The injury I see fall into his expression at that is deep and genuine, and it outrages me, because how *dare* he feel hurt? How *dare* he, after everything he's just revealed...all the lies and deceit?

"Clearly you shouldn't be here, girls," he says hoarsely, turning to the stairs instead of replying. "It's not helping things at all. Go back to your tutor, and tell him to keep a better eye on you."

Wren immediately bows her head in apology. She starts to descend the stairs again, gathering her sister on the way, only to stop in surprise in the next second.

"Let them stay, Fjord."

The terrible sinking feeling of betrayal returns to my stomach. This is a voice unheard tonight, but one I don't just have a *vague* recognition of, because I've known and revered it for seven years. Seven years I thought were given to me in good intention.

Sholto manoeuvres his way around the two Irving sisters, cresting the top of the stairs. His greying hair is pulled into its trademark leather tie, guilder's uniform pressed and sandalled feet light on the stone floor. He takes a quick inventory of the room, seemingly unsurprised and unconcerned by what he finds, even though I'm still holding my splintered arrow shaft under Levi's chin like I have any hope of actually harming him with it. Even though the world is upside down.

"Let the girls stay," Sholto repeats. "It would be prudent to introduce everyone, don't you think? The others are downstairs waiting...and I strictly forbid you to harm them, Skye. We need to talk. There is much to tell you."

"More lies?"

My voice is meant to sound scornful, but it doesn't. It just wobbles dangerously. Sholto hears it, and seemingly has little empathy for it, fixing me, like *always*, with a stern look down the bridge of his nose. "Compose yourself, and drop that arrow. Let me tell you of your mother, Saffron. She was a member of the Aeolus Dynasty; Nixen of the storm winds, as Fjord said. I knew her from the day she was born...and her mother, and grandmother...and beyond."

My berserk pulse picks up more speed. "What?"

"I've been known to your family for a very long time, Skye. Since before the Impurity War."

"You were *alive* during the Impurity War?"

He nods. Horrified heartbeats pass, and then I take a physical step back, my spine hitting the wall as if to physically remove myself from what's just been revealed. The unused arrow shaft falls to my side, my hold suddenly as listless as the eyes of the opponent I *meant* to hurt with it are. There are no words to express my shock at hearing Sholto say that, even after the huge, unreal things I've already been told tonight. The Impurity War was hundreds of years ago, which makes him...hundreds of years old.

"Do I even know you?" I ask, and this time my voice does break. Shatters. "How could you not tell me this, Sholto?"

"There are reasons."

"Tell me them. Tell me what could justify something like this? Hiding the fact you're ancient from me? That you knew my mum? That...that I'm from Elysium, and a demigod...?" I turn to Fjord. "Why didn't you tell me? How *could* you not tell me?"

"There are reasons, Skye," Sholto repeats, before Fjord can give what looks like another apology. "I will tell you them, in time, but first would say I'm sorry that Saffron is no longer with us. I was fond of your mother. We believe her death is embroiled in the assassination attempts inflicted on Elysium's dynasties, but there's also a much bigger narrative behind all of this, and it's still being told to us. There is much left uncertain. I know you're upset and confused, and recognise why, but I think when you hear the full story – or rather, as much of the story as we know – you'll understand why all of this happened as it did. You'll understand why we kept you in the dark."

"No," I shake my head furiously. "I trusted you, Sholto. I trusted you, when you took me in off the streets. I was so young and skinny and hopeless, and you lied. Every second of every day, you lied to me about who you were, and who I was. When I was having breakfast, first slept in a *bed*, learnt how to read...which I'm still so terrible at and always will be because I'm a bad reader and you're a bad man! You're both bad men! I don't understand! I'll never understand, because it wasn't true and it wasn't honest. I've been...more foolish than a fool. Than a fool fooling around. So foolish. Too foolish. It doesn't happen that way to beggars and thieves, does it? No one takes them in without an ulterior motive, and goddesses, I just...I just don't..."

I have to stop before I succumb to something of utter distress, something to bring me to my knees. *Everything* we've shared over the years now feels false. The joking, the fighting, the fatherly and brotherly love...it all becomes twisted and violated and wrong. Even the concept of a year suddenly seems fraudulent; for after walking this earth for hundreds of them, the timeline of my life must feel like a weekly schedule to Sholto. Insubstantial and insignificant...not worth *telling* me about.

"I'll never forgive you for this," I whisper. "Never. And I never want to see either of you again. I need to go. Now."

If Sholto feels repentance or worry over those words, he doesn't show it. He just stands there, regarding me with passive brown eyes, wearing a carefully ambiguous expression on his face. His silence screams indifference...and I truly think my heart might be breaking.

I think it's already broken.

I still remember stealing his wallet in The Eastern Harbours the day he met me. I still remember the first time I stepped inside his kitchenette in the Guild, in *awe* of it. I still remember passing the first meal he cooked for me out of the window, giving it to the best friend hiding behind his open shutters; the best friend true and tough enough to check up on me in my new home, who to this day still lives on the streets and that I *miss*. I still remember learning to spar with wooden spoons on the worn, tiled floor, and then fighting with my fists, and then knives. Then my *bow*. I remember it all, and it's *all* a gods damn lie.

That thought is suddenly too much to bear. I move to leave before I do actually fall down. Move to run from the two people I used to view as family, but who are suddenly stranger than strangers, bringing with them a foreign world shoved violently in my face. A world I'd once yearned to know...right? Did I not dream of visiting Elysium, just days ago? To look upon Nixen? To quench my desire for danger by experiencing something forbidden? The cruel irony of this situation is not lost on me, and I guess you *should* always be careful what you wish for...

"Levi," Fjord utters in a low voice as I lurch towards the door, fumbling the lock. "Please."

I look frantically over my shoulder and flinch, legs trembling, pulse sky-rocketing, thoughts overrun by the brittle edge of fear...because the Guardian is suddenly right there in front of me again, moving impossibly fast to be so. Woodsmoke hits the back of my throat as he lifts a hand, palm landing high on the door to push it shut.

"I'm not going to hurt you, Skye," Levi states quietly, and how many gods damn times has he said that tonight? Not enough to have me believing it.

"I need to leave right now," I exclaim hoarsely. "Right now. This second. Let me go."

"We can't," Fjord says, moving our way. "It's not safe for you on the streets, Skye. Not when you're this upset and our enemies are hunting us. Please give me a chance to explain further, and *please* believe me. It's not safe for you out there. We're just trying to protect you."

I don't listen to him, because who would? I try to wrench the door open again but it doesn't move, even when I pull roughly on it...pull with all my might. I twist back to Levi, breathing hard. The words *I'm not going to hurt you* echo mockingly in my ears, and you'd think I'd see proof of them in his eyes if they were true...but I don't. They're granite, storm clouds, with *nothing* in them.

"Let me leave," I exclaim tightly, and gods, it's embarrassing how close to a sob it is. I turn to Fjord, barely seeing him through the tears. "If he means me no harm, and *you* mean me no harm, you'll let me leave! N..now!"

His expression twists into immediate grief and regret, but it's Sholto who responds. His voice is so low I don't recognise it, or the blurry, unforgiving look on his face.

"This is for your own good, Skye. With Xa—"

I don't let him finish. I duck beneath Levi's arm, slipping through his hold even though he shadows me, clearly pre-empting the move. Somehow...I'm faster than him. Faster than I've ever been in my life, and you should know it's months before I move like it again.

Months before I realise I *can* move like it.

I flee towards the Irving girls by the stairs, partly because they appeared in the house from somewhere, which means there's probably an exit downstairs...but mostly because I don't think Levi will throw his knife with the two of them in his sights. Or maybe he would, if he's sure he'll hit his target.

The thought is cruel.

This night is cruel.

"This is for your own good."

Never, *never* are those words as simple or as innocent as they sound, especially when said by a man who lied to me for seven years.

I rush for the bannisters, readying myself to leap over them, but Fjord is suddenly there to intercept me, hands held out as if to calm me. "Skye, *please* listen to us. Xavier Ar—"

Unnatural wind volleys into the room through the open window, battering our loose garments and knocking over the amphorae huddled in the corner of the room. They topple to the floor, thick terracotta smashing into hundreds of pieces.

Wine spills.

It looks like blood.

The open window.

The final escape route.

I veer towards it, every nerve ending in my spine tingling as I sense someone moving in behind me. Terror rises when I realise they're about to seize me around the waist *just* like they did in the Medical Syndicate, only thank every goddess Levi doesn't get to me. There's the fleshy sound of two people colliding as both Fjord and he try to stop me but get in each other's way. Someone grunts out a curse, one of the girls gasps...and it's enough.

I don't break stride when I reach the window, springing off the ledge and into the night, jerking the hood of my cloak up. My feet pound over the ash laden rooftop in fury and fear and disbelief, their sound urgent and desperate and *lost.*

I feel so lost.

Ruffian

"You're from Elysium. And you're a demigod."

The words repeat in my mind over and over and *over* again like some mad, feverish cantillation, only there's nothing therapeutic about this phrase, and the more I think it, the less coherent it becomes.

I pelt across the rooftops, putting as much distance between myself and the safe house, and everyone in it, as I can. The familiar itch of windblown ash is a welcome plague upon my lungs, grounding me and telling me that this is real.

This is all horrifyingly real.

How could Fjord and Sholto keep this from me? One of my parents a god, the other a nix of the wind; a *dead* nix of the wind? The Impurity War being instigated by The Sabirs? It hurts so much to know what they've concealed from me, and it's also embarrassing. I feel foolish for not knowing who or what I am, and more for believing their lies about who and what *they* were. Would I have gone my whole life without realising the truth had Fin not asked me to go to the Medical Syndicate tonight? The thought makes my hot belly writhe.

And how is any of this even possible? Don't demigods have powers? All the heroines and heroes do in the legends...but I don't. I'm just short and scarred, with a terribly distracted mind and a mouth that almost always sounds like a child. What does that mean? That I'm powerless? The runt of the litter? Is that why no god has ever shown up on my doorstep and claimed me as their child? Why

I was abandoned on the streets of Ioxthel for so many years? Why Fjord and Sholto never told me the truth?

The miles scorch under my feet with just as much vigour as the thoughts blazing internally, but eventually I grow too weary to continue, and I suppose that's a fact of life, isn't it?

Nothing can last forever.

Even the fake family you make for yourself.

I stop on a rooftop, muscles cramping so badly I have to brace my hands on my knees, lungs violently sucking in air. Alcázar lies shrouded in morning fog far to the west, and the streets below are also misty and quiet. Behind, I hear gentle waves lapping at the shoreline and the scant sound of voices; probably fishermen back from a night trawl, readying themselves to go straight to the tavern. A salty breeze teases wisps of hair from my braid, and the feel of it is so familiar and bittersweet.

I straighten to standing and raise my head to the sky, struggling to ease my breathing against a suffocating wave of nostalgia. Tears rise like the tide, and I let out several silent sobs.

Desperation.

Relief.

I couldn't tell you why they're given, because I don't know anything in this moment. Somehow, that's ok. Unconsciously my legs have taken me back to the streets where my first memories take root. The streets that were my home before Sholto found me, seven years ago, and where my best friend still lives, and thrives.

The Eastern Harbours.

I haul my heavy limbs to the sea front and squat on a rooftop busy with washing and spice vessels, watching as the sky brightens and the harbour master ushers in the first merchant ships of the day. I don't have to wait long until I see an unruly head of curls I know just as well as my own greyish pelt. He's strolling idly along the main harbour's promenade, a sweet pastry in one hand and a small cat cradled in the other. Loose navy pantaloons and a pair of brown leather sandals that somehow always evade any ash stains set off his olive skin; and it could be he steals a new pair of shoes every day. Wouldn't be surprised. A green headscarf is draped half-heartedly over his neck, as if he couldn't be bothered to wrap it properly around himself this morning, yet I know that when he stands before any guilder – pockets heavy with pilfered goods and expression as beguilingly innocent as a lover shot by one of Eros's arrows – that scarf will become the only disguise he needs to save himself from the cells.

My heart swells at the sight of him, the euphoria a thousand times stronger than anything I've ever felt before, or ever will.

This is Tristan Knight.

He's the king of Ioxthel's street ruffians, my oldest and dearest friend, and the boy true and tough enough to hide behind the shutters of Sholto's kitchenette in the Guild, when I had my first meal there.

I watch as he wanders down the quaint harbour with a boundless spring to his step, dipping his head in greeting to the early risers and skipping around coils of rope and chain. He bows deeply to a young girl as she steps ashore from a merchant ship, grinning when she blushes. I know the ease with which he carries himself conceals the alertness of his eyes, and have no doubt he's scouting his surroundings for opportunities. I keep watching him, waiting, hoping...

He brushes past a floristry stall, murmuring a greeting to its owner as she bends down to retrieve a bunch of blooms from her water bucket. Next, he passes by a couple of vendors struggling to put up their awning. He steps around a nearby pothole in the street, dancing in a circle as if to regain his footing.

My eyes narrow.

Suspicious behaviour.

Quick as lightning, and entirely too fast for anyone but those paying keen attention to him, I see him steal another pastry and a plush leather satchel from their stalls. With a slip of his hand inside those loose, navy pantaloons he leaves a small origami swan and the sprig of blossom he just lifted from the florist on their counters; woefully inadequate payment, but payment nonetheless, for his light fingers.

He doesn't miss a beat throughout the whole ordeal, continuing on his way with the satchel over his shoulder and the pastry in his mouth, and the cat still clinging lazily to his arm.

No one notices a thing.

A laugh that's really a sob spills from my sombre lips, and the swelling in my chest spreads. This act is so completely him – so foolish, fickle and fantastic. Tristan has a heart of gold, a mind sharper than wit herself and an untethered, dangerously daring spirit. He's full to the brim with life, and *everything* you could possibly wish for in the very best of friends. I've never, ever been more desperate to be in his arms and to feel his warming presence – and as if he senses my thoughts, his head turns in my direction. Despite my hooded form and the distance between us he recognises me immediately, and the smile that breaks across his face is glorious. I drop from my rooftop and patter towards him.

"Good morning, little wolf cub who shines brighter than the moon she loves so much," he cajoles, taking the fresh pastry from his mouth and offering it to me. "I stole you breakfast."

"I'm not hungry."

With a slight of his hand into his pockets, he holds out another of his origami swans. "How about this fellow? Want him? Freshly folded last night..."

This gesture – so familiar, so bittersweet – causes my expression to crumple beneath the hood. Tristan sees it, because he sees through everything with me. He very quickly pushes the fabric down, blue eyes sobering as soon as they examine my pathetic expression of distress.

"What's wrong, Wolf?" he asks, moving in closer. "Talk to me right now. Why're you unhappy? What's wrong?"

"Everything," I whisper brokenly. "Are you busy this morning?"

"What kind of a stupid question is that?! I'm never busy where you're concerned, especially if you're *weeping*..." Tristan shifts the cat to his shoulder and hooks his elbow through mine. "This way. Let's go home."

We wander down the shoreline some way, reaching a smaller secondary harbour whose shores are littered with upturned fishing boats, crispy seaweed and broken crab shells. It's always deserted of people excepting the ruffians who've made their home here, only no one is around now. Dawn is an unusually busy time for the city's best pickpockets.

Tristan pops his black cat down on the shells and busies himself with examining one of the larger overturned boats. I watch him, eyes stinging with sea-spray and another form of salt water, and heart just so overwhelmed. I love this boy more than I love life itself. The dusty jawline, the deep olive skin and the hint of dimples above full lips that, misleadingly, give Tristan an air of boyish innocence. Drinking in the rugged charm of his features is like sipping on trust and nostalgia, the most profound shelter.

He soon lifts the side of his chosen boat up, heedless of the splintering wood, "Hop under, will you? There's a candle in my pocket we can light if it's too dark."

I've been beneath an upturned fishing boat many times throughout my life, most of them before I joined the Guild, and most of them hiding spots *from* guilders. I don't even think twice. I just crawl in and cross my legs, still trying to hold back tears.

"You coming?"

Tristan isn't speaking to me. I watch his cat raise its bottom high into the air in a long, languid stretch. He yawns, showing us his sharp, fang-like little teeth...and then promptly turns away, the tip of his tail twitching. He starts picking his way through the damp shells and pebbles, perhaps in search of breakfast, but definitely not in search of our company.

Tristan snorts at him, and ducks beneath the boat with me. Daylight filters through holes sure to leak water into the vessel if it were ever to float again, but it's still a little gloomy.

Seconds pass with only our breathing for company. I hear Tristan rustling through his pockets; a warm, solid arm jostling against mine as he settles beside me.

"Do you like my new satchel?" he asks to the darkness.

"Yeah," I croak. "What made you steal it?"

"I have a new alter ego who likes this sort of thing."

"Oh...cool. And the cat?"

"Tiberius?" Tristan strikes a match, illuminating his face. He's looking at me already, grinning. "Hello, Wolf."

Despite everything, I feel my lips soften. "Hey."

He lights the candle. "I found Tiberius a few weeks ago. He also likes to take a morning stroll along the harbour front...followed me all the way here one day, snuck beneath my blanket, and now won't leave me alone. I'm growing fond of him. He reminds me of this tiny little human wolf cub *years* back who did the same thing..." He taps my knee with the sweet pastry. "You sure you don't want this?"

I shake my head. "I feel sick to my bones, Tristan. Like I've been drinking old, grotty blood."

His lips purse. "That doesn't sound good, Wolf. Talk to me. What's going on?"

"You won't believe it."

"Try me."

"Fjord and Sholto have been lying to me. The entire time I've known them. They're from Elysium, and they just spent the night telling me I am, too. They told me I'm a *demigod.*"

Tristan's eyebrows shoot up. "Oh. That's unexpected. Uh...tell me everything?"

That's exactly what I do. I tell him of last night; from my trip to the Medical Syndicate on Fin's request and my fight with Levi there, to the other Nixen, the safe house, the truth about the Impurity War, Fjord's story on Elysium's assassinations and the last, missing member of the Aeolus Dynasty...me. I tell him they knew my mothers before they died, and then I quote Sholto telling me, *This is for your own good, Skye* upon my request to flee the safe house. I tell him how the entire evening feels like it's utterly ruined me.

Tristan is a marvellous listener. He lets me talk unhindered by interruption, but I see my own burning questions glinting in his eyes and I feel his wrath brewing. I spare him no detail and I spare *myself* no feeling; so when the tears tumbling from my eyes turn to these horrible, ugly, gut-wrenching sobs I don't fight it, just fall sideways into him and let him hold me through it.

"How could they keep this from me?" I sniffle, what seems like hours later. "How *could* they? About my mothers...this past life. And how is it possible, anyway? How have I not known I'm Nixen? A demigod? I mean, do you think it's true, Tristan? I'm not dreaming this am I? I haven't gone mad? I'm worried the Guardian, Levi, might have dropped me on my head earlier..."

Tristan's expression is full of sympathy. "You're not dreaming and you haven't gone mad, Skye, but I would first ask *you* that question. You were the one there. Do *you* think it's true?"

"I...don't know. It's unfathomable, all they've told me. The truth about the Impurity War, Nixen *not* being the enemies everyone thinks they are, the part where I'm a demigod, my mum being called Saffron. I just...in my mind it's all so scrambled."

"Understandable, but...forget your mind for a moment. What does your gut tell you?"

"To believe it all."

"Me too."

Of course. We're basically the same person. "I hate them, Tristan," I sniffle bitterly. "I trusted them."

"We both did, Skye. I'm so sorry."

"They'll be looking for me. They didn't want me to leave the safe house."

Tristan makes a low noise. "They won't find you. I promise you. The ruffians will hide you, and shield you. We'll fight with you. "

Tears of gratitude sting my eyes. "Thank you. I think we need a plan."

"For hiding you? Shan't worry about that, Wolf. I can basically fit you in my pocket."

"I meant longer term, actually. If it *is* true that Nixen aren't the enemies we thought they were, then what do we do about them being in the city? What do we do about Fjord and Sholto lying to the *entire* Guild? Lying to me? What do we do about there being Guardians here?"

Tristan thinks on this. "We need more answers, don't we? We need more of the story. They told you there was a lot more to tell, right? Then let's find it out. Let's spy on them. Do you remember where the safe house is?"

I nod.

"I'll have ruffians watch the building, and watch Fjord and Sholto in the Guild, too. We'll give it several days for things to quieten down, to survey how the scene settles, and then we'll spy them. Spy on them *good,* Skye, in the deep of night under moonlight...just like you like it. We'll spy so good they won't know what's hit them."

My throat is so tight I barely get the words out, "I love you."

He squeezes my shoulders. "I love you too. I'm so sorry. I can't imagine what you're feeling right now, but you must know you have me. You have the ruffians. We'll get through this together." He gathers me closer. "Do you want to hear some decent news to help soothe this terrible wound...because I have something to share if you want to hear it?"

I heave a shuddering breath. "I do want to hear it. I want to hear all about you, please. No more on my mad world that's upside down."

He gives me a small smile. "The Queen has a new bodyguard. No one really knows where he came from, but everyone is in awe. He's apparently a legend, or so my mole in the great fortress tells me...hence my stealing the leather satchel this morning. I've decided to broaden my disguise repertoire to include *healer* too, just in case Xavier decides the king of Ioxthel's streets needs to be taught a lesson. No one attacks a doctor, do they? No. It's genius. A mad good idea..."

I pull back sharply. "Xavier?"

"Is Ruby's new bodyguard," Tristan supplies, grinning impishly. The expression soon falls at my aghast reaction. "What's wrong?"

I tell him about my recent trip to spy on Ruby's Council in Alcázar, and my run in with the young blonde man shrouded in obnoxious mystery and sadistic mirth, there.

"Well, seems like you know who he is now," Tristan muses when I finish. "I'm sorry you clashed blades, but look on the bright side...you evaded him, which makes you better than a monarch's personal guard."

"But...but he knew my name, Tristan. He called me Skye...and he knew of Fjord and Sholto, too."

"Oh," Tristan's eyes widen. "Σκατά. Really?"

I nod unhappily. "What should we do? If Xavier knows my identity and caught me spying on Ruby then that's bad news..."

"I'll have my mole burrow through Alcázar as well he can, and to listen out at the Guild to see if you're in trouble? I mean...you say the man you saw was undercover that night, spying?"

"He looked like it."

"So it might be a different Xavier to Ruby's bodyguard?"

"Maybe," I say slowly, but I don't believe it. The coincidence is just too great. How many Xaviers *are* there in Ioxthel? "I think I should probably be very worried. I *am*, but I'm also stuck on this night. Fjord and Sholto being from Elysium. Me, a demigod..." I swallow tightly. "This week is just something else."

He kisses my temple. "Yes. It is. Good thing you're right where you should be, sitting beneath a damp, rotting boat by candlelight, nestled safely in your best friend's arms."

"Yeah," I sniffle. "I've got you."

"You have. Always. And don't forget that together we're invincible, Skye. We'll get through this, just like we get through everything. I swear to you with everything in me, we'll get through this."

He sounds so sure, like a child full of naive optimism and imprudent resolve...only Tristan is no longer young and he's never been a fool.

We sit this way for hours, our backs against the sides of the flaking upturned boat, damp pebbles digging into our numbing bottoms and knees resting against one another's, just like they did when we were children. Tristan mumbles the day away, talking of ruffians and stargazing and finding himself a sweetheart. Tiberius soon scratches on the outside, begging to be let in. He smells of fish and it's absolutely revolting. Tristan snorts out a laugh that turns into something much *much* more, and goodness, it's my favourite sound in the entire world – as rich as olive oil and freshly turned soil, as husky as the nutty wheat fields that surround Ioxthel's walls. I feel it tingle down my spine, warming me, buoying me, and only start sinking when it ends. The sobs soon turn into a violent need to shriek of the injury I feel Fjord and Sholto have inflicted by deceiving me. I almost let it out, but then Tristan gathers me impossibly close and presses another firm, lingering kiss to my temple. He doesn't say anything further and he doesn't need to. The embrace is enough...and in the flickering orange glow of our upturned boat that smells of seaweed and fish, with my best friend's skin forever warming mine, the misery and fury lessens.

Past Life

Ioxthel's rooftops, six days later. My senses are wick ready to be lit by the gloriously cool resolve of moonlight, my sobs long-passed...or so I'm very firmly telling myself. Here and now, it's not the time for crying. It's the time for spying good. For learning more of this mad story by unveiling the lies and ulterior motives, and summoning long-overdue truths.

Tristan is beside me, of course, hissing to a little ruffian girl huddled on her haunches on the streets below us. There's an immediate answering whistle from Akira - very soft, and just one note ascending.

"Check the back, will you?"

Footfalls patter away, even quieter than the breath of air she just puffed from pursed lips, and you should know that every single ruffian in Ioxthel knows how to whistle like that...knows the language pioneered by a genius who can't read or write himself but usurps everyone else by creating his own damn *dialect.*

We can't see Akira leave, but I can picture the scene exactly - a scrawny little girl scampering down the alley, wayward tendrils of dark, dirty hair escaping the deep blue headscarf she's all but submerged in, knees and palms scraping the rough stone walls of the buildings she passes. A wolf cub melding itself effortlessly into the shadows. She's the youngest of Tristan's ruffians, but also his favourite. Wiry, wily and unwaveringly loyal, just like all his crew are, but Akira has an edge, and there's something impossibly staunch in her ability to do, or even pre-empt, Tristan's bidding. She's gutsy, unapologetic, apoplectic at her circumstance in life...the *perfect* combination for a ruffian. I would know, because I used to be her.

She's not the only one here with us tonight. Three more of Tristan's pack are on neighbouring rooftops, and more loiter in the nearby streets, waiting to respond to the faintest whistle of summons...the first hint of trouble. It's been almost a week since I ran from here; Fjord and Sholto's safe house. True to his word, Tristan has kept me hidden from the world in the forgotten harbour, and also the dilapidated fountains he sometimes uses as a base just off the main oceanside promenade. The ruffians have been watching Fjord and Sholto in the Guild and here, surveying how the scene settles whilst I figure out how to be hungry again...and now it's our turn to wait and watch and spy good.

I tell myself I've no idea what's going to happen tonight, even though I do. Listening to clandestine meetings under starlight is my speciality, but there's only so much information one can glean from a conversation without prompting it, or summoning it. I know I am the summoner in all of this, which means talking to Fjord and whoever else is lurking in the small, bare building before us.

Which means...entering it.

Tristan might sense my worry at the thought, or he might be feeling the same, because he suddenly leans into me and mutters, "Everyone else is in position."

"Good."

"Are you ok?"

"Are you?"

"Skye..."

"I'm fine," I spare him a glance. "Totally fine. The finest I've been this fine year."

Tristan doesn't look impressed by the rebuff, but foregoes replying. Akira's whistle soon sounds again, but it's different this time; low and wavering, like a subtle warning. Tristan listens to two more rounds of the pattern before translating to me...or rather to *you*, because I know his dialect like the back of my own hand...

"Someone just entered the upstairs window, but not Fjord or Sholto. Akira has never seen him before."

Just moments after he says this, the washed blue door on the safe house's second story opens. This person *is* Fjord. One hand is on the scimitar at his hip, the other resting on the doorframe as he scans the surrounding rooftops.

"Skye?" he calls softly. "I know you're out here, and I know Tristan is with you, too. I know those whistles, sometimes enough to think I understand what they mean."

Silence.

Neither Tristan nor I reply to him, although my friend does lean further into me, whispering *very* quietly, "What're we doing, Wolf?"

"We know what we're doing," I hiss back. "I'm going down there, and you're staying here listening out for me."

"Are you *sure* you don't want me with you?"

I always want you with me, Tristan. "No. I'll be fine. But listen for me? Look out for me?"

"We'll be seconds away," he vows.

I rise from my haunches and move silently over the roof, pausing just before I reach the edge. Fluttering awnings brush my limbs like they've done twelve thousand times on missions like this, only they don't feel like companions tonight. They feel like the hands of ghosts gone long before my time, ushering me towards uneasy truths and broken friendships and daunting futures I'm not sure I ever want to hear about...but I have to, don't I?

I have to know more.

I drop to the outer steps of the safe house, landing on my toes. Despite the ruffian headscarf I know Fjord immediately realises it's me, and his hazel eyes are stark with relief. I'm a fool, because I still think of them as familiar, and I still think to believe them.

"Good evening, Skye," he offers sincerely. "It's very good to see you. I trust you're well?"

The formal greeting is Fjord down to the ground, as is the well-worn but immaculately polished tan leather breastplate over his pressed white shirt. I told you of this, the first time we saw him together. He's always so well presented, always so genteel and earnestly spoken...except he lies for *years* about big things, like the fact he's from Elysium and I'm a damn demigod.

"Is Tristan coming in?"

"No," I growl. "Him and his crew are waiting to ambush you if necessary. You won't know what's hit you. Who's inside? Bad people?"

"Uh...no. Jay, a nix you haven't met yet but might have seen from afar in the Medical Syndicate last week. He's a tutor to the Irving sisters, Wren and Ember, though they're not here. Levi just arrived, too."

"Sholto?"

"No, it's just the three of us. Jay, Levi and myself."

I digest that information, wondering what to think of it. Part of me is glad Sholto isn't here, because I think I'd be doubly mad looking at his stupidly composed face. The other part is frustrated. I want and need to interrogate him, to summon truth and information until my ears bleed.

"I cannot imagine how you're feeling at the moment, Skye," Fjord says, perhaps seeing an opportunity in the silence. "I just want you to know I'm so sorry for it. I never meant to hurt you in hiding this, and I cannot express my regrets for it enough. I cannot express that you're *safe* here, too. With me, and Levi. And Jay. We're not your enemies, and I'll never let you befall harm. I think of you as family, Skye."

"Know what I think of you as?" I bite out. "A liar, Fjord. A gods damn liar, who speaks so damn well you don't see through his words to the falsities behind them. You just believe him. With blind faith. Like someone more foolish than a fool themselves. That's me. More foolish than a fool...and you're the liar."

He has the audacity to look upset by the stupidly uttered words. His mouth shuts against further apology, and with a heavy sigh he reaches behind himself for the door.

The salóni is as I remember it, with its copper pendant lanterns, wicker chairs and single diphros stool. There's the staircase in one corner of the room and a reduced number of wine amphorae in the other, because if you remember the wind knocked over quite a few last time.

I immediately notice Levi standing by the window, and someone vaguely recognisable in one of the chairs; the male nix from the Medical Syndicate's herb garden, with his hair cut low to his scalp and a very broad frame. Visible now with proximity and the warm glow of indoor lighting are his features. Full lips, deep brown eyes, soft cheeks and jawline, just a hint of grey to his beard, and dark skin. He's years older than the other two, but he's bouncing both his sturdy knees up and down vigorously like an overexcited child, moving them to some urgent, unheard drumbeat. They stop the second we start examining one another. I don't imagine he sees much in me, because the ruffian scarf is draped heavily over my face, but I expect my eyes tell him enough.

I'm angry.

Upside down.

"You must be Skye," he says, voice smooth and deep, and with that lilt to it that's definitely not Ioxthelian. "I'm Jay. Tutor to the young Irving girls, whom I believe you met last time you were here."

Yes. I well remember Wren and Ember...but I don't tell him that. My eyes bounce to Fjord making his way towards the other wicker chair, and then Levi. His cheeks are flushed, like he's just been running through the night air, and I bet you he's the one Akira saw entering via the window. Is he bowing to me? I think he might be, inclining his head in that way, but it looks odd as if he hasn't done it for a while – and regardless, the courtesy is lost on me.

"The girls are beyond Ioxthel's walls now," Fjord says, stopping by the other chair but not sitting. "They're staying there with Idris, a Guardian-in-training, and their uncle, Yusuf Irving. His Guardian, Rose, is also with them. You might have seen her in the Medical Syndicate with Jay? She's around his age. Quite small?"

Perhaps. I remember a slender lady with weapons glinting beneath her lilac cloak and greying hair gleaming in the moonlight. I don't mention so, though, holding my silence.

"I'm also staying there for the most part," Jay adds, "but I was growing restless this evening, and decided to pay the boys a visit. It's been a while since they were both in the same room with me, and I miss having diligent students, because those girls...those girls are trouble."

He flashes everyone a fond smile, including me. One knee starts jigging energetically, maybe expectantly, but I still don't respond. I've barely taken a step inside the room and Fjord seems worried by it, probably because I'm never stationary and I'm *never* quiet. He's hovering by his seat, unwilling to sit down – playing the gentleman every bit as much as I'm playing the fool.

"Please say something, Skye," he entreats after long moments of awkward silence. "Please sit down? Make yourself comfortable?"

My nostrils flare indignantly at that, as if I could *ever* be comfortable here, with him. With Nixen. Woodsmoke and sea air tickle my senses when I do, and a wave of nostalgia hits, tugging me back to my childhood on the eastern streets. Within seconds, I know *exactly* what, or who, transported me there...and pivot with dizzying speed to the window. "You've been in The Eastern Harbours!"

Levi might look surprised. "Yes, I have."

"You've been spying on me!" I turn to Fjord in disbelief. "He's been spying on me!"

"Yes," he admits with a sigh. "I asked him to."

"You what?!"

Another sigh. "I asked him to mind you and Tristan in the harbours because I'm worried for your safety at the moment. That's all there is to this. No foul intent. I asked him to go there simply to protect you."

"Why should I believe you?!"

"Because we're friends? And because Levi is my Guardian, Skye, which means he lives to protect those dear to me. I swear to you, you are safe with him...safer than you could possibly imagine."

He watches me with beseeching eyes that make him look so much younger than he actually is. Letting out a low noise of frustration, I shove the scarf down from my mouth and turn back to Levi. He straightens from the wall and squares his shoulders, obviously anticipating an address.

"How did you find us in the harbours? *Where* did you find us? Did you follow me? After I ran from here?"

He nods.

"You've been...there the whole time?"

Again, he nods reluctantly.

Horror riots through me, my belly writhing with unease and total violation. He's been spying on us the *entire* time without our knowing? For six days? Whilst we ate? Slept? Washed? Gods, that's a terrible prospect. I thought I'd been hidden. I thought I'd been *safe,* with just my best friend...just us against the upside down world.

Tense moments pass before Levi's expression opens to something very grave. "I apologise if I've made you uneasy, Skye. That was not my intention."

"Of course it's made me uneasy! You've been spying on us without our consent! That's a horrible invasion of privacy!"

"I'm sorry."

"It was me who told Levi to remain hidden," Fjord is quick to inform me, "and therefore me who should take responsibility for your disapproval, Skye. I would tell you again it's for your safety, and that alone. No foul intent. Levi is simply there to protect you, and he's entirely honourable in it. He would never act in a way that would hurt your dignity or encroach upon your privacy more than absolutely necessary. You can trust him."

"After what happened in the Medical Syndicate? After you *lied* to me for five whole years, Fjord? After I thought I was *alone* with my best friend? Just us? Against the upside down world?" I glare at them both. "No, thank you. I won't be trusting either of you. Ever. As in...never. That's what ever means, here."

"I'm sincerely sorry for what occurred between us in the Medical Syndicate too, Skye," Levi says, and you should know his voice isn't rough with *feeling*. It's just rusty, like it hasn't been used for a long time – like that weird bow. "I would never have intercepted you had I known who you were, had I known you weren't someone I needed to worry about. I'm sorry for your unease."

"You don't look it," I bite out furiously. "You look like nothing, like there's no life in you. Sound like it, too."

Mm, that was mean, but I'm struggling to reconcile the fact he's been there the *entire* time, and Tristan and I didn't know. My palms shift over my bow, eyes just as restless taking in the threat. He's wearing his leather shoulder harness again, but like last time I don't see many weapons there; just two straight daggers that must be from

Elysium, because Ioxthelian blades are always curved. There's a thin leather cord around his neck, falling well below the "v" of his shirt, and though I can't see what hangs from it I'm immediately reminded of Fjord's hourglass pendant, the one he sometimes fiddles reverently with and *never* takes off.

In fact, you should know Levi reminds me of Fjord in several respects. Both have the height and strength of a fighter, with brown hair and modest features – though Fjord's are sharper, strikingly expressive and far more transparent. Transparent and...sad, right now.

"Please don't take your ire out on those who don't deserve it, Skye. If you need to be angry, be so at me. Not Levi. He's done nothing wrong."

"He attacked me in the Medical Syndicate, Fjord!"

"He didn't really. He just stopped you escaping because he didn't know who you *were.* We've been over this."

"Have we? Shame for you, then. I still don't get it. Still don't believe you, and never will again!"

He sighs heavily at this, and finally decides to drop down into the second wicker chair. He starts rubbing the heels of his palms into his eyes as if *he's* the one stressed and exhausted; the one lost trying to navigate an entire world that's been overturned so damn fast. "Should I just start talking?"

"Yes," I snap. "Start talking, Fjord. It's not like I've been waiting for five years to hear the truth, is it?"

Another sigh. "Do you remember what I told you about the Impurity War of four hundred years ago? About how it was The Sabirs who waged genocide on Nixen with a great, godly weapon? Well...it's the same weapon that Ruby is searching for now, the same weapon you heard her talk about when you were spying on the Council in Alcázar. It's been lost ever since the war, and no one knows where it is. No one except the one person who hid it, Sholto's father."

Sholto has a father? "What is the weapon?"

"The Torch of Prometheus."

Right, this is another big piece of news. Prometheus is a Titan, one of the forbearers to the twelve gods and goddesses of Olympus, of whom Zeus is now king. Most of Prometheus' brethren were entombed in the deepest recesses of the underworld, a place called Tartarus, when they were defeated by Zeus's forces during the Titanomachy; an age of endless battles that shook the world and shifted power to the Olympians many, many eons ago. But, Prometheus was amongst those titans who *allied* with Zeus, and he was rewarded for his loyalty following the war with the task, the honour, of creating mortals.

So humankind came to be.

Prometheus crafted mortals from clay, and loved us dearly. In fact, he loved us so much he stole the element of fire from Mount Olympus, the great kingdom of the gods and goddesses, and gifted it to Earth to keep us toasty and warm, hearty with the joy and passion of life's vigour. Zeus, as you might imagine, was enraged by the theft. No longer in good favour, Prometheus was cursed by him to spend eternity chained to a rock face, where every day an eagle would peck out his liver. The poor immortal titan would recover overnight, his body regenerating itself, only to be subject to the torment and agony and grossness all over again the next day – until one of Zeus's better known sons, Heracles, freed him.

That's a funny notion, if you think about it.

Father and son, acting in opposition.

The Torch of Prometheus pertains to the original handful of fire the titan first stole from Mount Olympus to give to us mortals. It's supposedly so powerful it ignites everything in its path – fast, before the intent to blink an eye has even been sent for. So *if* Fjord is telling the truth about this, and Ruby *is* searching for it, then we should all be worried.

"We've no idea how The Sabirs got their hands on the Torch last time during the Impurity War," Fjord goes on. "It's a horrendous thought to think they might be able to do so again. Another swathe of land set to waste like The Nether? Another million beings swept off the face of the earth?" He shakes his head. "It's a terrible thought. And it's pretty clear Ruby is making plans to find the Torch. We believe she wishes to solicit Wivern's help in that endeavour. The Crown Prince and Princess are travelling to Ioxthel for negotiations, and lead the entourage expected to arrive in the city tomorrow. We think war is going to be waged on Elysium again."

I think about that. "Is this why Nixen are suddenly in Ioxthel? To stop them?"

"Uh...not really, actually. Technically, everybody besides Jay and Levi are surprise guests. They're not supposed to be here."

"Technically, it's sort of my fault they *are*," Jay confesses from his wicker chair. "Unbeknownst to me, the girls, my students, and their Guardian-in-training, Idris, followed me through Elysium until it was too late to go back...and in turn, their very worried uncle and his Guardian, Rose, followed and found us." He snorts, only to immediately heave a sigh. "Those girls. They're far too inquisitive for their own good, and quite a few people besides themselves usually suffer for it."

"Why are you and Levi here, then?" I ask, and then without waiting for a reply, "Why are *you* here, Fjord? And Sholto? Why have you been here for years in enemy territory?"

"You," he replies quietly. "We're here for you, Skye. You've very important...and not only because we love you."

I ignore the flutter in my chest at that. "Because I'm a demigod?"

He nods slowly. "Because you're a demigod with a *prophecy* to her name, and because your mother, Saffron, was Sholto's student and friend, and your surrogate mother was...my real mother."

I blink. "What?"

Wariness brightens his eyes. "My mother was the one who fled Elysium with you, Skye. Melody Winters. She raised you for a time."

"You told me my surrogate mother passed away?"

"She did."

"Your mother...passed away?"

"Yes."

I stare at him, vision tunnelling. "When?"

"I'm not exactly sure. Sometime after you both fled Elysium, and before your first memories on Ioxthel's streets begin."

"You lost a mother?"

"Yes," Fjord repeats quietly.

"She fled with me and left *you* in Elysium?"

"Yes. She left to protect you, Skye, but somewhere along the way she must have fallen. We don't know how or why, though we're trying to."

"Did you...did you know she left Elysium with me? Last time you said only one person knew, and that was Sholto?"

He nods. "Sholto was the only one who knew. Myself and my family didn't know."

"You didn't know?" I echo, dumbstruck. "Why your mum left you there?"

"No. The two of you just disappeared from home one day."

I truly don't recognise my voice. "Home?"

"Yes. For the first five years of your life, you grew up in my household. I don't remember much from that time because I was also young, but I know Melody raised you with us as a foster child, and I remember the day you left."

"Us?" I say faintly.

"Me and my brother, Kieran," he explains, and immediately lifts a hand to rub his sternum, as if he has heartburn. His fingers slip beneath his collar, finding the hourglass hanging there and holding it. "Kieran has also since passed, though. There's no us anymore. There's just me. And," he glances to the window, throat working, "and Levi, who was also around growing up. His parents were Guardians to mine, and family friends. We all lived with the Nereids on the western coast of Elysium. Technically, I still do."

I can't breathe. "Your mum raised me? With you and your brother?"

Fjord nods, watching me as if he knows the storm brewing inside me, except how could he? Overwhelming feeling hits hard, spinning the upside down world off-kilter again. Shock? Disbelief? Grief? Despair? Desperate, lost hope? I don't even know what it is this time, but it's huge. I've spent my *whole* life wondering who I am and how I ended up on Ioxthel's streets; neglected, forgotten and alone. Fjord is telling me now that I had a household, a home, back in Elysium before I ended up here? With him and his brother, and his mother? Was it loving? Was it safe?

Goddesses, I can't breathe.

I can't understand.

I can't...stand.

I feel myself sit down. Right there and then, I just plop down on the floor in front of the door, bow clattering a little in my haste.

"Why don't I remember?" I ask, but I still don't sound like me. I sound utterly lost – and muffled, too, because the heels of my hands are suddenly in my face, trying to shove the tears stinging my eyes back in. "Why don't I remember Elysium or travelling here, or *arriving* here? Or you? Or your brother? Your mother?"

"I...don't know," Fjord replies, voice suddenly very gentle. "Nor does Sholto. The only explanation is that you were still very young at the time, not yet five years old. Even I barely have memories of you with the Nereids at seven."

"Or she might be blanking trauma," Jay interjects in a deep voice. His chair rustles as he rearranges himself in it. "I apologise if the interruption is disrupting, but I felt the need to add that. I am a tutor of many things, including medicine, and especially medicine of the mind. We talked of this didn't we, Fjord?"

"I don't think now is the time," he mutters back.

Deep-rooted tension has suddenly taken up residence in my temples, pounding with every haunted beat of my heart. Trauma? What does that mean? What kind of—

"Did I have the scars?" I blurt out roughly, still speaking into my hands...still shoving tears back inside with them. "When I lived in Elysium, did I have my scars? As a child?"

"No," Fjord says, almost reluctantly. "You didn't."

"So...so *that* kind of trauma? Is that...what you mean?" I swallow tightly. "Ok. Fine. Wow, that's fine. I'm so fine. I'm so damn fine."

Is this real?

Or is this a dream?

It has to be. I feel like I'm floating, sinking...drowning. I haul in a juddering inhale that contains no air, just waves of overwhelmingly difficult feeling to identify and navigate. My thoughts start tumbling, like wolf cubs writhing over one another for their mother's milk, submerged just as soon as they manage to surface. Now I can't think. The world is upside down. Everything is wrong. I'm...lost.

"What about the prophecy?" I force out. "You mentioned a prophecy to my name?"

There's a very long pause. "I wonder if we should talk about everything else tomorrow, Skye. We've covered a lot already tonight, and you appear fatigued, like you might wish to sit down? Here? In a proper seat? My seat?"

I lift my sore head, eyesight bleary. Fjord is standing by his wicker chair now, a crocheted blanketed in his hands...and I think he means to give it to me, only I'll *boil* if he does.

I'll suffocate.

"You told me I should stay until the end, Fjord," I say. "To hear the full story. I need to hear it."

"I did say that," he acknowledges, sounding regretful, "but I didn't appreciate how huge what I'm telling you is."

"I need to know."

"I understand that, but it's very late, and perhaps we should reconvene tomorrow over breakfast. In fact, there are refreshments downstairs in the kitchen if you'd like something n—"

"I need to know!" I insist, shocking myself with my urgency. "I *have* to know, Fjord! Please tell me! *Please!* This is my life! My world upside down! I need to know!"

Two short, sharp whistles immediately follow my outburst. It's Tristan checking in on me, and I should answer him, but all I can do is stare at Fjord, my chest heaving in tight lungfuls of...pain. He has to finish explaining this to me, because I have to know of my lost past. Of my future, in a prophecy.

Of everything.

"Levi," he warns in a low voice, and my pulse jumps with it. At first I think he's urging his Guardian to stop me from fleeing like last time, even though that's the very opposite of what I want to do right now, but then I heed the footsteps thudding quickly over the rooftop.

I scramble to my feet and lurch forwards, legs shaking with shock and horror and unpreparedness...only it turns out Fjord isn't calling Levi to arms - he's warning him *not* to engage.

I watch the Guardian hesitate briefly, before moving into the room towards the wicker chairs, closer to Fjord. Just seconds later a figure drops to the window ledge in a low crouch, a large green headscarf shielding everything but his eyes, and the salt stains on his ankles glowing in the moonlight. There's a bejewelled, Guild-issued dagger in his hand – one of mine, given to him years ago.

Tristan takes the quickest inventory of the room, eyes seeking me out immediately. "Wolf?!"

"I'm ok," I breathe.

"You didn't answer my whistle!"

"I was getting round to it."

"Not fast enough!"

"I'm sorry, Tristan."

He makes a low noise, slipping slowly from the ledge onto the stone floor. The dagger is held aloft, eyes sharp and flighty over the room's occupants like he expects them to pounce. There's the sound of more running feet from above us, but they stop as soon as Tristan whistles. His eyes are a deep blue, shadowed by worry and concern as he makes his way over to me – like he knows how utterly wretched and lost I'm feeling.

"Who're your friends, Fjord?" he asks in a low voice.

"This is Levi, my Guardian, and Jay, a former tutor of mine. And this is Tristan," Fjord explains to the room. "He's a street ruffian, and Skye's best friend. I take it your people are outside?"

Tristan nods absently. "I hear you're Nixen."

"Yes. I'm a Nereid, descended from the sea nymphs."

"You lied to Skye for five years."

Fjord runs a hand through his hair. "Yes."

"I hear you're sorry about it?"

"Very."

Tristan faces him, observes him for long seconds. "You should be grateful Sholto is even less in my favour than you are, or we'd be in a different situation right now...one where I refuse to believe you on principal." He lifts a defiant brow, finally pulling down his green scarf. Just like me, something tickles his sense of smell. He looks quickly to Levi, nostrils flaring, "You've been to The Eastern Harbours. I can smell the air on you."

Jay shifts uneasily in his seat, his restless knees picking up tempo. "By Zeus, it's like they really *are* wolves."

"Did you know?" Tristan mutters to me.

"Only when I walked in."

"It's for Skye's protection," Fjord speaks up, looking a little weary having to say it again. "Levi was there to keep her safe, Tristan."

"She's perfectly safe with me."

"She's not."

"Oh?" Tristan doesn't like that. "Do tell me why?"

"Xavier Archer, the man Skye crossed paths with in Alcázar last week, is no regular Ioxthelian. He's actually a rogue Guardian, and he seeks to *injure* people like Skye, not protect them. He's an awful man."

"A Guardian, is he?" Tristan seems to take this new information in his stride. "Why is he wheedling his way into favour with Ruby Sabir, then? I hear she's hunting the Torch of Prometheus, the weapon her ancestors used *against* Nixen during the Impurity War, contrary to what all the history books tell us...but you're telling me her new prized soldier is one of you? That's quite a convoluted situation."

"I wouldn't call him one of us," Jay inputs, voice dropping spine-tinglingly low. His knees stop jigging, too. "He's from Elysium, but he's no brethren to anyone here."

"'Her new prized soldier...'" Fjord frowns deeply. "What do you mean by that, Tristan?"

"Rumour himself tells me The Queen has a new bodyguard, and his name is Xavier. He's the talk of the town."

Fjord turns sharply to his Guardian. He says something in the strange language I can't understand, his features visibly paling.

"What're you saying there?" Tristan asks quickly, voicing my own question. "What tongue are you speaking? Sounds...weird."

Fjord stays locked gazes with his Guardian for long strained moments, something silent passing between them. Reluctantly, he turns back to us. "It's Ancient Nereid, Tristan. Levi and I learnt it growing up. We're just discussing Xavier Archer...and I must tell you that as brilliant as you and your people are, you are no match for a rogue Guardian, especially one playing games in politics. Especially one as vindictive as Xavier."

Tristan thinks on this. "But your Guardian is? Better than him? A match for him?"

"Without a doubt."

"I've fought Xavier," I say, finding my voice. "I fought him just days ago in Alcázar and," *fled like steam from a kettle,* "I won. He's not that dangerous."

"He is dangerous, Skye," Fjord insists. "Very dangerous. I will not rest easy knowing he's in the city."

"Why did you let me spy on Alcázar the other week, then?" I volley. "Why have I been free to walk around for my entire life here without protection?"

"I found out Xavier was here only when you told Sholto you'd met him spying on the Council. Neither of us would *ever* have allowed you to go to Alcázar that night if we knew The Rogue Guardian was there, and I would *never* have let you walk around alone. It's very concerning Xavier is meddling with Ruby, Skye. Her intentions are bleak, but he is the worst of the worst. I can't stress that to you enough."

"So as long as he's in the city I'll need protection? Guarding? Is that what you're saying?"

"Yes."

My teeth flash. "That's silly! Tell me why he's such a threat? To me, especially?"

Tension settles in Fjord's frame. "It's...not just to you, but you're especially dear to me, Skye, and especially important to the rest of the world. Keeping you safe is paramount."

"If I was dear to you, you wouldn't have *lied* to me for five years, Fjord, would you?! No. You're bad, and I'm a fool."

He sighs at this, finally dropping the crocheted blanket he's still holding for me over the back of the wicker chair. He takes his time finding his next words, like mine are still hurting him.

"Your absence has been noted at the Guild, and not just by Fin and Enye. Your Staff Sergeant is thinking of reporting it to her seniors...to *my* seniors. You either need to return to duties soon or keep an excessively low profile in Ioxthel from now on. Whatever you decide, Levi will be guarding you, with or *without* your approval...and with or without your approval too, Tristan. You can damn me for it, and you can misunderstand me for it, but I'm unmoved. Keeping you safe is everyone's top priority, Skye, and especially mine. It's my only priority, to be honest. I won't let you fall to harm."

"I don't need protection, Fjord," I hiss. "Least of all from any of you! I trust you less than the distance I can spit a cherry pip, which is not far, because I'm just as awful at that as I am reading! So...I don't want it. *I* won't rest easy knowing that's happening just like *you* won't rest easy with this rogue Guardian in the city. You should revoke the order."

"I'm not ordering Levi," Fjord says. "I never do. This is a favour, and one he's already agreed to honour."

"But I don't agree to it!"

"I'm sorry for that, but I'm unmoved. I love you, Skye, and I won't have you in danger."

"You being serious about that, Fjord?" Tristan speaks up suddenly, voice low. "Is he seriously bad? Is she in danger?"

Fjord's expression turns grave. "I give you my word and my honour, Tristan. Nothing I'm saying is a lie. Xavier is a horrible man, and he lives to ruin good people. I just want to keep Skye safe. Having Levi look out for her is the only way to guarantee that. I swear to you."

My friend stares at him, eyes sharp, searching. I'm not sure what he finds there, but I think it's a little more progressive than my own damning observations, because he nods very slightly and lifts an arm over my shoulder. "You say Ruby is going to negotiate with Wivern? That's why their entourage is visiting the city?"

"Yes. We believe she's hoping they'll join her in moving out against Elysium in return for her help dealing with troubles within their own borders. Unlike Astyros, Wivern is plagued by breaches from The Nether, and there are severe casualties for it. They're getting desperate for solutions."

"How do you know this?"

"Levi was in The Cold Kingdom for a few months before he travelled here. While there, he made himself privy to a few poignant discussions between Wivern's officials."

"I see," Tristan spares the Guardian a brief glance, his arm tightening around my shoulders. "You mentioned a prophecy about Skye just before I dropped in."

"Yes, I did."

"What's it about?"

Fjord shifts his weight. "This is where Sholto's part of the story starts. He'll tell it much better than I will, because he's one of the only people to have heard the prophecy first hand. I'll tell you it's why the truth was concealed from you for so long, Skye. There are grave reasons for why it was, and I hope, when he furthers the story for you, things will be a little more understandable...a little more forgivable."

"They won't," I rebut strongly. "I'll never forgive you."

He looks like he expected that answer. "I would like to ask you what your plans are for returning to the Guild, or not?"

"I'm returning tomorrow."

"For the entourage?"

"Yes."

"You know you're on the wall?"

My eyes narrow. " *Yes,* Fjord. I know. I haven't forgotten."

"Ok. Levi is registered in the Guild as a soldier back from the Front, and he's your new patrol partner. You'll start duties together the day after tomorrow on a 2 pm."

"What of Enye?"

"She's already switched partners temporarily given your absence over the last week. The change will be made permanent."

Oh. Gods, no. "You can't do that, Fjord! Enye and I patrol together! We're partners for life!"

"I'm truly sorry, Skye, but this is for your safety. You'll still be able to see her around the Guild when off duty – though I would have you swear you won't tell her, or Fin, any of this. Tristan is different, obviously, but you *must* keep who you are and who we are a secret from the Tsitak siblings. You'll risk your life and ours if you don't. Maybe even theirs."

"I won't risk anything!" I reply angrily. "They'd never hurt me. Enye would never hurt me. Fin would never hurt me."

Fjord's expression falls into something very unhappy at that. "Some truths are just too big for people to handle, Skye. It's a risk you mustn't take yet. I spoke with them both today to ease their worry, and told them you've been feeling unwell, hence why you haven't been on duty. I thought it was the best excuse, and one that will hopefully relieve your Staff Sergeant's disapproval too." His brow furrows. "Please give me your word you won't tell the Tsitaks, Skye. I'm begging you not to be irresponsible. My mother didn't leave her homeland and her family just for you to throw that sacrifice away, years later. Nor did Sholto, and nor did I."

"The Tsitaks would *never* hurt me," I repeat, voice shaking. "How dare you suggest they would! They're good, honest people who care for me, which is more than I can say for you. You're *not* good, Fjord! You're bad! A liar! A Nixen who didn't care enough to tell me I didn't have a mother!"

"Please give me your word."

"No," I say, horrified to feel tears springing to my eyes. "I won't, Fjord. You don't deserve it."

"Please, Skye. I'm begging you."

"I won't!"

We stare at one another, and I hate that I see honesty and heartbreak in his own eyes; eyes that *are* begging me not to tell others about this. I hate that I feel so torn between anger and rebellion, and a deep, irreversible hurt...a longing not to be so lost, and so estranged, from him. I hate that Tristan gathers me impossibly close into his side in the very next second and drops his lips to my temple, murmuring, "Let's keep this to ourselves, Skye. Keep it between the two of us to keep you safe."

"No," I whisper, but it's lacking strength and resolve, and I hiccup straight after it. It's not long before I turn and sink into the only arms I have faith in any longer, shoulders slumping in defeat.

"Thank you," I hear Fjord say hoarsely.

"Don't think this means you're in our favour," Tristan replies in a low voice. "I'm still angry at you, Fjord. Really pissed off. Don't think it means we're on the same side yet, either. The ruffians will be everywhere. Watching you. Watching *you*..." He turns briefly to Levi, and pauses for effect. "Consider yourselves warned. We're not on the same team...yet."

Fjord nods slowly. "I understand that."

The arms around me tighten. "Let's go, Wolf. Get some sleep. I'm exhausted."

I swear to you, my heart breaks the very moment I step over the threshold of the salóni's weathered wooden door and into the balmy night air. It splinters in two, because I thought I had a brother in the boy behind me - the same boy who would buff my armour at the end of every week, and save a seat for me with his big, intriguing friends. The gracious Lieutenant who would *always* shorten his strides for my stupid little legs. I thought I had a brother, but I was wrong.

Wivern Entourage

I should be excited about having foreign visitors in Ioxthel. It's unprecedented in my lifetime for the two mortal kingdoms of Astyros and Wivern to be meeting like this; and my ghostlike self would usually be singing from opportunity, alive with the prospect of seeing members from another kingdom's monarchy in the flesh.

It's not.

This just feels like yet another strange event set to muddle my thoughts and tug on my energy levels, and I don't see myself spying on them anytime soon. I don't see myself doing anything other than crying, and sleeping. I'm so...confused. Not only from what Fjord has revealed to me in the last week, but also about the city's guests themselves. If this state visit really is about waging war on Elysium – waging an unjustified war – then what on earth am I supposed to feel about it?

Where do I stand?

Which side am I on?

I don't remember Elysium and I don't identify as half-nix even though apparently I am...and yet I've never really felt Astyrosian, either. I've never trusted Ruby, and the rhetoric she weaves around herself – the rhetoric that enacting divine order should have no fear of retribution. It's a ruse to cover fouler intentions and one I'll never abide by, but I don't trust Fjord and Sholto anymore, either. So where do I stand on war being waged against Elysium? Do I even need to know where I stand? Or do I just need to sleep? To forget? To push everything away?

I have something that might help you with this, Skye, my counsel speaks up quietly. *A question, if you don't mind me voicing it.*

Hi, I reply immediately. *Missed you. I don't mind. What's the question?*

Is war ever justified? Is the loss of life, the bloodshed, the grief and the greed, ever truly justified? No matter who the enemy is...no matter what the perceived cause is?

It takes me a moment to answer. *No.*

Then I think we both know where you'll eventually stand on this. Eventually?

Yes. Give yourself time to sleep, will you? To forget and push everything and everyone away, until that doesn't work and you suddenly realise you want to gather them impossibly close again.

I frown. *I don't think I'll want to do that.*

No? Well, let's see. Together.

Together?

Yes, Skye. I'm with you, always.

I know, because you're in my mind.

Yes. She might sigh. *I'm in here.*

"Is war ever truly justified?"

This is the question ringing in my ears as I walk along Ioxthel's northern rampart, the fortified wall severing the city from mainland Astyros. I'm keeping a weary eye out for Enye, because if you remember we were both issued duties on the wall by Lieutenant Jensen last week in the bouleuterion. I've yet to see her. It could be her duty has been moved entirely now we've been switched as patrol partners, which is just horrible.

It's not just Enye there's no sound or sight of. Fjord, Sholto, Levi...none of them are around, or so they'd have me believe, and so I hope. Pretty sure that's a foolish wish though, and that Fjord's Guardian is lurking somewhere in the shadows, supposedly watching over me.

I slept badly last night, even with Tristan crashing on my bed in the Guild with me. I feel depressed. Numb, but also somehow overwhelmed by bleak emotions, and teetering on the edge of a mindset that seems worryingly fatalist.

I don't want to be that way.

At all.

I find my spot in the ranks of guilders on top of the wall, and just like I thought, there's no Enye waiting for me. Dampness springs to my eyes, little to do with the ash-riddled wind playing games with the hair and uniforms of guilders up here. For once, I can't complain about that, because it dries the tears on my cheeks quickly.

Everyone waits for the entourage in silence, looking through the rampart's low crenels for a glimpse of Wivern on the shimmering horizon. The view of Astyros before me is flat, sandy and dogged by a heat haze, as it always is. The kingdom suffers from drought further inland, and consequently most of its population is concentrated in Ioxthel, the capital city built upon a rocky outcrop of land that protrudes into the sea in the shape of a chipped oyster shell; the chip being The Eastern Harbours where Tristan and his ruffians dwell.

I've often wondered if this is why The Sabirs garner so much power here, and have done for so long. With their lands on the knife-edge of drought and famine, it takes only one slip of the hand that wields supply to tip people into death and disease.

Their hand.

Thus...we do their bidding, and we bow to their power. I believe it's really *fear* that The Sabirs' pedestal is built from – and if I'm right, their reign won't be as infallible as they hope for. True loyalty is never built from terror, and true power is never garnered through despotism, but instead through respect. So are they, The Sabirs, also teetering on a knife-edge? The knife-edge between repression of their people, and the people's resulting rebellion? And...why am I thinking of this? What's the point? I've forgotten it...just like I wish I could forget the good times with Fjord and Sholto.

Forget how much I loved them.

Love them.

The sun is nearing its zenith in the sky when Wivern's riders appear, their obscure, blob-like forms rippling in mirage. Everyone atop the battlement shifts restlessly, and continue to do so for hours, because it seems to take the entourage ages to reach the gate. Time. It moves slower as soon as you will it to speed up...and let's call that the curse of impatience. It's something we're all plagued by – though perhaps not Ruby Sabir, standing regally before the city gates to greet her guests. *She* isn't shifting restively like everyone else. She's cool and collected and alone, excepting General Marco flanking her.

There's no new, shiny bodyguard.

No rogue Guardian.

No Xavier Archer.

One of Wivern's central riders dismounts in front of the Ioxthelian leaders. This must be Raul Wenslus, Wivern's Crown Prince. His armour is a finely polished silver, and the cut of his deep blue cloak much more streamlined than I'm used to in Ioxthel.

The rider next to him also dismounts. She's similarly garbed, but there are two short swords crossed on her back instead of a long sword at her hip, and a dust scarf covering half of her face. I think this must be Princess Aoife Wenslus, Raul's sister and a notorious strategist for Wivern.

The three royals share a deep, courteous bow before exchanging pleasantries. In minutes, Ruby is laughing; her frenzied jubilation unmistakable to me. It's as if she's high off expectation, mad on the prospect of war-mongering.

Several minutes of unheard conversation pass before Prince Raul and then Princess Aoife mount their horses again. At Ruby's order, the heavy city gates swing open. Every other sentry on the rampart pivots to face in the opposite direction to their neighbours, until half of us look beyond the city walls and the other half mind the entourage as it wends its way through the streets, led by General Marco. My duty is to watch the rest of Wivern fall into step behind one another and enter the city gates, but not to watch them disappear into the city. I wish I could, if only to try and spot Tristan and his ruffians – for over the *clip clop* of horse hooves and the clinks of foreign bridle-wear, I can hear his people whistling softly to one another.

Excepting the sight of Princess Aoife's twin swords, I find myself underwhelmed by the entourage's arrival when we're eventually relieved of duty. I weave through groups of chattering soldiers returning to the Guild, half looking out for Enye but also half hoping I don't see her. I'm a terrible liar, and I'm so very close to breaking down it's pathetic.

Do demigods lose their minds?

I feel like I might.

I sleep better that night, but wake up feeling just as depressed. Empty, but also full of pain. I almost don't get up, tempted to spend the day under the covers stewing in my hurt and confusion. In the end I force myself out of bed – or rather, my counsel forces me. I dress mindlessly and drink stale water from the pitcher on my nightstand before heading out.

I'm walking past the mess for patrol – with Levi, let's not forget – when I see not Enye but her *brother* standing in the quad outside, chatting with a group of young Captains.

We spot one another at the same time.

Fin freezes mid-sentence as I falter mid-stride, and then struggle to reinstate them as he breaks off from the group and jogs over. His eyes are sharp as he approaches, hair ruffled by the warm breeze...expression striking. He stops before me and moves as if to embrace me, but seems to think better of it at the last moment, instead offering me a hasty but really smooth bow. I watch him straighten up, thinking how it's nice to be bowed to, isn't it? Nice to be bowed to, and not *lied* to for five damn years.

"Hi."

"*Hi*," he echoes, a little incredulously. "Are you alright? Where have you been for the past week?"

Cue me being a terrible liar. "Nowhere."

"Nowhere?"

"Yeah."

Fin frowns, maybe at my dull tone. His mouth opens and closes, as if he doesn't know what to say back to it...except he must, because Fin is *never* lost for words and least of all around me.

"What happened the other night?" he eventually asks. "We were due to meet by the library?"

Oh gods. We were, weren't we? We were due to meet to steal a book, go back to his room, talk about what I'd managed to spy on in the Medical Syndicate, do other fun stuff...and I'd wholly forgotten about it all, in the wake of everything else.

My shoulders slump with guilt and disappointment, something fierce stinging the back of my eyes and throat. Let's forget Enye. I might well breakdown and lose my mind right here, right now, in front of my long-time crush instead.

How embarrassing.

"I waited for you?" Fin presses when I don't reply. "For hours. What happened?"

"I...wasn't feeling well," I provide lamely, and so inadequately. "I'm sorry, Fin. I should have told you, but I wasn't feeling well and haven't been for the past week."

His eyes dip, studying me. "Were you in the infirmary? I looked for you there. So did Enye, and Sergeant Hajjar..."

"I wasn't there, no," I say, thinking on the spot. "I've been staying with an old friend out of the Guild, but I'm fine now. I just felt tired. Needed to rest."

"You felt tired?"

"Just...tired."

Fin hesitates, and then he does reach for me, his hands slipping to my shoulders. His palms are warm and gentle as he pulls me closer, searching my features. "I thought something terrible had happened to you, Skye. We both did. Why didn't you tell us where you were?"

I didn't know I should. "I am sorry. That was bad of me. I just...you know...just needed quiet."

"Quiet?"

"Yeah," I mutter. "You know?"

He frowns more, like he doesn't know...especially because this is me we're talking about. I'm never quiet. "Is something wrong for you to need that? Something up?"

"Nothing is up."

I try for a smile, but it either resembles a pained grimace or something horribly goofy, and inside I feel like screaming. Fin doesn't look nearly fooled, either. "I spoke with my sister yesterday about the switch in patrol partners you guys are having. She's just as upset as you are, not least because she hasn't *seen* you for over a week, Skye. But...I have a feeling this is more than that, isn't it? Something *is* up, and I would ask if you'd like to tell me about it? If I can help?"

Goddesses. My broken heart soars at the offer, and at his earnest expression. "No," I reply hoarsely. "There's nothing to help with. It's all good. I'm good. But...thank you for offering. That's...nice." *If I'm being honest, I fancy you more than ever now.* "Very nice."

"It's all good, is it? Even with Fjord?"

128

Nope. "Yes. Why would you think it isn't?"

"Because he was the one who switched you guys out as partners, and because..." Fin glances behind me. "He's coming over, looking tetchy."

"What?!"

I twist at the waist, eyes widening. Sure enough, Fjord is quickly making his way along the stone stoa adjoining the Guild's bouleuterion, heading right for us. He's moving with purpose, drawing attention from the surrounding guilders...or maybe it's Levi beside him, doing that.

If I didn't know Fjord's face as well as my own, I'd say the two of them were brothers. Just like I noted the night before last; both have dark hair, tall and strong builds, pleasing features...and that leather cord hanging from their necks, disappearing under their shirts. They're even mostly in sync with one another as they jog down the few steps to the quad, and for some reason that makes me feel even more miserable.

Oddly left out, too.

"Good m—"

"What's up between you and Skye?" Fin interrupts. "Why is she so upset?"

Fjord stills, eyes darting to mine and back to Fin. I can tell he's unsure of whether I've just told him *everything*. "I...expect she's troubled by the change in patrol partners."

"So is my sister."

"I'm sorry for that."

"I believe you, but they're still upset and I find I don't like that," Fin eyes his friend closely, then offers him a short, belated bow of greeting. "How're you? Wivern's officials treating you well?"

"Uh...I've yet to meet them, actually. That's on today's agenda, in Alcázar."

"Hope it goes well. Who's your friend?"

"This is Levi Silverstone. He's recently back from the Front, doing time with the foot soldiers to recuperate."

"Ah," Fin swiftly steps forwards and offers Levi his hand. "Fin Tsitak. Nice to meet you."

"And you."

"How's it being back?"

"Good, thank you."

"Caught up on the usual?"

"Yes."

Excepting the notable absence of his Elysium accent, Levi's voice is like it was the other nights I've seen him – rough and rusty, like he's just woken up from *years* of sleeping.

"I take it you're something to do with the girls being separated?" Fin asks. "Skye's new patrol partner?"

"He is," Fjord supplies, "but only because Skye and Enye have been together for far longer than usual patrol partners. Their Staff Sergeant, Yasmine Hajjar, suggested it was time for a change, particularly after Skye's absences last week. Levi's return provides a good opportunity to switch things up."

"Have they met before today?"

"Twice, yes."

"Yeah? How was that, Skye?"

I open my mouth, shut it...glance to the others. What on earth am I supposed to say to that? I offer Fin a small nod, pressing my lips together to stop from spilling the truth, or sobbing.

Just like that, everything about him softens in sympathy. I see him start to mistake this entire situation, perhaps my entire week of truancy, for nerves and trepidation.

It kills me.

I want to scream.

"Twice is good," he says encouragingly. "Right? What did you do, go for drinks? Did he buy for you?"

"He...he..."

I look away, to Fjord. He's watching me, a bleak shadow in his eyes like this is hurting him to see. If I wasn't feeling so numb, I'd be so angry at that. How dare he feel hurt when this is entirely his doing? How dare he feel remorse when Fin, his good friend, is so ignorant – so oblivious and gallant, picking up the conversation when I don't reply because he thinks I'm quiet because I'm nervous and he's trying to *help*, just like he said he'd do earlier.

"How was the Front for you, Levi? I hear it's tough at the moment. I hope you're not back here because you're injured?"

"No, I'm not. Thank you for asking."

"I have friends out there, and wish they were so fortunate to be unharmed. Perhaps you know some of them?"

"Perhaps, yes."

"Must be nice to rest up for a bit? Though, you should probably know this one is feisty, especially when she breaks up a tavern brawl or two..." Fin nudges me gently with his elbow. "I'm a little jealous, Skye. Most foot soldiers would chew their arm off to patrol with a Fronter."

Levi isn't a Fronter! I want to shout. *And I'm not a foot soldier! I'm a ruffian-nix-demigod who is totally upside down!*

"Do you want to go for drinks tonight after your patrol? Wind down together? Maybe we can make up for the time we lost last week?"

"Sorry, Fin," Fjord interjects quickly. "I need Skye tonight. We should go over logistics with Levi. Things aren't quite set in stone yet, and it's either with me or Sergeant Hajjar tomorrow...and I'd rather avoid the inevitable disciplinary that will occur if that happens. Unlike

Yasmine's newfound approval of your sister, she isn't impressed with Skye's truancy."

Fin hums. "I know Yasmine isn't impressed. She's not impressed with most people, but then I think if Skye really *was* unwell, she might be excused. I'll vouch for her, you know. Soothe Yasmine's obsessive need to uphold the rules..."

"So will I, but I'm afraid I still need Skye tonight."

Fin shrugs, and nudges me again. "How's tomorrow looking, then? You free?"

"Yes, in the evening."

"Stop by my room?"

"Ok."

He smiles a little. "Ok. Well, maybe I should let you get going. Nice to meet you, Levi. Mind your wits are as sharp as they were on the Front, will you? Skye is feisty but a bit out of sorts. She might need help ducking tankards."

"I'm not out of sorts, Fin. I'm fine."

He shoots me a disbelieving look, and twists with sudden seriousness to Fjord. "Might ask *you* for drinks soon to talk about this, Winters. It's not nice seeing the girls upset or nervous."

Fjord hesitates, then nods. "Good day, Fin."

"Good day, Lieutenant."

He bows to both Fjord and Levi, and then me, reaching out afterwards to tap the tip of my nose with his index finger.

"Bye," I mumble.

"Hope you don't play truant for me tomorrow like you did last week, trouble. I'll be waiting for you."

He holds my gaze as he leaves. We all wait until he's well out of sight before even thinking of moving. I look to Fjord, throat thick, disposition deeply wounded. He appears incredibly weary himself, rubbing an unhappy palm down his jaw.

"I asked you not to tell him anything, Skye," he says quietly, as if explaining himself. "You gave me your word."

"I told him *nothing*."

"You looked upset? And he seemed to know of it?"

"I'm upset because I'm upside down, Fjord! The world is upside down, and I hate lying. I'm *bad* at it. That's how Fin knew something was up! Not because I told him. I was hardly speaking, because I'm just...so bad at lying. And I'm upset," I'm horrified when my voice breaks. "I'm *upset* I forgot he wanted to meet the other day because of everything going on and that's bad of me. And it's bad of *you*, interrupting us. Lying to me. You're bad."

Fjord sighs. "I'm sorry you still feel that way. I hope after tonight you might think differently."

"What's happening tonight?"

"Sholto wishes to speak with you to tell you his part of the story. It's why you wouldn't have been able to meet with Fin. And...I apologise, but I must bid you a swift good day, Skye. I'm expected in Alcázar to greet Wivern's officials now, and you're due on patrol." He stops and bows to me, weary eyes suddenly full of...hope? "Please will you look out for each other today? Will you look out for Levi for me?"

I scowl. "He's the Guardian, isn't he?"

"Yes, and you'll be entirely safe walking beside him, but we all need someone to look out for us. Please would you, Skye? For me?"

My scowl deepens, and I open my mouth to retort back – to deny the request and ridicule it – except I don't. It's such an odd thing to ask of two strangers, especially when I'm beside myself with injury and the *last* thing I want to do is anything for Fjord.

I look to where Levi stands by his side, unspeaking, with no expression. He wears two daggers today, both Guild-issued and winking at his hips. They're slightly curved at the tip like most

Ioxthelian weapons, and not at all like the straight blade I glimpsed in his shoulder harness on that first night. He seems, dare I say it, very Ioxthelian right now, especially with his dark hair; though I don't miss the way his skin is blushing and browning beneath the sun, as if it hasn't been in it for all that long.

I'm not sure what the weather is like in Elysium, but I imagine it to be cold and dreary, like my mood and the weathered grey of Levi's eyes...which I still get *nothing* from. Or his features. Get nothing from those, either. They're just dull, subdued, untrustworthy, older than mine. Maybe even older than Fin's, and he's taller, which means he probably walks fast.

I look back to Fjord, mouth opening again. I *mean* to damn his request, to damn them both, but that's not what comes out at all. "Yes, I'll be a Guardian to your Guardian, Fjord."

He looks incredibly relieved. "Thank you, Skye. That's very good of you."

"Just...make sure you don't speak to me ever again. I can't deal with it, Fjord. I'll fall off the edge of the upside down world and never be seen again."

The Prophecy

Sholto doesn't meet with me that evening like Fjord implied he might. Instead, he greets me at the Guild's gates after patrol ends and escorts me back to my room in Delta barracks.

"We'll talk tomorrow evening," he explains.

"I have plans."

"Cancel."

Not a chance in the underworld. "Why can't we talk now? I'm not tired."

"I am, Skye. It's 2.15 am and it's been a long few days. Get some rest. You'll feel better for it, and I'll be able to explain things more exactly."

It's now tomorrow evening. I don't feel better. Sholto's kitchenette is lit by several thick, stubby candles. There are two painted terracotta cups of red wine on the rickety wooden table. He sits on one stool, me opposite him on the other. His wine is half gone, mine is untouched and will remain so. Though I'm thirsty for information, I'm also hoping to get through this quickly.

I haven't cancelled on Fin.

As soon as this is over, I'm going to his.

Sholto has expressed no sentiment of remorse for *anything*, but he has castigated me for being sharp-tongued with the first thing I said to him this evening, and for scraping the stool obnoxiously loudly over the kitchenette's stone floor. I don't care, though. Long gone are the days when I revered his ability to temper *my* temper, or his fathomless wisdom. The idea of it revolts me now – to think of how I let him shape me as a young girl, *knowing* what he was sitting on.

"I would appreciate it if you kept the satirical remarks to a minimum, Skye," he begins after minutes of quiet consideration, as if he knows my present thoughts. "It will make explaining things easier, and quicker. There's a lot for us to get through. What I'm about to tell you changes the course of your life forever. It ruins your expectations and hopes for the future, and you must respond to the altered state of play quickly and on reflex, just like I've taught you.

"We begin with me. I grew up many hundreds of years ago in the great kingdom of the gods and goddesses, Mount Olympus. Why? My father is one of the four sentinels to Zeus's throne. One of the four great ancients to Elysium's Guardians. His name is Zelos. You will have heard of him from legend."

Uh...

Yes, I've heard of Zelos.

Everyone has heard of him. He's the embodiment of zeal, envy, dedication and rivalry. A winged being who stands sentry to Zeus's throne alongside his brother, Kratos, and sisters, Nike and Bia, all of whom are children to Styx, the supreme river deity in the underworld.

He's also the *father* of Sholto?

"Before my journey to you here, Skye, I lived in Elysium mentoring young Guardians, as is the role of all the sentinel offspring. This is how I met your mother. She was destined to be leader of the Aeolus Dynasty, one of the twelve houses collectively ruling Elysium. Saffron didn't want to be a stateswoman, however. She wanted to be a Guardian – or so I first thought. It's not custom for anyone but those descended in some way from Zeus's sentinels to become one, but Saffron was incredibly headstrong, and she didn't believe in predetermined dispositions and destinies based on whom she derived her blood from. She fought her way with wile and wealth into training, and was mentored by me for some years until she was ready to protect her own family. She was quite magnificent despite not heralding the blood of a Guardian, to her utter delight. I believe *she* believed she was proving something to Elysium, showing them that blood isn't everything...and in many ways she was. With time, however, it was revealed she had an ulterior motive for persuading me to sharpen her senses and hone her hunting prowess; and that was, quite literally, to *become* a huntress. Your mother's ultimate goal in life was not to be a Guardian, Skye, but instead to serve the great goddess of the wild, Artemis. And serve her...she eventually did."

My eyes widen, heart picks up speed...lips silently usher the goddess's name. Artemis, as in Goddess of The Hunt, Keeper of The Wilderness, and Minder of Childbirth, Death and Disease. Daughter of Zeus and twin of the sun god, Apollo.

My mother served *Artemis?!*

"Saffron left Elysium and her family behind to join Artemis's hunting team," Sholto explains. "That family unfortunately fell prey to the assassinations of last decade. I believe Fjord told you of this last week, and mentioned that *you* are now the last member alive in the Aeolus Dynasty, Skye. You have a very prominent role in Elysium, and I will tell you of it soon. First, we must move onto greater things – the prophecy.

"Some twenty years ago, amidst the wreck and ruin rife in Elysium at the time, your mother briefly returned to her kingdom with a newborn baby girl, and left her – you – with a dear friend. This friend was Fjord's mother, Melody Winters. Thus, you grew up not in the lands of Aeolus, in the very northern reaches of Elysium, but instead on its western coast with the Nereids. I should tell you I don't believe this happened because your family were at greatest risk of losing their lives to the assassinations, Skye. I think Saffron wished for Melody to raise you regardless, in secret and with love. And...she did. You were fostered by her for just under five years before she fled with you, leaving her sons and her duties behind. Everyone that knew her was perplexed as to why she would leave Elysium without so much as a goodbye, including myself. I was...very fond of Melody and she of me, and thus it pained me greatly to know she'd disappeared with undisclosed reason. But then, just over ten years ago, I was very unexpectedly gifted a visitation from the great Oracle of Delphi – and all the secrets, all the undisclosed reasons, were revealed to me. The beginnings of an epic story started to unravel. Are you ready for it, Skye?"

Am I?

I've a feeling...no.

"The Oracle told me she'd prophesied of a lost demigod who would rise from the ashes to hold and heal a broken and inglorious world. She'd heard how a fierce warrior would use their silence like thunder to fight alongside the gods, and to fight against them; when all is ablaze with fire and wrongs are chosen for the right reasons. She'd *seen* how a phantom of retribution would defy the curse of their own mind to save everyone but those who once kept their sanity. The Oracle had, without a doubt, prophesied of Elysium's saving grace, and more, the Olympians' only hope. Thus, it instantly became clear to me why your mother left you, Skye, *hid* you in Elysium with her best friend, and why that friend ran without so much of a warning to me. Saffron must have told Melody of the prophecy, and entrusted her friend to keep you safe...to keep you from harm. I knew in my bones that the wisp of a child with amber eyes I'd met only a handful of times was the demigod spoken of in prophecy, and I knew I had to find you. So, I did."

Sholto pauses then to take a sip of wine, his gaze dark, fathomless and venerate. Feeling punches me in the chest, not only at this utterly overwhelming news, but because I've seen this look on him before every single day, usually when he watches me spar with Fjord. Is this what he was thinking of, when he did?

Our mothers?

The prophecy?

The world's saviour?

"Fate is fickle and tenacious and unkind, Skye. It finds you no matter where you hide. It found your mother, and I believe it enabled me to find you...and it will, without question, shadow your footsteps until this prophecy is complete. And so, you see, this changes *everything* you once thought you knew."

Another sip of wine. Another look to remind me that he thought of this *every* day...and he never told me.

"Oracles are agents of prophecy, vessels of divination said to be enlightened by the spirits of the sun god, Apollo, and the ancient titaness of good council, Themis. As I'm sure you well know, they *see* the possibilities and probabilities of the future, sometimes dream them...but anyone fortunate enough to receive their wisdom will know how infuriatingly opaque they are about those insights. They're notorious for weaving tales about distant futures with few particulars and obscure definitives, and though they never lie, they always speak in riddles. This prophecy is no different, but there are two things that strike me in it...two strings of fate already starting to unravel. The first is *a lost demigod who would rise from the ashes.* This is of course you, Skye, rising from your ruffian life on Ioxthel's ash-laden streets...and eventually leaving them behind for good. Then there is, *when all is ablaze with fire.* This, I believe, pertains to humankind's greatest weapon being lit and wielded, the Torch of Prometheus. It pertains to that which Ruby Sabir is seeking to use against Elysium as we speak, just like her ancestors of four hundred years ago did. And so *now* do you see what I mean when I say everything changes for you, Skye? Do you see how irreversibly huge these truths are?"

Yes. Except... "What do you mean by telling me I'll leave the streets of Ioxthel behind for good, Sholto? What does that mean?"

"It means you are to leave this city and this kingdom with myself and the other Elysium folk when the time is right. You are to depart from your past and embark on fate's journey for you."

"Why?"

Sholto's gaze sharpens to something very definitely discerning, and highly disapproving. "Do I really need to tell you that, after everything I've just explained? You hold the twelfth seat amongst the dynasties of Elysium, Skye. You sit on the kingdom's ruling council, and you are a demigod prophesied to save the world from wreck and ruin. I highly doubt you can fulfil those duties here in Ioxthel, sweltering lazily in the incessant heat."

I frown. I'm many things – many stupid things – but lazy is not one of them. "How exactly will I save the world anywhere? That's a very big task, Sholto. It sounds ludicrous saying it out loud."

"Does it?" He smiles tightly. "As I said, oracles converse in riddles. Usually, it is only time that unveils the solution. Time and thought...the latter of which you are not doing right now, Skye. I see it in your eyes. You're speaking and feeling without thought, on impulse. You'd do well to do as I teach you and master yourself into something steady and considered."

My nostrils instantly flare with indignation. That's unfair, isn't it? This is huge news – perhaps the *biggest* news one could ever receive, besides the time you're told your mother is dead and your dad is a god. I'm surprised I can even speak anything, let alone piece a coherent sentence together, let alone have it sound *considered.*

"You told to me to respond on reflex, Sholto," I reply stiffly. "I'm in shock. This *is* my reflex."

He takes another sip of wine. "Not the one I taught you."

It's ok, Skye, my counsel speaks up, heeding the volatility surging in me. *Keep pressing for answers. The Torch of Prometheus might be humankind's greatest weapon, but information is their oldest. You must wield both of them throughout this destiny. You must be the winner, here.*

I take a deep, deep breath. "When will the time be right to leave Ioxthel, Sholto?"

"In the next few months, I expect. Fjord has business in the Guild, wooing Wivern's officials and being our eyes and ears on the inside of Alcázar. I've a father to get in touch with and the oath of Ruby's Council to witness, and decipher. We both have that to do, Skye. We *all* have a map to find and hide once more...and then we leave. For Elysium. Or for the Torch first, depending on where it lies. I will know more when I speak to my father, for he was the one who hid it following the Impurity War, and is thus the only being alive who knows where it presently is."

This piece of information passes right over my head. Right over it, like I imagine storm clouds would if it ever rained in Ioxthel. So does the opportunity to grill him on the Impurity War he was alive for, four *hundred* years ago. All I heed from what he just said is that I'm expected to leave Ioxthel really damn soon.

I'm not up for that.

"I think you should sit with this and process it before you say words you'll go back on, Skye," Sholto says quietly. "I still see it in your eyes. You are not thinking."

"I'm *never* leaving my friends," I vow, ignoring him.

"You are."

"I'm not."

"You *are*, Skye. You don't have a choice."

I get to my feet with enough force to knock the stool over. My hands and voice shake violently, and those emotions start spiralling. My counsel's guidance be damned. Sholto's lessons be damned. I don't want to be the mistress of myself in this moment – I just want to scream.

"I'm never going *anywhere* with you or your brethren, Sholto. Never. I don't trust you, and I don't trust a destiny bequeathed to me by...by a witch I've never met who weaves tales with few particulars and no definitive outcomes! Why should I?! You can't blame me, hiding everything from me for seven years. I won't do it. I won't leave. I won't be in the prophecy. No way."

"They're your brethren, too," Sholto reminds me mildly, meeting my furious gaze with ease. "And you will be in this prophecy, because you *are* this prophecy. Sit down, Skye. I still have more to tell you about Elysium and your place amongst its ruling council. I have more to tell you of The Fates, and the world of the gods and goddesses...and of your mother, and her life with Artemis." He nods to the hands fisted tightly at my sides, and the empty spot over my right shoulder; a spot I wish so badly *wasn't* vacant in this moment. "You should know that the silver bow I gifted you years ago was hers, Skye. It was Saffron's. Every huntress of Artemis has one and only loses it when they die. It's why I know your mother is no longer with us – because she lost her bow."

Shock.

And rage.

"How *could* you?" I accuse, my voice low and splintered. "How could you be so cruel as to sit on this for *years* and not tell me, Sholto? You know how desperate I've been to know of my past. To know of my family. You know I'm the stupid way I am because of it. I don't understand how you could?"

"I was warned by the Oracle of Delphi not to reveal the truth until the time was right, Skye. And, from my own judgement, I believed it best to let you grow into this destiny. I was right. I don't regret keeping you in the dark. This is too much for a young, starving girl to handle. Too much for you to handle even now, it seems."

"I can't even look at you. I'm so angry, Sholto. So hurt."

"Because I retained the truth until you were ready to hear it?"

"Because you *lied!* You violated my trust! I was so young when you took me in, starving and...and so lost and sad. I followed you around like a puppy, believed in you like a dog does their master. Blindly, embarrassingly besotted, totally dependent...and you took advantage of that!"

Sholto's expression pinches at this. "Would you rather I didn't give you a full childhood with Tristan, Skye? Told you of this the day you met me? Would you rather I'd torn you away from the only streets you've the wherewithal to remember when you were so small people could toss you around like the dead fishes you used to steal from the harbours. Would you rather I'd done that, taken you to Elysium, and let them *gut* you there?" He shifts his kylix of wine over the tabletop in agitation, the only slip of composure besides a firm voice I've seen this evening. "I did it to protect you, Skye, and I do this now to protect Elysium and the gods and goddesses. If you don't realise that, quickly, then fate has slipped her strings and we're all doomed. Please don't tell me I've wasted years on the wrong child by sulking...and don't force me to force *you* to set out on this journey."

I stare at him, speechless. Is it me? Is it me with my incensed, impulsive mind, or is he twisting the situation back on itself, saying it's *my* fault I'm so angry I can't breathe and *my* foible in biting right back at the hand offering me poisoned meat.

"Don't force me to force you."

The words are just as twisted, and as wrong, as those he said on that first night in the safe house; insinuating that detaining me against my will was for my own good. It upsets me even more hearing him utter something so corrupt tonight, because it means it wasn't just a one off.

My hands twitch, and before I heed what I'm doing I've reached for the kylix still filled with red wine on the table. I honestly can't tell you what I'm going to do - whether I'm going to pick it up and throw it down my throat, urging the giddy rush of alcohol to my senses...or if I'll throw it over *him*.

I do the latter. Wine splashes across Sholto's chest, smattering his white shirt like blood flying from a flogging whip. He stills, supposedly in disbelief, and his lips disappear into a line of stark disapproval, his eyes darkening to near black. Precisely and with deliberate slowness, he puts both his palms on the table and pushes himself to standing.

I back away quickly.

Sholto isn't an overly tall man, but now he seems to grow impossibly large with each unfurling inch of his spine; his shadow expanding throughout the entire room. His stool scrapes over the stone floor, quieter than mine had been when I pulled it roughly and obnoxiously out on arrival, but somehow the sound grates more. It lasts for longer too, becoming a thick, wayward entity between us.

I see no relic of the foster father played by him for the last seven years. I just see someone to be resented and feared, and something feels like it breaks further in me for it. Tears spring to my eyes, unstoppable, just like the heart starting to thud unevenly against my ribs...ushering me to leave, to run from fate.

"I'm *very* disappointed in you, Skye," he says in a low voice.

"Get used to it," I sob.

Then I pivot and flee from his kitchenette.

Hoax

I knock frantically on Fin's door, lungs heaving with exertion, thoughts wild with disbelief at Sholto and all he's disclosed to me tonight. Sweat stings my armpits from the balmy night air and from fear that he might be following me here...wine-stained shirt like a violent battle wound, red and glossy beneath the moonlight. I look over my shoulder, expecting him to be there lunging for me to take me back to his kitchenette or even further afield – beyond Ioxthel's city walls, never to be seen again except by destiny herself. I thank every god, he isn't. There's no one out in Beta barracks besides me, and Fin.

"Hi," I greet breathlessly as the door opens. "I'm so sorry I'm late. I'm so sorry."

Fin pauses with his welcome on the tip of his tongue. I've no doubt his next breath is filled with fresh air and spilt wine, and maybe the bitter frenzy of my panic, too. I hope he doesn't ask about any of it. I hope he isn't going to turn me away.

"I'm sorry," I repeat earnestly. "It's—"

"Only a quarter past midnight."

"Yeah."

His eyes search mine, then drop the length of me. "You ok, Skye? You seem flushed."

"I'm...fine. Can I come in?"

He steps aside and lets me enter, still watching me closely.

"I meant to spend the evening here," I explain, starting to speak so fast the words run into themselves, until even I can barely understand them. "I meant to, but Sholto wanted to talk to me about something, so he talked and I listened...but I meant to be here, and

I'm sorry I wasn't given everything last week. I wasn't playing truant, I swear. Sholto just wanted to talk and—"

"It's fine."

"And I'm really sorry."

"You're fine, Skye," Fin repeats. "This is fine. It's good to see you any time of day or night."

"I meant to be here earlier, but Sholto wanted to talk."

"You've just told me that. I believe it."

His brows furrow in slight confusion, and maybe concern. He lifts a hand and tugs gently on the end of the braid falling over my shoulder, offering me a small, reassuring smile. I feel myself inhale sharply from stress and...overwhelming feeling.

He has no idea of what I've learnt these past weeks, or how shocked I am by everything tonight. He has no idea I just threw wine over the man I used to think of as a father, the man I respected for his honesty and integrity; and how profound a shock it is that he's *not* those things. He has no idea I now feel like I have an hourglass upturned over my head, counting down the days, minutes and seconds until that man expects me to *leave* Ioxthel. To save an inglorious world. To search for the Torch of Prometheus. To...lose my mind to insanity.

I squeeze my eyes shut, telling myself to forget it. Let me be hoodwinked by Fin and his magnetism tonight. Let me fall prey to this new hoax of quickened breath and hot skin and intimacy I'm suddenly exploring with him. Just let me forget everything.

The hand fiddling with my plait stops, slipping to my cheek. I feel Fin step closer and open my eyes. He's looking grave now, gaze bouncing over my jittery form with open intent to unearth *everything* that's wrong. "What's going on, Skye? Why're you so distressed?"

"I'm not."

"Are you unwell still?"

146

"No," I heave a deep breath. "I'm not distressed or unwell. I just...want to forget."

"Forget what?"

"Everything. Except this."

"This?"

"You."

His furrowed brows lift in surprise. Without warning, he picks up both of my wrists and tugs them around his waist. My cheek lands on his chest as he wraps is own arms around me, the weight of them warm and protective. He smells of black pepper and a day moving about in the sun, and gods, everything in me starts to respond to it.

"This is the best I've felt all week," he says in my ear. "Just so you know."

"Me too," I reply hoarsely.

"You sweet talking me, Skye?"

"No. That's totally your prerogative in all of this. Sometimes I think you were made to sweet talk people."

"I've never sweet talked you before."

"I don't believe that."

"You wouldn't. You're a pessimist."

My eyes squeeze shut again. It's as if he knows I need to hear it all – the banter, the wit, the guile. "I think you're an egoist," I manage to get back. "Big one. I'm embarrassed for you."

Laughter rumbles through me. "Ouch, I felt that. You're colder than Enye was during that bouleuterion meeting, when she told me to get lost and sit with my own friends..."

"She had a point."

Another deep hum of laughter. "How're you doing, troublemaker who is very good at ducking tankards? Forgetting anything yet?"

"Yes."

"Does it have something to do with being in my arms?"

Everything. "Not really."

"You sure?"

"Yes."

"Interesting. Might test that theory..."

He drops his arms from around my shoulders. I miss their comfort immediately, until his fingers start tugging the white blouse from my trousers, and the first thrill of dry, hot skin brushes mine. His palms settle on my waist, drawing me in. My pulse starts going wild, limp hands landing on a hard stomach. Shivers race down my spine when his lips brush my ear, so hot.

"Nothing to do with me, you say?"

Seconds pass before I feel myself lean into him, arms slipping to the small of his back. I don't speak, just press closer...and I think that's answer enough. The hands on my waist shift, smoothing their way down to my hips and then up, fingers spreading over ribs I wish weren't so sharp. He rests them there for several seconds, both of us just breathing...and then Fin pulls back.

Pure exhilaration hits my lower belly when our gazes meet. His eyes are smoky, mercurial, full of something that tells me he's thinking of the next steps; and that intimidates me a little bit, because he's the first guy, and this is only our second time.

"Remember that book we were due to steal from the Guild's library last week?" he asks, voice lower than it was before. "Well, when you didn't show, I took the liberty of stealing it without you. Read some of it tonight, waiting for you..." I watch as he walks towards his bed and sits on the edge of the mattress, then leans over to pick up a leather-bound book lying idly by his pillow. His eyes flit up to meet mine as he does, their hue still hooded. Heart thumping and throat dry, I meander closer. He starts flicking through the pages, humming vaguely, then stops and looks pointedly to the spot beside him. "Seems a bit empty, doesn't it?"

I stare a him, eyes wide, and lurch forwards and sit down, immediately falling into the dip his weight makes on the bed. The entire length of our thighs touch...and he has the nerve to blink down at me in surprise, as if he didn't *know* that was going to happen, settling this close to him.

I flush. "What's the book about?"

"Guess."

My brows pull together. "I don't think I can, Fin. The Guild's library might be shoddy, but it's big."

"Go on. Just try. One guess, Skye. Humour me."

"Demigods?"

"Huh. Wrong, but I'll give you a point for inspiring my next pick. I'm hoping you'll be there for it, too. I hate slipping past the guards alone, because I don't have to. They just let me walk in. And, you know, it'd be nice if you weren't late for our date."

"This is a date?"

"Maybe," he says lightly, shutting the book and dropping it gently into my lap. "Go on then, troublemaker. Quench your curiosity."

"'The Mishape...Mis*haps* of Eros, God of Desire'," I quote the title with difficulty, and huff out an involuntary laugh. "I probably should've guessed that, actually."

"Why's that?"

"I think only you would pick out the book on Eros, Fin."

"Really? Well, I suppose it is quite predictable. People like reading about people they can relate to..."

He grins, stretching his arms straight up and arching his back. I pretend I'm not watching him, or the strip of hard, bronzed stomach he flashes by doing so - and look away quickly when he drops an elbow over my shoulders, the move so damn predictable.

It still works.

"It was either this or a healer's catalogue of depressingly fatal hemlock cases, Skye. I know which one I'd prefer to forego...but in hindsight I think it's best if we get on with something quite pressing before we read it together. Warm ourselves up for it, you know?"

His fingers start tracing idle, nonsensical patterns on my upper arm, edging closer and closer to my collarbone and to the braid hanging there. The entirety of my body becomes hot, my heart ridiculously flighty, and no longer from running here. No longer from fleeing a future about saving fiery worlds or fighting the gods.

This is all Fin.

"What do you think, Skye? Read it later?"

"I think..." *Yes, definitely.* "I'm thinking of how Delta barracks' bathroom mirrors are embossed with Eros around their edges, actually. I bet yours are, too?"

"I don't know," he replies, tone wry. "I don't look in the mirror, because I'm not an egoist."

My laugh never leaves my lungs. His fingers have started trailing up and down the slope of my neck, pressing to my pulse for long, stuttering heartbeats, before repeating the pattern all over again. On the third pass I feel myself swallow involuntarily, and I know Fin doesn't miss it from the way he stills. He lets out a low hum, so quiet I might imagine it, before he picks up my braid and fiddles with the ends.

"You're quiet tonight, Skye," he murmurs. "Want to tell me why?"

"There's no reason."

"No?"

I shake my head. He tugs the small tie out of my hair, loosening the strands, and then his fingers move to my jaw, nudging it towards him. He's right there, sea-green eyes so bright, searching mine before dipping. Seconds pass before he leans in, hot lips pressing to mine gently. He stays there for long seconds, very still, like he's thinking hard on something or just memorising the feel of my mouth on his. I know that's what I'm doing, until my racing heart feels like it's about to explode and I can't take it anymore. I lean forwards, increasing the pressure, and am immediately met by him. His other hand slides under the curtain of hair freed from its braid, slipping past my cheek to the nape of my neck. He holds me to him as he opens my mouth, stealing my breath. I let him, fingers tightening around the book still in my lap, heart pattering out this heady, intoxicating rhythm that solicits me to solicit more; like this kiss is a drug, and I'm spiralling. The book falls to the floor with a dull *thud* as one of his hands drops to my hips, tugging me towards him. I stop thinking, and clamber really, *really* quickly - impossibly quickly - onto the bed and then him, sitting in his lap.

Fin pulls back, blinking at me in surprise. "How...did that even happen?"

"I don't know."

One side of his lips kicks up. Slowly, he drops his hands back to my hips, the weight of them deliciously warm, and pleasant. "Ok. Well you can do it again, anytime you like. I just have one question for you before I lose my cool."

Do you ever? "Yes?"

"Have you and Fjord made up?"

Instantly I feel myself lock up. "No. We haven't. We're..." *never going to make up about this.* "We're not speaking."

He nods, as if he expected that answer. "I would ask if that's why you're so distressed tonight, then?"

"I...I'm not distressed." *Lie.* "And I don't want to talk about this. Don't want to talk about Fjord or...anything. I just want to forget."

"I know," Fin says, quite gently. "But I'm worried, Skye. You played truant for a week without telling *anyone* where you were, and you haven't even tried to see my sister since you returned, even though she's just as upset by the switch up in patrol partners as you are. You're quiet, look tired, and you show up at my door really late tonight as this little bundle of fear and hurt." His lips press together, eyes so firmly holding mine I couldn't look away even if I wanted to...and I do want to. I want to hide, because I'm so bad at lying, hopeless at withholding sentiment from my expression, and tonight...tonight I'm feeling it all. "Something is wrong, Skye," he insists. "I want to know what it is, so I can help."

"It's so beyond help, Fin," I whisper, then gulp the words right back in with a sharp, shallow inhale. His brows slam down, torso leaning back from mine in shock, because goddesses, even to me that sounded bleak. I stare at him with wide eyes, then lean in and plonk my mouth on his, gripping his tense shoulders and neck to pull him back to me. He barely moves, and I can tell his mind is racing, stuck on what I just said.

I'm an idiot.

"Skye," he mutters around my quick, sloppy kisses. "I still want to talk."

"I don't."

I try to pull him to me again, and when that fails lift my hands and start loosening the ties on my shirt...then think better of that, or rather don't think at all, and drop them, fumbling with the top of Fin's breeches. His hands *fly* from my hips to grip them, stopping me instantly.

"Gods," he says in a gruff, exasperated voice. "I want to talk to you, sweetheart. Don't do that."

"But—"

"I want to understand this. How can I help? Do you want me to talk to Fjord? Or your new partner, Levi? Is he still making you nervous?" He squeezes my hands. "I have some weight in the Guild, Skye. Not as much as Fjord, but I could mention something to Sergeant Hajjar about the change in patrol partners. Inform her of how it's getting to you. Or Enye could try. She's shadowing Yasmine at the moment, and is definitely in good favour with her."

Surprise courses through me. "I...didn't know that?"

Fin's expression briefly brightens to pride and fondness. "We think there's about to be a switch up in Guild roles. Hajjar is pleased with Enye, and wants to see if she's ready to fill bigger shoes. Likely *her* shoes. It's good for my sister in many ways, but I know she'd prefer to patrol with you. I know she'd be happier doing that. She's worried you're not speaking to her because you're upset Yasmine chose her and not you, Skye. She cried to me at dinner."

Guilt punches me *hard* in the gut. "I'm not upset with her at all. I didn't know about this before you told me, but I'm pleased for her. Really pleased. Don't mention anything to anyone, Fin. I'll speak with Enye soon, but I don't want her to patrol with me. Not if she's climbing the ranks in the Guild. No way. Please don't say anything. I would really not like that."

"I—"

"Please don't, Fin. Please. I need you not to."

His lips press together, clearly frustrated and unwilling, but eventually he sighs. "Fine, I guess I won't mention anything to Yasmine, but I *am* going to speak with Fjord, Skye. I don't like how this went down, without either Enye or yourself knowing about it. That's not right. I'm surprised he even let it happen given how close the two of you are. Which is...another question I should ask you but...won't."

He finally releases my hands, shaking his head a little. They fall limply between us, but now I'm not fuelled by an urgent need to distract him, to lose myself in something reckless – now I'm actually *thinking* – I feel my cheeks heat with embarrassment. Gods. I don't know what I'm doing – in any part of my life, but especially here with this. Does he expect me to do something after obviously meaning to do it just seconds ago? Did he expect me to do it anyway, tonight?

"May I?"

One of Fin's hands slips to the small of my back, the other lifting between us to tap the tip of my nose, and then it hovers over the hastily, half-loosened ties of my shirt.

Mouth dry, I nod.

His lips tip up on one side. "Thanks."

I watch him deftly pull on the ties until they undo completely, fingers gently parting the fabric. He stops before he does anything else, the hand in the small of my back pressing me closer, until our lowers halves are well settled. I inhale softly, then exhale in surprise against the pair of soft, sensual lips suddenly parting mine.

"Forgetting anything yet?" he murmurs there.

Goddesses, yes. "A bit."

"Something to do with me?"

"Everything."

"Good."

Without warning he stands, turns, and guides me down until my back hits the mattress. My pulse jumps as he hovers over me, knees besides my hips, one hand denting the feather pillow by my head, the other coasting down my sternum to where my shirt is untied. Those sea-green eyes meet mine, filled with something that tells me Fin knows full well there's a terrible secret lingering unshared beneath the surface that he intends to find out, but also something softer –

something that speaks of one time shared together beneath the fragile flair of moonlight...and now another.

He pauses again before going further, even though he's already asked once. "May I?"

"Yes," I whisper. "I would like you to."

He offers me a very small smile, and then lets his body fall and his fingers drift...and we both know we're heading somewhere soon. My muddled thoughts find their way to safer waters as meaningful moments turn to minutes, turn to more. The overwhelmingly warm, pleasant weight of him over me, our shaking exhales, skin on skin, slow lips and deft hips...

They're all hoaxes, painting the perfect escape.

Until I leave.

Wreaking Havoc

The next day is a bad day. Despite everything with Fin, I'm not in a good mood. In fact, I think I feel *worse* than if I hadn't gone to his after Sholto's kitchenette.

Guilt.

That's what I feel – for escaping with him, and hiding everything from him whilst I did.

After lying awake for half the night fretting, I leave before he wakes up and search for Enye at breakfast, only to forgo actually *seeing* her when I spot Sergeant Yasmine Hajjar by her side, and realise that I'll just feel more guilty lying through my teeth to her, too. I end up stalking my room alone, stewing in worry and hurt and rebellion. Last night's news was just too much. I'm *not* leaving my friends. I'm not leaving Ioxthel. Prophecy be damned. Ruling a kingdom be damned. Everything and everyone be damned...

Tristan doesn't show up throughout the day, which inevitably means he's actually busy, something I can't fault him for. Though I don't doubt other ruffians are minding me, I want *him*. I miss him dearly, and feel pathetic for it, because it's been one day since we saw one another and I've been able to offload my burdens onto his steady shoulders. One single day since I've been anchored to him, my forever saving grace...yet I feel impossibly adrift, lost in an ocean swell of shock and unease and hurt, and hating it.

When the bells chime 6.00 pm I realise I've been in here the entire day, and I'm late for my night patrol. I almost forgo duty and get back into bed, but then think I'll go utterly mad with just myself for company. Hastily, I throw on my armour and daggers and hurry to the gates, but I don't stop when I see the guarded Guardian waiting for me there.

156

Upon levelling with my busy strides in the square abutting the Guild Levi greets me with a hushed *Good evening,* just like his quiet *Good morning* yesterday, and then that's it. I get nothing else from him, ever.

It vexes me, and it unnerves me.

I'm aware I never entertain any form of communication with him, not even a greeting in return...yet I think my situation is different to his. I think my silence is justified, because I'm not the enemy in disguise within Ioxthel's walls. I'm not the lethal Guardian with strong shoulders and wickedly sharp, straight daggers hidden somewhere on him who's sworn fealty to Fjord; a Guardian you'd think might wish to gain my trust, or at least my good favour, given everything in the Medical Syndicate last week, and given how adamant Fjord is that he and his brethren are not my enemies.

Levi doesn't seem interested in that. He doesn't seem interested in anything. He merely walks beside me in silence, usually just shy of my right shoulder – with very little expression ever found on his face and very little discernible feeling in his body language. He's watching our surroundings for sure, but just what he sees in them is impossible to know, and his eyes are just...so grey. Sometimes pale, sometimes dark, usually favouring soft heather, but always overly weathered and subdued. Or I guess another word I'd use for them is weary...which is sort of beside the point. The point is, his thoughts are indecipherable, and his propensities for silence and indifference unnatural.

We're on a southerly patrol route tonight, ironically very near the Medical Syndicate where we first met and had that horrible tiff. The streets are quiet, lulled to sleep by tired travellers and tradespeople dragging their aching feet and pitiful wares home, but you should know my feet aren't tired. Gone is the Skye of a few days ago, drained of all energy, numb with overwhelming distress. We're angry today after last night's news of the prophecy and leaving my friends, and my feet are stomping over the packed ground like a wolf cub on a mission to wreck and ruin.

I look sideways, and don't even try to pretend I'm not scrutinising Levi. His profile is materially pleasing, a collection of modest features that despite housing absolutely no sentiment are distinctly softer than the regal lines and edges to Fjord's face, especially cast in the setting sun's mellow glow. I can see the leather cord around his neck, tucked below the "v" of his shirt and the Guild's leather breastplate. I want to know what hangs from it, if only to confirm my suspicion that it's similar to Fjord's hourglass. Does it have something to do with their friendship? Or Levi's fealty to him, as his Guardian? And what does fealty even mean?

Like I said, no one knows much about The Guardians of Elysium except the fact they're supreme fighters protecting the Nixen from...something. Sholto told me a little of their heritage last night, but I still want to know more. I want to know why Fjord has one. And, there's that part about the eternal tie in the history books. Is *that* what it means to swear fealty?

Skye, my counsel mutters, heeding the storm brewing in me. *I would urge you to be steady, today. Nothing good is ever said or done in anger. Breathe through it, surpass its challenges, and be the most gracious version of yourself you can.*

Goddesses. Does she even know that's the *worst* thing she could say to me right now?

Ignoring her, I bat my way violently through a washing line that's half fallen in one of Ioxthel's ash-riddled gusts of wind. I keep staring at Levi's profile. Obviously. I'm being *obvious* about it, and yet he tolerates the scrutiny for well over a minute before he spares me a glance.

"Is everything ok, Skye?"

"No," I say bluntly. "I'm thinking in anger. Getting nowhere."

He waits for me to elaborate, but *I'm* waiting for him. "Is everything ok?" is the only thing outside of his greetings, and outside of our first few encounters in the Medical Syndicate and safe house, that he's ever said to me. He's not trying to sound Ioxthelian right now, and the lilting accent from Elysium is back...the roughness to his voice still there. It's always so hoarse, like it's suffering from disuse or a sore throat.

"Thinking about?" he eventually prompts.

"Guardians."

"What would you like to know?"

Perhaps why you're so damn silent? So reserved? "Sholto told me you're all descended from the four sentinels to Zeus's throne on Mount Olympus, and that *they* are the offspring of the river deity, Styx? That his father is one of those sentinels, Zelos?"

"Yes."

"How does it work? Being a Guardian? Swearing fealty? What *is* fealty? Is every Guardian assigned to one person? There can't be enough of you to go around?"

"No, not everybody has a Guardian. We're prized in Elysium, and people drive hard prices. The highest bidder usually wins; and these are typically members of the Nixen dynasties, the wealthy and powerful. You'll find most Guardians working for them. Fealty means sworn, unfailing loyalty."

I think on that. "You're saying someone *buys* their Guardian, and then that Guardian swears fealty, unwavering loyalty, to them?"

"Yes."

"That's very stupid. Loyalty isn't something you can *buy*. How much did Fjord pay for you? Hard price?"

"I swore fealty to a friend with no payment."

"How often does that happen?"

"I suppose...sometimes."

What a helpful response. I gesture to the leather cord around his neck, "The hourglass Fjord wears, do you have one too? Is it something to do with your fealty to him?"

He might look very slightly surprised. "Yes."

"What's the significance of it?"

"It's filled with sand from the Nereid settlement back in Elysium. It's our vessel of fealty, tied to where we grew up...and where you grew up for a time."

"For the first however many years of my life that I have no memory of, maybe because of trauma to do with my scars?" I mean to snort out a derisive laugh, but the same throbbing from the second meeting in safe house has started up in my temples. It's like my mind doesn't want me to think on the past I don't remember – like it's stopping me from doing that. "The history books mention something about the eternal tie," I continue with difficulty. "What is that? Why is it important?"

Levi doesn't reply to this, nor does he give me any sign he's even going to. He's examining the dusky, narrow streets ahead, seemingly absorbed by them even though there's nothing remarkable there besides the setting sun. He doesn't even look like he's *heard* me.

"The eternal tie," I grate out. "What is it, Levi?"

He blinks. "Uh...it's a string that ties itself between a Guardian and their ward, tethering them together mentally, physically, and spiritually. It's rare."

"Like a soulmate?"

"Of sorts, yes."

"So it's not the same as fealty?"

"No. Swearing loyalty through fealty is consciously done by a Guardian, or consciously solicited by whoever wants them to serve. When Guardian and ward are tethered, neither party have a say."

"What are you?"

"I've sworn fealty to Fjord."

"Yes," I say, a bit impatiently. "But was that always the case? Since forever?"

Levi hesitates. "No."

"So what have you *been?*"

He hesitates again, this time for longer. His entire disposition is excessively guarded when he does speak. "I suppose I've been many things."

Wreck and ruin. "Have you, Levi? What's your story then? What *things* have you been? How's your life gone so far?"

"It's gone ok. There's not much to say."

"No? But you've still been many things?" I stare at his soft profile, gaze hard and challenging. "Now I'm intrigued, because I think you're lying about something."

Skye, my counsel speaks up quickly. *I'd urge you to read the signs and be gracious.*

The signs just make me want to interrogate him more, I hiss back, internally of course. *Make me want to push him until that veil over his face slips into sentiment and he gives me* something *to work with.*

Don't pry.

Why?

Do I ever lead you astray?

Do I ever lead you astray? I throw back slyly. *Nope. Never. I'm a great leader. Objective. Rigorous. Mature.*

Please just trust me, Skye. Someone's story is theirs to tell in their own time, and theirs alone. Don't pry with this. Be gracious.

Both my brows raise at this. Again, it's probably the worst thing she could say to me in this state, and I open my mouth to defy her wishes – except I don't end up probing Levi on his history. I suddenly think of a better plan than prying, and that's *spying.*

I'm good at spying.

"Do Guardians train?" I ask him instead. "Or are you born with super special powers?"

He lets out a low breath, maybe one given in relief. "There's something called The League of Guardians in Elysium, an organisation governed by the children of Zeus's four sentinels. They're incredibly long-lived, and spend their time mentoring young Guardians – training us."

"Like Sholto?"

"Yes, as the child of Zelos, Sholto mentors. He trained Rose and your mother, I believe. He was the original founder of The League some years ago."

"I see." *The long-lived liar failed to mention that bit last night.* "And what exactly do Guardians train to fight? What're you protecting Nixen from?"

"We fight what their world has always been plagued by, which is now worsening. Creatures from The Nether – daímōns and wraiths."

"Aren't they one and the same?"

"No, although they're similar. Daímōn is a very general term for a spirit. They can be either good or bad, or both I suppose, whereas wraiths are a very specific type of daímōn. They're hollow shells of the souls they were when alive, and inherently evil. They're most commonly what we fight."

"So wraiths are ghosts?"

"Of sorts, yes."

I can't help but find that a little ironic, given my pastime. "You protect Nixen from ghosts?"

"Not all ghosts. Some have their soul intact. These don't classify as wraiths, and they have no interest in harming the living, so we subsequently have no interest in fighting them."

Oh, I see an opportunity here. "You had an interest in fighting *me* the other night, Levi, when I was ghosting. You went to *kill* me."

That's a total exaggeration, and we both know it...but Levi still slows his steps and says, very sincerely, "I must apologise to you again, Skye. I'm sorry for what happened at the Medical Syndicate. Though my intent would never have been to kill you, I wouldn't have subdued you as I did had I known who you were."

"You weren't going to kill me?"

"No, I wasn't. I wouldn't have harmed you, either."

My eyes narrow. "What were you going to do then, getting that close behind me? Tuck my hair behind my ear? Ask what soap I use?"

He spares me a glance, and I know he knows I'm provoking an argument. I mean, it's not a huge mystery given how low and daring my tone is – given how the scowl on my face is so deep and furious I can barely see him beneath my eyebrows.

"I will apologise again, Skye," is what he replies, bowing his head in deference. "What happened between us in the Medical Syndicate is not how Fjord wished for us to meet. How I wished for us to meet."

I let slip a dark laugh. "Oh? He wanted us all to have dinner together, did he? To wait until I'm *silly* off wine to tell me he's from another kingdom and lied to me for five years, and to tell me I'm the daughter of some odd god in the sky who probably couldn't think up a name for me so just stuck an *e* on the end of wherever he was for good measure, then threw me from the heavens because the gods don't like strays or people with weird scars on their skin. They're all perfect, aren't they? Perfect beings. I'm not perfect. I can't tie my shoelaces, and I say the wrong thing. I eat with my mouth open too. I'm not perfect. That's great dinner table talk. I would have really liked it, learning the truth from the lies whilst silly off wine. Would have sicked up all my food in shock, too." *Whoops. That's gross.*

Stop talking. "I would have liked that, Levi, so much. Best thing that's happened to me all lifetime, and this is the second. Having someone shadow me through my own streets because of some rogue Guardian who's nowhere to be seen. Where even is he, Xavier Archer? Why is he so bad? Where's the threat from him?"

I stop and pivot on my heel, searching our surroundings for him. Levi stops beside me, too, but he doesn't respond to my outburst.

His silence is *really* starting to get to me.

"You don't talk much do you? It's very rude. Unfriendly. Unhelpful. Not like I imagine Guardians usually are."

"Xavier is hiding from me."

"He's afraid of you?"

"Yes."

I think on that. "Is he really so bad? The worst of the worst?"

"Yes. I wouldn't like to think of anyone walking these streets alone, even if they are their own. He's very bad, Skye."

"Bad, because he's horribly shy like you, with eyes that are so dull they look dead and no one could *ever* trust? A voice like rust, too?"

Oh, man. That is *not* what I meant to say...especially because my own voice is so harsh and spiteful uttering it. I don't sound like me, and I immediately regret that. I watch with a rapidly souring gut as Levi quickly averts that *dull* gaze to examine the streets, the tips of his cheekbones flushing the unmistakeable pink of someone shamed.

You should be thoroughly ashamed of yourself, Skye, my counsel says in a low, disappointed voice. *Stop this spiteful nonsense and apologise to him.*

I don't.

Even though I should, I don't apologise to Levi, and it's perhaps my second lowest point in all of this shit...something I even lose sleep over in the coming weeks. And the first? The lowest of the low points? That'll be here for us all to witness in just a few short, glorious hours.

I move to leave, to flee from my guilt. "I would like to go."

"There's a tavern brawl brewing down the street. It's the other way."

There is? "I can't hear anything."

Levi nods, and continues examining the streets in steady surveillance, attention lingering on where I *know* there's a tavern in the distance. He turns back to me to see what I'll do...but he doesn't quite meet my gaze, because I told him his eyes looked dead, didn't I?

"What're you thinking?" I ask uneasily, fidgeting.

"I'm not really," he admits, and then sighs, as if he knows the response will frustrate me. "I suppose my mind is on the virtues of not talking much, and how it enables you to become a good listener. And on how I would never lie to you as Fjord's Guardian, even though I understand that will be difficult to believe."

"It is difficult."

"I understand."

"The world is upside down."

Levi digests that. "I understand."

I fidget again, shifting my weight restlessly from foot to foot. I still can't hear anything besides the usual low hubbub of evening life, but then I'm not really trying to. Everything is so noisy and so muddled in my mind that I haven't a hope of listening out for anything else. And Levi still isn't meeting my gaze, which makes me feel really bad. So mad at myself. Mad at my counsel, too, for being right in that nothing good is ever said in anger.

Apologise, she says sternly now.

I open my mouth, but nothing comes out. Even though I know it should. Even though somehow, I think Levi *does* understand that the world is upside down for me and I *do* know he wasn't going to kill me - or even harm me - in the Medical Syndicate.

I pivot on my heel and start in the opposite direction to the tavern, fleeing my guilt and unease. I don't stop when two strides later I hear the starts of a fight - glass shattering, voices raised - or four strides later when my counsel totally deserts me, storming out of my imagination in protest.

I miss her the second she leaves.

And I miss myself, too.

* * *

My awful, guilt-riddled mood doesn't improve throughout the rest of our night duty, or when we return to the Guild at dawn and find Fjord waiting for us just inside the gates, looking refreshed, genial and hopeful.

"Good morning," he greets, offering us both a deep bow. "How was patrol?"

"So bad," I mumble. "I'm mad, Fjord. Said the wrong thing, the worst thing, and didn't apologise for it. Nothing good is ever said in anger. Don't you know that? I thought I did, but I didn't. It was bad and I'm still mad...and I failed your request. I didn't act like a Guardian to Guardians at all. I was spiteful. I'm a bad person, like you were, lying to me for five years."

"You're not a bad person, Skye."

"Yeah, I am."

Fjord's eyes travel to Levi and linger there. "Right. Well...you're still both here, so that's positive. Might I have a moment of your time, please?"

"No," I say quickly, a little fearfully. "I'm mad, Fjord. I'll say the wrong thing to you. The worst thing. Won't apologise for it either because I'm a mad, bad person."

I lurch forwards and start hurrying past the mess hall towards the barracks. I'm not hungry for breakfast, which is a good thing because I don't feel like seeing *anyone* right now unless it's Tristan. Goddesses, I need to see him and tell him about the prophecy and the Nixen dynasties in Elysium; and about Artemis and my mother.

Still can't believe that.

Throwing a glance over my shoulder, I wonder if I should just go straight to the harbours without washing up, because I'm that desperate to see him. I see that Levi has disappeared from the gates, but Fjord is following me.

"Leave me be," I say, and it sounds like a plea. "I'm mad, Fjord. I'm going to do the wrong thing."

"I would still ask to speak with you, Skye. It will only take a moment, and it's quite important. Please?"

"No," I face forwards again, picking up my pace. "I don't want to talk. Ever. To Hades with the prophecy. I'm not leaving Ioxthel or Tristan. I won't. I need him in my life, and he needs me, so I'm not leaving. And I'm mad, so I'm going to say the wrong thing. You seriously need to leave me be."

Fjord is now level with me, matching my strides with incredible ease, because I'm so stupidly short. "I'm not here to discuss leaving the city, Skye, unless you wish to."

"No, I don't! Because I'm *never* leaving!"

"I...understand you might feel that. If you remember, I left my kingdom behind to come to Ioxthel five years ago. I left my Guardian behind, and both our troubles...so I know what it's like to go through something like this. I know how impossibly dreadful it feels, and I'm sorry you're experiencing it now. I would...would like to help you through it."

I start bounding up the barrack steps, emotion rising. "You don't understand, Fjord! How could you? Have you had someone lie to you for five years? Someone you thought you could trust?" I'm horrified when my voice breaks on the last word. "I trusted you like family, family you *knew* I was desperate for, and you took advantage of it. Of me!"

"I didn't mean to. I would never wish for that, Skye. I also trust you like family. I *consider* you as family, given everything with my moth—"

"*Stop* talking to me," I interrupt, pivoting to face him at the top of the stairs, hands forming tight little fists by my side. "I'm so mad at you, and I don't believe you. I don't."

Fjord stops too, and he's a brave man to stand on the edge of a flight of steps with someone starting to lose it before him, but he doesn't look fearful. He just looks pained, and earnest.

"Please hear me out, Skye. Don't shut me out. I never meant to hurt or take advantage of you. I'm not your enemy."

"You're not my *friend*, either."

He snares my elbow as I turn to leave, grip gentle...because *all* of Fjord is so damn gentle, isn't it? "I *am* your friend, Skye. I love you like a sister. That's never going to change, and I'm begging you, *please* believe me, and please don't shut me out. My mother, she loved—"

"Let me leave, Fjord! I'm so mad, and sad...and I'm going to do something bad! Lose it! I know it! I keep *telling* you it, so get off!"

"I just need to tell you something first. Sholto requested I did so, and it's important. Please let me tell you it."

"Get off!"

He doesn't. With the hand still gripping my elbow he edges us both away from the steps, so maybe he *is* worried I'll push him down them...or that I'll trip over my own feet and fall. That's probably more likely isn't it? Because I'm mad and sad, and losing it, not thinking straight. Not thinking at *all*.

It's here now.

The lowest of the low points – and in a moment of swollen frustration and impulsivity, of betrayal and anger and *hurt,* I bend my free arm back and throw my fist forwards.

Hitting him on the cheek.

Hitting Fjord.

The sheer unexpectedness of the move is the only thing that enables me to land the glancing blow. It's not a proper punch, but Fjord still shies away in surprise, his neck whipping to the side. He lets go of me immediately. I stumble away, heart lurching in my chest, gut swooping so low I feel like following it...feel like dropping to the floor in a pitiful heap.

I watch warily as he stands frozen for several long moments, then lets slip a shaking breath and turns to face me. There's no ire in his eyes, but there *is* shock, and great injury.

Great injury.

It makes me feel sick.

It makes me want to sob and scream, because despite *everything* I'm saying and doing, I still believe those eyes, and I still believe the sentiments splashed so genuinely over his face. I still believe he's sorry and sad just like me, and that he does love me. I...can't believe what just happened.

I just hit *Fjord.*

"I'm here to tell you that Lieutenant Jensen's oath with the Council is happening tonight in the Temple of Poseidon," he informs me in a very measured voice, as if I haven't just assaulted him. "Sholto wants you there to see what we're up against. I'm not in favour of it because I'm worried about Xavier, but Sholto is insisting. He'll wait for you beneath Ioxthel's bell tower at 11.00 pm. If you don't show there's not much he can do, but he'll be angry, Skye, and having both of you angry will be hard." His throat works as he watches me. Waiting for a reply? Or waiting to understand what just happened, to fully realise I *hit* him. "That's what I needed to tell you, but I would take the opportunity to say that I'm more sorry than you could ever know for this, Skye. I see how much hiding the truth from you has hurt you, and how foolish it was because of that. I regret it, deeply...but it wasn't just my decision to make, and revealing everything to you would've gone against both Sholto's and the great Oracle of Delphi's instincts. That's not to say I'm excusing m—"

"It sounds like you are!" I interrupt. "Sounds like you're excusing yourself from this dinner table where you reveal that I'm a demigod prophesied to save the world and you're from Elysium and you want me to make *friends* with the Guardian I just called horribly shy in spite! It's like you're just dropping a huge explosion of truth right next to the wild boar roasted with an apple in its mouth which I've never had the luxury of eating because I lived on the *streets* growing up, and now...you're leaving. Pushing your chair back and leaving, after dropping that explosion of truth, like it's not *you* that did it. Like you're not responsible for ruining the dinner. That is the hugest of excuses right there...or here....Fjord. Just one big fat excuse. Fatter than the boar itself..."

Mm, what an utterly ridiculous outburst. I say such stupid things sometimes, and I *do* them, too. Stupid, hurtful things that injure other people.

Fjord lets out a low sigh when I stop talking, holding my restless, guilty gaze. One hand rests lightly on the scimitar at his hip, the other reaches for the tiny hourglass hanging down his sternum, holding it in comfort. Wish I had my bow here to do the same.

"I'm not excusing myself, Skye," he insists. "I swear to you. I feel terrible, and guilty, and I'll never stop trying to express those regrets to you, or to regain your trust. I would go back and change this if I could. I'd listen to the people I respect most and tell you sooner...but you *have* to see that our actions are not without explanation. This story is shocking and worryingly dangerous, and we're just trying to protect you. That's why we kept this from you. To protect you. To shield you from a very dangerous destiny for as long as possible, and to let you grow up with your friends. We did this because we love you dearly, Skye."

"Well I *hate* you," I blurt out. "I hate you forever for this."

He flinches. Stares at me with more injury than I've ever seen – more than when I hit him. Something inside me cries out, wails like a child. I can't stop. Thinking and knowing I'm in the wrong is doing *nothing* to stop me, even though my gut is so nauseous I think I might actually be sick and the tip of my tongue is burning up with something spicy and bitter, because I'm lying.

So badly.

Tears spring to my eyes, falling rapidly. I'm hurting, and now *he's* hurting...and I can't seem to stop saying the wrong thing.

"You should cease trying, Fjord. You'll never recover my trust, and I just *hate* you for this. I'll never forgive you. I don't ever want to speak to you again, or see you...even for dinner with a wild boar. This friendship we had is lost forever. I never want it back. I'll run away if you try, and you'll never find me. Never."

Fjord seems speechless, and looks incredibly young all of a sudden – his eyes wide and his harmless features etched with distress and fear.

Fear that I will run.

And he'll never find me.

"I will not stop trying," he eventually gets out in a very hoarse voice. "I will never give up on you, Skye, because you're family to me and you always will be, but I hope you feel better soon. Please think on Sholto's request about the oath tonight if you can bear to, and be assured I'll leave you alone for some time. I won't pester you...even for dinner with a wild boar. I bid you good day."

He turns quickly without looking at me, and my expression crumbles as soon as he does. Silent sobs hitch my chest so violently I struggle to breathe through them as I watch him jog stiffly down the stairs, disappearing from sight. Everything in me hurts. From the swooping motion in my gut, the heavy, hollow *thud* of my broken heart, my stinging nose and eyes; to my stupid temper that feels as unspent as the gaudy riches hoarded in Alcázar, but at the same time so utterly exhausted.

This was a bad day, and I made it so.

The Oath

11.11 pm.

The bell tower.

It's still the bad day.

Sholto is loitering on the shadowy fringes of the square abutting the Guild, just like Fjord said he would be. He's difficult to see, not only in his stealth, but also because the moon is hidden behind a rare mass of smoky clouds; it's pearly, luminescent sheen veiled *just* like everyone's intentions seem to be these days, including Ruby Sabir's.

I'll tell you now, I'm not here for Sholto. I'm here because I've never trusted The Queen or her Council, and because hunting fickle secrets in the dead of night is what I do.

Living for the next hustle.

Living to ghost.

I'm telling myself tonight will be no different to normal, even though I'll have a lying amateur beside me, and even though I feel so very far from my usual, dizzyingly exhilarated self. Instead, my mood is bathing in the midnight black of my cloak. I feel weird about things with Fin, doubtful of what on earth is going on between us; bad I haven't spoken to Enye when she's worried I'm upset with her. I feel even worse about being mean to Levi and hitting Fjord earlier.

Worser than worse.

But...I'm telling myself, and you, to forget all of that bad stuff, because I'm so full in my muddled messy mind that I can't cope with it, and I need another to help me. That's when things will get better, isn't it? When I can offload my troubles onto Tristan's strong, steady shoulders...and though I haven't even seen him yet, I will soon.

He's just busy.

I'm just adrift.

But it's temporary. Things will get better, and though it's a bad day, it's not *all* terrible. I know the other ruffians are here, lingering in the gloomy recesses of the streets Sholto and I are due to walk through to travel to the Temple of Poseidon, watching over me and minding our passage. Minding my past mentor – the master fabulist, the long-lived liar, the *amateur* ghost...

"Skye."

My eyes narrow, feet faltering over the dark, dusty square. That tone is just like it was when I fled his kitchenette two nights ago having flung red wine over his white shirt – low and disappointed.

I'm still furious.

And afraid.

I peer into the gloom, watching Sholto's small but billowing form dispel the shadows beneath the bell tower. He's wearing a cloak tonight, a novel sight.

"You're late," he states stiffly. "I said 11.00 pm."

Yep. Decided I'd make you wait because it's a bad day...and I had trouble tying my shoes, like usual.

I obviously don't respond to him out loud with this, and I'm absolutely sure he wouldn't care for it, anyway. He merely pivots silently on his heel in our intended direction. It's clear he expects me to follow, and though I'm half tempted to ditch him just to damn those expectations, I don't.

We wend our way quickly through the streets, sharing the shadowy sills of Ioxthel's squat, shabby sandstone houses with Tristan's ruffians to avoid the night patrols of guilders. Sholto doesn't comment on the roguish sentries there, and nor they him. They just watch on with beady eyes, saluting me...condemning him. When we hide from a second pair of patrollers, I tell myself not to wonder what

174

happened with the tavern brawl I refused to attend with Levi last night when we were on duty ourselves, but I do. I feel impossibly ashamed of my behaviour towards him.

Unsurprising, my counsel speaks up, and it's the first thing she's said to me since she stormed out of my mind. *No one is immune to the plague of guilt, Skye, especially when their tongue is bitter with spite. I'm severely disappointed in you for not apologising.*

Me too, I mutter. Then, a little begrudgingly, *Nice of you to show up.*

Sadly, I never really left...and let's call that *the plague of fate.* There's a pause, and a sigh. *It is done, Skye. Let's not dwell on any of this now. You need to focus.*

What if I didn't want to? What if I just made this bad day the worst *day.*

I'd say you're a fool, she responds with another sigh, *because you've arrived.*

Oh.

She's right.

We've reached the Western Peninsula, where the fortress of Alcázar and the Temple of Poseidon dominate the craggy cliffs. The land between the two sites has eroded, leaving a thin, treacherous path through the waves, lit by sparse flares. Sholto and I forego using my preferred ghosting route, the forgotten water outlet beneath the wisteria-laden battlements, instead skirting the perimeter of the fortress by hastening over it's rocky, oceanside foundations. They're deserted – too irregular underfoot, and too prone to disappear beneath storm swells, for sentries to patrol.

The Temple of Poseidon itself is small and remote, but by far Ioxthel's most impressive architectural masterpiece. Astride a stack of weathered rock beaten relentlessly by waves, it adopts the highest point in Astyros; if you can really term it part of the kingdom when it stands so resolutely in the ocean. Sparing moonlight shines over half the building's marble pillars and sculpted friezes, embedded with thousands - upon thousands - of glossy, grooved seashells. The excessive grandeur is a suitable tribute to Ioxthel's patron, The Sea God, Poseidon - or so the monarchy tell us. They would, right? They used *our* money and *our* labour to build it many hundreds of years ago, and then they're the only ones allowed to worship in it.

Twelve figures are already gathered at the base of the stone-cut staircase rising up to the temple. Each holds a torch of fire in one hand and the tether of a small, domestic animal in the other. The poor souls are bleating so mournfully they're giving the frenzied seagulls circling overhead a run for their drachmae, as if they know what's to happen. As if they know sacrifices are to be made tonight.

"Be quiet and vigilant, Skye, and stay behind me," Sholto mutters when the Council start traipsing up the stairs, following the only figure with their hood down - no doubt Ruby.

I watch his cloak swirl with a menacing mind of its own around his ankles, my ire rising at the blunt order; but I do follow him, and I am quiet and vigilant. We stick to the stairs' bends and hollows, staying out of sight - and behind us in turn is someone else doing the same. She's a tiny, lone figure slinking silently up the damp steps, a wolf cub forbidden from following her older siblings on their hunt...but following nonetheless. It's Akira, Tristan's favourite little ruffian girl.

Upon arrival at the temple, the Council halt just short of its entrance and bow before an altar also adorned with thousands more glimmering seashells. They very quickly start performing a meticulous sequence of prayer, purification and libation led by Ruby - though this is not, Sholto informs me, as it should be.

"Usually on ground as sacred as the Temple of Poseidon a high priest or priestess will direct ritual proceedings," he mumbles, voice barely audible over the crash of waves below and the Council's sinister hum of prayer above. "It is wrong for The Queen to be leading this."

Lieutenant Jensen is the last to be purified and pay his respects to the altar. I know this because Ruby pushes his hood down as he kneels before her. Shadows from a nearby fire bowl flicker over his face, making it difficult to discern his expression, but I can tell he's nervous from his shaking, jerky limbs, and there's an edge left unspoken to the crimson smile Ruby gives him – something well pleased, and highly foreboding.

The sacrifices are next, and each is completed efficiently and reverently. The animals are washed with water and barley before their throats are slit and the warm, metallic smell of blood fills the air. The scent is as harrowing as the cries from the live animals awaiting their fate. Washing them before sacrifice is supposed to show their willingness to be part of the ritual, but that's not what I hear in their whines and whimpers...and you and I both know if they were to slip their tethers, they'd flee from here like sea spray from surf. They'd probably flee *into* the sea spray and surf, stormy waves be damned.

Singed flesh soon replaces that of salt water and blood as the sacrifices are skinned, dismembered and tossed into the fire bowls. Eventually the meat will be eaten, but only after the main ritual proceedings have taken place.

The Council now file up the temple's steps, their monotonous prayer growing more vigorous with every stride, until it reaches its zenith in the very centre of the small, opulent building. One by one they sink to their knees, place both hands on the floor and bow their heads in worship...and so far, in case you *didn't* know, this is all as you might expect from a sacred ritual. Unremarkable, and a little dull to describe to be honest...

Until it's not.

The moment the last Council member's knees touch the marble floor, a deep, menacing rumble roils through the air. Seconds later the ground beneath my feet lurches right and then left, jolting Sholto and I violently into the altar we're now creeping past. The very foundations of the temple seem to shift, slabs of marble cracking like the fractured glaze of a pottery vase. Thunder booms overhead so loudly it rattles my bones and looses scree from the cliff, the debris swiftly swallowed by the ocean below...an ocean that suddenly looks *much* closer to us...?!

Frozen in disbelief, I watch as a huge wave crashes into the rock face to our right, shaking the temple to its core and peppering Sholto and I with cold, salty spray.

"They're not honouring Poseidon in his own temple," he explains over the roar of wind, earth and water. "This ritual is not for him, and the god is angry. This quake is his doing."

"Poseidon?!" I breathe incredulously. "Is he here, then?"

"I doubt it, and I doubt it will last long. Quickly now, Skye. Follow me."

The earthquake and small tsunami grumble to a stop as we creep nearer the temple and scale its foundations, hiding in the thick shadows of a marble pillar. The Council are still kneeling in a circle, but Ruby and Lieutenant Jensen now stand gingerly in its centre. In Ruby's hands is a large golden goblet, incandescent from the glow of a nearby fire torch. Her eyes are wide, perhaps seeking to understand the recent quake, or seeking to *defy* its perpetrator – and whichever it is, the expression doesn't last long. Deep garnet liquid is dribbling over the backs of her hands, no doubt spilt from the goblet. She flinches violently, features twisting in pain, and quickly wipes them in the folds of her cloak.

This, it seems, also means something important to Sholto. "Keep an eye on that goblet, Skye. It doesn't hold what you think it does."

"It is time," Ruby states, her voice ringing out over the Council's low, eery chants. She hands the vessel to Lieutenant Jensen with what would be a laughable degree of reverence, if any of this were funny. "Drink, Lieutenant. Fulfil your oath in the name of the ancient gods and goddesses."

"In their name," he mumbles, lifting the goblet to his lips. For a few hefty swallows, nothing happens. It's as you might expect from someone drinking wine in prayer, albeit someone who *really* likes the good stuff...until it's not.

Jensen's hands suddenly start quivering, minutely as first, and then violently. Manically. He chokes and wrenches the goblet from his mouth, shaking his head as if to clear himself of a stunned stupor. Red spittle flies from his mouth, and at first I think it's the wine...but then his limbs grow rigid, and he staggers sideways with the goblet held aloft. I see the liquid streams from his eyes, nose and ears, too.

Jensen is bleeding from his orifices.

Horrified, I start forwards – to do what I don't know, because it's not as if I know *anything* about medicine, and I never find out anyway. Sholto jerks me back by the hood of my cloak, throwing his arms around my shoulders and pinning me to his front.

"No, Skye," he orders gruffly in my ear. "You stay here."

"We have to go!" I hiss, struggling. "He's dying!"

"As will you be if you go in there."

"But we have to stop this, Sholto!"

"No. We have to *understand* this. The Lieutenant is drinking ichor, the blood of the gods and goddesses. It is fatal to mortals. I've no doubt he knew this before he drank from the goblet, and he has thus sealed his own fate. The question is why he has done it."

"That doesn't mean we shouldn't try and undo it!" I exclaim. "That we shouldn't try to help him!"

"There is no remedy for this," Sholto insists in a low voice. "Nothing we can do to help. Trust me. Once ichor passes a mortal's lips, they are irreversibly lost to the world. It's highly corrosive to even touch, as you must have seen when it spilt over Ruby's hands. Please turn, and watch. I need two sets of eyes on this."

I do turn back to the temple, and I do watch; not because he orders me to, but because I feel impelled by my own morbid horror, and also...I can't look at him. I'm utterly shocked by Sholto's attitude towards what's unfolding, the death of a fellow human. I know he's four hundred years old, but does that automatically pave the pathway to apathy? To nonchalance?

No, my counsel mutters, even though I'm not talking to her. *It does not, Skye, but I'm with the son of Zelos on this one. It's too late for the Lieutenant, and there's nothing you can do for him.*

I watch helplessly as Jensen falls heavily to his knees in the middle of the chanting circle, convulsing violently. Blood drips onto the pearly marble slabs around him, smattering like ink would to parchment from the nib of a quill...or like blood from a flogging whip. Ruby now darts towards him looking panicked, but not because she's worried for him, and not because she's doing what I can't and moving to *help* him, either.

"Drink!" she shrieks, seizing him by a meaty forearm and wrestling the goblet back to his lips. "Finish this. You *must* finish this quickly!"

Her voice echoes through the temple, shocking in its fervency. When the sound fades, the Council are still uttering their chilling prayer and Jensen is choking on the liquid, the blood, being forced down his throat. Then, Ruby stumbles back a step. The Lieutenant's tormented eyes widen...and every muscle in my body locks up.

There's no missing the newly iridescent glow of his irises, their sheen brighter and hotter than the depths of the fires lining the temple's perimeter...and so unnatural. Fury and fear explode in my gut at the sight, on instinct, because although I don't entirely understand what's happening, I know in my bones it's *bad.*

This is really, really bad.

Lieutenant Jensen throws his head back in a silent, spluttering scream, and from his mouth pours...smoke, I think? The murky vapour instantly smothers the temple's interior fires, twisting with vigour through the air, seemingly propelled by itself. As it does so, the empty goblet falls with a clatter from Jensen's limp fingertips, and then he also hits the floor.

Unmoving.

Ruby springs forward, this time wielding a censer; something similar, if not identical, to the one she used two weeks ago to bless her Council in Alcázar. She tramples over Jensen's body in an hasty attempt to swipe the vessel through the air and collect the writhing smoke. Bones break sickeningly underfoot, and if the fallen Lieutenant wasn't dead before, he is now.

My revulsion expands.

So does my fury.

Now *I* feel like burning brighter than the extinguished temple fires, setting this whole building ablaze. Setting this *peninsula* ablaze. Righting wrongs. Erasing evils. Destroying everyth—

"Skye...?!"

Sholto quiet exclamation is like thunder in my ears. His arms instantly fall from me, just as my counsel also ushers a quick, shocked warning.

Be still, Skye! There's nothing you can do now!

I don't know if she's right. Without Sholto's grip on me, and only the goddesses themselves know why he let me go, I really think I might storm into the temple. I might engage with Ruby, razing those intentions redder than her name to the ground. Destroying everything in my path before the urge to blink an eye has been solicited.

Burnin—

Skye! my counsel snaps, very fiercely. *Listen! Watch! Be still!*

Jolted by her vehement tone, and disoriented by the hot riot of energy brewing in me, I find myself doing as she wills. A horrible, deathly silence has filled the temple and its surroundings. The Council have stopped their prayers, perhaps in the very same second Ruby snapped her precious censer shut, locking in the smoky substance vomited by Lieutenant Jensen. She stands over his crumpled, contorted form with an air of mad exhilaration to her, and no sign of remorse.

"It is done," Sholto breathes grimly from where he hovers behind me. Close, but no longer touching. "This was a summoning, Skye. The vapour the Council called upon, channelled by Lieutenant Jensen, was a spirit. Or part of one. I am sure the next oath will be soon, and I am sure we will hear of it shortly..."

He's right.

"Next month," Ruby address the group breathlessly. "Next month, on the full moon, we repeat this with our second representative from the Guild. I trust she is ready...?"

She waits for one of the kneeling figures to nod their bowed, hooded head obediently. Something about the action is unnervingly familiar, but I can't pinpoint why, and I don't have the wherewithal to think on it right now. Ruby is looking pleased by her response, and reaches beneath the folds of her cloak to hook the censer safely onto her waistband. She picks up the golden goblet tipped forlornly onto its side, wiping its rim carefully but somehow without finesse or reverence – like it doesn't really matter now it's empty.

"Excellent," she says, smiling. "Well, my patrons, it is done. Let us feast together."

The Council immediately rise from their knees, descending the temple steps to the shell-laden altar and leaving their fallen member's broken, bloodied form behind.

"Come, Skye," Sholto mutters as they do. "We should go."

"What about Lieutenant Jensen?"

"He's dead. We can do nothing for him."

I swallow tightly. "We should check, Sholto. We should check for a pulse. Or...we should help him pass into his next life."

"After undertaking a ritual such as this?" Sholto's hands land on my upper arms, urging me to turn. His expression isn't as stern as his tone, but it still brokers no room for debate. "After such a ritual as this, Lieutenant Jensen will never reach the destination in the underworld he wishes to, Skye, no matter who minds his passage there. There is nothing left to do."

"But—"

"Do *not* argue with me," he says firmly. "Leave with me. Now."

I'll be honest with you, I regret letting him persuade me to leave. Perhaps there *is* nothing for me to do for Lieutenant Jensen, but I swore I'd never cave to Sholto's wishes again, and yet here I am, doing just that.

We creep past the Council gorging themselves on charred meat and wine, descending the slippery stairs and climbing over the peninsula's jagged rocks without a word. A soft whistle sounds as soon as we hit the streets beyond Alcázar, no doubt Akira. I spot her loitering on a nearby rooftop. She turns without further communication and leaps to the streets below, and I bet you anything she's going to find Tristan to tell him what we witnessed, to tell him how *bad* it was. It is, for selfish reasons, a very good thing – busy or not, he'll be visiting me tomorrow.

Sholto and I return to the Guild in silence, and I find myself too preoccupied to refuse him escorting me back to my room. My mind is still in the temple, staring at Jensen's etiolated body...cursing Ruby for whatever sins she's conducted tonight. Cursing Sholto for stopping me stopping her. Cursing myself for letting him do it, and for being so *bad* today...

Hitting people.

Hurting people.

Hurting myself.

"Tell me what happened back there," Sholto requests as we start up the barrack steps, him before me. "Please."

"I don't know what you mean."

"When you wished to storm the temple and I stopped you. What happened?"

"It's just as you said. I wished to stop Ruby, and you stopped me. You manhandled m—"

"No," he interjects, a little impatiently. "I meant...your skin became very hot beneath my hold. Burningly so, and instantly. I do not understand how or why, if you didn't ignite your ichor."

What the what now..? "Ignite ichor?"

"Yes. You didn't do that, so I don't understand..."

He stops walking and talking so suddenly I bump into him, then totter down a stair or two muttering dark expletives. Sholto doesn't seem to hear it, instead twisting to look down at me with a very strange expression on his face, his right foot yet to land its next step as if it mirrors the cloud of his suspended thoughts.

"I'm not following you, Sholto," I admit, when the seconds pass by and he doesn't say anything further...just stares at me. "What exactly do you mean by, *ignite your ichor?*"

"It *cannot* be so?" he mutters to himself, clearly still not hearing me. His brows pull together, something fast and furious turning over the brown depths of his eyes. They bounce between mine, as if searching for something...something on instinct I'm not sure I want him to find?

"What cannot be so, Sholto?" I press.

"No..."

"What?!"

Tense seconds pass before he remembers himself, turning rigidly and restarting up the stairs. "Never mind, Skye. It's late. You should sleep. We'll be meeting soon to discuss what happened tonight with the other Elysium folk, inevitably in the safe house, and probably sometime in the next two weeks. I will inform you of when, and expect you to attend. I also expect you to travel with me to meet my father, Zelos, when he responds to my attentions."

"Zelos?" I frown. "Why're we meeting up with your dad?"

"Do not call him that. We are meeting with *Zelos* because he hid Prometheus's Torch following the Impurity War, all those hundreds of years ago. He is the only being alive, to my knowledge, that knows of its whereabouts...thus it's essential we talk to him. I told you this in my kitchenette two nights ago, before you left in disgrace?" He stops as we near my room, this time less suddenly. He's no longer looking strangely shocked or perplexed. "You've seen for yourself tonight what we're up against, Skye, and even wished to stop it in the heat of moment...albeit recklessly. Malevolent intents are being put into play, becoming enshrined in reality through ritual, and The Queen is masterminding it. Tonight was the first of no doubt many, many deaths we will witness together, and so you *must* master your feelings. You *must* journey down the strings our fates have woven for you, without rebellion and without needless ire. If you don't, you disappoint not only myself, but *your* self...and the world."

"Thought I'd disappointed you already," I say back quickly, but it's lacking bite because I can still smell sea spray and smoky meat in my hair from the oath, and his words make me uneasy.

Sholto's expression pinches. "Yes. You have disappointed me."

We stare each other down. Before me, I see the vigour of someone pretending not to think furiously; someone four hundred years old who I thought I knew, but don't and never did. Someone I resent and feel bitterness towards. Someone who hurt me so horrendously badly...and who I can't see myself ever forgiving.

He hasn't even said sorry to me, has he? Excepting that first meeting in the safe house, when he told me my mother was dead...Sholto hasn't apologised for his lies. Hasn't admitted it was *wrong* of him to conceal everything from me.

Now I'm thinking of my mother, Saffron. Huntress to Artemis, and whose silver bow I carry on my back in this very second. What of my father, too? He doesn't stand before me, like I pretended to myself he did for the last seven years. Not even *close*...because if you remember, my father is the god no one knows the identity of. The *god*. Which makes me a demigod, doesn't it? Duh. We knew that already, but how do you even reconcile news like that? How do you become ok with it? I still feel in a haze of disbelief over it – over everything.

"Goodnight, Skye," Sholto offers crisply, when neither of us has spoken for minutes. "Sleep on all we've witnessed together tonight, and on your irascible temperament towards me. I expect you to realise this is bigger than the injuries you feel I've inflicted upon you by protecting your younger self, and you should know I do not ever expect to have wine thrown over my shirt again."

"You deserved it."

The words slip from me before I can stop myself, and even though I mean them...I regret saying them as soon as they come out.

"Mind your manners," Sholto warns in a very low voice, after a *very* fraught pause. "We have a long path ahead of us. You do not wish to provoke my wrath before we've even set out, and I will *not* tolerate insolence from you - not when Elysium, and perhaps even the realm of the gods and goddesses themselves, Mount Olympus, is at stake. Tonight's foul happenings were meant to be an awakening for you, a summons to reason from the slumber of your needless ire and rebellion."

"Don't tell me to *sleep on it all*, then," I throw back tightly. "If you want me awake for it. Mixed messages are the work of Hades...of witches, too."

Sholto shakes his head, lips pressed into such a firm line they blanch of all colour. "You disappoint me with that remark, Skye, and you disappoint yourself. I will not repeat myself again. Mind your manners. I will *not* tolerate insolence from you."

He leaves promptly without his usual bow of respect, the hemline of his cloak still meddling menacingly around his ankles, just like the spirit summoned by the Council meddled menacingly with the temple fires, extinguishing them. Just like my own unease at Sholto's warning is meddling with the fires inside *me*, provoking them in the very same instant it works to dampen the flames...to tame my ire and injury and rebellion. He speaks the truth, doesn't he?

Tonight *was* foul. Ruby's intentions *are* red, and what's happening is clearly bigger than the injustices I feel I've been dealt by Fjord and Sholto. I *am* being summoned to reason, to destiny, but at the same time...I can't get over the fact that Sholto hasn't apologised, or that Fjord, the guy I truly thought to be the most honest, honourable person in the entire world, lied to me about really important things for five years.

They're small cruelties, when placed besides death and devastation and destruction. But for me? In me? They still feel so big. How do I let them go, and is it *right* for me to let them go? To forgive? I just don't know, because I don't know anything anymore. Sea from stone, right from wrong, fire from fury...

The world is upside down, and I feel like I'm falling off it.

Mess

Unless you're a ghost, it's impossible to give someone the slip forever. I *am* a ghost, a phantom of the night hunting the secrets of your life, beckoning those dark desires stashed away in the shadowy corners of your mind like cobwebs in a pantry. I swear I *am* one, but only when shrouded in moonlight. Only when holding my silver bow...which is why when walking to breakfast in broad daylight without the weapon, without any form of cloak or armour, it's inevitable I *don't* manage to give Enye the slip.

It's eight days after the Council's fatal oath in the Temple of Poseidon. I'm on a rest day, and have every intention of spending it with Tristan in the forgotten harbour full of crab shells, upturned boats and memories, or maybe on the streets with him, depending on how busy the ruffians are. Pilfering goods, stealing from the rich, giving to the poor...whatever it is, I'm down for it, but I *do* need breakfast first and I *do* need to shake off the soldier suddenly tailing me.

The stiff, sleepy muscles between my shoulders lock at the sound of Enye's voice, raised in volume, filled with purpose. You should know this is the third time she's called my name, now.

It's the third time I've tried to ignore her.

"Skye?! *Stop* running! I know you can hear me?!"

I can tell she's started running herself from the jingle of her dagger belt, following me down the steps of Delta barracks. I've barely picked up my own pace when she levels with me, passes me by...and stops to stand right in my path. There's a very wounded and shocked expression on her face at my behaviour, which soon morphs into something fierce and determined. Both her full lips and hips tilt to one side, and she folds her arms, staring me down.

"Hi, Enye," I mutter.

"Hi," she says with emphasis. "I have so many questions for you, the first being why in all of Hades underworld are you avoiding me?"

"I'm not."

"You are! Big time. I haven't seen you for weeks, and I know we're not patrolling anymore, but I never see you at breakfast or lunch or dinner...and now I know why. You're going *early* to miss seeing me, aren't you?!"

"If you must know, I haven't really been going at all. I'm not very hungry at the moment."

On instinct, her gaze sharpens. "You look...tired."

"Thanks."

"Just being honest."

"Did I teach you that?"

Her brows now drop into a deep scowl, but I don't miss the way her nose twitches, holding in the begrudging smile that always threatens to slip loose when Fin pops up where and when he's least expected to, or when I make a quip that's quick, and rooted in the history of our friendship together.

"So, *are* you heading to breakfast today?" she eventually presses. "Please don't lie, Skye. I've been missing you terribly, and I've been so worried you're upset with me."

"I'm not upset with you. Really, truly not. I've just been busy and tired, and..." *losing my mind.*

"Right," Enye says slowly. "But are you going to breakfast now?"

There's really no possible way out of this, is there? "Yes, I'm going to breakfast."

"Good. So am I."

An awkward moment passes with neither of us moving, before we fall into step together. The act is bittersweet. We used to do this daily, first walking to the mess for either breakfast, lunch or dinner

190

depending on our patrol routine, and then we'd hit Ioxthel's streets – Enye talking nonsense about putting extra notches in her dagger belt, and me musing on what it would be like to be a *silent* nightingale. Then we'd discuss the ins and outs of her family running their vineyard beyond Ioxthel's walls, which would inevitably lead to us making plans to sample wine from different taverns around the city to find out where theirs had been sold...plans that would somehow *always* end up with Fin joining us, too. Master of the hoax. *Great* at buying drinks to soothe the wound of being Enye's unashamedly overbearing older brother.

But we don't do that anymore, do we? We don't walk and talk, and we certainly don't eat together. Is that because I've been trying to give her the slip for weeks? To avoid having a conversation that will no doubt be riddled with lies? Or is it simply because the paths of our lives are diverging, and we're drifting?

That's a depressing thought.

Naturally, I wallow in it.

"How is shadowing Sergeant Yasmine Hajjar? Is it good? Better than patrol?"

Enye hums. "I knew you were going to ask that first."

"What's wrong with the question?"

"Nothing, except it's the *hardest* one of the lot, and a total diversion tactic."

"So? Answer it."

She takes a deep breath. "It's going well. It's interesting, seeing how duties change with a new title. There's so much delegation higher up in the Guild. Lots of politics. But...to tell you the truth, Hajjar scares me a *little* bit. She's very intense. I can't imagine ever being like that if I'm made a Sergeant, because I'm not really a tough nut, am I? Nope. Soft shelled all over. I think she likes me, though. I know she does...and so does her brother."

My brows raise. "What now?"

"Yeah. I think he likes me."

"*Like* likes you?"

"Yep."

"Name?"

"Vishnu Hajjar," she supplies, her lips twisting into something that could be a grimace, could be a grin. "Funny how his name suits him. He's quite posh, and proud. But...I think I like him? He's a healer, and we've been going for drinks."

Wish I'd known this sooner. "That's really cool, Enye."

She clears her throat. "Yeah. So, that's my life. Shadowing Yasmine is going well, and I think a boy might finally fancy me. Now it's your turn, Skye." Pause. "Fin spoke to me."

Oh, great. "I asked him not to. Said please and thank you, and everything."

"Yeah. When does Fin ever do what he's told?"

"Whatever he's said to you—"

"That you're upset with your uncle and Fjord, perhaps not only because we've been switched as patrol partners?" Enye levels me with a knowing look. "Don't tell me not to believe what he said, Skye. I can see for myself it's true, and so can he. He also didn't need to tell me that you *don't* wish for us to be partners again, for the sake of me rising ranks in the Guild. I know you well enough to know you'd want this for me...and that you wouldn't be *this* upset about not patrolling together anymore. Want to talk about it?"

"Nothing further to say," I respond quickly. "I'm a bit miffed, and I miss you...but I do want this for you. So bad. Maybe badder than you."

Her expression turns bland. "Funny. I wasn't talking about my career, and I think you know that. What's going on with Fjord?"

"Nothing."

"Skye..."

"Let's go back to the part where you said Vishnu Hajjar *liked* you, Enye. What does that mean? What happened?"

Enye's unimpressed expression heightens further, but so does the sweet tilt to her mouth. I can tell she wants to talk about it. "Yasmine's duties took her to Alcázar a few weeks ago, talking to the fortress sentries there. Something to do with the city's Wivern guests...or so I assume, because Lieutenant Jensen was also there, and I know he's conducting liaisons between the Guild and the entourage along with Fjord. Or, he *was.* Yasmine says she hasn't seen him in over a week, and no one knows where he is. Apparently General Marco is worried."

Yeah, I think darkly. *Yasmine won't have seen her senior, nor Marco his second, because Lieutenant Jensen is dead.*

"There was a feast afterwards," Enye goes on. "Yasmine's brother Vishnu was there, because although he's a healer in the Medical Syndicate he also works in Alcázar. We started talking. Or rather, Yasmine got me talking to him. He asked me for drinks the next day, and I said yes. He's training to be The Sabirs' personal physician...has even tended to Ruby herself."

My heart does a funny flip. "What?"

Enye gestures for me to enter the mess hall first. "Yeah. It's impressive, and a bit unbelievable that we'd go on a date. He's...to tell you the truth, Skye, he's very proud, and I'm not sure I like him that much, but I think I like him enough to...you know..." She grins sheepishly. "Do *that* for the first time."

Something uncomfortable settles in my belly. "That is...impressive that he's tending to Ruby, but not unbelievable you'd go on a date. Besides his pride, how were drinks with him?"

"As good as our breakfast is going to be," she quips, handing me a pitcher of water from the spread table, then picking up a round boule of bread and a huge bunch of grapes herself. "Know why?"

I watch her profile carefully. "Why?"

"The conversation really flowed, *just* like it's going to do this morning. Let's get back to you, Skye. Why're you moody?"

Ugh. "I'm not moody."

"That's a lie. You're so down I can't see through the thick clouds of shit surrounding you."

"It's not a lie," I insist. "I don't lie."

"You do, and it is."

"It's not."

"It is."

"It's *not.*"

She slides into an empty stone bench and places our breakfast on the small table between us, clasping her hands together. Her lips, twisted in annoyance and thought, suddenly soften. "Maybe moody is the wrong word. Please talk to me about why you're *upset*, Skye."

"I'm not upset."

"Yes," she sighs heavily, "you *are*. You forwent duty for days. You've been giving me the slip for weeks, and you are so quiet. And tired. You look tired. Fin noticed it. I've noticed it. Honestly? We're both worried. You usually ramble like an idiot, and I say that in the best way, but you do. Usually say the stupidest stuff and yet you're not now. Why are you not yourself?"

"I'm still talking," I say defensively. "Still saying," *bad, horrible things to very quiet, guarded Guardians,* "really stupid stuff."

"Not nearly as much as you normally do."

"Well," I think on that briefly, then immediately shove a huge handful of grapes into my mouth, and dip a stale hunk of bread into the water pitcher and shove that in, too. "I was taught it's rude to talk with my mouth full. That's probably why."

She sighs in exasperation. "Skye."

"Mhm?" I mumble around the food. "Yesth?"

She sighs again. "I just want to help you. We just want to help you. My brother is *worried*, Skye. Fin is...really damn worried about you. Do you even know how unusual that is?"

My heart jumps, but luckily it doesn't change my answer. "There's nothing for you guys to help with, Enye. Thank you for offering, but there isn't."

"That's just...another gods damn lie," she grumbles, turning to our breakfast and ripping off a hunk of bread for herself. She doesn't eat it though, just turns it over despondently in her hands...and I think I hate myself for it. It's no longer just Fjord and Sholto culpable for their lies and deception, is it? I'm right there with them. It doesn't matter that I gave Fjord my word I wouldn't tell anyone about this, because this obscurity feels like it's *my* decision.

How can I tell the Tsitak siblings I've recently learnt I'm a demigod, and also a nix of the wind...and that there's been a prophecy made in my name about saving the world? How can I tell them that the men I considered family, and everyone else considers family for me, too, are technically enemies in Ioxthel? Only they're not enemies. Which would lead me onto our warped history detailing the Impurity War, and how it appears The Sabirs, our monarchs, are really the evil ones here by committing genocide on Nixen hundreds of years ago. Which would necessitate me revealing how I've spied and ghosted on Ruby and her secret Council for the last seven years, and recently witnessed an oath in the Temple of Poseidon that killed Lieutenant Jensen and, Sholto thinks, summoned a malevolent spirit. Perhaps a spirit related to their quest to find the Torch of Prometheus, the weapon used against Nixen by

The Sabirs four hundred years ago. Four hundred years ago when, funnily enough, Sholto was *alive* because he's incredibly long-lived as the son of Zelos, one of Zeus's sentinels.

Gods.

Goddesses.

It sounds utterly ludicrous in my head, let alone what it would do out loud. How can I say these things to them, if the opportunity arises? I *can't* really. Not without difficulty. Not without risking them feeling hurt by what I've hidden from them for weeks, and inevitably unsure of how to view me thereafter; just like I feel hurt by and unsure about Fjord and Sholto, and just like Enye now feels hurt by me *not* telling her everything.

And I know neither her nor Fin would hurt me upon learning the truth. I know they wouldn't, but I fear they might not like me for it and I fear – in quite a worryingly obsessive way – that Fin won't want to do stuff with me anymore. The last thing I want to do is ruin what's only just starting, because it's the only thing I feel I *do* still have in my life, besides Tristan. I want to hold onto my friendship with Enye and these dalliances with Fin – to protect them and covet them. Except it's not the same now I'm sitting on half-truths and untruths, is it? It's not the same, because *I'm* not the same and life isn't the same, and nothing good *ever* comes out of a lie. Nothing good. This is such a messed up situation. A muddled, impossible storm cloud of thought to be in...

Yes, my counsel mutters, unsolicited. *It is. Might this go some way towards explaining why Fjord and Sholto were wary of revealing the truth to you?*

Inwardly, I frown. *Sholto told me they lied because the Oracle of Delphi forbid them to tell me of the prophecy until the time was right, and he judged he wouldn't tell me until I was ready to handle this...which is a silly excuse, and one he has no remorse for.*

196

But Fjord is remorseful, Skye, she reminds me seriously. *He's very, very sorry. He even told you he'd have gone against Sholto and the Oracle's judgements if he knew this would be the result. If he knew you'd feel so injured and resentful...and estrange yourself from him.*

I'm not estranging myself! I say in indignation. *This is his fault! His doing!*

Predetermined destiny is no one's fault but those of The Fates themselves, actually, she says, a little primly. *Think on that, will you? And stay present for Enye. If you want to protect and covet your friendship with her, you better start acting like it.*

Grumbling something indiscernible around my huge lump of soggy bread, I swallow thickly, "It's just difficult, Enye. It's difficult to talk about. It's not that I don't want to...and not that I don't love you for asking."

"But we're your *friends*, Skye. If you can't talk to us about something difficult, who *can* you talk to?"

Tristan, I immediately think, but don't say it because she doesn't know who he is. Neither her nor Fin know the ruffian king is my best friend, and that I'm a thief turned soldier but will really *always* just be a thief. "I know you're my friends, Enye. I love you. Please can we move on? I just...really want to move on. Want to talk about you and Vishnu and your first time? Please?"

She watches me searchingly, lips pressed together in a firm, stubborn line. Eventually, because she's a good friend where I'm not, she relents. "Yes, fine. Let's move on. Just please don't give me any more of your weird evasiveness, Skye. I still want to eat with you every day even if we're not patrolling together. And...whenever you're ready, Fin and I are here to listen." She reaches over the table and grips my shoulder, shaking it fondly and encouragingly. "We're here for you, Skye."

Don't make me cry. "I know. Thank you."

"How about we go for drinks soon? With Vishnu and Fin?" Her hopeful expression twists into a quick grimace. "Except, you should know that's not even a question. You're *definitely* coming to drinks with us. My brother hasn't met Vishnu yet, and he's for sure going to be a menace. Going to be overprotective. I need you there to quieten him."

"When would this be?"

"Next week, if you're free?"

I try for a smile. "Yes."

"Let me know your patrol schedule, and I'll speak to Vishnu about his work. Or...it might have to be the week after next, actually, because he works at the Medical Syndicate *and* Alcázar. He's very busy, and likes to tell me that, because he's proud but he's also nice, and I think I still want to...you know. Because I haven't yet, and...I need to."

She gives me yet another sheepish smile. I struggle not to sour my own in worry over her talking about doing this with a healer training to be Ruby's personal physician...and good thing I do try, not least for Enye's sake, but also because over her shoulder I see Vishnu's sister herself striding through the mess towards us.

With dark hair, almond shaped eyes and a slender but sturdy frame, Sergeant Yasmine Hajjar is quite typically Ioxthelian. She's older than both Enye and I, unwaveringly good at her job and a mighty abider of rules – which is why this conversation will no doubt be a bad one for me, and the goddesses only know how I evaded it for so long.

Mhm, my counsel murmurs. *The* "how" *has a name, Skye, and we've just been discussing him. Don't play the fool. You're smarter than that.*

That is ru–

"Skye," Yasmine barks, interrupting my reply.

I look up innocently. "Sergeant?"

"It's a desired surprise to catch you here this morning. Don't think you've slipped my mind. You and I need to discuss your truancies of two weeks ago. Walk with me."

"Yes, Sergeant Hajjar."

She offers a quick bow to Enye. "I'll meet you at the gates, Tsitak."

My friend bobs her head, throwing me a sympathetic glance behind her back. She mouths, *See you for breakfast tomorrow?*

Yasmine and I exit the mess together, walking briskly towards the stone stoa running the length of the Guild's meeting rooms and offices.

"Let's cut to it, Skye," she says, stopping by the doorway to the bouleuterion. "I'm disappointed that you skipped duty. It was almost a weeks' worth of patrols you forwent, without explanation. I've been told you were unwell by both Lieutenant Winters and Captain Tsitak, and yet I remain dubious. There were no reports to an onsite healer from yourself, as the Guild's strict sickness protocol states there should be, and you were nowhere to be found all week...certainly not in the infirmary, nor in your quarters. Can you explain yourself?"

"I *was* unwell, but staying with a friend."

"Can they vouch for you?"

Yes. Tristan Knight would vouch for me until his dying breath, but you're not going anywhere near him. "He's a cloth merchant," I lie quickly. "Out of town now."

One dark, disbelieving eyebrow arches high. "Of course. Well...I'm aware of the friends you keep within our institution, Skye. Lieutenant Fjord Winters makes a particular habit of looking out for you, but leniency doesn't become the Guild, and it certainly won't do your future any favours. Nepotism is a dangerous antidote to failure. Do you understand me?"

Yes, I do understand her. More than once over the last five years, my reputation as Fjord's special sparring partner and Sholto's "niece" has saved me from punishment – my recent truancy, and lack of retribution thereafter, being a case in point. What Yasmine doesn't realise is I've never really had future aspirations for myself in the Guild, and I certainly don't now.

"I understand you, Sergeant Hajjar," I offer dutifully. "Very well. Maybe too well?"

Impossibly, the dark brow inches higher. "Then you'll understand why this is your last warning before a strike. I'm watching you, and you'd do well to watch yourself, too. With features as easily recognisable as yours, it's hard to slip surveillance. Mine is resolutely on you." She gives me a very odd, strained smile. "Know that some strikes land harder than others, Skye."

Instinct rears to life in me, raising my heart rate. Was there a double meaning to the way she said those last words? In Ioxthel, a strike is a public display of physical discipline given by senior Guild officials, most commonly a flogging. When Yasmine's flimsy warning to me expires, it seems I'm destined for one. It will hurt, and I don't *want* one, but that's not why I'm so unnerved.

I can't help thinking she meant something more by it, especially when I watch her astute brown eyes snag on my scars, taking in those easily recognisable features. I'm biting my tongue hard to hold in my rebuttal and defence, both begging to be let loose – every muscle in my body locking up to stop itself reaching for the daggers at my hips. The latter is a very strange reaction to have towards Yasmine, and now I'm thinking *furiously* on it. Thinking on how instincts never lie. Thinking on how her brother is a healer, training to be a physician for Ruby Sabir herself, and on Yasmine's increased duties in Alcázar with Lieutenant Jensen...the first victim of the Council's oath.

Who is the second to be?

Also a member of the Guild, right? A *female* member of the Guild, who bowed her head obediently when called upon by Ruby in the Temple of Poseidon, in a manner that felt *very* familiar to me at the time...just like Yasmine Hajjar is bowing her head now, though admittedly to utter a dark warning and not to display obedience.

My gaze drops to her wrist, seeking the elusive emblem of Ruby's Council I've never been able to discover; the one I told you of when I first started narrating this tale. Yasmine wears a leather fencing glove, but is that the tip of a white scar I see, poking out from beneath it? Something branded on her skin by a hot poker? Gods, I think it might be. I tilt my head to the side to see better. It looks like the tip of...a sword, or spear?

Or an arrow?

"Eyes up, soldier!"

I jerk my gaze to Yasmine's at the sharp order, swallowing. "Sorry, Sergeant Hajjar."

"Don't push me, Skye. You seem bent on giving me reason to punish you. Is that right?"

"No, Sergeant Hajjar. I'm sorry."

There's a fraught pause. I'm not sure she believes me...and I'm not sure I trust her. "You're dismissed."

I salute her, then turn stiffly and walk along the stoa. Every muscle in my body is still urging me to draw weapons, or at the very least *not* to give her my back. I hold my breath until I'm at the walkway's end, right by the steps leading to the quads outside the mess, then risk peeking over my shoulder. Yasmine is still watching me from the bouleuterion's entrance, the weight of her stare as heavy as the riot recently unleashed upon my instincts.

Alice Bamber

Heist

Unless you're a ghost, it's impossible to give someone the slip forever. I *am* a ghost, a phantom of the night hunting the secrets of your life and beckoning those dark desires stashed away in the shadowy corners of your mind like cobwebs in a pantry. I swear I *am* one...but I'm also a thief, living in the good name of the hustle and the heist, and today, I don't even *want* to give someone the slip.

It's noon.

Now sixteen days after the oath took place.

I'm on another "rest" day...ha. I've already breakfasted with Enye, talked about having drinks with Vishnu and Fin next week still, because as she anticipated her new suitor is incredibly busy with his work in the Medical Syndicate *and* in Alcázar, tending to Ruby for a third time. I'm sceptical of him, and ever more so of his sister, Sergeant Yasmine Hajjar, but haven't told anyone about it. Haven't spoken to Fjord, either, but *have* battled with my counsel over him - over how sorry he obviously is for everything, and how I'm pretending not to feel like she's right.

It all feels strikingly familiar, like we've been here before or like I'm *stuck* down one of those burrows in my mind...even more so because although I'm not presently in the vicinity of the Guild and I've totally abandoned trying to evade Enye these days, I'm still being followed by a soldier. Chased by one, even.

By several.

Five minutes ago, Tristan and I were hiding outside the Shrine of Offering, a small temple located fairly near the Guild to the north of the city. We'd been hiding there all day, waiting, watching...spying good. It's now dusk, and the sun's plump, fiery orange bottom is kissing the dusty horizon beyond Ioxthel's walls. Our plimsolled feet are kissing the streets, too, barely touching them as we flee from the guilders that *should* be minding the daily transfer of silver drachmae from the shrine to a small but sturdy wagon waiting beyond its stone steps; soon to be pulled by the poor, hot, fly-riddled chestnut mare all the way to the Western Peninsula.

To Alcázar.

Only, the guilders *aren't* minding the transfer of silver coin, and they're certainly not minding what else goes into the wagon...which may or may not include a little wolf cub with dark, dirty hair and knobbly knees, and an uncannily strong throwing arm.

No.

Shame.

They're not minding her, because unfortunately the guilders are no longer on duty in the shrine. They're no longer even within earshot of it, because Tristan and I are leading them all on a *very* merry chase, executing a ridiculously elaborate game of cat and mouse through Ioxthel's narrow, winding streets and flat, step-like rooftops...and yet it's so funny, because the only people catching up in all of this is *us*.

"So I have news on Yasmine Hajjar," he puffs out as we veer right down a side-street together, footsteps in sync and bodies weaving their way rhythmically through the lines of colourful flags and washing hanging dozily overhead. "My people have been following her everywhere."

"And?"

"And her duties *have* increased in Alcázar, just like you thought they had. We've even seen her with Ruby's favoured new guard a few times, although you should know we don't see much of him. He's an enigma. Meant to ask if you've heard any more about his history yourself? *The Rogue Guardian* as Fjord called him..."

"No."

"No?"

"No, I haven't heard more about Xavier, or why he's apparently so damn dangerous."

"You still not speaking?"

I feign ignorance as we race up the outdoor steps of a house, then haul ourselves onto its roof. "To who?"

"To Fjord."

"Nope."

There's a pause. I can feel Tristan's gaze on the side of my face. He gets a mouthful of awning for not watching where he's going, but so do I, and he's still looking at me when we gain speed again. His eyes, the only feature I can see around the swathes of dark green ruffian scarf bundled over his head and neck, are the soft kind of shrewd, a deep blue that speaks of understanding and counsel.

"What?" I huff breathlessly through my own bulky scarf, facing forwards again.

"You look tired."

My teeth flash. "*Thanks*, Tristan. Like you can see with me wearing this thing."

"I see through everything with you."

"Gods, I hope not."

He puffs out a laugh. "What're you thinking?"

"That's my question for you. Insulting a wolf is never wise."

"Huh. Good one. I'm thinking I want your thoughts, *Wolf*."

"On what?"

"Mostly on Fjord."

"Why?"

"Because I've some of my own, but this is *our* problem to solve, and both our minds need to come together..."

He stops suddenly to leap over two adjacent rooftops in quick succession, and I immediately follow suit. There's a little girl on the second, staining her hands the same shockingly burnt orange as the setting sun as she sifts spices between lidless stone vessels. She freezes when we pass her by, and *flees* when she hears the shouts of outrage from the guilders following. We're still in their sights, but the cloud of ashy residue behind us is thickening, and they're lagging. They're seriously lagging, because it's not as if the rooftops are their terrain or their hunting ground, is it?

So sad.

Too bad.

"Wolf?" Tristan presses when we start brushing shoulders again, striding out. "Tell me your thoughts?"

"I'm angry. And hurt."

"So am I, on your behalf."

"I'm upset."

"That he lied?"

"For *five* years," I say heatedly, though it comes out muffled through my scarf. We leap over the balustrade forming a railing to our rooftop, rare in Ioxthel, and down into a small courtyard below. My feet echo my tone as we start running again, soles stamping heavily over the pockmarked mosaic floor like they wish to chip more of the marble tiles, which wouldn't be *so* inaccurate... "For five years Fjord knew who I was and where I came from, Tristan, and that I lived in his *household* back in Elysium when we younger, and he never told me."

"Yeah."

I grumble. "Yeah?! What kind of a response is that?!"

"One that means I'm thinking, Wolf. Give me a second, please, and chill yourself out."

We burst out of the courtyard and back onto the streets, narrowly missing a collision with a wagon of pungent dried meats loitering there. The bearded vendor blinks in surprise as we race past, then slowly, surreptitiously, pushes his wagon to the side so that it encroaches further into the entrance we just exited from – as if he *knows* we're about to steal from Ruby, and he's in favour of it. To be honest, with us wearing these scarves, I wouldn't be surprised if he did. The ruffians are known by everyone these days.

As we hare down the new street, Tristan deep in thought and me deep in...I'm not sure what frame of mind...I peer over my shoulder. It's at least twenty seconds before the guilders start struggling around the vendor's wagon, so we're definitely losing them.

"Ok..." Tristan has found his words, albeit breathless ones. "Would I be right in saying you're feeling *more* upset over the past life you don't remember, and Fjord and Sholto keeping that from you, than you are about this random, mad prophecy telling you you're a demigod, and that you'll hold the world on your tiny but mighty shoulders?"

I face forwards again. "Yep."

"I guess I understand that, but I'm now more worried about the other side."

"About the prophecy?"

"Yes."

"Why?"

He lets out a grunt. "Akira told me the oath she witnessed in the Temple of Poseidon with you guys was horrible. If that's what you'll be up against in this destiny of yours, then I *really* don't like it, Skye. It's dangerous. I don't want you in danger, don't want you anywhere near it, especially without me..."

Tristan also glances over his shoulder briefly, checking on the guilders, before snatching my wrist and tugging me into the murky shadows between two buildings. I wobble on the balls of my feet, startled by his stopping us so suddenly, and again when he pushes us both down onto our haunches.

"Which brings me back to your thoughts on Fjord, and I suppose his Guardian. My people *can't* find out much on Xavier, but I believe Fjord when he says he's a serious threat. He might have lied to you for five years, but you *cannot* deny he cares for you, Skye. He loves you. Sincerely. I see that...seen it all along."

"What're you saying, Tristan?"

"I suppose what I'm really wanting to ask you, when I ask for your thoughts on Fjord, is *despite* the hidden life, and despite his roots growing up in another kingdom...do you trust him?"

"No," I growl, immediately and vehemently, and feel my flushed cheeks turn very red in rebellion of the lie. Tristan sees it, or maybe he doesn't with the deep shadows here and my ruffian headscarf.

Maybe he just knows me so well.

"You can still trust people who hurt you, Skye," he says, more gently. "No relationship is without faults and scars."

"Ours is."

"Well, yes," he admits. "It is. But...that's different. We're different, aren't we? I think I do trust Fjord. I trust his love for you, and his intentions to keep you out of harm's way. Giving you his Guardian is proof of that. If I'm being honest? Knowing you have someone else looking out for you and loving you amidst this mad new life fills me with relief."

"But...but he..."

I stop my feeble defence with a noise of frustration, because unlike Tristan I never work through my words before I start blurting them out, and I have no idea what to say next. Out of *nowhere*, or maybe everywhere, I suddenly feel like bursting into tears. I feel like swaying forwards and pressing my temple to Tristan's shoulder and letting it all out. I really hope I don't – this is *not* the time for that.

"What're you implying, Tristan?" I finally manage to say, voice pinched and tight. "Where are you going with this?"

"I'm...not really going anywhere," he admits, puffing out a laboured sigh. "I'm just musing, or I guess I'm processing things. Tend to do that when I run, and I think I'm ahead of you, because obviously it's easier for me to be. This is *our* problem, but out of the two of us I'm the one most on the outside, looking in. It's not me the prophecy is about, is it? And it's not me with a past life in another kingdom..." He shifts forwards on his haunches and slips a hand beneath my scarf, gripping the nape of my neck. It's slick with sweat, and I can feel his frayed leather bracelets sticking to my skin...and that's a bit gross. "I'm sorry, Skye," he says seriously. "I'm upsetting you, and I'm not meaning to. This isn't what today is about, either. Today is about pilfering goods, and giving to the poor. Living for the hustle and heist. So...you ready?"

"Was born ready," I grunt out. "And so were you. Don't know why you stopped us in the first place?"

He glances through the shadows back to the streets beyond. "I'll go right, you go left. Let's split up and loop back around. I think we lost them...and I bet you twelve bags of silver Akira is in position now."

"Not going to gamble on that, Tristan, because I think it too."

Despite the headscarf, I know he throws me a grin at this. We rise together from our haunches, pausing just before we part ways.

"Love you, Wolf," he says softly. "Love that I still get to do this with you."

"Love you, too."

We flee our hiding spot. I feel Tristan disappear more than I see it, because we're looping back to the shrine in opposite directions. My heart starts out an increasingly insistent rhythm, something faster and more furious than before, and that's partly because today *is* about pilfering goods and giving to the poor, living for the hustle – and my giddy, reckless nature loves that.

But honestly?

It's mostly beating so fast because I don't have Tristan's hot, steady and familiar presence beside me any longer and...what did he just say?

"Love that I *still* get to do this with you."

Still. Because it's expected that I leave Ioxthel for the prophecy and this destiny, isn't it? That's what Sholto said had to happen. *Leave Tristan.* I don't want to, but he just sounded like he thinks I will. He thinks I will stop doing stuff like this with him, that we won't be together forever – which means from here on out, he thinks we're on borrowed time.

* * *

When I say Akira has a strong throwing arm, it means she does. She throws better than a fully grown, fully trained guilder throws punches when sparring with their rival peer...especially when she's stealing things.

I catch the fifth bag of silver drachmae lobbed by her from the back of the wagon to the rooftops with a hefty grunt, feet stumbling to maintain my balance. When they find their running rhythm again they feel heavy and lethargic, like walking through marshland sludge, and that's because I'm weighed down, literally, by thousands of silver coins.

Each time she throws a bag to me, I catch it in the rudimentary scarf-sling tied over one shoulder, then snuggle it against my belly as one might a baby. Tristan is on the roof opposite me, catching his own bags of silver straight into the leather satchel he stole that day in the harbours; the one he told me was for his new disguise as a healer. It drops several inches each time the treasure lands in there, evidence to the weight of the coins.

I'm *slightly* worried.

Slightly.

Partly because, despite not having a scarf tied over my mouth any longer, I'm not sure how many more bags my puny muscles and lungs can handle before they both give out of me. I'm small and wiry, and not made for carrying heavy things. I'm also worried because I think one of the bags is overflowing, or the scarf has split under the weight of my hoard and I'm leaving silvery coins like a trail of breadcrumbs behind me, ripe for a guilder to follow. That's not good, but I guess it's not like they know where the trail started, or that there's anything *to* follow in the first place.

When they returned, breathless, sweaty and besides themselves with anger over the street ruffians who melted into nothing...melted into the streets they *plague*...the wagon had been fully loaded with no problems. Loaded with silver coin, and with another special sort of cargo...who throws another bag to me now, hurling it through the air. It arcs high over the rooftop, cartwheels fast, before hitting me square in the torso and knocking the air from my lungs in a sharp, forceful exhale. Thankfully the grunt is obscured by the wagon trundling noisily over the uneven streets below, but Tristan stills hears me.

Wolf senses.

They miss nothing.

"You ok, Skye?"

"Think I'm...reaching...my limit..."

He catches his next bag of drachmae easily. "I'll find you when we're done if you want?"

"Might be best."

"Τα λέμε, τότε," he says, jovially.

See you, then.

I spare him a suspicious glance and find him doing the same with me, though his is sly, and impish. He still has his scarf tied around his face, but I can tell he's grinning.

"Shame though, Wolf," he remarks lightly. "I'll be richer than you."

"Shut up."

"Rude."

I grumble, but forgo a retort as he jumps to the next rooftop. I veer left, parting ways with the wagon, and don't last long before I drop to the narrow streets below and slow to a walk. Gods. This silver is heavy, and I'm ridiculously out of breath. Madly exhilarated, too, especially knowing that this will *all* go to those who need it most; delivered in the depths of night by Tristan's ruffians onto the worn, rickety tables of Ioxthel's most crowded households.

I wonder what it would be like to watch someone wake up in the morning and drag their weary bones from a shared, itchy bed with too few sheets and too many bugs, to find the small leather pouch resting unassumingly on the table...and then I wonder how it might feel to *be* the person to wake up in the morning and see glimmering proof that for the next year there's enough coin to buy food and cloth for my family.

Thinking on these things makes me think of times, in the early days, when I'd wake up and find a different kind of treasure on the table – one that, at least to me, was just as valuable.

Breakfast.

Made by people I pretended were my own family. It would always be stale bread and grapes with water, or sometimes even watered down wine if I'd been good the day before. Sholto would be there in his kitchenette clearing up after us, and then two years later Fjord would be there too, polishing my guilder's armour for me and always leaving me the unbruised fruit. He'd talk to Sholto about important adult things. Things that went straight over my sleepy head, but that in hindsight might have been well disguised musings on life back in Elysium...because little did I know then what *they* knew about me, and what they were hiding.

Manipulation.

Deceit.

Lies.

Love, my mind volleys suddenly, and for once I'm not sure if it's my counsel speaking, or my own wisdom. *Lessons. Listening. Support. Sparring. Tireless endeavour to be there for you. Tireless resolve to cross entire kingdoms and leave behind their own troubles, their own loved ones, to find you.*

Out of nowhere, or everywhere, the wish to burst into tears springs forth again...and I nearly do. I feel the salt water sting my eyes, feel the rush of prickles up my nose. How wrong is a wrong if it's done for the right reasons? How evil is an injury that's inflicted in good will? How unforgivable is a lie given to protect you?

To protect *me.*

"Skye?"

Oh *gods.*

My flighty feet trip over themselves in panic and surprise, but I still manage to fling my free elbow out towards the sudden, unwelcome sound of my name behind me. The voice that utters it is quiet, rough, lyrical and...too late, I realise it's now *familiar.*

Fortunately, my hit never lands. Levi moves so fast he blurs, stopping my strike easily...and his grip doesn't even feel firm on me, even though elbows are sharp and I'm fast and forceful when I want to be. Quick as lightning – though obviously that's an exaggeration, and obviously however fast I am it's nowhere near as fast as him.

"What're you doing?!" I exclaim hoarsely, peering through bleary eyes *way* up at him, because he's tall and I'm so damn small. I'm almost *crying*, too, which is just not on. "Levi?! What're you doing?!"

He lets me go immediately, bowing his head. "Forgive me. It was not my intention to startle you. I thought you knew I was walking behind?"

I did know you were there, I'm about to say in what's very blatantly a lie, but decide not to. I also decide against, *No. I didn't know you were there, because I was lost in a storm of exhilaration and triumph, and trying to navigate a moral labyrinth of wrongs done for the right reasons and lies given to protect me and panic and pain and confusion over what to think and how to feel and who to forgive!*

"Why would you think that?" I eventually get out, sniffing thickly. "That I knew?"

He steps back and bows *again*, this time in greeting? Only it looks funny. Rusty, and awkward, especially on someone who's just proved themselves capable of moving faster than lightning strikes.

"You were sighing," he explains. "I thought in aggravation at my presence."

"Oh...I wasn't sighing at all. No sighs here. Must have been the wind." *Lie.* "But now you mention it, what *is* your presence doing here?"

"I'm guarding you, as requested by Fjord."

"I'm in danger right now?"

I glance around the tiny, deserted alleyway, gaze sceptical. It's bare and blissfully cool, suggesting the sun's rays might only ever reach it in the evening...the perfect place to slow a thundering heart and wheezing lungs, manifestations inherent to a ruffian heist...which brings me onto Levi, the guarded Guardian who is *not* out of breath like me but *is* sweating, like he's been running fast and far after a wagon of silver...

"Were you following us, just now?" I exclaim. "Have you been doing that the whole day?"

Levi nods. "I've been where you've been."

"On the heist?"

"Nearby."

"Nearby?"

He nods again. My eyes narrow in discontent, and then in an act of pure stupidity – one fuelled by giddiness and surprise and maybe just a bit of drama for your sake, but probably *not*, I should tell you, fear – I use my free hand to brandish my dagger at him. "You're not going to report me to the Guild, are you? Or Tristan? I won't let you do that."

Levi's gaze dips to the blade and back to mine, searchingly. For once, he offers me an expression – it's utterly perplexed. "No, Skye. I'm not going to report either of you to the Guild. I would have no wish to."

Duh. Of course not. Levi is an enemy hiding in our ranks, isn't he? "Talking to Fjord counts, though," I say quickly, to cover up my blunder. "That counts as reporting us, because he's a Lieutenant...in the Guild."

"I suppose I should change my answer to you, then. Fjord will be interested to hear of how your day was, and I will undoubtedly fill him in."

"Why?"

"I don't believe you'll do so yourself."

My brows slam down into a deep scowl. "He's spying on me through you, isn't he? That is..." *just what I want?* "Terrible."

Rich talk from you on spying, my counsel mutters, raising a brow.

I raise one back. *Look at all this silver, though. I am rich right now.*

Levi is quiet before me, obviously seeing no need to respond to my remark...or not knowing how to. He's examining my scowl with no expression himself besides the impression of thought, and you should know this is the first conversation we've had since that bad day a few weeks ago when I called him shy and told him his eyes were dead, then went off in a guilty strop. We genuinely haven't spoken at *all* on our patrols excepting his hushed, formal greetings at their start, and they still unnerve me...mostly because I feel *very* odd about my behaviour on that day.

The flush of exertion in my cheeks immediately heightens with deep shame thinking on it...and I'd prefer not to do that. Not to think on it. Not to think on anything, really, including the fact that Levi is right and I *won't* tell Fjord about this heist, because, as Tristan and I examined earlier, we're not speaking. Haven't done for over two weeks. I haven't even really glimpsed him, which makes me think – and I know I'm not supposed to be doing that – of that one time two *years* ago when Fjord's duties with the Guild took him beyond Ioxthel's walls for several months. Excepting that, this is the longest we've been without seeing each other. Two weeks, that feel more like lifetimes. *Strange* lifetimes, because it's strange we're not sparring together every day, and that my armour is shoddy because he's not polishing it for me because we're not speaking. Strange that Fjord hasn't *tried* to speak with me, hasn't sought me out? But...that's fine, because it's what I want, isn't it? I told him I wanted him to leave me alone.

Told him I hated him.

"Why did you stop me, Levi?" I ask, to divert myself from *that* horrible thought. "I assume there was a reason? The stars tell me there's a reason for everything, even though I don't believe them. Don't believe in destiny, either, and especially mine. They're witches, oracles. I'm sure of it. But...did you have a reason now? For this? For stopping me?"

"I had a reason, yes. There's a meeting in the safe house scheduled now. I'm here to tell you of it."

"Now, as in *now*?"

"Yes."

"Why is this the first I'm hearing of it?"

"I was supposed to inform you of it this morning."

"Why didn't you?"

"I judged it important not to interrupt you."

"In what way?"

His eyes drop to my rotund stomach shrouded in Tristan's ruffian scarf, and the sparing drachmae littered like breadcrumbs over the dusty street behind me, then lift. Their hue is the usual weary grey, not at all shiny like my silver coins, and...is it me, or does the skin beneath them look tired, too? Or is it just the shadows here? Or is it his freckles, because he *does* have a few of them, smattered sparingly under his eyes.

It's true that the more I see of Levi - nearly every day, on our ridiculously silent patrols - the more I realise he *is* like Fjord in looks, but he isn't.

Dark hair, yes.

Tall, steady build, yes.

But Levi's features are definitely different, the planes and angles of his face, and even his frame, a little sturdier than Fjord's, and yet softer...not quite so proud, or sharp, or set to grind *swords* like Fjord's are. I suppose that's not a new realisation, because I told you it before on our first patrol together, but I wouldn't mistake them for brothers now.

There *is* still that pendant both of them wear, though, hanging on a thin leather cord beneath the "v" of their shirts; the hourglass that has something to do with Levi's fealty to Fjord. It's supposedly filled with sand from The Nereid settlement back in Elysium, isn't it? Now I've a headache, thinking of the infancy I no longer remember, and my journey here to Ioxthel that I've absolutely no recollection of either. Is the amnesia from trauma, like Jay suggested? Youth before memories take root in one's mind, like Fjord thought? Or something yet to be deciphered...perhaps *never* to be deciphered.

Just like the fate of Fjord's moth—

"Skye?"

"What?" I reply quickly. "I'm listening. With four ears."

"The meeting is on the oath," Levi says, or perhaps repeats. "Sholto's father has also been in touch. He's organised to meet tomorrow, and Sholto wishes you to be with him for it."

Sholto's father being Zelos, right? The embodiment of rivalry, jealousy and zeal, and one of four sentinels to Zeus's throne on Mount Olympus. The person who hid the Torch of Prometheus following the Impurity War, all those hundreds of years ago, and the only soul alive according to Sholto who knows of its location.

How could one possibly forget?

"It's now?" I verify again. "The meeting?"

"Yes."

"Will you force me to go even if I say no? Like you tried to force me to stay in the safe house the first night we met?"

Levi takes a moment to respond. "No, Skye. I won't force you to do anything. The only reason I prevented you from leaving the safe house was the matter of your safety on the streets, especially after the shock of everything that night, and how much there was left to be explained. I would apol—"

"You didn't prevent me though, did you?" I interrupt, more rudely than I mean to be. "I escaped. Ran away."

He bows his head. "Forgive me. I should say I tried to prevent you, and would apologise for it causing you unease."

"I wasn't uneasy. Demigods don't *get* uneasy, Levi. They're just fast, like me. That's the reason you didn't catch me, isn't it? Because I'm fast when I want to be..." I hitch my belly of silver coins higher as if to prove my point. I'm pleased at the impressively rich jingle they give, and look up at him with defiance and burning self-importance. And then, to my dismay, I feel my mouth twist into a *very* impish grin. Something almost...friendly. "I'm really fast, Levi. Bet you I'd win in a race through these streets against you, even if your strides are long and good at dealing with spiels on oracles that are really witches."

Mm. Given how quickly he stopped my strike just now, and how easily he caught me in the Medical Syndicate on that first night – how easily he must have kept up with Tristan and I today, too, and without us even knowing it – that's a very foolish dare to make towards him.

I regret it.

But I also don't.

Levi blinks twice at the boastfulness; not quickly, but not sleepily either. He does that sometimes, and I'm starting to think it's one of the only mannerisms he doesn't have the wherewithal to hide. *I* just don't have the wherewithal to know what it means, and he's definitely not about to share it with me, is he?

"I would not force you to be present at this meeting," is what he replies to me – thankfully ignoring the bold dare. "Nor would I force you to be at any meeting thereafter, but I suppose I would advise you to attend them. Your presence is sought by everyone, and especially Sholto. He'll be angry if you refuse him."

I hum. "I don't mind if he's angry at me, because he's already angry and disappointed." *But maybe I should be at the meeting to tell Fjord about my suspicions on Yasmine? Just to say that, though.*

Not to say sorry for hitting him, or that I miss him. "But that's all I needed to say, Levi. I wasn't thinking anything, and definitely not about Fjord."

Skye...

What?

My counsel's sigh is long-suffering, and highly exasperated. *You're tiring yourself out by being this way, sweetheart, and I would urge you to try and work through it. Remember? Like we discussed on the day Wivern arrived in the city. Sometimes we push people very far away, only to remember how much we want and need them nearby. Is this perhaps time to realise that, and stop being this way?*

I feign ignorance. *Being what way?*

Pretending to be angry at everyone and everything...and especially Fjord, the surrogate brother of your dreams who loves you dearly.

I wrinkle my nose, because I don't know how to reply to that without admitting she's right. *Sweetheart?* I echo instead. *You've never called me that before.*

She hesitates. *Have...I not?*

No. You haven't, and good thing, too. It's a stupid term. Untrue. I don't have a sweet heart. I'm...spiteful. Say the wrong thing to Levi, do *the wrong thing to Fjord by hitting him.*

No term of endearment is stupid, and I think you'll find you have a very generous heart, Skye.

Even though I'm angry at everyone and everything?

Even though you're pretending *to be angry at everyone at everything,* she amends lightly. *Yes. That you have half your weight in silver weighing you down right now in readiness to give to the poor is testament to that.*

Yeah?

Yes.

I grin at her, unable to stop myself, then realise I'm also grinning outwardly and promptly *do* manage to stop myself, because Levi is still here, and I must look utterly demented smiling blithely at the blank wall behind him.

"Uh, are *you?*" I quiz quickly.

"Pardon?"

"Are *you* angry at me, like Sholto is?"

Levi takes in the brandished dagger still held tightly in my left hand. I have the distinct impression he's reading me like a book, and I bet you twelve thousand of the silver drachmae I'm struggling to hold that I'm an *open* one.

"No," he says seriously, dropping his folded arms. "I'm not angry in the slightest, Skye."

"Even though I called you horribly shy, the other week? Said your eyes were dead and your voice was like rust?"

Whoops. Where did *that* come from? The smugness of mine is now entirely gone, replaced by something appalled. I wish Enye were here to witness the stupid things flying out of my mouth.

"Even though, Levi?" I press, when he doesn't immediately respond. "Even though I said those things?"

"I am not angry with you, Skye."

"Is Fjord? That I hit him?"

"No, he isn't."

"Why hasn't he spoken to me, then? Why hasn't he tried to see me or spar with me?"

Those weathered eyes search me again. "I believe he thought you didn't want him to, Skye."

"I didn't," I lie immediately. "I don't. I don't want him to speak to me ever again...not even for dinner with a wild boar and an apple in its mouth. But I guess...I guess I need to speak to *him.* I need to tell him one thing. About...things. Will he be there? At the meeting?"

"He will, yes."

I pretend to think hard on that, as if I haven't already made up my mind. "I need to find Tristan and give him these before we go."

I hitch up my hefty sling of silver. Levi nods in understanding and turns towards to the alley's entrance, his expression growing distant...or even more distant, I should say. "He's several streets to the west. He's looking for you."

"How do you know?"

"I can hear him."

I blink in surprise. My thoughts hare back to that bad day I'd sealed the fate of. *"I suppose...my mind is on the virtues of not talking much, and how it enables you to become a good listener"* is what Levi had said to me then, and...I think he was telling the truth.

Now I'm back to thinking on him not talking much, and me calling him *horribly shy* in spite. It was very wrong of me to say that to him like I did, as if being shy is something dishonourable. It's not, and regardless of how angry I'd been, or how quiet and unforthcoming he'd been, I shouldn't have suggested it was. I was wrong to say it, and to walk away from the tavern brawl he'd been right about because he's a good listener. I know these things, and I swear to you I almost mumble, *I'm sorry I behaved badly on that bad day.*

I almost do.

"How long have you known Fjord?"

"My entire life."

"Your entire life? Since birth?" I don't even wait for his answer. "So you were around then? You must have been."

"Forgive me. What do you mean?"

To Hades with the headache I get thinking on it... "When I was with the Nereids, before Melody left with me? You lived there? With them?"

"Uh, yes...I lived with the Nereids, but like Fjord I was young and remember very little. I was also away for the majority of each year training."

"To be a Guardian?"

"Yes."

"What age does that start?"

"It varies."

"Well, when did you start?"

"Very young. Four."

Oh, that *is* young. It explains why he's faster than me. "We start at twelve in the Guild, but I've sparred with Fjord every day, so I'm..." *hopeless at focusing.* "Though not any longer. We don't spar any longer, because of everything, which is..." *not good.*

I hum out a sigh, shifting my weight restlessly from foot to foot – partly because the scarf sling full of silver is hurting my neck, but mostly because great goddesses, was I ever lying earlier. I want Fjord to speak with me. I want us to spar together again. I want him to be missing me like I'm missing him...even though I hit him and told him I hated him.

"What do you remember?" I press Levi to distract myself. "I don't remember anything of Elysium, or of that time. What do you remember?"

"I remember the Winters' household very well, and returning home one year to find Fjord and...his brother...had been joined by a little girl. A little sister. I have a vague memory of meeting you, but I very often sought out tutoring lessons on my holidays with Jay, the Sylvan tutor, and I doubt we spent much time together."

A little sister.

I stare at him, unblinking...but not unfeeling. Then, in a sudden, intense outburst that reminds me of a young child unsure of everything and everyone but desperately hoping for something good

– a *very* little sister, maybe of the same age as the one he met... "Do you swear on your life you're telling the truth, Levi?"

He's definitely surprised by this. "I would need to know about what, exactly, to swear that."

"Everything."

"Can you be more specific?"

"About...what you just told me. About their household, back in Elysium. The Winters' household. And...and also about me being in danger with this rogue Guardian here, Xavier. The person you're protecting me from. And...and Fjord."

"I don't know what you mean by that last point," Levi responds slowly. "But the others are true. Would you elaborate, please, on what you mean about Fjord?"

Was I really like a sister to him, and Kieran, his brother? Was I like a daughter to Melody? What about his father? Where is he in all of this? Mine is a god. Is that true? Sometimes I'm dubious and in disbelief, because no one knows who he is. And...was it a home in Elysium? Was it loving? Was it safe?

I fidget uneasily, because no way am I voicing those desperate hopes out loud only to have them shattered. Levi is waiting for me to respond, and I'm just staring at him, staring up into dull grey eyes that look like weary, weathered rock. Totally lifeless. Except...that's not true. There *is* something discernible in them for the first time, something patient and understanding.

Levi looks kind.

I hitch my belly of coins up, flushing. "I can't elaborate on Fjord right now because of things made from glass. Where is Tristan...please?"

He takes a moment to focus. "Still west of here. He's becoming restless and would appreciate finding you. I would ask what "things made from glass" means, Skye? I'm at a loss of how to interpret it."

"Oh..." *Just my deepest, dearest hopes. Just things that can utterly ruin you.* "Things that break if you drop them, or someone else drops them. Like...hearts. They're glass. And hopes. Also glass. What're you thinking? What're your thoughts?"

"I...am thinking of someone I used to know," he offers, quite awkwardly. "And I'm also thinking of Fjord."

"Good thoughts?"

"Yes."

"So you're not angry?"

I get another expression for this – it's unhappy. "I'm not angry in the slightest, Skye. I would now ask why you think I am?"

"I don't know. Don't know what to think about anything these days, least of all you because you never speak to me, and there was that day on patrol when..." *you were being unforthcoming and I was being terribly rude, but shouldn't have shamed you, not least because you're not really shy, are you? You're just reserved and excessively guarded, and kind.*

Levi opens his mouth and shuts it, I think trying to understand what the unfinished sentence of mine is. "I've been especially quiet with you on patrols because I thought you'd prefer silence, Skye, and I was particularly awkward during your last interrogation because the topic of conversation was very difficult for me, and I was having...a really bad day. I suppose I don't usually speak much, but it's not personal to you in any way. I give you my word and my honour in this. I'm not trying to be unhelpful, and I'm not angry. I just...don't usually speak very much."

"You had a bad day?"

"Yes, I did."

"I think...that's my fault?"

"No," Levi shakes his head. "I assure you, my mood had nothing to do with you."

"Even though I said what I did? Called you shy? Said something about your eyes and voice?"

"Though your remarks took me off guard, my mood had nothing to do with you," Levi repeats. "I would apologise if that thought has troubled you, or if you believed my silence thereafter was given in anger. It wasn't."

I grimace. "I don't think *you* need to apologise, Levi, because..." *that's what I need to do here.*

I still don't say the words, and it's as frustrating for my guilty conscience as it is my guiding conscience...my counsel. I don't finish the sentence with anything else either, just observe him.

Strangely, I believe Levi entirely.

I get nothing from him but weathered, tolerant eyes, and his voice is exactly as it usually is - rough, rusty, and unnervingly toneless - but it's also somehow undoubtedly honest. Which means I now have so many more questions. Why was the topic of conversation difficult for him on that patrol? What made his day bad, and his mood sad? And why doesn't he usually speak much? Does there need to be a reason? No. It's fine to be quiet, but I think there's something behind all of this. There's a story left untold, and yet it's impossible to guess it...

Huffing out a little sigh of frustration, I finally test the waters with a single, short ruffian whistle; and bless him, there's an immediate answer from Tristan a few streets over to the west. He is restless, and he does want to find me.

Just like Levi said.

Instinct & Heart

It turns out the safe house has two entrances. Beyond the outdoor steps leading up to the washed blue door of the salóni on the second floor is a very small courtyard which multiple houses seem to share, and multiple streets feed into. There's a set of worn wooden doors with cross bracing there. Dry gnarly vines creep over the sandy stonework, fluttering pitifully in the balmy evening breeze; like wilting hands, waving in a disenchanted greeting for us. The place is deserted...excepting the small figure already squatting on her haunches in one corner.

Akira appeared with Tristan when he found Levi and I in our little alleyway. You should know the ensuing encounter between my best friend and Fjord's loaned Guardian was significantly different from their last. Tristan made no threats. Didn't stare at Levi damningly...although like me he did stare, his deep blue eyes sharpened by something scrupulous and shrewd.

Unearthing intents.

Measuring trust.

Levi showed little expression and no unease at it, and he didn't say a lot...but it's true he did offer to help me hand over the heavy bags of silver snarled in my green ruffian scarf, and he bid Tristan farewell with one of his rusty bows when we left. *And* he did give Akira one of his Guild issued daggers when on a strange whim – and I expect a very giddy high from the heist – the little girl asked for one.

She flaunts it proudly to us now from her corner, mouth splitting into a mad grin. She's seemingly completely unfatigued by the stunts she pulled this afternoon, and then there's me...giddiness totally dissipated by the overwhelming riot of emotions vying for control over me, and trying desperately not to drag my feet. It's like I'm wading through ocean sludge, like every step is a fight for me to become unstuck...to find my way out of the rabbit hole I've been lost down.

I manage a fond nod to her as Levi gestures me towards the wooden doors, and focus on the soft thrum of voices filtering into the courtyard. They stop as we near, replaced by the sound of a bolt being slid aside.

It's Sholto. "You're late, Skye."

"That's my fault," Levi responds. "I didn't tell her of the meeting soon enough."

"Oh?" Sholto raises his brows, and doesn't offer him a bow...even though the younger Guardian gives him one. "Interesting and unlikely. Skye is notoriously bad at promptness. You are not."

My mouth prepares to defend myself, but that's not what spills out. There's no retort, and no ire and rebellion, to my dismay. There's just me coming unstuck, and muttering somehow almost *nervously*, "What's in there, Sholto? Behind you?"

"The kitchen."

"Who's in there?"

"The Elysium folk."

I look up at him. "Who are they?"

"Yusuf, chief of the Sylvans back in Elysium and uncle to the Irving sisters, along with his Guardian, Rose. She's a former student of mine. The youngsters are upstairs in the salóni with Jay, their tutor, and Idris, their Guardian-in-training."

"What about Fjord?"

"Yes, he's here too...though why you should ask about him is beyond me, given your obvious loathing of us *both*..." Sholto makes it clear he's been made privy to what happened the other week on the barrack steps, and is disapproving of it. He takes a moment to observe the damp wisps of hair that have escaped their disintegrating braid and the rest of my sweaty, dishevelled attire. "Explain to me why you're late, Skye, and in such a state. It's rude to keep guests waiting."

"Trouble on the streets," I mutter, in the very same moment Levi repeats, "It's my fault. I didn't tell her of the meeting soon enough."

Sholto purses his lips, and even though technically both answers are true, I can tell which of us he blames from his sigh as I brush past into the *kuzína...*and more fool him for it.

More fool me, too, for losing my ire and rebellion.

Or for holding onto them for so long?

Just like the salóni upstairs, the safe house's kitchen is small, dark, well-worn and basic. There's a wooden table stained by knobbly candle wax dominating the stone floor, where Fjord and another man are sitting nursing black and orange terracotta kylixes; small, bowl-like wine vessels. Beyond this, opposite me, is the staircase Ember and Wren crept up on my first visit here. I can hear very, very faint movement above, no doubt the youngsters themselves. Immediately to the left of the kitchen doors is an exposed stone wall, to its right is a plain clay oven, leant against by a woman with a sprightly frame, greying hair and eyebrows that – just like her past mentor's – rise expectantly as she watches me enter. I recognise her vaguely from the night in the Medical Syndicate's herb garden. The night *everything* changed.

Both men at the table stand. My eyes immediately stray to Fjord and linger, and I'm not just thinking about how I won't be able to speak to him in private tonight about Yasmine – not in such a small space with so many people. I'm not just thinking about that, because my stomach is suddenly so hollow and nauseous it's impossible to ignore, and my eyes are searching frantically for a little red mark on his cheek from my hit. Reason tells me it will be long gone, because it's been *weeks* since we saw one another.

Weeks since we spoke.

For fear of very suddenly bursting into those long-overdue tears, I focus on the stranger. He has a trimmed beard and red hair styled back from an expressive face. Freckles cover every non-bearded inch of his creamy skin, offsetting rich green eyes, and there's an air of grace to him – an impression of dignity that immediately cements itself when he steps forwards and offers me his hand. Just like his face, a sea of pigment coats the skin across his knuckles, disappearing beneath the pleated ochre shirt he wears. In this attire he looks like he's attempting to emulate a spice trader, but his red hair won't do wonders for that guise in Ioxthel. Nor, as you must know, will convening for clandestine meetings with his brethren, the city's enemies, under the fickle flair of candlelight...

"Yusuf Irving," he introduces in Elysium's clipped, lyrical accent. "It's an honour to meet you, Skye. I'm Ember and Wren's uncle, and this is my Guardian, Rose Walsh."

He nods to the woman leaning against the stove. I look down at his hand, wondering if I should entertain the pointless diplomatic gesture. I do, but I let go *very* quickly to fiddle with the hilts of my daggers. I think everyone is expecting me to speak, to reply to Yusuf or offer some kind of greeting to the room, but I don't. I just watch as he retreats to the table once more, and pretend not to notice Fjord offering me his seat.

And that's a good question, isn't it?

Where to settle.

I intend to loiter by the door, but Levi is presently rebolting it for Sholto and standing sentry there, and there's little space for two. It leaves me the stove, where Rose is, the upturned wicker basket by her feet, or the bottom steps of the staircase. Or awkwardly hovering along wall, like I'm doing now.

"We haven't started," Sholto tells us as he drifts towards the table. "Yusuf has been filling Fjord in on political life back in Elysium."

"Thus, we're a little tired," Yusuf provides with a weak smile.

Sholto returns the expression, gesturing to Fjord's still vacant seat as he takes his own. "Are you sitting?"

"Thank you, no. I think I'll stand."

He moves towards Levi, and even though he doesn't look at me as he passes by, I know what he's doing. He's leaving his seat at the table open for me even though I won't take it, because he's ever the undying gentleman who lies and that I *hit...*

"Right," Sholto spares me a glance of reproof, like he *knows* what's going on in my head. "Let's set to, then. I'm sure you've all heard by now that my father has responded to me. Skye and I are travelling to meet with him at the Temple of Thetis tomorrow."

"The Temple of Thetis?" Rose queries.

"Yes. It's an ancient hilltop site that lies in ruins perhaps half a day's ride beyond Ioxthel's walls. The two of us set off at dawn tomorrow, to be back by nightfall. Or so I hope. However, this is not what I wish the meeting to detail. We ha—"

"Why there?" I interject.

"Pardon?"

"Why are you meeting your father at the Temple of Thetis? Why not here? Or somewhere else in Ioxthel?"

"You'll have to ask him that, Skye, when *we* meet with him. It was Zelos who chose the ruined hilltop site, perhaps because he's always been fond of Thetis and her life story. I should warn you that my father does not descend from Mount Olympus often. Let's just say he'll make a spectacle of it tomorrow. And *now* let us move onto today's topic. The Council's ritual proceedings were over two weeks ago. It's a shame we haven't all been together before now to discuss them, but I suppose we've been making headway in other matters."

He looks briefly to Fjord brushing shoulders with his Guardian by the door in a manner that makes me very curious, and at a total loss of how to interpret.

What other matters?

"The oath Skye and I witnessed was fatal, as I highly suspect all future oaths will be. During the ritual, Lieutenant Jensen drunk the blood of the gods and goddesses, ichor. Coupled with the Council's prayers, this solicited the summoning of a spirit, soon after captured by Ruby Sabir in her silver incense vessel..." Sholto goes on to explain the smoky substance vomited from Lieutenant Jensen in more detail, and how his eyes glowed shortly before he fell, as if lit from within. "This is why I believe the ritual was a summoning," he says. "There are signs his body was briefly possessed by the spirit upon drinking from the goblet."

Yusuf frowns. "Mortals summoning a spirit? That is rare, is it not?"

"Indeed," Sholto nods. "Summoning a spirit is no trivial endeavour and requires great effort – great energy. Ruby's Council are thus conducting the ritual accordingly. The Temple of Poseidon is a spiritual pool rife with energy, just as any profoundly sacred site is. The same logic can be presumed for their use of ichor. The life force of the gods and goddesses is perhaps the greatest, purest form of energy on earth if you can get your hands on it. Finally, they're performing the ritual in a series of separate liturgies every time a Council member undertakes their oath. Thus, these three things – standing on sacred ground, using the power of ichor, and performing the ritual incrementally – will eventually enable them to summon the full spirit."

"So how have the Council acquired ichor?" Rose asks. "And whose spirit are they summoning? If they're searching for his Torch then might it be Prometheus?"

"The reality is it could be the ichor of any divine being who shares deity heritage," Sholto explains, "and not necessarily a god or goddess themselves. This brings me onto my next point. The Council is expected to meet again for their second oath on this month's full moon. My plan is to discover more about all of this then, and to find out how many of these oaths we can expect. There are twelve members of the Council, so will there be twelve rituals? These are the kinds of clues we need in order to solve this puzzle...the puzzle of just who exactly they're trying to summon to earth. Rosie, I believe you'll be useful in this."

Rose nods. "It'll be like old times, old man."

"Yes," Sholto spares her a smile. "Only the stakes are higher, and you are no longer a student of mine." He turns to Yusuf. "Are you happy to be without your Guardian for an evening?"

"I expect so. We'll have Idris, of course, and Jay is almost as nifty with a sword as he is a quill..." Yusuf glances up to the ceiling briefly, to where we can hear the faint murmur of voices. "It's no surprise that's something the girls are particularly interested in."

"Then it's sorted. In two weeks' time, Rose and I will witness the Council's second oath. Now, onto the ground tremors I mentioned to some of you."

"You really believe Poseidon smote his own temple?" Fjord speaks up from the door. "That's big."

"I believe the god of seas, storms and quakes was displeased with the activities of the Council, yes. I wouldn't, however, call what he did smiting. It was more of a grumble, a warning to Ruby and to all of Ioxthel that he is angry."

"So, Poseidon was expressing displeasure, but not enough to ruin the site or stop the ritual altogether?"

"Yes."

Fjord folds his arms, brow furrowing. "That's typical godlike behaviour, isn't it? Refusing to interfere with mortals unless absolutely necessary."

"Indeed."

"At least they're aware of what's happening?"

"I hope so, Fjord. I expect to know for sure when I speak with my father. He is, of course, privy to life on Mount Olympus being Zeus's sentinel..." Sholto suddenly fiddles his kylix of wine over the worn wooden tabletop, like he's agitated. "I expect to know more on many things, really, including why there is a map to the Torch of Prometheus in such carelessly close proximity to those who would desire to wield the weapon. Why there is a map in the first place. I admit, it really doesn't make sense to me. My father is many things, but foolish or forgetful he is not."

Yusuf takes a healthy sip of his own wine. "What do we think the map is? Something drawn with quill and ink?"

"I cannot believe it would be," Sholto says, but he sounds unsure. "Zelos wouldn't do such a thing, for he would have no need. Yet...I've no idea what the alternative is. Does anyone else have suggestions?"

They don't.

"Have you seen the Torch yourself, Sholto?" Rose asks. "You were there during the war of old, after all."

"I've not seen the weapon with my own eyes, no, but I've seen its aftermath. Millions of lives lost in a stuttering heartbeat. A giant fireball of dust and debris that turns night to day and then day to night. An area larger than one hundred Ioxthelian peninsulas patched together...simply obliterated. Irreversible, insurmountable devastation. Colossal loss. This is the wake that the Torch of Prometheus leaves when lit by those who bathe in foul intention and dabble with unbound power. I'm not ashamed to say I deeply fear what will happen if it falls into the wrong hands again, or if we fail. If fate slips its strings, if we *allow* it to slip its strings, we are all doomed."

He looks over the room, eyes darkened by the unseen evils of the past. They end up on me and stay there...and they're not the only pair. Thick stillness has settled over the kitchen, the kind rife with grief and apprehension and the unmistakeable strain of furtive glances – stolen looks towards the fierce warrior prophesied to fight alongside and against the gods when all is ablaze with fire and wrongs are chosen for the right reasons, and towards the demigod who will, supposedly, rise from ashy streets to hold the entire world on her scrawny shoulders.

Stolen looks towards *me.*

I feel myself flush, and try desperately to solicit some form of brazen defiance to meet their stares...to disquiet *them* in turn just as they now do to me. I'd be a liar and a fool, though, if I didn't say I feel like I might be nearing the same page as Tristan was earlier, processing things whilst we ran. It's suddenly clear I haven't thought much on everything Sholto told me that night in his kitchenette, and again after the oath – I haven't thought much on anything past my fury and resentment of him.

Perhaps, even witnessing the horrors at the Temple of Poseidon together, that is understandable? Perhaps it's justifiable, because this is an impossible, insane situation to know how to interpret. I mean, have *you* ever been told you're destined to save the world? That your mum served the Goddess of The Hunt, Artemis? If so, tell me how I'm supposed to respond and what I'm supposed to feel, or who I'm supposed to trust.

Instinctually, my eyes flit to Fjord lingering by the doorway. This time, even with the nausea and regret and guilt, I can't look away. His brow is furrowed once more, expression etched in deep thought and worry...and from the way he's looking right back at me with those homely hazel eyes, with no pretence of furtiveness, I think it's worry for *me*.

Yes, my counsel agrees softly. *I would agree with that.*

What do I do?

What do you mean, Skye?

I shift restlessly. *Who should I trust?*

The answer to that lies in your *heart only, my sweet girl. I've no right to tell you who to trust.*

But—

Listen to it, she interrupts gently. *Over and above everything else...over and above me. You must listen to it, and believe in it. Trust in it.*

Trust in...my glass heart?

Yes, she murmurs. *Trust in your glass heart, Skye. Trust it will only ever lead you home, like it is right now...*

I blink rapidly back to the present. Fjord and I are still watching one another, hooked by the gravity of the other's gaze...by the years of friendship and feelings of family that I've told myself lie as *lies* behind us, but are still rising in me now as hopes made of glass, and I know never left him. My folded arms have relinquished their stroppy hold, my shoulders orienting themselves towards him as if I might *go* to him.

On instinct.

With heart.

"Well..."

I jump as Yusuf's polite, lyrical voice shatters the spell of silence cast over the room, and find myself turning jerkily back to the table.

Against instinct.

Without heart.

"Why did Scarlett Sabir, Ruby's ancestor, do it?" he asks Sholto. "Why would she wield the Torch and kill so many of us those four hundred years ago? What did Nixen do to her or her people to warrant slaughter?"

"Many in Elysium believe she was motivated by fear of our powers, and fear of the unknown," Sholto responds. "But I believe the devastation was so very great because Nixen were actually in the wrong place at the wrong time. I believe the Torch was meant to destroy the earth we walked upon more than our people themselves."

Over his shoulder, Rose frowns. "Why exile us from Astyros in the first place?"

"Orders."

"From Zeus?"

"No. From Zeus's predecessors."

This time it's Yusuf who frowns. "The Titans?"

"One of them, perhaps. Or even their forbearers."

"The *Primordials?* Good grief..."

The Primordial Gods and Goddesses. Deities born from Chaos, the intangible void of everything and nothing that existed prior to the creation of the universe. Beings such as Gaia, or mother earth. Ouranos, the sky. Aether, the air of heaven. Hemera, the day. Nyx, the night. Tartarus, the darkest depths of the earth. Beings that, to our knowledge, have either retreated into the very fabric of the dreamscape they themselves define, to watch silently as new generations of deities take their place, or were banished from the earth by their descendants...never to be seen again.

Until now.

"I do not know if my suspicions are true," Sholto confesses to us. "But I do know that failure in this quest is not an option. Mortals must not wield the Torch again, and we should do everything in our power to stop them. The lesser of two evils will need to be sought. Our loss given for others' gain. Impossible situations that leave irreversible scars on the human soul must be navigated, the sacrifices inherent to them made *without* rebellion, and without ire. We should be resilient to this. Prepared for it. And we should realise this is a time for selflessness. For endeavour in good for *more* than just one. This is not a time for wallowing in self-pity and loathing and depression. Μιλώ ειδικά σε εσάς, Skye."

I speak especially to you.

His eyes meet mine over the table again. I hold his stare, several snappy retorts stampeding over the tip of my tongue. Things like, "I'm never leaving Ioxthel with you," or "I'll never listen to your stupidly sage spiels again," or even, "So this meeting is really about reasoning with me, is it?"

The damning words never make it from me. I've lost my voice to unease, to thought and reason, just like everyone else. The kitchen is once again heavy with silent grief and a deep sense of foreboding, and yet *more* furtive glances snuck my way...and it's for this reason that very, very soft footfalls can be heard descending the stairs beyond the table.

One by one, people heed the noise and turn in their direction, but no one gets up. No one seems worried. Indeed, Yusuf looks like he expected to hear something like this...

Sagittarius

"Ember Nesrini Irving!"

Jay's low, deep voice rings out from the salóni, his heavy strides rattling the floorboards overhead. The soft footsteps on the stairs stop with a scared squeak, then a gasp – as if the culprit can't believe she's let slip the noise.

"Did you think I wouldn't notice you gone?" Jay asks, sounding only mildly disapproving. "You know Idris is terrible at distractions."

"Hey!" an unfamiliar voice exclaims.

There's another muffled squeak. The creeping on the stairs starts up again, this time with haste. Two little sandalled feet appear half hidden by a swirling lilac cloak as Ember treads gingerly but very quickly down the last few steps, still looking up over her shoulder for her pursuer. When she reaches the bottom she spins to face the room, eyes frantic with the type of giddy, zealous excitement only the youth bring with them.

From the table I hear Yusuf sigh deeply.

Rose, too.

Jay soon appears over the little girl's shoulders, looking impossibly broad behind her tiny frame. He has a leather notebook and lead pencil in one hand, a pair of dice in the other – but the only things he's rolling are his eyes.

"Excuse us everyone," he says, tone very dry. He glances down at the fiery head of hair below. "*Did* you think I wouldn't notice?"

Ember nods without turning to him. Her hands are wringing themselves into nervous knots by her stomach, but she also seems to be holding in a giggle. More footfalls sound. Wren and another figure appear on the stairs. I don't recognise the boy on the cusp of adulthood, but I'd bet it's Idris, their Guardian-in-training. His stature is short and strong and his skin dark, and he seems to be struggling with a smirk; though he soon schools it into something far more serious upon spotting Yusuf.

Ember's emerald eyes are still wide, drinking in the kitchen like she might gulp up water from a fountain. She seems particularly enamoured by the door, returning again and *again* to it.

"Hello," she eventually says, just to Fjord.

"Good evening, Ember."

She looks to Rose by the stove, spots the older Guardian's greying eyebrows arched in light reproof, and turns quickly back. She starts swinging her shoulders eagerly. "Good evening."

"Good evening," Fjord repeats, smiling.

She looks to his side. "Hello."

There's no reply.

"Hello," she says again, with more emphasis.

"Hello, Ember," Levi offers quietly.

"Good e—"

"No, Ember," her uncle interrupts sharply. "We've talked about this."

Her toothy grins falls a little. Reluctantly, she looks away from the door. Her attention flits around the room like a nervous bird, perhaps searching for the next suitable person to bestow her weird game of greetings upon...and that turns out to be *me.* Her mouth forms its sweet o of wonder when she sees me lurking by the wall and she all but lurches forwards, thrusting a hand into my stomach.

"I'm Ember," she introduces, voice young and breathless. "And you're the sky."

Uh...

I look down at the tiny hand before me, plump with youth and a childhood of plenty, and just *made* for getting sticky. Despite everything, I don't have it in me to refuse her.

"We've met before," she says, as she starts shaking my hand. "You were upset, and drew your bow on me and Wren...or Wren and me...Wren and *I*..." Her expression sobers for all of two seconds as she sorts out her grammar, before she giggles. "We interrupted that meeting, too."

"I'll have you know I haven't interrupted *this* one," Wren grumbles from the stairs. "This is *all* you, Em. You're so naughty."

"And I'll have you know I'm *very* good at distracting people," Idris tacks on. "Jay was wrong."

"I'll have *you* know that's the last thing you should feel pleased about, Idris," Rose immediately chides. "Guardians don't mess around, especially in hostile territory."

"This one does," Jay mutters, but he turns to sock Idris lightly on the shoulder. The act elicits another fleeting, poorly controlled grin from the young Guardian...and from Ember, too.

"You're the sky," she repeats.

"It's without the *the*."

Her grip tightens as I try to tug my hand from her, becoming surprisingly strong for someone so small. "Really?"

I nod.

She thinks very carefully on that, looking confused. "Well, you are the sky to me. You're...everywhere. Sometimes blue, sometimes grey, sometimes as fiery as my name. You're so breath-taking. I dream of you most nights when you're starry."

"You've got the wrong person, or *thing*, Ember. I'm not the sky, I'm just...Skye. With an e."

She thinks very seriously on that again, shaking her head. "I haven't got the wrong person. You're the sky and...I really like your scars."

"Ember!" Yusuf exclaims from the table, sounding horrified. He turns to me quickly, expression one of remorse, "I must apologise for my niece, Skye. She is terrible at manners."

I look down at Ember with her wide emerald eyes, her lips and cheeks as plush as the flesh of her palms...and sigh.

"Don't worry, so am I."

Her toothy grin reappears. Slowly, and then all at once, she starts shaking the hand she's still holding onto...but she looks to the door as she does it. "Good evening, Levi. How do you do?"

Yusuf stands so fast his chair topples over. "I am very sorry, everyone. We've digressed here, and I think it's time we got ourselves back where we belong, safely beyond Ioxthel's walls. It is *well* past the girls' bedtime."

"Ours, too," Sholto offers mildly, also standing. "Skye and I are up at dawn for our trip. We should get some rest too."

Yusuf looks grateful for the remark. "Wren? Help your sister upstairs."

She does so, giving me a wary sideways glance and a very small smile as she grabs Ember's shoulders, tugging her roughly away. "You are *such* a liability, Em."

"You just didn't have the guts to do it!" Ember hisses back.

"I'm too mature for games like this."

"Oh, you're so *not.*"

"I am! This was an important meeting, and you ruined it. You should be ashamed of yourself...and for talking to her like that. You're so stupid."

"Shut up."

"Will not," Wren volleys. "Get going."

They disappear upstairs with Idris. The rest of the group starts to disband; Rose and Yusuf saying their farewells to Sholto, Fjord and Levi gathering with Jay at the base of the stairs, brushing shoulders and talking in hushed undertones. It's unexpectedly the perfect opportunity for me to slip out through the kitchen doors by myself.

The world has darkened considerably since we arrived, to nightfall. The skies are clear, with the stars promising the city's gazers a good watch. Which constellation is shining brightest up there? I think it's Sagittarius. He's the centaur – half-man, half-horse – who gave up his immortality for Prometheus upon the titan's release from his eternal punishment of liver-pecking eagles. Remember? The punishment Zeus, King of the Gods himself, inflicted upon Prometheus for stealing fire from Mount Olympus and gifting it to mortals without his consent...and so, if you remember this as well, his Torch was born. Prometheus was released, or rather *freed* by Zeus's own son, Heracles, and then Sagittarius – or his name is really Kheiron when you're talking about him *before* he became stars – gave Prometheus his immortality. It's a bit ironic, given our discussion just now...a funny coincidence we're currently halfway through Sagittarius' month of the year and talking of the Torch, the very thing that landed Prometheus his punishment in the first place.

Heaving in a deep breath of warm, dusty air, I tip my head back and bathe my face in starlight. Do the heavens see me, like I see them? Do they ever bear witness to my shoddy, woefully irregular prayers? Do they know how to sort out someone's murky, muddled mind for them?

I feel stuck but also unstuck...stretched cruelly between two mindsets. They're very obviously brethren in the safe house behind me, aren't they? There's a deep friendship between Fjord and Levi, and seemingly Jay, too. An upright respect between Yusuf and Sholto that hails to diplomatic familiarity and maturity, and a history between Sholto and his former student, Rose. And Ember is just...annoyingly sweet.

The stars are veiled in the sky now, because my eyes are closed with the same questions from earlier floating before them...still unanswered.

How to respond?
Who to trust?
What to feel?

Behind me are folk from Elysium. Folk that I've been told for the entire lifetime I remember are evil and enemies. Admittedly I've always questioned that, and even hungered to see them and their kingdom for myself. But it turns out they're not evil. They're normal, and relatable...which doesn't mean I *trust* them, but it does mean I see they're not my enemies. I really do see that, but I just don't know what to *do* with it, especially because my ire, injury and rebellion are now seriously dwindling, like a feebly flickering flame licking at the barest stub of wick.

In their absence, what is there to feel? I've been lost to the emotions upon learning the truth on that fateful night in the Medical Syndicate. Refusing to find my way out of them, probably because they've been a coping strategy – a fiery form of protection from the cold unknown.

What do I feel, now they're leaving me? What *should* I feel? Daunted by the prophecy, and weirded out by being the daughter of a god? Worry over what's happening in the world, especially Ruby's warmongering against Elysium? Fear and unhappiness of the very deepest and most desperate nature over the potential prospect of leaving Ioxthel...leaving Tristan? They're all *cold* emotions. All things that remind me of a dark, forlorn childhood living in uncertainty; living on the streets before Sholto's kitchenette, without food or water or shelter...even without Tristan, for a time. Is *this* why I haven't been able to work through, as my counsel put it, pretending to hate everyone and everything? Because the alternative is even harder?

I'm praying to the goddesses now, asking them to tell me any or all of the answers to those questions, and to sort out my messy, muddled mind. I'm so tired of it. She was right in that too, my counsel. I'm exhausted pretending to battle with others when really the person I'm battling *most* is myself, and the person *losing* most in that is myself.

My eyes open suddenly, chin tipping down as a soft whistle sounds – a supple, wavering note. It's Akira, asking me if everything is ok. She's still on her haunches in the courtyard's corner, watchful and dutiful as ever...still totally unfatigued by our heist. I raise my hand and debate going over, but decide I need space to know what to do with these jumbled thoughts. Decide I want to slip through Ioxthel's streets back to the Guild and into my bed like I just slipped from the safe house.

Heaving in another laughably deep breath, one that actually fills my lungs with too much air and makes me need to cough, I start to do just that. Honestly, I'm not ready to be up at the crack of dawn for the trip to see Zelos. Not ready for a day alone with Sholto, either, because I don't know how to be with him, the four hundred year old man.

"Skye?"

I've made it only metres before I hear the sound of the safe house's kitchen doors opening and shutting. My steps falter at the familiar voice, and so does my pitiful resolve. I tell myself not to look, tell myself *not* to, but it's genuinely only the next second I peer over my shoulder. Fjord is jogging briskly down the street, with Levi following at a much more leisurely pace behind. I stop, waiting for the former on instinct, and with a heart that warms, despite everything, as he halts before me.

Our eyes meet.

Hold.

My stomach swoops, something heavy and unspoken tickling the tip of my tongue. *Sorry for hitting you, and saying that I hate you. Sorry for being moody. I miss you so much I feel sick.*

"Uh, so Levi told me you wished to speak with me?" Fjord begins, clearly oblivious to my thoughts. "I'm here, if you'd still like to do that. I would like for you to do that...if you wanted to?"

There's an awkward pause. I start fiddling obsessively with the hilts of my daggers, trying to find words...trying to select the right tone.

"I think the second Guild member due to fulfil their oath is Sergeant Yasmine Hajjar," I eventually get out in a small voice. "I'm fairly sure of it."

Fjord's brows lift. "Would...you be able to tell me why you think that, please?"

I do, explaining about my talk with Yasmine beneath the stoa last week, and about how her duties have increased in Alcázar, an account first made by Enye and later confirmed by the ruffians' surveillance. Then, I tell him of the scar I think I spotted on Yasmine's wrist, just where the elusive mark of the Council would be, and of how to me her mannerisms appeared alike to the hooded member nodding obediently in the Temple of Poseidon.

Fjord listens to it all, watching me intently with thoughts racing behind his eyes, and I know he's discounting nothing. "Thank you for sharing this with me," he says when I finish. "I'll think on it, and look into it."

I nod, and avert my gaze over his shoulder. Levi is taking his sweet time walking towards us, and I'm sure it's deliberate, as if he *knows* there's more I could say.

"That's all," I mutter, turning quickly on my heel. "I'm going back to the Guild now."

"Wait?!"

Fjord reaches out to catch my elbow, only to drop it immediately – either because my skin is still horridly sweaty from the heist, or because he didn't really mean to touch me in the first place. His expression tells me it's the latter, and that he's fearful of it inciting the same reaction in me as it did last time...

Me, hitting him.

Then feeling *terrible* about it.

"Uh...I just want to wish you a good trip tomorrow," he says. "We haven't spoken recently, but I was going to find you today even if you hadn't attended the meeting. Even if you didn't want to speak to me. I really hope the trip goes well, but I feel obliged to tell you I've heard Zelos has a reputation befit for one of Zeus's sentinels. He's dangerous and volatile, and I would urge you to keep your wits about you. I wish you weren't visiting him alone...or with just Sholto, rather. I wish you weren't...uh...weren't just going with him. That you had...another with you."

The fumbling way he corrects himself has me seeking his gaze. What is *his* heart telling him, in this moment? Who does *he* trust most in all of this? My stomach flips. All I see before me is sincerity, earnestness and affection...and you and I both know it's time to stop lying to myself. It's time to start finding ways to reconcile.

"Please be careful, Skye," he urges quietly. "I'll be eagerly awaiting your return, as we all will."

He looks fleetingly to the small shadow now lumbering from her hiding spot by the safe house – Akira – and then up towards the massive fortress dominating Ioxthel's Western Peninsula. The sigh he lets out at the sight sounds as fatigued, as frustrated, as I feel.

"That's what I wanted to say, but I must bid you a swift goodnight. Unfortunately, it's not my bedtime yet. I'm late."

Late? "Late for what? Where are you going?"

"Wivern's generals are meeting Guild officials in Alcázar tonight for a feast, and I've been asked to attend. It's the first of several nights of revelry over the coming weeks, firming up negotiations."

I blink in surprise. "You're going to Alcázar tonight?"

"Yes. With Ruby, Prince Raul and Princess Aoife, some of Wivern's senior generals...and your Staff Sergeant, Yasmine Hajjar."

More blinking from me, in both surprise and...horrible worry. This is big news, and I think it harks to the look Sholto gave Fjord back in the safe house about *headway in other matters.*

"The ruffians," I hear myself say. "If you need help, you should whistle for the ruffians. They know you. Trust you. They'll help you. They'll be nearby. And..." *I'm so sorry for hitting you, for saying I hated you. For being moody. I miss you so much I feel sick.*

Annoyingly, I stop just in time to prevent the apologies, and stare at Fjord with beseeching eyes, like a deer caught in the light of a huntsman's lantern...shocked, overly exposed, like *he* can tell me whether I should finish. His own expression is softening into something very definitely hopeful, but he also looks like he's thinking better of replying to me as he wishes. He's thinking better of letting me know *he* knows I'm very worried for him, and forgiving him, because he really does understand me so well. He'll think I'm probably furious at myself for saying the little things that I have, and letting slip I *don't* hate him. Letting slip some of the old Skye who rambles to him about everything and nothing and loves how he polishes her breastplate and sharpens her daggers for her and would do *anything* to protect him.

"Thank you, Skye," is all he says, offering me one of his unwaveringly gracious bows. "I'll remember that. Goodnight."

He turns to Levi, finally nearing. The Guardian isn't watching us, I expect to give some impression of privacy, and his profile looks...different. Looks wearier than it did in that shadowy alleyway earlier. There's a strain to it – like he's stressed or worried but trying to hide it. Fjord immediately sees something there too. Letting slip a tired exhale, he moves forwards to grip the back of Levi's neck with a firm hand. Then, in a gesture that surprises me a little but shouldn't, he leans in and kisses him on both cheeks.

"I'll find you later, Silver," he vows. "When I'm back from Alcázar. Rest up in the meantime. Did you read the book I gave you yesterday?"

"Yes."

"Was it good?"

"Yes."

"Do you need another?"

"I would not ask you to trouble yourself."

This in itself seems to trouble Fjord. He examines his Guardian for a long moment, then reaches up and runs a hand through his hair, tousling the short strands. The gesture is fond and nurturing, but Levi barely turns to him, his features growing even tauter; his attempt to hide whatever is lying underneath becoming stark, almost painful to watch. Fjord mutters something in that foreign language they use – Ancient Nereid, he'd told Tristan and I weeks ago in the safe house. He sounds determined and Levi looks...worse. Now Fjord is gripping his neck with both hands, forcing their gazes to meet. More speech I can't understand, but I think Fjord is reasoning with him? Or reassuring him?

The sight of them is unmistakably brotherly, and speaks of friendship, understanding and something intense. And when Levi, the meticulously guarded Guardian, finally lets slip that hidden expression watching Fjord leave – let's slip something of deep misery

– I find myself wanting to know what that intense thing between them is. Not because I see ulterior motive or fickle intent in their intimacy, or something else to damn and distrust Levi for in his guardedness, but because I see the *opposite.* I see something trustworthy. Something that speaks of love and the struggle to work through troubles together.

Perhaps most importantly, I see something powerful enough to remind me that prophecy to my name or not, mysterious deity blood rioting through my hot little ruffian veins or not, life's narrative includes all of us. The story isn't just about me and my troubles or my messy, muddled mind, because I'm not the only one who battles with them. Not the only one who's juggling strife and uncertainty – yet it's blindingly obvious I've been making it so. I've been making the story all about me.

That needs to stop.

The Temple of Thetis

I've never left the city of Ioxthel before. Obviously, I was born *outside* it in another kingdom, and I must have travelled *to* it aged five with Fjord's mother...but as you know, I don't remember either my former home or the journey from it, and I'm not about to risk the headache that always appears these days whenever I try to – not when the sun is already blistering the back of my neck and the soles of my feet feel bruised from the dry, packed earth we're walking over.

I'm thirsty, and feel foolish for it because I didn't drink anything when we left the Guild before dawn this morning, and obviously gulped down the entirety of my water skin at sunrise because of it, only to immediately realise Sholto and I have a *long* way to go – half a day on foot in the full sun – before we reach the Temple of Thetis. Not to mention the return journey.

It's now almost midday. We've been walking fast in total silence through the gnarly vineyards abutting Ioxthel's walls, wending our way to The Eastern Pass, a trading route hugging Astyros's coastline. It's so *hot*, and I've a feeling it's about to get worse – up ahead is the barren outcrop we're due to veer off the well-trodden road for. Our destination, the ruined Temple of Thetis, is just visible on its summit.

Sholto's pace has been quick and purposeful throughout the morning, and I can't see him letting it up even when we start our ascent. I hope he does, though, partly because my clothes are so soaked in sweat they're actually starting to weigh me down, but mostly because although we've been silent for the entirety of the journey thus far, I'm about to start talking.

Excessively.

Today is about gathering information. So is tomorrow, and the day after that...and the *weeks* after that. Gathering information, reading the other stories, pestering people with questions...because I'm good at that. I'm good at being rebellious and throwing tantrums, yes, but I'm also good at pestering people - which, if you think about it, makes me quite like a child. Quite like Ember, I suppose. But...that isn't the point of realisation I'm trying to reach in these musings, and it isn't what I'm trying to tell you, either. What I'm *trying* to tell you is that now my ire, injury and rebellion are leaving me, I'm strategising new ways for how best to deal with the heavy, icy stone of worry sitting in my belly at the thought of a very, *very* big destiny waiting for me, perhaps one without my friends. I don't want ice or any other form of coldness in my life. I want and need warmth; not necessarily from the sweltering sun overhead, but from the promise of a *forever* spent with my best friend. Warmth from the feel of Enye's steady hand gripping my shoulder, telling me she's *there* for me, and from the infectious mischief of Fin's smiles when he steals a book on the god of desire and tells me to tell him if I see the similarities.

No.

I don't want cold...but then I don't want to be so hot and angry at everyone and everything any more, not least because we've figured out this is *bigger* than just my story. So, I suppose what I'm trying to tell you, and myself, is that today marks a new phase. A page turn to a new chapter where I pester people with questions and learn how to start new little fires inside me that aren't so angry and injured, so that *if* Tristan or Fin or Enye aren't there when destiny, the cold unknown, comes knocking...I'm ready.

Sholto is ahead.

You should know he's positively *storming* up the hillock's steep, dusty slopes to the temple, so there's been no let up in his pace. He spares me a glance over his shoulder now, either because he somehow reads my thoughts and intentions in the silence - the quiet before the storm – or because I'm so withdrawn he thinks I've run back to Ioxthel. His breathing is slightly laboured, but not nearly as much as mine, and that's a little embarrassing given that he's over four *hundred* years old.

"Sholto?"

"Yes?"

"What's the history behind the Temple of Thetis? You told Rose it's ruined."

"I did say that. The temple was constructed in honour of the sea nymph, Thetis, one of fifty daughters to the ancient sea god, Nereus. Many years ago, the site was sibling to Ioxthel's great Temple of Poseidon. Unfortunately, it fell into disrepair after the Impurity War. We're following the old pilgrimage route between the two, though that too seems to have been discarded."

I look down to where my feet are stumbling over the dry, rocky earth, and see that he's right. There's nothing that even remotely resembles an animal track, let alone an oft-used path of pilgrimage.

"This is Thetis, mother of the famous demigod, Achilles?" I verify.

"Yes."

"She dipped him in the River Styx, didn't she? Held him by the ankle and *dunked* her own son in a river in the underworld to give him invulnerability."

"She did."

"This is Thetis, who defended Zeus from his siblings' rebellion despite him marrying her off to a mortal king against her wishes when he was her lover?"

"I think we've established we're thinking of the same sea nymph, Skye, for she's the *only* nymph with the name Thetis."

I'm quiet...for a few seconds. "You'd think Zeus would set a better example wouldn't you? On how to treat others?"

Sholto lets slip a quiet, humourless laugh. "I'd mind what you say next, if I were you. You're speaking of *the* most powerful being in the universe. The King of the Gods himself, and keeper to the throne of Olympus. He does not like to be slighted."

"That's sort of my point, though," I say. "Not the last bit, because I don't mean to talk *bad* about Zeus. He's obviously mighty. Really very impressive..." I hazard a brief, wary glance to the skies before going on, half expecting a lightning bolt to snake down and smite me. "What I'm saying is everyone watches him because he's so powerful, and I bet you everyone tries to imitate him, too. You'd think he'd have treated Thetis better and not married her off to some earthly heathen when she helped him fight to keep his throne, his *power*, and when the two of them were lovers. Don't you think? It's odd he'd do that. And wrong. You shouldn't marry someone off. Especially to a heathen. Especially if you're their lover. *Especially* if everyone is watching you do it."

"I don't think..." Sholto begins, but seems to rethink those words, and tries again, "There will be much to the situation we as bystanders to their relationship don't know, and will never know, Skye. Much left untold that might explain Zeus's actions and make them less deplorable."

"'Wrongs done for the right reasons, the lesser of two evils chosen...'" I quote some of his spiel from the safe house yesterday. "Is that what you're saying, Sholto? That Zeus was doing that stuff to Thetis in good intention?"

"Well remembered, Skye. That is what I meant."

Feeling smug, and happy this new strategy seems to be working – because that heavy stone of worry in my belly is very toasty right now – I get busy with my feet and elbows and put on a burst of speed to catch him up. My breathing suffers for it but that might be excitement, more than anything.

"Have you been here before, Sholto? To Thetis's temple?"

"Yes, many times. It used to be glorious, and I suppose still is in its own way. Magnificent views."

I look around. From up here, Astyros embodies the very definition of heat; the shrinking, sun-baked lands dusty and barren, the air thick with a haze that promises of hard toil to make ends meet. The city of Ioxthel is further south, a bustling fusion of spices and fishing boats and haphazard sandstone terraces rising before the ocean. She looks further away than I anticipate, and the distance unnerves me. Let's not forget I'm expected to *leave* her soon. To leave my friends and Tristan, and the only streets I have the wherewithal to remember, in order to travel to Elysium. Or to find the Torch of Prometheus. That's what Sholto told me back in his kitchenette, didn't he? Either we leave for Elysium, or we leave to find the Torch...and it fills me with yet *more* unease, because his father is the only being alive who knows where the weapon is. Hence today might well set in motion plans to leave Ioxthel...to leave Tristan.

"Why does your father like the tales of Thetis so much?" I ask quickly, scrambling for a distraction. "You said Zelos was fond of her. What does that mean?"

"He knows Thetis personally."

"Really?!"

"Yes, Skye. My father is sentinel to Zeus, thus he knows everyone personally. I suppose he's especially interested in Thetis because he relates to her journey in life. Relates to it, and thrives off it."

"In what way?"

"Thetis was courted by both Zeus and Poseidon. The rivalry endemic to such a situation, when a woman or man is sought by two suitors, is coveted by Zelos."

"Because he embodies it, right?" I guess. "He *embodies* rivalry?"

"Rivalry, strife, jealousy, hatred...Zelos embodies them all, and he lives to witness them in others. To enhance them in others, too."

I think back to Fjord's warning to me on the streets outside the safe house, telling me Zelos had a reputation befit for one of Zeus's sentinels. Telling me, indirectly, that he wished he was coming on this trip too...

"Is your father dangerous, Sholto?" I ask hesitantly. "If he's a sentinel, is he quite powerful?"

"Undoubtedly."

"So this trip is quite dangerous?"

"It might be, yes."

That's all he says. He doesn't reassure me, nor does he explain more of his father. It takes me a moment to find my voice. "I have another question, but it's not about Thetis. It's a bit random, actually."

"Why would you think that mattered?"

"I don't know. Just speaking out loud..." *Pretending I don't feel unsettled by you telling me your father is dangerous. Wishing Fjord was here, too.* "What did you mean when you talked about *igniting ichor* the other week? After we witnessed the oath together you mentioned it, but told me I hadn't done so?"

"Ah. I was referring to your ability to ignite the ichor in your blood. To call upon the energies and powers of the gods and goddesses. Everyone who shares deity blood can do so in order to heighten their senses and hone their abilities to fight."

I miss one of my busy steps in surprise. "Are you saying I can switch *on* the blood of the gods and goddesses inside me and...power up?"

"I suppose it is analogous to a power up, yes," Sholto sounds like the phrase is a bit crude for him. "As a Nixen, igniting ichor will enable you to better summon, and better wield, the element you have an affinity in."

"Which is?"

"You are a descendent of Aeolus, Skye, the master of the storm winds, and thus that element for you is..."

My eyes widen. "I can wield *wind?*"

"Yes."

"And...and as a demigod?!"

"As a demigod, you have the means to gather and harness very great powers from the gods and goddesses – with time and proper training, of course."

Man, that's cool! "Ok. Wow. Big news. Important stuff...but you're saying I *didn't* do it, didn't ignite ichor on the night of the oath?"

"You did not, no."

"Why did you think I had?"

"There are distinctive signs of ichor's use, and I was momentarily confused over one of them. I should've known better. I haven't mentored you in this."

"How *do* I do it, then? Use ichor? Ignite it? Call upon the energies of the gods and goddesses and power up?"

Sholto is silent for a moment, and then he does slow his pace – stops walking altogether and turns. "When you're ready to speak to me with less defiance, Skye, I might humour that question with an answer, or even a demonstration. There is much left for me to teach you now that the truth is known. Your potential is totally untapped...so I'll say again today what I did in the safe house yesterday. This is the time for moving *beyond* your own ire and rebellion, to rise and meet this profoundly important destiny bequeathed upon you by The Fates. This is the time to pursue your resilience and power for the good of others, to test yourself to your limits, and not to test the limits of my, or any other's, patience."

"I am moving through it," I get out in a small voice. "I'm moving through behaving angrily by asking questions. I'm getting unstuck."

"I see that," Sholto remarks, and he doesn't sound disapproving...except he sort of does. "Does your tone need to be quite so demanding whilst you do so though?"

"It's not meant to be," I mumble. "But...maybe it's because you haven't said sorry, Sholto. For lying to me, and for manipulating me as a little girl. You haven't said sorry for those things, so maybe that's why I might still sound not as I should. And...I'm quite excited. There's that, too."

"I haven't apologised because I don't see the need to," Sholto replies simply, and then upon seeing me looking taken aback, "For the last seven years I've housed, raised and mentored you, Skye. Indeed it is *still* my role to mentor you...we are *still* to journey through life together. As I've told you before, I spent those years without revealing The Fates' intentions for you in order to *protect* you. In order to let you grow. Don't think I don't see how, despite that, this is difficult for you to come to terms with. I do, Skye. I see it's a lot to understand, especially given your temperament...but in my eyes it doesn't warrant apology. And it doesn't warrant you bathing in undue sulk and wilfulness. I have navigated many, *many* surprises in my time, and instruct you now with insight. What should be *more* pressing on your mind than the anger and betrayal you feel towards me is the magnitude of just how much your life is set to change, and the gravity of all you must undertake with the prophecy. The injury and injustice you feel you've suffered from my duplicity should pale in comparison to the real troubles at hand, which is the potential fall of Elysium, and the demise of Mount Olympus. These are deep, inescapably *vast* troubles, Skye, of an ilk thousands of times more pressing than your domestic strife. I would urge you to see that not soon, but now. The world needs it's heroine *now.*"

He stops to fix me with a profound stare, a deeper, graver sort to those of instruction and counsel he used to give me during our sparring sessions...and yet the line of his lips softens slightly when he sees the torn expression forming on my face.

Torn, because I am starting to see it.

"I'll not apologise as you wish me to," he says, and even his voice is less strict now – more like it was when he'd chide me *ever* so slightly, but not really, for never buying lunch. "I'll not apologise, but I will offer you my candour. Just because these years have been spent with myself keeping you in the dark, it doesn't make them untrue, or undignified. It doesn't discount the times we've shared. I am fond of you, not least because you're Saffron's daughter, and not least because you're also now a student of mine. And it is *because* I'm fond of you that I instruct you as I do now. Firmly. Without tolerance of things that are childish and unhelpful to you...and given everything, unhelpful to the rest of the world. Trust me when I say I live in good intention, Skye. For you, and for the gods and goddesses. I always will. But you *must* get yourself together. You *must* stop disappointing me and yourself, and be the heroine we need. Not tomorrow, and not soon. You must be what we need now."

He watches me for a moment longer, then offers me a small bow of respect and starts up the hill again, leaving me behind to reflect on...so much. On him saying he's fond of me and sounding like he means it, and on him calling me Saffron's daughter. To reflect on the words,

"The world needs it's heroine now."

* * *

We walk up the rest of the hillock in silence, Sholto remaining some distance ahead of me...and so much for my intent to pester him. I barely see my feet traipsing over the uneven terrain, or the dusty sediment staining my damp ankles. It's gross, but you should know I'm sweating a *lot* more than usual, unused to having absolutely no shade from sail-like awnings or rooftop overhangs, or even the blissful reprieve of a cool stone wall half-cast in shadow. Anything would be a relief from the full sun baking the lands, blistering the skin over the back of my neck...robbing my tongue of what little moisture it has left.

When we reach the hill's summit there is – shockingly – a ruined temple, and it's not difficult to imagine what the former building might've been like. Modest in size, with marble plinths, pillars and friezes, it must have promised timeless pride and glory to the thousands of pilgrimages made here to offer homage to Thetis, the only sea nymph with that name, in the hopes she'd hear their prayers and *heed* them. And yet I can't help but think those trips were made in vain, and that those prayers lie strewn right alongside the temple ruins. It makes me feel odd if I'm honest, looking upon the tumbled friezes and pillars nestled by the hillock's own weathered rocks and sparse, scruffy foliage. It's like they sought refuge there...sought shelter as a stray mountain goat would from the fierce winds wreaking havoc up here. Winds that, let's not forget, Sholto just told me I have the ability to wield...which if I'm being even *more* honest with you might be why I'm feeling so odd.

I watch him walking the ruins before me, slowly climbing the temple's chipped steps. He stops when he reaches the top, right beneath one of two upstanding friezes. His expression is focused, eyes as flighty as the sparrow hawk battling the skies overhead. It's fluttering form swoops every so often to find a new vantage point or a new stream of wind to surf.

Until it starts fleeing.

Fleeing fast.

"With me, Skye," Sholto warns in a low voice, snapping his fingers at his side.

My senses prickle with unease. Hurrying up the steps to him on instincts I don't even question, the silver bow on my back whistling as I go, I search the hilltop for danger...for something dark and shadowy. Something of malevolent intent and envy and *zeal*.

Seconds later the earth ripples underfoot, kicking up a vast shockwave of sandy dust as something incredibly heavy and compact drops, literally *drops*, straight from the heavens. He lands in the middle of the ruined temple, an enormous figure resting on one knee, with his shaved head bowed as if in prayer and a single fist punched into the ground to stabilise himself. My heart lurches in my chest as two massive white wings snap open on either side of him, flapping lazily. He rolls his hung head, unwinding tense shoulders and a neck that seems to shimmer with gold...and then he looks up.

Chocolate eyes pierce mine, their hue smooth and shrewd and wholly familiar; except the face they belong to is too angular and the frame beneath it just too...enormous. There is malice in the man's features instead of diplomatic reserve, and his pink lips curl into a cruel smile that stretches taut as he looks beside me, to Sholto.

To his son.

Awash in the scorching sunlight, Zelos lets out a low, rumbling laugh that *sings* of danger. "Well, isn't this a surprise..."

Alice Bamber

Friend or Foe?

The embodiment of zeal, envy, emulation and rivalry appears aged, and ageless. The weathered creases imprinted in his face hint at long years lived, long battles fought, and yet it's impossible to discern how old he really is. His physique is that of a wisened fighter, definitely befit for a sentinel to Zeus, but his lashes are soft and full, professing the mischief of someone decidedly youthful; and his skin, a deeper shade of amber than the sunlight falling over his shoulders, is marked by none of life's usual blemishes of maturity. He wears a white toga tied around his hips and nothing else, making it easy to discern the network of veins sketched over his body – veins of liquid gold.

I'm not joking.

Literally, veins of liquid gold.

I've never seen anything like it before, and I wonder if I ever will. Have *you* seen someone with blood like that? It's a bit freaky, to be honest.

Excepting his brown eyes, Zelos looks little like his son, but I suppose he feels a bit like him. Everything about both of them is tangibly permanent, as if nothing could ever touch them, let alone harm them...something I've long witnessed in Sholto's presence and especially of late. Is it the air of assuredness that being hundreds, if not thousands, of years old brings them? Or just a family trait?

Unlike his son, however, Zelos carries with him a hostile volatility. An unpredictability. You can see it in the air around him, a thick aura of danger and violence, and a lack of inhibition to use them. It's blindingly clear my thundering heart isn't about to let up anytime soon, because there's *every* possibility it should remain ready for action. My instincts sharpen further as the second pass by,

262

each breath I haul in tightening with the realisation that it might be my last...it *would* be my last, if Zelos chose to stand against me. And...and that feels like a possibility as he cocks his head to the side, scrutinising his son in the way *the* top predator would his prey. I watch his tongue slip out and run itself over his pink lips, the act given in nothing but the name of anticipation, before his enormous white wings fold behind him and nestle neatly down his back.

He straightens, then *purrs.* "Hello, son."

"Zelos."

"Nice day to settle scores, is it not?"

Sholto shifts restlessly. "I'm not here to fight. I'm here for information."

"How interesting."

Zelos doesn't sound interested – he sounds dangerous. He licks his lips again before pinning his gaze on me; and I don't miss the way it snags on the scars marking the left side of my face. Two expressive eyebrows twitch and drop. He starts walking towards us, his footsteps shaking the ground...and if it wasn't clear before he stands several feet taller and broader than Sholto. Feet taller and broader than even Levi or Fjord, too.

"It's been a long time, Skye."

Goosebumps rush over my skin, a forewarning I'm stupidly slow to recognise. In less than a heartbeat Zelos stands just inches from me, his brown eyes consuming as they look into mine. Heat and the rich, sweet perfume of cloves and tree resin surround me, much like the scent of his son...and then his son *is* there, hauling me back to stand behind him.

"Keep your distance, Zelos," he warns in a low voice. "We're not here to play, either."

I stare at Zeus's sentinel around Sholto's stiff stance, my poor heart going utterly berserk. He just moved impossibly fast, covering a distance of at least ten metres in *far* less than the time it takes to even summon the urge to blink an eye.

"You've the nerve to issue me with an *order*, son?"

Zelos hums out something deep and lazy, a rumbling sound made for savouring...until it stops, and his expression falls into pure fury. His form becomes air once more as he pulls Sholto forwards by the shoulders and tosses him aside, like one would toss a fish out of its net in The Eastern Harbours. Totally without care, totally in control. Over the blood rushing through my ears and my own startled grunt, I hear him land clumsily on all fours. He whips around, but he's nowhere near as quick as his father. I get the sense that nothing in this world compares to Zelos...except, it seems, my own endeavours to summon not the blink of an eye, but my bow.

Yeah.

My bow.

You should know I've *no* idea how I drew the weapon so fast – as well as an arrow. No idea. All I know is that Zelos is back in my space, but this time he has its sharp tip poised over his heart, and my bowstring is cutting into the archer's calluses on my fingers, steady but ready.

The sentinel glances down in surprise, his brows rising. He freezes, barks out a loud, highly amused laugh, and spins out of Sholto's reach as his son picks himself up and hurries over to us. I swear I see Zelos flick his ear as he returns to the midst of the ruins, and in his hands...in his hands, he holds that bow and that sharp-tipped arrow.

How on earth did he get those...?!

Something blocks my line of sight; Sholto, returning to his protective stance in front of me and leaving very little space between us...because clearly last time, it wasn't enough. His back is covered in hilltop dust but he seems unhurt, and I'm too shocked to protest or outmanoeuvre him.

I look down stupidly at my empty hands, disoriented, unnerved and *terrified* that I didn't even feel Zelos take my bow, let alone see him do it. That I didn't heed myself draw the weapon in the first place is even weirder.

"We need to *talk*, Zelos," Sholto entreats. "Please."

The sentinel doesn't even spare his son a glance. He's too preoccupied examining my bow, handling it with a degree of reverence and ease that implies he's entirely familiar with archery. He pulls the string taught with two hooked fingers and takes aim, tendons rippling in his arms as he does so, and then he looses the arrow. It scuppers through the holes of a ruined frieze and into the sky, arching in an extensive, expert trajectory that never ends. The arrow just goes and goes and goes, until it disappears into the pale haze *high* above us.

"This is a very nice weapon, Skye, befit for a goddess...except you are not one. You're not even a Huntress to her." Zelos fixes me with a humoured look. "Did you steal it?"

It's difficult to find my voice for quite a few reasons...but mostly because my arrow, that I spent a good long time sharpening last night when I returned to the Guild from the safe house, is literally lost to the heavens.

"Steal it from who?" I ask hoarsely.

"Artemis. Did you steal it from Artemis?"

I shake my head, flinching when he appears in front of us again. He gazes at his son for a long moment, letting him clock his proximity, before offering the bow back to me.

"This weapon is that of The Huntress. I hope you treat her as well as she does you."

The Huntress?

As in...Artemis?

Hesitantly, in confusion – because Sholto told me the bow was my mother's – I reach forwards and curl my palm over its cool silver frame, strong relief coursing through me when Zelos readily relinquishes it. He stares at me for long seconds after he does, without reserve, then steps back and *finally* looks to his son.

"Talk to me, then. My time is short."

Sholto takes a deep breath...and dives *straight* it. "Where is the Torch of Prometheus?"

"Why're you asking?"

"Evils are moving against Elysium. The Queen of Astyros is joining forces with the Kingdom of Wivern, amassing an army. She's searching for the Torch, just as her ancestor, Scarlett Sabir, did those four hundred years ago. History is on repeat...and we are trying to stop it."

"Who is we? Yourself and the thieving demigod?"

"Amongst others, yes."

Zelos considers this for a moment. "You'll never find the Torch, Sholto. Nor will Ruby Sabir. Don't trouble your mind on the matter."

"I believe she will," Sholto objects, tone that of someone trying *very* hard not to sound short. "She's searching for a map to it, Zelos."

"Oh? What's that, then?"

"We don't know. Do you not, either?"

"I do," Zelos grins. "I'm just testing you."

"Where is the Torch, please?"

"I won't be telling you that."

"You would risk a repeat of the Impurity War, Zelos? You know what The Sabirs and their followers will do with the Torch in their possession. You know millions of lives will be jeopardised."

"I'm not risking anything," Zelos refutes mildly. "The Torch is perfectly safe. No one will ever find it, least of all a mortal...and I'll never disclose its whereabouts to you, either. Don't weep over it."

Sholto stares at his father with a darkening expression, and his father, in turn, curls his upper lip in distaste. His tongue darts out again, eyes honing as his pupils dilate – like he's closing in on a target.

"This is bigger than us, Zelos," Sholto murmurs to him in a low voice, as if he knows it. "This is much bigger. Please tell us where the Torch is so we can safeguard it from Ruby, and from anyone else who would use it for ill will."

"How do you know The Queen will use it for ill?" Zelos sounds surprisingly serious in his query, until he laughs. "Ruby is an interesting soul. I'm intrigued by her and her family, as you all should be...but she won't find it. I thought I just mentioned that?"

"She will with this map," Sholto grates out.

Zelos's grin widens. "There is no map to the Torch, Sholto. I was fooling you. Do you think I'd create something that would reveal the whereabouts of humankind's greatest weapon to them? You're growing simpler with age."

"What about a guide?" I speak up.

Zelos peers around Sholto to me. "Though I am interested in her life, I'm not going to *help* Ruby Sabir, or any mortal. Or any *being*. I'd like to see them try to persuade me, for they'd be dead before they finished their request. It begs the question of why the two of you are still here breathing..."

"I...didn't mean *you*, actually."

"No?"

I shake my head, fingers spasming around my bow, heart flopping all over the place. Gods, his stare is disconcerting. Dark, irreverent...unforgiving.

"Who did you mean then, Skye?"

"I...don't know. Just a guide to the Torch, but *not* you. Definitely not you, because I would still like to breathe, please. I mean...someone else, or something? Some kind of trail?"

"You speak as a huntress, following the tracks of her prey?"

Uh, well...no. But if I say yes, will you help us? "I'm just speaking out loud actually, Zelos. Musing. Randomly. I do that a lot. Especially right now, because I'm moving through anger, you see? By talking and questioning things. It's helping."

Zelos's head tilts further to the side. It takes me a second to realise how *stupid* I sound by saying that. Does a sentinel to Zeus need to know of my anger management strategies?

Short answer, no.

"That's interesting," he says.

"What?"

"How possible the impossible becomes when you've two minds working on the same problem. I see you in there, you know."

I shift uncomfortably. What is he talking about, seeing who in where?

"Nothing is impossible, Skye," Zelos furthers, and his eyes are staring straight into mine. Straight *through* mine. His voice also softens, losing its cruel edge. "Remember that, when times are hard, and remind those closest to you when they forget. Nothing is impossible. Time is there to be found and borrowed if only you bow to its glory. And...I *see* you, in there."

I see you, too, my counsel burst out suddenly. *The real Zelos. Buried beneath layers of bitterness and heartbreak. Lost, but recoverable by the right person with enough willpower.*

I blink in surprise. *What...on earth?*

Before me, Sholto finally starts to let his agitation show. "Stop playing games with Skye, Zelos. I wouldn't be here if this weren't serious...if this weren't essential. You're wrong. Time is not dispensable. We're running out of it, fast. Please tell us where the Torch is...or why its guide would be in such close proximity to The Sabirs? Ruby intimated it had been beneath her nose for years..."

Zelos is still looking at me. "I wonder how she knows that."

"Xavier Archer is working with her, or perhaps working *on* her. I believe he might be manipulating her, bending her will."

"Oh," Zelos snorts. "Well, that would be how she knows, wouldn't it? Pray, how is Xavier doing these days? Nike refuses to even mention his name to me...the son she disowned *long* before she had reason to."

Nike. As in...Zelos's sister? Another child of the ancient titaness and river deity, Styx, and consequently one of Zeus's four winged sentinels. The embodiment of victory herself. Unless I'm mistaken, what Zelos is saying is that she's also the mother of Xavier Archer, The Rogue Guardian who is worser than worst, and who Levi is supposedly protecting me from?

That's a plot twist.

"Xavier is no doubt excited to get his hands on the weapon of a titan," Sholto supplies stiffly. "He's wooing Ruby. Pretending to be her bodyguard."

Zelos snorts again. "I would *love* to see the little tike try to find the Torch. Nike would *end* him...not that she knows where it is, either."

"Zelos—"

"Your thoughts seem as frustrated as your voice, Sholto," Zelos interrupts firmly, his eyes suddenly taking on a dark, *dark* glint. His patience has expired. "Something pressing you need to get off your chest? An apology, perhaps? A settling of scores?"

Sholto's mouth opens and closes several times, his cheeks turning pink. "Don't be facetious."

"Do I not have good reason to be?"

"No."

"Oh?"

The thick tension between the two of them becomes near suffocating as they stare each other down. Neither yields, even when Zelos lets out a humourless laugh and turns to me. There's no wisdom in his eyes now, and no endeavour to find something of interest in mine.

There's just bitterness, and spite.

"You know, Skye, we've crossed paths with one another once before. You were younger and not, I'm inclined to think, with your birth mother at the time. It has me intrigued...who *are* your parents?"

"Uh...I don't know them. My mum is...not here."

"Not here? Saffron, one of little Artemis's fiery huntresses, dead?" His brows arch. "How interesting. Dad must be the god, then, and might I ask who? Who's dad, Skye?"

"I don't know."

That ghost of a rueful smile appears. "Do you not?"

I shake my head, staring at him. My flighty heart is picking up speed again, because something about his dark demeanour, his tone, this whole *game* he's now playing, raises the question of whether *he* knows who my father is. "Do you? Do you know who my father is, Zelos?"

The smile broadens, stretching tight and taut with savage enmity. He looks to his son again, and says pointedly, "Oh, I know who your father is, and I know more of your mother than you could possibly dream of, but I sadly won't be telling you about either of them. Not when there's something incredibly important my son needs to get off his chest first."

"There is nothing," Sholto denies.

"Mhm. Interesting. If that's what you truly believe, then we have a problem. One that should be settled..."

The two of them lock gazes again. I stare without really seeing either man, my eyes wide with shock and my hopes soaring higher and higher than my arrow lost to the heavens. I suddenly feel like my forgotten past might finally be within my grasp.

"When did we meet, Zelos?" I ask breathlessly. "You said we'd met before? When? Where? I don't remember you?"

"It was in Wivern, of all places. I responded to a friend seeking refuge there...guarded her briefly while she thought on how best to store borrowed time for those who might need it most in the future. The young girl she travelled with had amber eyes and salty hair. It's true the Nereids always leave an impression on —"

"Melody went to *you* when she left Elysium?!" Sholto interrupts sharply. "Why didn't you tell me this, Zelos?!"

His smile is grim. "It wasn't important. Melody had already disappeared when we last met...and I assumed you knew, Sholto, given how close the two of you were. Such good friends...no?"

I've never seen Sholto look so out of sorts as he does now. His ruddy cheeks tint further, but the rest of him blanches of all colour, as if he's in terrible distress or disbelief. He reaches for the skim at his hip, seemingly in preparation to draw the weapon...and I think he really *might.*

He really might draw arms on his father.

I watch him in shock, my brain puzzling through what's being said at breakneck speed, trying to decipher the energy they're throwing off. I mean, Zelos is telling us that Melody sought him when she fled Elysium with me? Clearly he, Zelos, was also her friend? Both were her *friend,* but a grievance lies in the matter.

"What happened when she came to you?" Sholto grates out. "In Wivern?"

His father hums. "I believe you owe me an apology before I tell you that, and even then I'll be disinclined. I lost faith in your integrity years ago, son, and now I finally get to see you suffer for your sins."

Sholto draws in a sharp inhale wrought with intent, and I don't think. I'm suddenly so worried they're about to fight and destroy my only means of finding out about my forgotten past...and we can't let that happen. I quickly forgo Sholto's shadow and step to his side, practically vibrating with unspoken questions. They're vigorous ones, filled with a lifetime's worth of burning intrigue and hope.

So many things, made of glass.

Ready to be shattered.

"What about me, Zelos?" I burst out. "Will you tell *me* what happened when Melody and I were with you? How old was I? Why were we in Wivern? What does storing borrowed time mean? Do you mean that literally, or figuratively? Was...was my hair really still salty? From the sea, I guess, because the Nereids are descendants of the sea nymphs, aren't they? And...what did *she* look like? Melody? Was her hair salty? Dark, like Fjord's? Did...did we..." *Did we seem like mother and daughter, even though we weren't really?*

"Why were you in Wivern, Skye?" Zelos smirks. "Perhaps to run away from the selfish, sinful bastar—"

"She chose me!" Sholto explodes. He totally loses his cool, drawing his sword swiftly and stepping forwards, slashing it through the air by his side as if to warm the blade up. "I have nothing to apologise for, Zelos! I wasn't selfish! I didn't sin! She chose me! She loved *me!*"

Stark, unbridled anger flashes over Zelos's face at this, and then I watch something *ignite* in him. The patchwork of veins sprawled beneath his skin starts to glow, like thin rivers of glimmering gold. They pulse with every strong, supreme beat of his heart, and there's suddenly a shockingly violent tug in my own pulse, too. My blood starts to pump faster and faster through my system, like something is pulling at it *hard.*

Summoning it.

"Melody did *not* choose you, Sholto," Zelos seethes, his voice dripping with a low, cold promise of violence. "She was shot by Eros, and you *knew.* You knew she wasn't herself, and you didn't stop!"

Eros. Son of Aphrodite. The God of Love, Sex and Desire. A troublemaking trickster known for messing with others' pursuits of the heart by shooting them with his magical arrows. The same being embossed on the edges of the Guild's bathroom mirrors that I *swear* I don't look in very often...and who Fin likes to think he's similar to.

My eyes flash to Sholto beside me. When he doesn't reply, doesn't *refute* his father, I feel my mouth drop open in shock. Eros *shot* Melody with his magical arrows, and affected how and who she loved. *This* is what Sholto was describing on our journey here, isn't it?! The parallels between Thetis's life and Zelos's are *real,* except Sholto is also embroiled in the matter, because it's father and son who are the two suitors vying for the love of one woman! They're the two men caught in a violent quarrel of jealousy and rivalry, but their lover is gone.

Fjord's mother, Melody.

Gone.

Feeling punches me in the gut, powerful and overwhelming...and I've no idea how it didn't hit home sooner. No idea how I've known this but not *felt* it. My mind hares back to that second meeting in the safe house, when Tristan and I were spying good and Fjord was first telling me of Xavier Archer being dangerous, and how Ruby was looking for the Torch of Prometheus...and of the time before his mother fled Elysium with me, when I lived with him and his brother, Kieran, in their household amongst the Nereids.

Mother.

Brother.

He lost both of them, didn't he? He told me his brother had "also passed" meaning....he's dead. What of his father? I've heard *no* mention of him in all of this, which suggests Fjord has also lost him? Which means that his entire family is gone. He's just as without kin as I am, but I *hit* him right after he said he loved me like a sister...

"We're done here," Zelos says abruptly, jolting me from my regrets and grief. He turns and starts striding away over the hilltop, veins of shimmering gold still pulsing, his pearly white wings snapping out on either side of him. They're so immense they almost span the entire width of the temple. "I never want to see you again, Sholto. I'll kill you if I do. Rip your sorry, sordid excuse of a heart from your body with my own hands and feed it to Poseidon's pesky underwater monsters, and I'll *enjoy* it."

"If that's true, then why did you meet with me today?!" Sholto volleys brazenly, totally unfazed by his father's threats. If anything, they just make him angrier. "You threatened to kill me last time we saw one another, and yet here we are. Both alive, both angry...neither one willing to apologise to the other."

"I met with you today because I foolishly hoped you were repentant!" Zelos throws over his shoulder. "But you're not, and never will be. You were *never* honourable enough to apologise, Sholto, even as a young boy. Hades has a very special place in the underworld for people who take advantage of a lover that's unable to give true, informed consent. Think on that whilst you fail to find your precious weapon, and pine for the days you lived without a soul bathed in sin."

His leg muscles tense to take to the skies, to return to the heavens from which he fell, those immense wings flapping faster and faster to gain flight...and I don't stop to think. I run forwards with as much gusto as my little legs can muster, thieving feet light over the dusty earth, buoyed by the swelling hilltop breeze...and then I do something really stupid. In fact, it's perhaps *the* most stupid thing I've ever done, in taking hold of the feathers on the edge of one of Zelos's pearly white wings and tugging with all my might. The limb feels soft and cool, like a pillow or a cloud...disconcertingly luxurious, yet somehow still incredibly sturdy and undoubtedly forbidden.

"Please don't leave," I breathe. "Zelos? Please? Can I just say something before you do? Just one thing. It will be very small. Smaller than me. Just one thing?"

There's a grunt.

A horrible, straining silence.

He falls back to the ground with a heavy *thud,* batting me sideways with his wing as he turns to face me. I hurry to regain my balance, surprised I'm not totally swept off my feet by the blow – because I think he could've sent me into the stratosphere if he wanted to.

The strained silence descends again. I stand there with my locked thighs quivering, like a deer caught in the glow of a huntsman's lantern...only today, the light is from Zelos's veins, literally *ignited* in gold.

He still doesn't speak, and nor does he move. He doesn't do anything but stare down at me with eyes of obsidian, cold and dark with raw fury. Fury for his son, and maybe for me, for touching his wings? Something tells me I shouldn't have done that, but by Zeus, is it ever too late now. I know my own eyes are wide and frisky, heart and better judgement begging me vociferously to flee from his path...but I don't.

I can't.

Say something, my counsel orders sharply. *For goddesses' sake, Skye. If you tell Zelos you wish to say something to him, then you need to say it to him! He's waiting for you!*

But I have no idea what! I exclaim. *I said that on a whim! A stupid whim! Help me?!*

Talk of Melody!

"She has a son!" I blurt out randomly, and much too loudly. "Melody. Your...friend. You know she has a son, Zelos? He's called Fjord. He's been living in Ioxthel for the last five years, sparring with me every day. He's *my* friend, and he's searching for the Torch too. He's part of the team Sholto mentioned earlier..."

Keep talking, Skye!

"Uh, so Melody...I'm sorry if you think she died because of me. I don't remember travelling with her from Elysium, but if I did I'd tell you about it. Obviously. Because...apparently you saw us? In Wivern? We could talk about that, if you wanted to? I know I'd like t—"

I flinch when he moves forwards, coming within inches of my jittery form. Sholto is instantly behind his father, sword poised...but the sentinel doesn't seem bothered. He just stares down at me damningly, searchingly, and I've a feeling he's debating whether to pick me up and toss me from the summit...to throw me into the glistening ocean *miles* below us, or maybe that stratosphere.

My counsel fidgets restlessly. *You must keep talking, Skye. Tell him of Melody's son, still living. Tell him more of Fjord.*

"I'm sorry for whatever happened between you and Sholto, Zelos. I don't really understand it. I didn't know of it before today, but I think Melody must have been very special? Her son, Fjord, is very special. We haven't been speaking to one another recently, because I've been upset with him for not telling me some stuff. Important stuff. Only *that's* not important right now and anyway...I think I forgive him for it. I know I do. There are bigger, more pressing things to worry about and I guess...I guess what I *really* wanted to say, when I just pulled on your wings and said I wanted to speak with you and say...uh...well I said I wanted to say one thing and it's been a few, but what I did really want to say is that I don't want millions of lives to end because of two broken hearts. I don't want this," I gesture clumsily between father and son, "to ruin the world. There's a prophecy about me. Did you know that? It says I'm supposed to *stop* that...to stop the world being ruined. Hold it on my shoulders, somehow. Gods know how. I'd rather it wasn't ruined, you know? Because I think that would make it difficult, or *more* difficult, than it needs to be. There'll be pieces sliding all over the place. Bits of soil getting stuck in my hair...and twigs too, because I never brush it. Please tell us where the Torch is? To help Fjord? Melody's son? And...me?"

"You've never been in love if you think the world isn't worth ending for someone," Zelos responds, his voice low and hollow. "Waging war, wreaking havoc, wielding devastation, they are only *ever* about pursuits of the heart. Ask any and all of the gods and goddesses, and their sentinels."

"Is that what you're doing by not telling us where the Torch is? Waging war? Is that what Melody would want, for you to do that in her name?"

He arches a brow.

I swallow hard. Gods, my throat is so tight, my bow horribly slick with sweat in my hand, but I *must* keep going. I think I'm getting somewhere. That last point was a good one, wasn't it? And something tells me Zelos is thinking on it.

"If Melody was anything like her son is now, I really don't think she'd want that. In fact I *know* she wouldn't, Zelos, because Fjord is so gentle. He's so good. Just the best person I've ever met. Good, gentle...gracious. Please will you help him? Us? Protect the Torch?"

Silence.

It stretches between us, but this time it feels different. It feels hopeful, because Zelos's jaw is working overtime, and those dark eyes are searching mine, as if to verify that what I just said about Fjord is true...to verify that Melody's son is my friend, and a wholly *good* man.

Thank the goddesses, he believes me. "Melody was searching for The Hesperides after she left Elysium. The Nymphs of the West dwell in Wivern's furthermost mountain foothills, and she wanted to hide you both with them in their gardens. She sought refuge with me for a time to devise the best route, and to ask for my advice on borrowing time...as I said. If you lived in Ioxthel throughout your childhood, I doubt either of you ever made it to your destination, but then I've been known to be wrong before and doubt is as fickle as The Fates are themselves." His gaze moves to the skies over my shoulder, that muscle in his jaw still jumping as he clenches and unclenches his teeth. He swiftly looks back to me, brown eyes so raw and dark and...pained. Heartbroken. "As for the Torch? It's guide? Look no further than yourself, Skye. The trail, the tracks you seek to follow, start with your very own footprints...and who knows where you'll take yourself."

Forgiveness

Sholto and I travel back to the Guild in near silence, just like the early stages of our outward journey. He seems pent up with anger towards his father and lost in deep thought, and *I* am lost to deep feeling, dwelling on all Zelos revealed to us about *me* somehow being a guide to Prometheus's Torch, and everything about Melody. I realise I need to see her son. Knew I did in the very same second Zelos first talked of the woman he loved and I truly comprehended that Fjord lost his *mother.* He lost the mother who left him and his now dead brother in the Kingdom of Elysium in order to flee to protect me...and then he himself left that kingdom, five years ago.

In search of her?

Or of *me*, the girl he said he loves like a sister? How did his brother die? Would he have died if Melody hadn't left? Did the three of us ever eat pulverised food together, or were they too old when my mother by blood, Saffron, first left me with them? Did we play with one another as children? Was their house with the Nereids warm, and safe?

Was it...my home?

"I trust you'll sleep well tonight," Sholto says as we stop by the steps to Beta barracks, where his quarters are. "You did well today. I'm impressed. I must freshen up, and then visit Fjord to discuss our findings. I'm hoping he's waiting up for me in his office. I'll no doubt call a further meeting in the safe house to discuss this, and you should expect to hear of it soon. *I* expect you to attend it on time, this time..." He waits for a response from me, and somehow, gods know why, seems satisfied by my highly distracted nod. "I would also expect you *not* to tell Fjord of what Zelos disclosed to you of his mother and myself. Not to upset him with it. My father lives to create jealousy and strife in the lives of others, and he unleashes ridicule to do so. Fjord deserves only the truth about Melody, which Zelos did *not* give on the summit today. Do you understand me? I would expect you not to harm Fjord by sharing this with him."

Uh... "I understand."

He holds my gaze for a long, searching moment, and seems satisfied once more by what he finds there...and seriously, only the gods know why. Or maybe the goddesses. Maybe it's *them* working their magic...just like it is throughout the entirety of this tale.

"Goodnight, Skye."

"Night."

I wait for him to crest the barrack stairs, then turn and hurry back the way we came, trundling beneath the stoa outside the Guild's meeting rooms. My steps are lumbering and ungainly with my bow hidden in the folds of my cloak, but I'm still fast, hastening all the way down the walkway, past the bottleutenon's entrance, into the corridor of private offices...right to the Lieutenants' section. My heart has been gaining momentum since we stepped back within Ioxthel's walls, but it's positively berserk by the time I patter over the marble floors to Fjord's office; the pulse in my neck thumping with so much force I actually feel faint. In a daze, I watch my hand raise and just hover there, my knuckles brushing the wooden door.

Do I? Don't I?

"Fjord?" I call quietly, trying for a measured voice in case he's in there but not alone; in there with someone like Sergeant Yasmine Hajjar. "I would like to speak with you, please. It's me, Skye. Your...your friend."

There's immediately movement behind the door. Someone tall and strong, wearing a plain white shirt and an even plainer expression opens up, but it's not Fjord.

Grey eyes look down at me, silent and steady, weathered but somehow so tolerant, and very definitely unsurprised – and I'd wager the excellent listener heard me well before I started speaking.

"Uh..." I hesitate. "Hey, Levi."

He inclines his head in a half-bow. "Good evening, Skye."

"Are you...uh...are you ok?"

"I'm well, thank you. And you?"

I nod a little. "Is Fjord in there?"

"Yes."

"Cool. That's...cool."

There's a pause. "Would you like to speak to him?"

"Yes," I croak, a little mortified by how hoarse I sound. "I would like that."

He steps aside, holding the door open for me. It quickly becomes apparent I've interrupted something...a meeting of the brotherhood. Fjord is settled behind his desk with his next words loitering on parted lips and a roll of parchment held in his hands. There's Jay, the Irving's tutor, sitting on the long, low seat hugging the right side of the room. His hands are hung between his knees, head twisted towards the door but expression still stuck on whatever came before – something of deep thought.

Fjord blinks in surprise at the no-doubt dishevelled sight of me, then seems to remember himself and swiftly stands in greeting, placing the parchment he holds on the desk. From this distance, it looks like a drawing of something. A building?

"Good evening, Skye."

"Hey."

"I trust you're well?"

"I'm..."

Tragically, I don't finish the sentence – can't. I just stand there, thinking of his mother and her lovers. Thinking of the brother from my dreams, and how much I miss him. I watch him shift uneasily at my silence, probably as he debates whether to sit down again or not. His gaze moves over my shoulder, to the door Levi is presently shutting and locking.

"Surely...you didn't come back to the Guild alone?"

I shake my head. "Sholto is on his way. He's freshening up first, then coming to talk to you, but I—" *I came straight here, because...do you know, Fjord? Do you have any suspicions about your mother's history with Sholto? With his father, too? Do you know I miss you dearly? Do you know I don't hate you? Do you know I think of you as a brother, like you think of me as a sister?*

Do you know I love you?

"I trust you're well, Skye?" Fjord enquires again, when yet again I don't finish my sentence, just stand there...tragically. "How was the trip?"

My eyes dart to the others, then back to him. I feel myself nod vigorously, like an imbecile, and it's a completely inappropriate response to his question. My fingers spasm at my sides, summoning their bow from its hiding spot in my cloak...summoning thought.

Do you know?

Do you—

"Do you..." I blurt out, then stop, my eyes wide and frisky heart *wild.* "Uh, do you..."

"Do I?" Fjord's prompts, when yet *again* I don't go on. He's watching me intently, suddenly very still by the desk...in readiness for the rest of my sentence, or for something more?

Something we're both yearning for.

Tell him, my counsel speaks up suddenly, surprising me. *Please, Skye. Forget what Sholto said. Will you tell him about Melody?*

"Do you know that Sholto and his father...they both loved your mother," I get out. "Melody. They loved Melody. They were *in* love with her, and they hate each other for it. Do...you know that?"

Immediately, Fjord seeks solace in the pendant hourglass hiding beneath the "v" of his white shirt. He's not wearing the tan leather breastplate that's so well worn but so well polished, but I see it over the back of his chair. It's meticulously maintained, just like my armour used to be when he'd buff it for me. He'd save the uncrushed grapes for me at breakfast, too, because he's the brother from my dreams, and in return I told him I *hated* him.

"I was aware Sholto was fond of Melody," he responds slowly, voice lacking volume. "But not that he was in love with her. Nor his father, Zelos. I didn't know that."

"Was your mother long-lived?"

"No more so than other Nixen."

"So..."

So that's something, isn't it? We stare at one another, and although we're both thinking the same thing, I'm the one who actually goes on to say it, urged by my counsel and by my heavy, hollow heartbeat that is so desperate *not* to be hollow any longer. And once I start, I don't stop. I just talk, rambling on and on like I do – like I haven't been talking to him for months.

Because I haven't.

"If Sholto was alive and active during the Impurity War, then he's over four hundred years old. I don't even know what Zelos is. That's...a mighty age gap between them and your mum. He has wings, Zelos. Did you know that? He has white wings. Have you ever seen him? He's big and...I think he almost threw me off the hilltop because I touched them. His wings. Very soft. But, he didn't throw me. Obviously. I mean I'm here, aren't I? He loved your mother, Fjord, and he intimated his son might have taken advantage of

Melody, because...I forgot to say, and I should've said it first, but Eros apparently shot Melody with one of his arrows. You know, the kind from legend, where they meddle with someone's heart? Eros. The God of Desire. The Guild's bathroom mirrors are embossed with him around their edges, but I only know that because...I don't know. It's not like I look in them often. Or *that* often. I'm not an egoist, like Fin. Don't care about my freaky eyes and scars."

I jerk my bow from its stash beneath my cloak and pluck the string, ridding it of chalky, hilltop dust. I sneeze when I do, twice, then start speaking faster.

And faster.

"I've read a book on him, too. Eros. Or...I read some of it. You know I struggle with books because of the jumbled words, but I believe it could have happened, even though Sholto told me Zelos lies...and he told me not to tell you. He did, but I am, so that makes me disobedient. I mean, what's new? And it also makes me unsure of him. Sholto. Do you trust him? You seem to. You're like a team, except *you* say you're sorry and he just usually gets cross with me. I get cross back. Although he told me he was fond of me on the way to the temple, because I'm Saffron's daughter and his student, so that's something isn't it? Fond of me. But...anyway he doesn't have a good relationship with his father. They *hate* each other. I told you that, didn't I? It's because of your mother. I know it is. And...we found out who might be the guide to Prometheus's Torch, the thing Ruby is searching for...and it turns out it's *me*, Fjord. *I'm* the guide to the Torch...but Zelos wouldn't tell us where the weapon was actually hidden, because he *hates* Sholto. And your mum...who he loves...she sought Zelos after she left Elysium with me. She sought refuge with him, because we were on our way to The Hesperides. That's apparently why Melody fled the kingdom, in order to search for The Nymphs of the West in Wivern's westernmost mountain foothills, only we didn't reach them. I don't know why. Obviously. Because I have no memory of that time, and I get a fierce headache every time I try to think of it. Like now. I suddenly have a headache thinking of it. But, uh, *anyway...*Zelos seems to. Seems to know of that time. And...of borrowed time. He spoke a lot about borrowed time, which I didn't understand. He said he knew who my father was, too. Talked of impossible things being possible, and told me to remember it and to remind people dear to me when they forget and...uh..."

I stutter to a stop when I realise I'm no longer standing before the door running my mouth, but instead moving back and forth through the room like I might *actually* run; thighs tensed in short strides, sentences and breath shorter still, dusty plait swinging between my shoulders. I'm heading straight for Jay sitting on the low couch hugging the side of the room.

I halt mid-stride, watching his jigging foot slow its tempo and his brows rise in something of great bemusement. It's obvious I must look quite odd...so I spin quickly to face Fjord.

He's staring at me, too.

Like I'm odd.

"I...didn't know if you knew," I hear myself say, very feebly compared to the tirade I've just unleashed on them. Heat rises to my cheeks. "About your mum. I didn't know if you knew. I ran here to talk to you against Sholto's orders. Which makes me disobedient...but what's new?"

"No," Fjord replies hoarsely. "I didn't know this of Melody, Skye. Thank you very much for telling me. For disobeying him."

"Did you get all of it? About what happened with Zelos, too? Quite a bit went down on the hilltop."

Fjord shares the briefest glance with the others. "Perhaps between the three of us, yes, though might I suggest we go over it once more to be sure?" He gestures to the plain chair before his desk and the brass pitcher of water there, or maybe it's wine. "You must be tired, Skye. Would you like to sit down for refreshments before you tell us what happened again?"

I nod.

Don't move.

Fjord hesitates, clearly unsure of that response, and heads around his desk and pours me a cup from the pitcher himself. He hands it to me standing up, eyes searching mine. I take it, *gulp* it down when I realise it's water and not wine and I've been thirsty for the entire day, then hand it back. He pours me another. I gulp that down, too...and four more after it, before wiping the back of my hand over my mouth and nodding vigorously to tell him I'm finished. Fjord takes the cup and sets it on the desk, every movement he makes smooth and inoffensive.

Unlike me.

"I didn't mean to hit you the other week," I reveal loudly. "I mean, I did...but I didn't. Not really. Not at all. Not *you.* I've been meaning to say sorry forever, losing sleep over it. Pretending I haven't, though. I've been pretending I'll—" *never forgive you.*

I stop, looking at him beseechingly just as I did outside the safe house yesterday...as if *he* can tell me whether to bolt, or whether to stay and finish this.

"It's ok, Skye," he offers very carefully. "It's all ok."

I press my lips together. Fiddle with my bow string. Sneeze, twice, then decide I don't want to sit down and start for the room's sidelines to put them all in my sights, only to stop when Fjord's eyes meet mine, right as I pass him by. Brown, or green? I never really know what colour they are, but they're pensive, humble and so *hopeful*, and all I see is faith in them. I see faith and good will and this earnestness that no one else I know seems to bring with them in life.

286

See someone I've known and trusted for five years...and still do. My lips suddenly start trembling for no reason, but for every reason, right?

The liar.

The Lieutenant.

The brother from my *dreams.*

Let's forgive him, Skye, my counsel says gently. *I think it's about time, don't you?*

Fjord looks like he might heed my thoughts. Knowing me, they're definitely written on my face. He moves forwards, seemingly against his better judgement...like he knows he shouldn't, knows he might scare the wild wolf cub away by doing so, but he can't help himself.

"Do you mean it?" I whisper, tears welling in my eyes. "Do you mean you're sorry?"

"Good gods, yes," he says immediately, his expression falling into the deepest kind of sentiment. "I have never regretted something more in my life. I've never felt more guilt or unease, hiding this from you, and I'll never make the same mistake again. I'm so sorry for it, and I *just* want you back on my side. I'm desperately sorry, Skye."

"I don't hate you. I lied, because I'd never, ever hate you. I...I lied about it, and I'm sorry I did."

This, it seems, is what Fjord has been waiting to hear. His torso lifts in a deep inhale, and then he raises his arms, too, the white sleeves of his shirt billowing out like the pillowy sails of the small fishing boats in the harbours, waiting to envelop me.

Hailing me home.

"Come here, please."

My bow and arrows fall to the floor with a dull *thump* as I drop the leather strap of my quiver, then bound the remaining distance between us and barrel into him with force...too much force. I bash my teeth as my face plants itself against the broad, flat side of his shoulder, arms sweeping around his waist. I don't care and Fjord doesn't either, easily stepping into the embrace and matching it. Goddesses, the feel of it...of an hug that's so warm, safe, steady and trusted...I don't know how I went on without it these past weeks. Or I *do*, because I had Tristan to hold me up, but still...

"Nice," Jay murmurs in his low, smooth voice. "That's nice to see."

Isn't it just? My counsel's response is so soft. *Yes. Very good, you two.*

My eyes squeeze shut against a wealth of tears, and Fjord's torso hitches sharply under me, then falls in a rumbling exhale that sounds full of relief.

"Σε συγχωρώ," I sniffle to him, voice muffled by his shirt. I press closer, positively burrowing into it. "I forgive you. I miss you."

"It is I who have missed you, Skye," he mutters hoarsely, bowing his head to rest it beside mine. "You've no idea."

"I do," I mumble. "I've even *more* of an idea, because I missed you more. It just...took me ages to remember it, and then when I did, I didn't show it. But I swear I missed you more. I'd bet with you on it. Silver drachmae, if there're any left from Tristan's heist..."

Fjord lets out a choked laugh. One hand slips to the back of my head, holding me to him. "There's nobody like you. I love you for it."

"I love you too. Were we a family? Back in Elysium?"

He pulls back, hand ushering my gaze up to meet his. He seems to *know* the question is built from a lifetime's worth of desperate longing, and his hazel eyes are warm and so *homely* for it.

I'd follow them anywhere.

I'd follow him anywhere.

"We were a family, and we still are," he vows. "You're family to me, Skye. Never, ever doubt that."

The tears that have been loitering in my eyes for days, or even *weeks,* finally escape their home at this, expression crumpling into something of a child overwhelmed by feeling – but I don't care if I look stupid or young in this moment. Nothing matters but those words, and the sureness behind how they were spoken.

"I tell people you're the older brother from my dreams," I hiccup. "Then I tell them I hope I'm not dreaming, because I want it to be real. I want you to be real. I want a family."

Fjord's own expression falls into something strikingly tender. He leans in and presses a firm, lingering kiss to my temple, then wraps his arms around me again and holds on tightly. "You're not dreaming, μάτια μου. This is real. We're family."

My little eyes.

Sweetheart.

I press closer. "Do you swear? On your life?"

"Yes, I swear. Never doubt i—"

There's a sudden knock on the door.

"Lieutenant Winters?" Sholto calls brusquely. "Is now a good time?"

Fjord tenses under me. "Uh...one second?"

"I need to speak with you, either in your office or mine. Our contact had information on...weaponry...that will interest you."

"Yes, one second," Fjord repeats with a little more emphasis. His arms shift restlessly around me, and he looks down as I pull back. There's something in his eyes he's trying to tell me silently, but I don't know what.

There's a pause from Sholto. "Are the boys in there with you?"

"We're just finishing up."

"So, my office?"

Fjord purses his lips, murmuring very quietly to me, "Don't tell him you've told us about Melody, please."

I nod. "He told me not to, so..."

He lifts a sleeve to hastily wipe my wet cheeks, then calls through the door, "Let's do it here. Silver, please will you...?"

Levi opens up. Sholto doesn't bestow him with a greeting, seemingly expecting to be let in without word or even a bow of pleasantry...even though Levi offers *him* one. He does, however, recognise Jay's presence, "Nice to see you. How's the tutoring going?"

"Well, thanks. Yourself?"

Sholto nods, his brows lifting in surprise when he sees me standing before the desk, scrubbing my face raw of tears. "And hello, Skye. I thought you were retiring?"

"Changed my mind," I say thickly. "I'm not tired. Not even a little bit."

He takes a moment to observe Fjord and I. "The world looks a little righter from where I stand, I hope."

"It feels it, too," Fjord replies quietly. He squeezes my shoulder, then slips away to his desk and starts rolling up the parchment he was discussing with the others before I interrupted them. He uses the scroll to gesture to the chair opposite him, "Have a seat, Sholto. You must be weary."

"I am fatigued, yes."

"How was it?"

"How much has Skye filled you in on?"

"Nothing, really," Fjord says smoothly. "We were discussing other things."

He looks to me, and you'd never know he was fibbing...never know the huge news he's just learnt about the man before him loving his mother.

He now gestures me to the cushioned chair he stands by behind the desk, but I shake my head. "You have it."

"Are you sure?"

"Yes."

He seems reluctant, but he does sit down there. I linger where I am, thoughts and feelings tumbling over themselves, itchy eyes bouncing around the room and snaring on my bow and quiver. I bustle over to pick them up, and then just...stand there. Sniffling. Feeling small and gawky, a bit like the scrawny oranges strewn prematurely on the ground of the garden quads outside – the ones stranded from their fat, juicy twins on the trees, all of them sweltering in the sun. Except, the only reason I'm so hot here in the office is the work of my own emotions, and the weight of too many eyes.

Immediately, I know I should've taken up Fjord's offer of his seat, because although this is a different room, I have the same problem as I did yesterday in the safe house. I'm stuck on where to settle. Where to stand. Where to *be* in this new group of people that are probably, definitely, going to become *my* group of people.

My brethren.

My pack.

I peek at Levi by the door, the loaned Guardian I still need to apologise to for being rude, and who *always* stands where I'd choose to be. By the entrance and exit, ready to respond to trouble. He's examining the room silently, but his eyes linger on me when he sees I'm watching him. His observations will no doubt be far more discerning than mine are of him, but I *think* I'm right when I say I see understanding brightening his dull grey gaze, especially when he shifts slightly to the side, making space by the door.

I debate it. I could well join him there, or I guess I could join Jay sitting on the stretched couch in the room's periphery. There's space there for three – maybe even four – of me.

I hurry over to the Sylvan tutor, sparing him a sharp glance. His hands are flat on the red cushion, fingers and feet back to tapping out one of their lazy, syncopated rhythms. He raises a single, thick, expressive brow when he sees me moving towards him...and the other when I pick up the tiny leather diphros stool by his feet and drag it across the room. I plonk it down ungraciously behind the desk, hide an impressively snotty sniffle, then hide everything but the top of my head when I plop down heavily on the stool myself.

Right next to Fjord.

Right back where I should be.

The Healer

Time is speeding up. It started a few days ago, right when Sholto and I returned from the Temple of Thetis and all was forgiven between Fjord and I. Now it's whizzing by at an unnaturally fast pace; seconds blurring to hours, blurring to days.

Maybe it's a by-product of me coming unstuck, in that I've built up so much momentum, gathered so much hot energy trying for something but getting nowhere, that when I finally burst forth from my little rabbit burrow of ire and rebellion, I burst forth fast and I don't stop...just keep *legging* it through everything I need to do each day, from breakfast to patrol to seeing Tristan, to stealing to sleeping...until the days disappear and *time* disappears, and there are just ten days left in Ioxthel.

Ten days.

Thank the gods I don't know that right now, because I think I'd cry harder than I did the night after Fjord and I reconciled, and that's not an option. I'm in public, in the balmy courtyard of one of Ioxthel's busier taverns getting tippled. We're here finally having those drinks Enye and I scheduled over breakfast all those weeks ago. She's sitting opposite me, with Vishnu her healer boyfriend-but-not next to her. Fin is opposite him, beside me, presently pouring me my *fourth* mug of wine. His gaze meets mine all too briefly when he does, sea-green eyes smoky and mercurial, but his expression is a mystery and has been all evening...and I don't know what to make of it, especially because he stayed over in my room last week for the first time but left before I woke up, just like I did the second time in *his* room. Except this felt different. This felt like a statement, an unspoken rule I should know how to decipher, and so does the way he's pouring my drinks for me tonight and knocking his knees into mine but barely looking at me.

Barely noticing me.

I let out a low breath, fidgeting to ease the sore backs of my legs over the wooden bench we're sitting on – sore because Fjord and I have started sparring again every day and it turns out demigods lose fitness, just like everyone else. I try hard to tune into the table's conversation and not the sound of Fin breathing beside me. Vishnu is saying some very, *very* big words to do with the anatomy of the human body. Or maybe it's the physiology. I don't know, and I feel quite embarrassed about that because Fin and Enye seem to be keeping up ok...him despite not even *looking* at Vishnu.

And I know what you're thinking.

You're thinking that despite my spiel just now, Fin must be looking at me with those mercurial sea-green eyes hooded by mischief and lust, because he's the master of the hoax, and he just poured me a full cup of wine...and because he walked me here, so I thought he was going to walk me home, too.

You're wrong.

So was I.

Fin isn't looking at me, and he's definitely not going to walk me home – and I have no bloody clue how to decipher those statements and rules I just told you about, because he's presently watching another *girl* by the bar. A girl he seems to know really well, and I'm fairly sure he's due to leave with.

She's pretty.

Prettier than me, and her figure looks like I sometimes wish mine did. Not scrawny, like an orange strewn prematurely on the ground from her tree, but a nice plump, juicy fruit who was fed and watered when she was younger, and is probably consequently also well educated, and so can read without the words sliding all over the page.

Healthy.

Enticing.

Not *me.*

I reach for my mug of wine and take a *big,* noisy gulp, forcing myself to focus on Vishnu instead of looking at Fin...instead of noticing how the entire length of our thighs are touching. His is big and solid, and I swear I'm *not* noticing it.

Vishnu, Sergeant Yasmine Hajjar's brother, looks like he was also well fed and watered when he was younger, and now enjoys schmoozing patients – or rather they him – on a daily basis. He has dark hair long enough to pull back into a low leather tie at the nape of his neck, and kind brown eyes. A kind face too, though it's accented by a very stern mouth; probably because it's so well worked, spieling long, funny words that I don't think I'll ever hear again in my life. I have a feeling he's saying them purely for show. There's a neat little moustache wiggling every time he speaks, and I think it must be quite strange to feel when Enye kisses him. Or maybe she's a better kisser than I am, and doesn't just plonk her mouth somewhere near a boy's lips and hope for the best. Maybe the girl by the bar is that, too.

A better kisser than me.

I can't help it. I glance at him, and find him adopting that lazy, arrogant sprawl you only ever really see on men, at least in Ioxthel. He's still watching the bar, fingers toying idly with his own mug of ale, and a suggestive smile tipping up the corner of his lips...and *they're* not stern. They're soft and sensual, and goddesses do I ever *not* like the thought of someone else kissing them, especially when our legs are literally touching right now.

As if he hears my thoughts, Fin glances sideways. He raises a brow, knocks his knee into mine twice, then lifts his mug and finishes it.

"Sorry to cut in," he says in a low voice that doesn't sound sorry in the slightest. "I need to take leave of you all. It's good to meet you, Vishnu. We should do this again sometime. Mind you walk my sister home for me...?" He waits for the healer to nod, and looks to Enye. "Bye, little one. Unfortunately you're paying for the next round."

"Like you'll let me," she throws back, smiling. It's a grateful one, not drenched in hidden frustration like it can be. Fin has been on unusually good behaviour tonight, maybe because he's been making bedroom eyes at the healthy, enticing girl who isn't *me* across the tavern...and that's not fair. "See you later? Tomorrow?"

"Yep, sometime after midday."

He pushes up from the bench and slides several silver coins her way – his money after all for the next round. Then he reaches over the table, and me, to shake Vishnu's hand in farewell. I get a whiff of pepper and musk, and alcohol, before he moves to leave...only to turn back at the last moment, as if he *forgot* me. He nods to the mug of wine clutched white-knuckled in my hand.

"Don't have too many more of those will you? Enye will have to carry you home. You'll do her back in."

"Shut up," I get out, and I'm beyond grateful I sound so unaffected, because inside I feel cold and unsettled and rejected, and really worried that something important and hopeful – to me at least – is ending before it even started.

Worried isn't even a strong enough word. I'm *fearful* that this thing between us is literally not a thing anymore, and that someone who isn't mine and never could be is about to become someone else's. I thought *I* was going to be the one leaving with Fin tonight. I thought *I* was going to be the girl he tipped up his lips suggestively to and hung a strong, lazy arm over the shoulder of to walk home.

I whip my head back to the others and force myself not to look at him as he does something I *don't* want to see by the bar, something

296

that's nowhere near a careless plonk of his lips on hers, ignoring the horrible feeling souring the wine in my belly. In dire need of distraction, I down most of the full mug he poured me, choking on the liquid.

Better that than my emotions.

"He's an idiot, Skye," Enye mutters in a low voice, drawing my attention across the table. She's twisting back from watching the bar, and I can tell she's only just realised why her brother left...why he's been on such good behaviour all evening. "A gods damn idiot. Don't think on it except to know he'll feel terrible tomorrow about leaving you."

I take another huge gulp of wine, trying to stop my expression wringing itself inside out...because I don't think Fin will feel terrible tomorrow at all. The knee he just bumped starts bouncing neurotically to warm itself up in his absence, seeking to take my mind off the brutal, irreversible feeling of total rejection.

I turn to Vishnu, wiping the back of my hand over my mouth. I bet you it's stained as red as Ruby's hands...hands that, let's not forget, the healer is in the habit of tending to as her physician. "So...I was really liking hearing about you, Vishnu. Hearing about your work in the Medical Syndicate? And Alcázar? That's super impressive. Knowing so many proper words and important people...it must be tiring?"

Vishnu's kind expression brightens to something proud and gratified, clearly benefitting from my flattery.

He has no idea I'm using him as a distraction.

Have been all evening.

"Yes, Skye," he replies. "I'm humbled to say I've recently been entrusted the care of the royal family as their lead physician. My duties are, for obvious reasons, concerned particularly with our

Queen. She's a phenomenal woman in need of the highest quality of care, as all her predecessors before her have been."

"Because they're so important as the kingdom's rulers?" Enye asks, looking and sounding intrigued. "Or because they're unwell?"

"Because..." Vishnu stops himself, seemingly facing a dilemma between revealing more of his prowess to us and protecting the confidentiality of his patients. Thankfully the former wins out...and without much of a delay, too. "Because none of us are immune to troubles of mood and mind, even those who live in fortune under the glowing light of fame and prestige."

"Troubles of mood and mind?" Enye frowns in thought. "Do you mean mental health, Vishnu?"

"I might, yes."

He smiles vaguely at her, smoothing a hand over his hair to slick it down. My eyes snare on the little white mark on the inside of his wrist as he does so...a mark that's half hidden by the burgundy healer's shirt he wears. It's quite different to the start of something I spotted on his sister's wrist beneath the Guild's stoa, some weeks ago, but at the same time it looks *similar* in that it's been branded onto Vishnu's skin by a hot poker. My gaze narrows, then darts up to his. Thankfully, he's not watching me watching him, but instead asking if Enye wants another drink. My stomach twists with unease, just like it did when my friend first told me she was dating Yasmine's brother, personal healer to Ruby...

I suddenly wish Fin was still here.

Not for my sake, but for Enye's. I thought she bought me along to this meeting to stop him inappropriately interrogating Vishnu; to dampen the pesky, protective older brother vibe he normally gives off. It usually drives both Enye and I berserk...but tonight I'd have welcomed it, because I have a feeling Fin would be able to see through Vishnu with no problem. He'd be able to safeguard his sister against someone I think might be sketchy.

But that's the problem. Fin hasn't been the protective older brother tonight. He's been very quiet, pouring me drinks, bumping his knee with mine...but mostly staring at the girl by the bar who's prettier than me and he seems to know *well*. Now he's left with her, leaving Enye alone with Vishnu and me behind...rejected.

"Please tell me your history, Vishnu?" I probe suddenly, a little desperately. "Your childhood?"

He seems a little taken aback, but obliges me. "I grew up here in the city with Yasmine and my father. He's a scribe in Alcázar, well renowned for his work on viticulture, hence why Enye and I hit off so well at the start. Her parents, as I'm sure you're aware, own a vineyard beyond Ioxthel's walls. My mother sadly passed away giving birth to me. She was a healer...and I like to think perhaps I do her proud following in her footsteps, living in her good name."

"I'm sure you do, being a physician to The Sabirs. That's very impressive." *Do I do my mother proud? Getting drunk? Being jealous? Running my mouth too often? Losing myself for* months *down a rabbit hole of ire and rebellion?* "What's it like, then? Being their healer in Alcázar? Hard work? Rewarding? I bet they pay well..."

"My experience healing The Sabirs is limited, actually, because I'm fairly new," he admits. "But I suppose I've recently surmised that the hardest scenario of ill health befalls those who live with the curses placed upon them by their heritage...or those who struggle through the aftermath the actions of others have dealt them. No one enjoys being cursed, you see, for there is nothing to be done about it...unless you have a mind of genius, and a knack for playing fate." His lips twitch, as if he wishes to smile but doesn't. "The Sabirs have experienced all types of ill health throughout their years ruling, and

Ruby suffers many troubling symptoms. She is still a phenomenal woman however, perhaps even more so because of that."

"What kind of symptoms?" I press quickly. "Of mood and mind? Mental health?"

"I'm afraid I can't tell you that, Skye. As her physician, I'm interested in improving our queen's life, but not in talking of it. I am a great believer in protecting the dignity of my patients. The dignity of any human."

I find myself fidgeting impatiently at this, warm wine sloshing around in my belly. I can't fault him for saying what he has, but I want to ask him why he chose to disclose *anything* on the matter if he truly lives in the name of confidentiality? I don't say anything, for Enye's sake, even though from the way her eyes slide to mine and linger I wonder if she's thinking the same thing.

We've been doing that a lot tonight, whenever I emerge from my vexed, distracted thoughts on Fin. Locking gazes, finding solidarity in each other's presence, doing what girlfriends do best. I think she's been asking for my silent opinion on Vishnu most of the time, but *this* time I know she's giving me *her* thoughts on him...and thank the gods, given what I've just seen on his wrist, she's saying, "*I know. He's quite proud, which isn't my type. I'm not so sure about him anymore. Not sure if I want to...you know...for the first time.*"

I think it's a very good thing she's reached that conclusion by herself...but inevitably I then think, so *stupidly*, about how if I'd gone home with Fin just now it might've been my fourth time with him. I need to stop talking about him, don't I? It's boring. I sound stuck again, only this time down a new rabbit hole. I need to not be there. Not be stuck. So I think...I just need to stop thinking?

I reach for the brass pitcher of wine and splash the rest of its contents into my mug, then polish that off, not even tasting the warm, spicy alcohol as it slides down. I tell myself very, very firmly not to think about what Fin is doing with someone else right now as it hits the rest of tonight's consumption in my belly, and instead to focus on rearranging my own plans, because obviously they've changed, and obviously I don't want to go back to the Guild. Don't want to be anywhere *near* there.

I think I want, and need, to be with Tristan in the harbours...to tell him how I'm feeling. Just to *tell* him it, and then that be the end of it. I certainly don't want to know why I'm feeling this way, because knowing Tristan he'll know that and readily share it with me – understanding me better than I understand myself. I don't want to know. I just want to see him, tell him, and hug him, and that means heading to the eastern streets over the rooftops when Enye, Vishnu and I finish up here. And, I suddenly realise, that also means I should find Levi and tell him of my change in plans. I'm *sure* he's somewhere nearby, watching over me like Fjord requested, protecting me from Xavier Archer. Remember? The Rogue Guardian and Ruby's new bodyguard who is apparently the worst of the worst, except we still don't know why, and we haven't seen him since the very start of this tale, that morning in Alcázar.

I should tell Levi something else whilst I'm at it, too. Should finally tell him that I'm sorry for that bad day when I called him shy in spite and told him his eyes looked dead, and was just...rude. Not only on that day, because at the start of every single patrol he's met me with one of his quiet greetings, a sincere *Good morning, afternoon* or *evening*, and up until the Temple of Thetis I've ignored him.

That needs to change.

Tonight.

Now.

Sorry

Turns out trying to get yourself onto the rooftops when drunk off maybe an entire brass pitcher of wine isn't easy, even if you're a well-seasoned ghost-stroke-demigod...and especially if you're sore.

In body, and mind.

And heart.

I've just left Enye and Vishnu walking back to the Guild, telling them I'm retracing my steps from patrol earlier because I dropped my dagger. It's a really stupid excuse, but I think Enye was too grateful to notice. She's definitely got cold feet for doing stuff with Vishnu tonight, and somehow needs to tell him that. Having me there would be mighty awkward, and besides, it's not so late she'd insist I walk home with them, and it isn't like I can't take good care of myself.

Or...is it?

I move to standing from rolling myself over the edge of the roof, hurriedly brushing down my knees and straightening my shirt's collar, trying to keep my balance as I do so. I might sway several feet to the side as I do, because goddesses I'm actually very tipsy. I start stuffing the wayward tendrils of my hair back into their braid, fingers fumbling all over the place and snagging in the knots. I'm probably ruining it more, but I want to be at least vaguely presentable for him. I want to show him I'm serious, and sorry.

"Levi?" I whisper-shout, searching the shadows. "Are you up here? Watching over me? Being a Guardian?" There's no response. No sound or sight of him, just the gentle breeze ruining my feeble attempt to patch up my braid, and the unmistakeable smell of ash cooling after a long day in the sun. I wait for a few seconds, still notice nothing, and slowly start stumbling over the rooftop. "I'm on my way to find you. On my way to right wrongs and talk to you, I guess. To ask a question or two. Or three. If you're not busy? If you don't mind... "

There's a soft puff of smoke and minerals from behind me. I turn fast, wobbling on the spot, and then there he is – steady shoulders edging their way through a washing line of fluttering sheets, sections of his white shirt glowing in the sparing moonlight overhead. His entire being is shrouded in mystery and magnetism, or that's what my mind silly off wine thinks. He might look surprised to see me up here, or he might not. Might look concerned, might not. It's difficult to tell with Levi, especially when I'm drunk.

"Hey."

"Good evening, Skye. Is everything ok?"

"Yes," I nod vigorously. "It is. It's just...I don't know if you heard me just then, but I have a question. Or two. Or three. For you?"

He comes to a stop in front of me, waiting for them. I stare up at him, lost in the mystery and magnetism. I start wondering why I've never just *looked* at Levi before without intent to unveil his unwaveringly guarded expression, or back in the early days, to strip down his defences in defence of myself. Why I haven't just regarded him as someone really important, really *dear* to Fjord. Someone with a beating heart, a mind full of thoughts, and a soul fuelled by hope, just like any other human. Someone who is quiet and steady, enigmatic and obviously incredibly loyal – and who is seemingly very selflessly giving their time to watch over me.

"How're you, this evening?" I ask earnestly. "Are you hungry? Happy? Sad? Lonely? Enchanted by the moonlight, like I am? I'm always enchanted by her. *Love* her."

He examines me closely, eyes lingering on the flush in my cheeks. It must be quite obvious if he can see it in that beautiful moonlight, or maybe he's staring at me because I have red wine all over my mouth, in which case my earlier attempts to look presentable are utterly futile. I want to tell him I'm not being friendly just because I'm drunk, but I'm not sure he'd believe me.

"I'm well thank you," he responds seriously, because Levi is never not serious. "How're you?"

My heart feels odd, knowing Fin is with another girl right now, but I'm pleased I've finally looked at you as someone very important to Fjord, and thus by extension...me. "I'm ok," I say with a shrug. "I have another question...the original one. Do you mind if I ask you it?"

"Not in the slightest."

I nod, then out of nowhere stumble a foot or two to the right. Levi shoots forwards, reaching out to mind my balance for me; although thankfully I manage to catch myself before I'm in any danger of falling. Or maybe I don't, actually. Maybe that's him, gripping my shoulders.

Whoopsie.

"You ok?"

"Mhm," I give him a very sheepish grin. "I'm good, thanks. Do you mind if I ask you a question?"

He blinks. "Not...in the slightest."

"Cool."

Seconds pass with me just smiling up at him, like a weirdo, and him clearly waiting for me to speak, before we both realise he's still holding my shoulders.

His hands lift.

The night air feels quite chilly.

"Uh..." I clear my throat. "Is it ok if I stay in the harbours with Tristan tonight? I assume you'll be there if I do, fulfilling Fjord's favour and all, and I wanted to ask you if you'd mind before I just upped and went because...I haven't before. Haven't asked you if it's ok what I do even though you're following me around on *and* off patrol. And I suddenly thought, down in the tavern...that one there...that it's not right for me not to talk to you. I *should* tell you my plans and ask if they're ok with you, because you have to go where I go, fulfilling Fjord's favour and all...and you have a beating heart and a mind full of thought and a soul fuelled by hope that probably...well, it probably hopes not to be here right now, doesn't it? So, this is me doing that. Asking if you'd mind if I go to the harbours tonight to see Tristan? Do you mind?"

"I don't mind if you go there tonight, no."

"You sure?"

"Yes."

I open my mouth to reply, then press it into a line of thought. Am *I* sure he's sure? His expression is sincere, eyes subdued but serious and...that's it. That's all I get from him, because that's all I *ever* get from Levi.

Is it odd I still trust him for it?

Perhaps not, given he's Fjord's Guardian and best friend – which is, if you think about it, another thing that should push my guilt riddled belly and tongue into overdrive. Levi is Fjord's Guardian and *best friend,* and yet he's stuck with me...stuck guarding the girl who's been really rude to him and who, before now, has been ignorant, insolent and ungrateful for the favour he's fulfilling.

I'm ungrateful, aren't I?

Regardless of my scepticism over the threat Xavier poses to me, and therefore the need for Levi to play warden here, that doesn't mean I need to be blind to the time he's putting in. The effort involved in it. The selflessness. Because here I am, tipsy from too much of the wine Fin poured for me, still hot from one too many soft prods down my spine on our walk to the tavern, and then hot in a totally different way thinking on him doing that with another girl *right* *now...*and here Levi is on the rooftops, without food or drink, or friends.

Without protest, too.

I suddenly feel extremely guilty, especially when my focus drifts and I see the skin beneath his eyes is tired, just like it was that day in the alleyway. His entire presence looks so steady and pieced together, well presented in a way that puts me to shame, but at the same time he's so weathered – like he's been beaten, is *still* being beaten, by some relentless, invisible force that only ever leaves a mark on the inside.

On the soul.

I've no idea what it might be, or why I suddenly think I see *sadness* in his gaze. Those grey irises I always tell you are weary, dull and subdued...?

They now look full of sorrow.

Full of grief.

Why do I see that? Because my thoughts are the fumbling yet still profound shade of someone feeling silly from wine? Because I'm looking at him for the first time, as someone with a beating heart and a mind full of thought, and a soul fuelled by hope? Or because the moonlight has finally unveiled something secret of Levi to me? A piece of the puzzle.

I've no idea which it is, or if it matters that I don't, but you should know I really do think I see grief and sorrow in his eyes, and I'm still staring right into them, and he's staring *right* back...wholly untroubled and tolerant of my gawking. He's simply waiting for me to say something further, isn't he? Just like he did on the day of the heist, he seems to *know* what's going on inside and that there's so much left unsaid that's important for me to share.

And in the profound, fumbling way of someone silly off wine, it strikes me that in being quiet all of the time unless requested otherwise, Levi isn't just listening to how others speak. He's listening with all his senses and especially his eyes – deciphering the silent, unique language of others by unearthing their true story. He does it, my tipsy brains likes to imagine, with the unhurried endeavour of someone studying the endless, ever-changing plotline of a book...and I realise I'm *behind,* aren't I? My single drunken realisation tonight about the weary, grieving grey of his gaze is swallowed by the wealth of knowledge he must have gathered on my story, because I'm a *loud* narrator, and he's been reading me since we first met.

I just know he has.

"Did you hear what Vishnu was saying about Ruby's family?" I ask, my stupid brain selecting something important to blurt out, and yet not the most important, the most pressing, thing I need to say to him.

Which is, simply, *I'm sorry.*

Levi hesitates. "I heard some of your conversations, yes, but not intentionally. I feel it would be remiss of me not to listen in sometimes, to check in."

"Yeah. I understand." *He thinks I'm accusing him of eavesdropping, doesn't he? Only I'm not.* "It's just...Vishnu mentioned things about The Sabirs' medical history that I think are important, and I'm thinking of telling Fjord about them. I just wondered what your thoughts were? If you thought anything of it? If you were checking in when we were discussing it, that is? About mood and mind and mental health?"

"I think it's definitely wise for you to talk to Fjord. He'll be interested to hear of it."

"Yeah?"

Levi nods.

I nod, too, and then frown. "And...you probably won't have seen it from the rooftops, but I think I saw a marking on Vishnu's wrist like his sister, Yasmine, has. Only this one looked a bit different...so I'm a bit worried he's also part of Ruby's Council, and I just let Enye walk home with him by herself. I suddenly think that's bad of me? That I wasn't thinking straight. Still am not. I had quite a lot of wine, you see, because Fin poured me too much and then *left* with someone else..." I heave a tight breath, looking up at him with woeful eyes. Getting drunk tonight was apparently a bad decision, because it's made me incredibly morose.

Quite weirdly infatuated with staring at him, too.

He's really handsome.

"I'm a bit worried, Levi," I repeat. "For Enye. She's going home with Vishnu. Or not really, because he's not her type, but he's still walking her home by herself. Anything could happen."

He seems to understand I'm asking him, without asking, for advice. "Should we perhaps take a detour to the Guild over the rooftops and mind her steps back home?"

My brows lift. "That sounds good, but also like it should've been obvious for me to think of?"

Levi doesn't pass comment on this, which is very kind of him. "Could Tristan and the ruffians also be of help to you? Might they watch over Enye for the next few weeks, especially if she's with the healer, just as they've been doing for you?"

"You mean...they follow her?"

"Or him, yes. To make sure she doesn't befall harm, and to address your suspicions that the healer might be a member of Ruby's Council."

"Yeah," I say, nodding slowly. "They could...and would, if I asked Tristan. That's a good solution. The best solution. The ruffians are the best. They'd keep her safe. So...I'll tell Tristan when I see him, and he'll immediately send Akira, bless her. She still loves that dagger you gave her on the day of the heist, remember? Right after you helped with the silver and I didn't thank you..." I hum sheepishly, shifting from foot to foot. I hope I stay in one place, but it's difficult to know – my senses are way off. "And then I think I'll tell Fjord about Ruby's medical history tomorrow, and Vishnu's mark. Or you should tell him if you see him before me, but we'll probably see him together won't we, if you're spending the night in the harbours with Tristan and I. You sure you don't mind going there, Levi?"

"I don't mind, Skye."

We make haste over the rooftops, easily finding Enye and Vishnu walking home. I'm right in that she does have cold feet, and they say goodbye just outside of the Guild's gates with only a brief kiss. As soon as she's within the premises and the healer is more than a few streets away, I feel much better. I turn to leave, wobbling, and find Levi right there – close enough to touch. I think he's quietly minding my balance for me again, which is really nice.

We don't speak as we start for the harbours, but my mind is whipping up a storm, thinking about all I still need to say to him. I end up loitering on the edge of several rooftops, each time waiting to leap over the streets in the hope he'll jog *beside* me instead of behind, like he usually does. And Levi, the guarded Guardian who listens with his eyes, quickly understands my intentions and joins me. He obliges my hope, because he obliges everyone, doesn't he? He does their bidding. And that makes me think, what does he hope for? In his soul? What does he want for? Does he ever get to pursue it?

Why is he sad?

Tristan and his ruffians are gathered in the forgotten harbour when we reach the eastern streets, loitering in the same bay of broken crab shells, upturned boats and life-giving memories that I first told my friend about *everything* changing. Tiberius, his black cat, is stalking languidly over their sprawled legs, pestering little Akira most of all. There are too many dice games simultaneously at play – and consequently a *lot* of blasphemous language. Tristan glances up when Levi and I crest the roof's edge, light from a squat, fiery iron barrel giving his features a scrumptious orange glow. He's strumming a soulful tune on someone's broken and no doubt stolen bouzouki, watching his people do their thing, but he stops and raises a hand when he sees me, dimples peeking out.

Levi is beside me, examining the twisting, moonlit streets below and the glistening ocean beyond, but I know he knows I'm watching him. He spares me a glance when the seconds pass by and it becomes clear I'm not leaving imminently, because I have more I need to say...and this time I'm *going* to say it.

"You don't have to stay up here and keep watch," I offer. "You could be with the ruffians if you wanted? You could rest with us, sleep with us? We wouldn't mind. I'll find you an upturned boat, one where you won't be disturbed, and one that doesn't smell of fish. You can have my blanket, too. Tristan keeps it separate for me so Tiberius doesn't do his business on it. So, it's clean...or as clean as me."

Levi is very clearly *not* enamoured by the offer, but is trying hard to figure out how to refuse it without hurting my feelings. Or I think that's what's going on inside his mind. Difficult to tell with him, especially when I'm drunk.

"Thank you, Skye," he settles on, "but the rooftops offer a good vantage point, as I'm sure you know. I'll rest easier up here."

"Are you sure?"

"Yes."

I glance down to the courtyard. Tristan has started strumming his bouzouki idly again, feigning patience. I wave to him, signalling I *see* that he's acting up with that slow, monotonous strum, and stalling myself. "I guess I'll just find you in the morning then, when I'm leaving?"

"I'll be here."

"Yeah. I...don't doubt it. At all. Not one bit." *Stop stalling!* "I have one more thing to say before I go, Levi. Before I leave you in peace. It's not a question, which...I hope is ok? And I should've said it to you weeks ago, but I'm going to do it now, because I heard somewhere that sincerely spoken sentiment is always better than nothing, even if you sound stupid saying it." *Heard from my counsel, that is.* "So, I'm going to do it. I'm going to say I'm so sorry for calling you shy last month, and for being really rude to you for...ever. Since we've known one another. This has all been a low point for Skye. For me. I'm really sorry for it. Sorrier than sorry herself, in fact."

I offer him a rueful smile, totally deserting my intentions to jump from the roof's edge. My palms shift restlessly over the hilts of my daggers as I stop in front of him, forcing myself to finally do the important thing.

The right thing.

"I'm sorry," I repeat seriously. "It was spiteful of me to call you shy, and my better judgement told me not to say it, not to say anything because I was angry, but I still did. I have no excuse. It was just bad, and a bad day, and I'm really sorry for it. And...I know I've been insolent lately, working through stuff. You'll have witnessed that a lot patrolling with me, watching over me, but I regret that day most of all, punching Fjord and saying you were shy and that your eyes looked...dead. They don't, and there's nothing wrong with being quiet, but there was *everything* wrong with how I said what I did, like it's a *bad* thing. Like it's dishonourable not to speak much. It isn't. I should never have suggested it was. I've wanted to apologise to you for a while. Longer than you might think. Definitely longer than that. Even when we stole the wagon of silver and I wasn't speaking to Fjord

I was feeling really bad, and then *you* apologised which was just...so wrong. Even on that bad day, right after I said it, I was feeling guilty. I bet you didn't know that, although none of this is important, least of all that last point...about me being pleased you didn't know that." *Don't say it, Skye. Don't say...* "It's not like I'm trying to *best* you in hiding my feelings, is it? No. I'm really not, Levi. My counsel would sigh if she knew I'd even thought that whilst apologising, because it sort of detracts from the sincerely spoken sentiment, doesn't it? Not that I *have* thought about it...trying to best you in hiding my feelings. I haven't. Not really. It would be a pointless endeavour anyway. I'm an open book, or at least a book you've read quite a lot of, and you're not...mostly because I'm terrible at reading." *Stop talking!* "Uh, so what's important is giving the apology, and that you know I'm really sorry. I'm really hoping you'll forgive me. The moon showed me you for the first time tonight, and I suddenly realised, really belatedly, that you're very important to Fjord which means you're very important to me, too. So...I think I need you to forgive me? Please? I am very sorry. You're important to Fjord, so you're important to me. I'm really sorry."

Goddesses. How tiresome was that? I force myself to focus on the hot flesh of my fidgeting palms to stop from running my mouth more. Levi is quiet for such a long time I'm really not sure if he's going to respond, but then he does and it's totally in my favour...and we should both thank the moon for that.

Or maybe just him.

"There was never much to pardon you of, Skye, but thank you for your sincerely spoken sentiments. You're entirely forgiven."

My eyes widen. "Really?"

"Yes."

"Truly? Entirely?"

"Yes. I see that you're experiencing an exceptional number of shocks in your life. There's much being asked of you in all of this, and it's difficult for you to handle...as it would be for anyone. I understand that."

"I don't," I say quickly, and very lamely. Then I sigh loudly, "I don't understand a thing, Levi, but that's not a good enough excuse for being rude to you. Having a bad day doesn't give someone the right to be spiteful even though I acted like it did. I'm not good like that. I just run my mouth, especially when I'm tipsy. Not that I was tipsy on that bad day, and I swear I'm not just being friendly and apologising to you now because I'm drunk. I'm not even drunk..." *Lie.* "I've been meaning to say it for weeks...and I knew if I told you that, if I told you I wasn't doing this just because I'm drunk you wouldn't believe me...but I've gone and said it now haven't I? But I swear this is a long time coming, and not just happening because I had too much wine. I swear on my life. I've lost sleep over it for about thirteen nights in total, which is one for each of the gods and goddesses, then one for you. The most important..."

"Skye..." Levi's reserved expression softens into something I *want* to say looks quite endeared, and maybe a little exasperated. "I would take your word without your life, and I would ask you not to trouble yourself further on this. Not to lose sleep. You're entirely forgiven."

"Yeah, but I need you to know it's not because of the wine."

"I believe you. Please don't trouble yourself further. Besides, I would still apologise myself for what happened in the Medical Syndicate between us. That was a wrongdoing of a far greater magnitude than a simple disparaging remark, and I think if anything, we're even."

"Oh," I hum. "Those waves met shores long ago, Levi, so if *you* don't mention that, then I won't mention *this.* Calling you shy. Being sorry for it. Ok? Let's just say all the waves met the shores, and all is forgiven. Because it is? We're good?"

I offer him a hopeful smile, pleased when he gives me a single nod in return. I then have to bite my tongue hard to keep from blurting out the questions positively burning it's tip. *Why is it you're so quiet? Why is your voice always rough and rusty, like you're unwell? Why are you so guarded? Why are you sad? What's the story left untold?*

I think I almost draw blood trying to hold them in, and I make no pretence in trying to unearth their answers in observing him. I don't get far, and that slightly soft, endeared expression is gone again, but I suppose now I've seen it I can't unsee it. Levi really does look tired, as if he's weighed down by something relentless – like his soul is weary. How old is he? There's something to his face that makes me think he's outgrown his youth, surpassed the early austerity of sprightly adulthood...so he's years older than me, but not *so* much. Under twenty-five, definitely, and the more I stare at him, the more I see good nature in his features. They're modest and regular and forgiving, even if they are blanketed of sentiment. I see someone very enigmatic...mysterious and *impossible* to read, but still straightforward? Someone I know where I stand with, and that's somewhere *safe,* isn't it?

Safe and respected.

And...he's really very handsome. Dark hair, those freckles under his eyes, features modest and regular and forgiving, much softer than Fjord's beautifully sharp bone structure and jawline...and I know I've already told you all that, literally just now, but I suppose I'll say it again. He's very handsome, especially with his white shirt falling in a deep "v" like that and his cheeks flushed pink from the night air. Or is he embarrassed by us talking of his quietness again? Somehow that's just as lovely as the ruffled hair Fjord sometimes subjects him to...

The bouzouki strumming in the courtyard below suddenly increases in tempo, like Tristan is finishing off his song with a flourish. Only he's not. He just keeps going and going and *going*. It's a sign he's getting really impatient, but he just looks like a madman, strumming like that. He's so stupid. In the best way. I'm going to miss him more than everything, more than *everything*, if we leave Ioxthel.

If.

When...

I have to hide a very sudden, very sad expression. "I should go, Levi. Tristan will bother us if I don't go to him soon. Or *you*, rather. He'll just bother you...though you should know you're growing on him, and he likes that you're watching over me. Give it a month and he might even serenade you with that bouzouki. He likes doing that, especially to guys. He's looking for a sweetheart, too...not that that would be you. Do you like guys or girls, Levi? Or both? Or neither? Don't answer that. Not my business." *Will we be here for a month longer? I hope you say girls.* "I'll see you in the morning, but if you need something in the meantime just pop down. Except...mind the crab shells if you do. They can be quite sharp even with plimsolls or sandals on, and sometimes, mostly when I'm silly from wine, I worry they're not empty and I'll be nibbled on in my sleep. Death by tiny crustaceous monsters..."

Death by tiny crustaceous monsters. Great goddesses, who says something like that? Seriously? No one does. Not even when they're drunk, or the main protagonist in a book.

Levi doesn't immediately respond to it, and even though I don't blame him at *all* for that, the sight of him standing there silently and patiently, without food or friend or protest, tugs at my heart. I can't unsee it, now. He's submerged in something – something of sorrow and grief, and of a story left untold that I know you and I both wish to hear, and to be there to witness unfold.

"I'm pleased you forgive me, Levi," I say, trying for a quieter, earnest voice...one where I don't slur my words. "Very pleased the waves met shores. I'll bid you fare thee well, now."

"Goodnight, Skye."

"I hope you sleep well up here, with the moon. She's good company, even if she does gossip. Or...maybe I should say I hope you *Guardian* well? Ha. Don't let the crabs eat me, will you? I either want to die saving someone's life in battle or saving the world, or not at all...you know?"

Honestly? Do *you* know that I don't think I've *ever* sounded so foolish in front of someone as I'm starting to sound in front of Levi Silverstone...maybe because I'm speaking for the two of us. I hum sheepishly again, but if he thinks the remarks are even a little bit weird he doesn't let on. He just bows his head slightly, offering me a silent, gentle *fare thee well,* and maybe even an assurance of my safety from crabs. The gesture is every bit as gracious as those which Fjord usually gives, even if on Levi it looks less tamed; rough round the edges just like his voice. Was I blind to the courtesy before? Or did I just not hang around long enough for it? Or did I not *deserve* it?

Stupid.

I'm stupid.

But...growing less so.

Jealousy

There's someone walking through the gardens behind me, just shy of my right shoulder. I can hear him rifling through the pages of the book the two of us just picked out from the Guild's shoddy library, but every so often he stops doing that, reaches out, and tugs gently on the end of the braid swinging like a pendulum between my shoulders.

I won't lie to you.

I like that he's doing that, because it means he's probably watching it sway...and tonight, in the starlight? I'd say my hair is more silver than the dull, mousy colour of dust it can sometimes favour, which maybe, *maybe* makes me a tiny bit enchanting? Just like the full moon blessing us from the heavens above.

I'm pleased about it. Pleased it looks silver, because I want to be enchanting. I want to be someone *someone* can't look away from, and not simply because I have freaky amber eyes and scars like lightning sprawled over the left side of my face, neck and torso...scars that yesterday I could've sworn spread a bit after my shower, like a river tributary finding its way through new territory, or water dribbling through pebbles. Some of the marks are now wrapping around the side of my hip, down to my left buttock...something I don't know if *someone* will notice.

I hope he doesn't.

Or...I hope he does?

I think I hope he *does*, because it's not like I care if he sees it tonight and thinks, *"That's different to the last girl I was with...the pretty, plump one from the tavern who's a great reader and an even better kisser."*

No.

I don't care if he thinks that at all, or that he deserted us at drinks the other night for her. It doesn't matter. Never mattered before, even when I saw him dancing with a *guy*...so why am I unbelievably jittery tonight? Why am I *nervous* walking in front of him, thinking I must look ungainly or scrawny or gawky? Why do I jerk, hyper sensitive to his touch, when he next pulls on my braid, his knuckles brushing my spine and drifting lower to the small of my back...where he prods me gently.

I don't know.

I tell myself it doesn't matter.

"I have two questions, Skye," Fin murmurs from somewhere by my head, his tone so *light* like he's absolutely worlds away from me, somewhere cool and collected and unflustered.

My voice sounds weird. Squeaky. Like a mouse caught between a rock and a hard place, or a star struck by...a brighter star. "Two questions?"

"Yes, if you'll permit me to ask you them?"

"If I'll permit you..." I throw him a funny, flushed look over my shoulder. "Go on, Fin. I do permit you. What're the questions?"

"The first relates to the news that reached me of you and Fjord being back on good terms. I saw you sparring the other day, and was pleased to see you both looked...friendly. How did the two of you reconcile?"

Had to be a difficult question first, didn't it? "He said he was sorry."

"For what?"

"Is that your second question?"

"Mm, no."

"So..."

Two warm, gentle hands land on my waist, steering me left down one of the quad's walkways – away from the pair of guilders patrolling the interior of the gardens. "So let's just say if you're quick with me, Skye, I'll be quick back. You sure you want that?"

I feel my spine tingle, the weight of his hands doing funny things to my lower tummy...and the realisation that we're heading deeper into the gardens doing funny things to my heart. "Fjord said sorry for lying to me about something," I supply. "But he didn't mean to lie, not really, and I believe his apology. So...everything is forgiven."

"Everything is forgiven?"

"Yeah."

"Good to hear Fjord's sins go unpunished by you. That makes me hopeful for myself. Stop here, will you? I think this section looks promising."

"Promising for what?"

"Examining the statues."

He moves in close behind me, until his front *just* brushes my back. I can feel him breathing, feel his steady heart heightening those tingles down my spine, until I'm almost quivering with excitement. One of his hands slip from my waist to my stomach, lying flat there, and I thank *all* the goddesses I don't jerk at the touch.

"Looks a bit of a sorry chap, doesn't he?"

"Very downbeat."

I think he's talking about the statue of Poseidon we're standing a few metres in front of. The God of Seas, Storms and Quakes is wearing a toga tied over one shoulder and resting his three pronged trident staff against the other, and his expression is especially stern and morose...but I only know this because I've seen him before. I'm not examining the statue right now, or the way the vines running wild and free through the scraggly gardens have climbed the hefty plinth to tickle Poseidon's bare, pearly feet. From the way Fin's hand is starting to move, I doubt he's giving it his full attention, either.

I hold my breath as he rubs my belly a few times, petting it. "Feels like you had a nice dinner tonight, Skye, but it would've been nice if you didn't insist on playing hard to get with my sister by *refusing* to allow me to sit with you in the mess. It hurt my feelings."

"I wasn't playing hard to get."

"No?"

"Nope."

"How do you figure that?"

"I'm...not to be got."

"Not to be got?"

Gods. That sounded so stupid. "Yeah. Not to be got."

"Hm. Interesting. That sort of brings me onto my next question."

"The second one?"

"Yes," Fin's tone turns even more playful. "The boy who'd like to think he *got* Enye...her temporary suitor. What did you think of him?"

I don't trust him, being Yasmine's brother and tending to Ruby Sabir. "Vishnu seems nice, I guess. Smart, and he obviously loves his job. He didn't stop talking about it, did he? Using lots of big words that I didn't understand, which was embarrassing. Sometimes I think I'm stupid, because..." *I can't read well, or tie my shoelaces. Not like that girl you left with the other night can.* "Because of things. But did you? Understand them? The big words?"

Fin shifts behind me, moving in closer. Warm breath brushes my ear, and I just *know* he's looking down in front of us, watching his hand. "Not all of them, no. Don't be embarrassed, Skye."

"I'm not embarrassed."

"You just told me you were?"

You're so close I'm not thinking straight. "Did I?"

"Yes."

He leans over my shoulder even further, humming a little, and then those idle fingers pinch the folds of my shirt, untucking it. Deftly he slides his hand underneath, and this time I do jump when our skin touches. Flush. Quiver. And Fin is still worlds away, somewhere cool and unflustered that must be *alive* with fellow hoodwinkers.

"Want to know what *I* thought of Vishnu?" he asks, dropping his chin to the top of my head. "I think Enye needs to find a new boyfriend. He was far too smooth. I don't trust a guy who pretends his intentions are pure, talks big words but plays himself down so much, especially when he's wooing my sister."

I let slip a breathy laugh. "Wooing?"

"Yes. It's when you try to impress someone before you *got* them. When you do foolish things, and think them, too."

"I know what wooing means, Fin, but who even uses that word these days?"

"I do, and I imagine Eros does, too. What's wrong with it?"

"It's just...a weird word."

"Is it?"

"Yes."

"Is it?"

"Yes..."

His hand is on the move again, sliding slowly from side to side in tiny movements, then venturing high. I stop breathing. I'm not wearing anything under this shirt - no breastwrap - and from the way Fin stills behind me, I can tell he figures that out *very* quickly. He lets out a low noise, his chin dropping from my head to my shoulder. His lips press to my cheek in a surprisingly sweet, chaste kiss.

"Have a suggestion," he murmurs.

"Yes?"

"Want to read our new book here?"

"Uh..."

That is not what I expected him to say, and nor is what he does next what I expect him to do, because we start going *backwards...*or so I think, at first. Should know better really in the company of the master of the hoax...but that's what being hoodwinked does to you.

You forget things.

Important things.

The book replaces his head by mine, pages stirring my hair and eyelashes as he lets it fall open. I feel myself blink rapidly, letting out a funny laugh. "You mean literally read it *here,* Fin?"

"Why not? Poseidon looks like he could use a pick me up...and it's sort of about him." He flips through a few pages with his thumb, the hand on my stomach starting to smooth over my skin again, modest and gentle. "I have one request of you though, if you will?"

"What is it?"

"I need you to listen."

"Of course I'll listen."

"I expect you'll try. But if you *don't* manage to, by some twist of fate or hand, I'm going to find a few inventive ways to remind you of the virtues of mental rigour. Do you think that's fair?"

"I think *inventive* is quite a vague word, and you wouldn't agree if the tables were turned."

"Wrong, actually. I'd say yes to anything you wanted to do."

"I'm dubious."

"Shouldn't be."

Really? I bite my lip, trying to think on it...and not, as I should be, thinking on how utterly *stupid* I am to let this happen when a few weeks ago he left me hanging in the tavern for another girl.

Right in front of my eyes.

"Ok," I sigh. "Read the book. What's it on?"

"I'll let you tell me that in a few minutes. It'll be a test on how well you're listening. Yes?"

Goddesses help me. "Yes."

He starts reading. Immediately I'm lulled into something exquisite listening to his low voice, my pulse thrumming steadily but every so often putting on a burst of speed, excited for what's on its way. We've done this three times now, and I'm lying to myself if I say the feelings swelling in me don't have *layers* to them. Layers of fondness and friendship and something words don't do justice to.

I'm enchanted by Fin.

I was the first time I saw him on Enye's thirteenth birthday, even though I know I wasn't to him. I was too young. But I hope I'm somewhat enchanting to him now. Hope his excitement has layers to it too, instead of being just physical. Just fun. Because I fear it *is* just those things for him – and the way he left with that girl in the tavern, almost *forgot* to say goodbye to me, only confirms that fear.

Thankfully, or maybe not, I stop thinking completely as he starts driving me to distraction, his hand rubbing my full belly a few times before edging higher. His palm is so warm, dry, gentle...and now it's so high the tops of his knuckles are brushing much softer flesh. I stop breathing as he turns over the page with his other hand, jostling me ever so slightly. His touch lingers innocently where it is before circling back down my sides. He does it four times, and on the fifth I jump when he hits the last of my ribs and presses in, tickling me.

"My bad," he says huskily. "Hit a sweet spot."

I swallow tightly, urging a retort to the tip of my tongue but nothing comes, and every wish for it is lost to the night breeze when he starts up again, voice a soft murmur, the tips of his fingers replacing his palm as they drift to my belly again, tap the fullness there and then start memorising higher territory...and higher still. My breath hitches sharply, because this time he's not idle, or innocent, there.

"Fin..."

"Mm?"

"We're in public."

He drops his head beside mine, voice thoughtful. "Wouldn't call this public, Skye, and you're not listening very well. This is my first inventive way to remind you to work on your mental stamina."

I jerk a little at his fingertips' next gentle tug, and mean to say his name in protest...but it doesn't come out that way. It comes out breathy and lost. Fin shifts restlessly behind me. There's a soft *thud* as he closes the book with one hand.

"Don't think I'll be reading any more of that. Turn around, will you?"

Heart jumping, I do, trying to fix an easy expression on my face. I can tell my amber eyes are bright and glazed with excitement; and Fin's are mercurial, sea-green, smouldering. He holds the book out for me to take, and as *soon* as I do he leans down, picks me up by the backs of my thighs and sets me down on the plinth of Poseidon's statue. He settles between my legs, hands sliding to hook behind my knees, tickling me again...and I'm thinking he did this *fast,* just like he promised.

"Didn't know it was possible for someone to fit so perfectly into my hands," he says, pressing a soft kiss to my cheek, "until I met you."

"Ugh. Swe—"

"I know you're sweet," he interrupts, moving to kiss my other cheek. His hands search for mine without looking, taking the book and setting it somewhere on the plinth beside us. "Too sweet for me."

"I'm not sweet. I'm..."

What even am I? Stupid for letting this happen? Lost in your charm, snared like a doe in the light of a huntsman's lantern?

"Feisty?" he provides.

"Yes. That. I'm feisty."

"Trouble?"

"That, too."

I feel him grin against my ear. "And tell me, do I feel as perfect to you as you do me? Do I feel unique?"

"It's difficult to know," I say, shivering. "This is my first time having someone in my hands."

Fin stills. "The first?"

"Yeah..."

My cheeks catch fire as he pulls back sharply. The look in his eyes tells me he's surprised, a little worried, and I suddenly think it was a really really bad idea, sharing that. "Why didn't you tell me, Skye?! If I'd realised...and I didn't realise, that night..." He trails off with a frown. "Wait, I'm your first and only, right? Since we started?"

Gods, what do I even say to that? What's the right answer? The *cool* answer...because what I just told him was *not* cool, was it?

Lying isn't coo—

"No," I fib, before my counsel can finish her sentence.

Fin blinks again. "No? I'm not your only? There...have been others? Since this started?"

I nod, trying to fix a blank expression on my face...and I think he's trying to do that, too. The hand at nape of my neck shifts restlessly and then lifts, only to return immediately...and then Fin pulls me to him, his mouth landing on mine without reserve. Words flee me as he immediately forces my lips open and inhales deeply.

Goddesses.

The feel of him against me is swiftly growing so pleasantly familiar. The heat, the firmness, the faint scent of pepper and sweat that's *all* Fin...I think I'm losing my mind.

My hands tighten, gripping him and pulling his head down. He doesn't resist, and I lose even more breath at the first wet touch of his tongue against mine. I wriggle impatiently, bringing us together and eliciting a low grunt from him. The sound seems to be as involuntary as the hectic rhythm my heart is starting up, and then sense flees me. Just...vanishes. I suddenly have the ingenious idea of doing that again – of moving my lower body with his to further this, even though we're hidden but not *that* hidden, and the guards are due another walk through of this section soon. My hands grip his neck more firmly, lifting myself a little. Fin's mouth toughens against mine, the hand behind my knee pulling me in. Seconds turn to minutes, and we're both breathing heavily. I'm burning, shaking, and he's so tense, so expert...until he lets up. Stops kissing me, stops moving entirely, and I *feel* him start to smile against my lips – the act slow, sly, humoured.

Then he bites me.

Hard.

The noise I make is more than breath, rising in pitch. Something surprised, excited, worried. I break away with difficulty, one hand moving to his shoulder and flattening as if to push him away, only for some reason it doesn't do that. It just fists into the fabric of his shirt, pulling him *closer.*

Sense, ruined.

Vanished.

He drops his forehead to mine, his exhales fast but not nearly as desperate, as lost, as mine. "You ok, Skye? Need to slow things down? Take a breather? Too much trouble for you?"

"No," I gasp, wetting my sore lip. "I just...don't want someone to see or hear us."

"They won't."

"They might!"

His temple rolls over mine as he tilts his head to the side. The hand behind my knee carefully lowers it, then moves to his shoulder, weaving our fingers together and squeezing. "Have another question for you."

How do you even think of them right now?! "Ok..."

"Is there someone in particular you wouldn't want to see us? That you'd want to hide this from and keep this behind closed doors for? Your second?"

"What...do you mean?"

"I mean this is chill between us, but if it was becoming so—"

"You mean *you* have someone you want to hide this from, don't you?" I interrupt, pulling away from him sharply. I hit the back of my head on Poseidon's gargantuan kneecap in the process, but don't even notice. "That girl from the tavern? Yeah, I imagine you wouldn't want *her* to see us now, Fin. Totally imagine that."

His eyes snap open, brows rising high. "We were talking of you actually, but is that jealousy I hear in your voice?"

"No! I'm not jealous. I don't care who else you're with." *Stop there. That sounded good. Convincing.* "I don't, because I'm not jealous. Not even sort of. But...but it would make me think...it *does* make me think..." *Who's better? Who do you like more? Will you stop this with me for someone else? Is this the glimpse of an ending before it even started?* "Uh...it just makes me think."

"It makes you think?"

I'm suddenly so hot I'm sweating. I fidget in his hold, then quickly try to divert the focus off me. "What about you? Do you ever get jealous?"

"Do I need to be jealous?"

"What do you mean?"

"I mean, do you have another suitor, Skye? Someone I need to worry about? Your second, maybe? Third?"

"Uh..."

The hue of Fin's eyes clouds. He presses me more firmly into the statue, puts both hands on the plinth beside my legs and leans in. The move is slow and deliberate, and would be intimidating on someone I knew less. Or, to be honest with you, I'm a little intimated right now.

"*Uh...*is a very interesting response," he says, voice low. "Perhaps one that should be replaced by *Fjord* now the two of you have made up?"

My expression twists itself into something of utter revulsion. "Urgh. *No,* Fin. You serious?"

His jaw tightens, eyes bouncing between mine with shameless scrutiny...and gods, he *is.*

He is serious.

I shift restlessly. My sense is no longer quite so lost to his guile at the thought of... "*Not* Fjord, Fin. He's honestly and *literally* like a brother to me. Can you never imply that ever again, please?"

"But you *do* have someone else?"

No, I don't. There's genuinely nobody...but you *do, so I'm going to pretend like I might.* "Would you be jealous if I did? Worried?"

"Maybe," he mutters, and then grins. It's playful with a tough edge, just like the hue of his eyes and his voice. "Know why, Skye? Because it would make me *think.*"

I stare at him.

He stares back.

Something tense settles between us, and it's not the zesty language of lust. We're getting nowhere in this interrogation, because we're not trying to? I mean, what's the *point* of this? Why are we talking about this? And why is there an edge to him, suddenly? I go to hop down from the statue's plinth, frustrated and flustered and immediately feeling the need for space, but a gentle hand at the base of my neck stops me.

"Where you going, trouble?"

"To...read the book."

Fin examines me closely, unfooled – because he knows I struggle with reading – then picks the tome up from where he set it down, *right* beside me. "It's here. You don't need to go anywhere to read it...especially because I'm starting to think you have experience in the matters it deals with."

"Matters?"

"Yes. Since you failed your earlier test, it's clear you weren't listening. I'll reiterate for you. The book is all about Thetis, the sea nymph who doused her son in the River Styx to bless him with invulnerability, and who was courted by two suitors. Two *gods*, in fact. Poseidon and Zeus."

Shock and suspicion riot through me. No one in the Guild besides Fjord knows Sholto and I visited Thetis's ruined temple the other day to see Zelos...but this *can't* be a coincidence, can it?

"Why did you choose that book, Fin?" I ask carefully.

He shrugs. "I've no idea. It felt slightly warmer than the others around it in the library, and it fit perfectly in my palms...a bit like you do when you're not trying to run away from me."

"Sw—"

"It's not sweet talk," Fin interrupts, tone easy...but with that damn edge. "Never is, Skye. Upon further thought, I *first* picked this book up because it felt right...but I *chose* it for us because Enye and I went out for drinks with The Queen's new bodyguard the other evening. He spoke of Thetis, then. Mentioned he knew two people ensnared in a love triangle just like she was...and that brings me *right* back to what we were talking about."

The pit of my gut twists with unease. "Drinks? With The Queen's new bodyguard? With...Xavier Archer?"

"Yep, that's him."

"You've met Xavier?"

"I've met him twice, now. First time he talked of Thetis, second time he told us to expect big happenings for the Guild soon. Told me to expect duty away from home in Wivern. He's interesting, impressive...sexy."

"Sexy?"

"Bit like that sound you made earlier, and your new patrol partner."

My eyes widen. "I don't know...what you mean," I say, very belatedly and *very* awkwardly.

Fin hums darkly. "There we have it, Skye. The other suitor. Your second."

Oh, gods. "Levi isn't my other suitor or my second, Fin! Don't go round saying that. He's not!"

"Defensive?"

"Yes, because it's not true, and I don't want you spreading rumours about him!" *Not least because he's an enemy within Guild ranks, and needs to keep a low profile.* "It's not true. Don't go round saying it!"

"No?"

"No! Just drop it, ok? Why're we even talking about this? Why did you even ask?"

He watches me for a long moment, *still* overbearingly in my space, before finally leaning back. He swipes up the book in one hand, and offers me his other. "You know what? I'm not sure. Let's go, Skye. To somewhere people can't see us so that we can finish what you started."

"I didn't start it," I say shortly, distractedly. Short, because he's in a really weird mood tonight, and it's making *me* feel weird. Distracted, because he just told me he went for drinks with Xavier, The Rogue Guardian Levi himself is playing warden to me for, and who is supposedly very bad. Only...we still don't know how or why he's so evil, do we?

"You did start it," Fin is refuting mildly as he helps me down from the plinth. "You started it by fitting so well in my hands. Makes me want to do foolish things with you...and think foolish things, too."

"Think foolish things?"

"Mm."

That's all he says, but he squeezes my hand a few times before dropping it, then throws me one of his mischievous, lopsided smiles *without* an edge...which instantly fades as we exit the library quads, heading for the stone stoa outside the Guild's offices and meeting rooms.

He gives an odd, cold laugh. "Με δουλεύεις."

You're kidding me.

Bewildered, I follow his gaze there, and immediately recognise Fjord's silhouette standing by one of the walkway's marble pillars. He's not facing us, instead looking out over the moonlit quads – but I'd be very surprised if he hasn't heard our footsteps approaching. There's also something small and decidedly *bookish* held in one of his hands, suggesting he's been in the library recently and thus walking through the gardens, too. I hurriedly straighten my shirt and smooth my hair down, expecting him to turn and greet us, but he doesn't. He just stands there, facing away but definitely waiting. I've a feeling he's been waiting for some time, and it's suddenly *very* obvious he needs to speak with me.

I glance sideways as Fin brings us both to a stop before the stoa's steps. He's watching Fjord without the usual friendly expression on his face. I wait for him to look at me but now *he* doesn't either – just keeps staring at Fjord, a muscle in his jaw jumping and the line of his shoulders filled with something like determination.

"Fin?" I begin hesitantly. "I think I need to reschedule tonight. If...you don't mind?"

"You serious, Skye?"

I nod warily, "I think Fjord needs to speak with me. I think he's waiting to do that."

"Speak to you about what?"

"I don't know."

"Well, let's go and find out, shall we?"

"Uh..." I catch his elbow as he moves forwards, darting onto the stoa's bottom step to intercept him. "I think it needs to be just me, Fin. You know. Just...me and him."

"You and him?" Fin's brows rise, and then he lets slip that funny, low laugh again. There's no humour in it. "Wow."

My cheeks heat. Gods, I'm ineloquent sometimes. "I didn't mean it like *that*. I just...think it might be personal stuff, you know?"

"No," he says shortly. "I don't know, but I'd guess it's the stuff that had the two of you not speaking to each other for *months*, right?" His nostrils flare, tense shoulders squaring. "What's going on, Skye? I'm not stupid. I know there was more to your argument than a simple lie, and I know there's still more going on. What *really* happened the night I asked you to go to the Medical Syndicate? It all started then."

I swallow tightly. "Nothing happened that night and...there's not more to this. Not more going on."

"There is. You're lying to me."

Yes. It's killing me. "I'm not. I just...I'm sorry, but I just need to speak with Fjord by myself. Please? I'll make it up to you. I swear I will, but..." I bite my lip in frustration, then bounce forwards and wriggle my arms around his waist, trying to distract him from interrogating me further. His body is stiff and he doesn't return the hug, but at least it gives me a few seconds to sort out my expression into something believable. To erase the terrible guilt I'm now feeling. "I'll see you later?" I ask hopefully, pulling back.

"Will you?"

"Tomorrow? I hope you have a good night."

"Me too, Skye. Feels ruined now."

"I'm really sorry."

"Don't be."

My stomach sours more, the belly full of dinner and lust suddenly replaced by icy stones of worry. There's such a bluntness to his voice, like he's really pissed off. It makes me say something....foolish. "Maybe you should find the girl from the tavern, Fin. Your hundredth? Make trouble with her just like you did the other week, when you left me."

His eyes darken. "Yeah, maybe I will. I'm not sure she'd ever drop me like I'm something dispensable."

"But...that's what you did to me," I defend, cheeks flushing. "You just left me at the tavern, Fin. You almost forgot to say goodbye to me, and you *left* with another girl right in front of me!"

"Did I?"

A muscle in his jaw jumps. He looks away, his eyes falling past me to the walkway again. I want to turn around to see if Fjord is watching but realise that would probably be a bad decision. Several strained seconds pass between us before Fin sighs in frustration, slips a hand behind the nape of my neck and presses his mouth to mine. It lingers there; hard, hot, and not remotely modest. He doesn't look back when he leaves. Nor does he bow to Fjord when he passes him beneath the stoa, even though his friend greets him.

My conscience roils with unease as I watch him walk out of sight feeling deeply torn – unbelievably guilty for lying, but also pissed off that he doesn't seem to think he dropped me the other night. Heaving a deep breath, I hurry up the steps to Fjord. He looks like he's feeling bad too, and like he understands a little of what just went down. He looks like he's just pulled triple duty, actually. There are shadows beneath his eyes, hollows to his cheekbones that hint at stress or tension yet to be expelled. I've a feeling it's because of something far deeper than my own strife.

"Skye," he greets as I approach, offering me a gentle bow. "I'm very sorry to interrupt your plans."

"That's...ok."

"Sholto has called a last minute meeting in the safe house to discuss important matters, and I'm to escort you there. We should leave as soon as possible." He hesitates. "Do you need anything first? Your cloak?"

"No, I'll be ok. It's not cold."

"You sure?"

"Yeah."

Love that you take the time to check that, though. We fall into step together, walking quickly. In just seconds I feel like there's something missing...except it's not my cloak. Not my bow or quiver, either, though both would be a welcome weight on my back, one to hopefully replace the terrible burden I feel for everything with Fin.

In desperate need of a distraction, I nod to Fjord's hands. "What's that?"

He lifts the book between us. "It's for Levi."

"Does he like reading?"

"He loves reading. I've never met someone who goes through books like him."

"That...makes total sense."

Fjord gives me a bemused look as we pass beneath the Guild's gates, heading out into the square towards the bronze armillary sundial. It's arrow is very strangely pointing right for the full moon looming large and luminescent over Ioxthel. You should know I no

334

longer feel even a *little* bit as enchanting as her. I just feel like a liar, and a bad friend.

A bad...girlfriend?

"Makes sense, how?" Fjord queries.

I shrug. "I don't know. It just does. Levi definitely seems like a reader, doesn't he? Quiet, pensive, humble..." In my periphery I see Fjord give me that look again, and fidget. "Uh...not that there's any one *type* of reader. They're everywhere, aren't they? All sorts of readers. Some loud, some quiet. Some big, some small. Some old, some young. Some humble, some proud and pretentious. I just...I guess what I'm saying is I think reading suits him. Levi. It suits him. And all the other readers, too. Because they're everywhere, and there's no one type..."

You have to laugh at me. Fjord looks a little like he wishes to, except he doesn't - maybe in goodwill towards me, or maybe because there's definitely something else preying on his mind. Searching for a distraction for *him* now, I look around and suddenly realise what's missing. There are two shadows behind us, but no Guardian.

"Where *is* Levi, Fjord? Why is he not with us?"

"I asked him to run to the harbours for Tristan."

My heart flips. "Is he ok?"

"Yes, but I thought he'd want to be at this meeting, and I think you'll want him there, too. We're discussing leaving Ioxthel, Skye. In the next few days."

The pit of my gut swoops dizzyingly low. "The next few *days*?!"

"Yes."

"Why?!"

It's a stupid question, but Fjord understands it. "Things with Wivern are progressing, negotiations on alliances firming up. They've all but agreed to go to war on Elysium with Ruby. They've also just had some surprising news from home, and it's taking the

Prince and Princess back to Wivern sooner than anticipated. They've asked an entourage from Ioxthel to leave with them, returning Ruby's diplomatic gesture."

My voice sounds strangled. "I think Fin mentioned that just now. Said that...that Xavier told Enye and him of rumours about duties away from home in The Cold Kingdom."

Fjord's neck whips in my direction. "Xavier?"

"Went for drinks with Fin and Enye, recently."

He stares at me, face pale and features further hollowed by stress. "I need to speak with Fin about that."

I'm not sure he'll like it if you do. "What is so bad about Xavier, Fjord? Why is he so dangerous? Why is he called The Rogue Guardian? Why...why is Levi guarding me from him?"

Fjord grimaces...and doesn't answer me. "Yasmine is dead, Skye. You were right. Sholto witnessed a ritual in the Temple of Poseidon with Rose tonight, and she was the second member of the Council to fulfil her oath. She met the same fate as Lieutenant Jensen. It's my belief Enye will take her place in the Guild as Staff Sergeant of Delta, something that must've been orchestrated by Yasmine given how she asked Enye to shadow her for the past few months." Deep breath. "Speaking of the group set to travel to The Cold Kingdom...I've been asked to lead the entourage by Ruby."

"What?!"

He nods tensely. "The unwelcome news has sped up proceedings with Wivern, and they're set for a final night of revelry two days hence, and set to leave four days hence. The Queen asked me tonight to honour my duty to the Guild and escort them home with a small company of our soldiers. I'm to think on it until the next meeting."

"But...you know your answer?"

"I do, yes."

I barely find my voice. "I'm going with you?"

"This is what we're set to discuss tonight. I have a feeling Sholto is unsure of the best course of action – of whether everyone else will come to Wivern, or return to Elysium."

"I have to go with you," I say forcefully. "To Wivern. I *have* to be with you."

Fjord glances at me. "Forgive me, I meant everyone as in Yusuf and his brethren. Sholto certainly wishes for you both to travel with me to Wivern...and I wish for it, too."

"So I'll be with you?"

"Yes."

Relief courses through me. "So what's the unexpected news for the Prince and Princess?"

"Their youngest sister Liberty is very unwell back in Wivern, and has been since the day they left. News of it only reached them yesterday. Understandably, they're worried for her and return to spend time helping look after her." He stops, catching me by my elbow. "I'm so sorry to spring this on you, Skye. You should know I also feel shocked by how fast things seem to be happening. There are matters I still have to attend to before we leave. And...this isn't all we're set to talk of tonight, either. If you remember, we're also yet to discuss your meeting with Zelos in Thetis's ruined temple, which means I have something to request of you." He waits for me to acknowledge him. "I would ask you, please, to still have Sholto think you haven't told me of my mother...that you haven't told me of Melody, himself and his father being involved in some kind of lover's quarrel. I don't want him to know that I know."

"Swear on my life I won't," I vow immediately, earnestly. "He'll never know I've told you until you tell him, Fjord."

"Thank you."

I nod, and suddenly find myself fighting back tears. "I don't want to leave Tristan. I think I'll die."

"I know," he murmurs, hands slipping to my shoulders and squeezing. "I know, Skye, but I swear to you it won't be forever. You both have important journeys to embark on. Him here, as the *true* King of Ioxthel, and you as the world's small but mighty saviour." He offers me a very soft, wry smile, expression alive with gentle feeling. "You're quite a pair, and will remain so always, but you're temporarily finding different roads to the same destination. I'm with you for yours, Skye. You know that. We'll journey this together. Get through it together."

"Because...we're family right?" I mumble hopefully, heart swelling with love. "We'll always travel the same road as family?"

"Yes, sweetheart. We will."

Wivern or Elysium?

The others are already at the safe house when we arrive, loitering in the crumbling courtyard outside the kitchen's worn wooden doors. Tristan is throwing stones against the shutters of the surrounding houses, their walls presumably devoid of residents given how no one is storming out to curse him. He turns quickly when he hears our feet scuffing over the dry earth, throwing arm poised. One look at his expression tells me he knows what this meeting is about, and one look at *me* no doubt tells him I'm *very* close to tears.

"Got you something for the memory pool, Silver," Fjord murmurs to Levi as Tristan and I embrace, then jostle with one another to enter the safe house first, pretending so *hard* we're not both terrified of what's soon to be put in motion.

"You didn't have to do that. You know I'd never ask you to trouble yourself."

"No?" Fjord sounds tired. "Well, I didn't. It's nowhere near a trouble to get you a book. I hope you enjoy it."

He ruffles Levi's hair, then hands him his gift and holds the door for him, like he works for the Guardian and not the other way around. I watch, intrigued, as Levi lets the book fall open and studies the pages. He doesn't do it for very long before he nestles it in the folds of his arms, like he's squirrelling it away for later – hiding it from thieves, perhaps. Then he takes up post by the door Fjord is bolting behind them and starts observing everyone just like he usually does; quietly, unobtrusively, wearing an expression of nothing.

Silent.

Guarded.

Handsome, too.

My mind jumps back to the library quads...to Fin suggesting Levi was my second suitor. I still want to defend that statement in earnest, because I *don't* want those rumours flying around.

I barely know Levi.

Obviously, my first impressions of him were very wrong, and increasingly I realise I like him a lot. He's nice, and he's Fjord's Guardian and best friend...but I seriously barely know him, and I *do* think he's quite handsome, so is that also why I'm being defensive? Trying to hide it from Fin, and from myself? Goddesses I hope not, and not least because you can find someone handsome without fancying them, and Fin is...good. What's going on between us feels good – not forever or exclusive, admittedly, but momentous, because he's my first and he's so charming. A bit possessive tonight, though. And why would I worry about finding Levi handsome if that good thing with Fin isn't exclusive? If I *know* he does stuff with other people? Saw him leave with another girl in front of my very own eyes?!

Hot frustration rises in me, volleying with the worry and unease souring my stomach over the thought of what we're set to discuss here tonight. Fin frustrates me in so many ways, but I do feel terrible about cancelling on him. How can I remedy that? How *will* I make it up to him, like I told him I would?

I sigh heavily, only to immediately try to hide it when Levi's eyes flit to me, fussing around the table with Tristan...like he heard me make the noise. He probably did, didn't he? He is *the* excellent listener, after all.

I greet him with a strained smile; not because I find him handsome, but because since the night I said sorry I've been trying harder to be openly grateful for the favour he's fulfilling in following me around Ioxthel...and I've also been trying to make up for all the times he offered me a quiet greeting before patrols and I ignored him. I stretch the smile a bit more at the thought, then start to feel foolish because I'm not sure he can see my expression in the dim candlelight here. He probably thinks I'm just staring at him, or grinning dementedly – but then he greets me one of those rusty half bows, something really more of a nod of recognition than anything. Still, it's not lost on me or my pulse, and Tristan doesn't miss it either, possibly because he also received one upon his earlier summons from the harbours.

"No ruffian manners there, Wolf," he mutters in my ear, dragging out the last of the kitchen table's rickety wooden chairs. Sholto and Fjord are already occupying the others, with Rose standing by the stove. "You sitting?"

"Not sure," I say, turning to him. "I never know where to *be* during these meetings."

"I think you should sit."

"Well, I don—"

His hands land on my shoulders to steer me down into the seat. He settles himself standing behind me, and I can hear him rustling around in his pockets, probably counting how many of his origami swans he has left for today – the ones he leaves as pitiful payment to the vendors he steals from, if you remember.

"There you go," he says, holding one out for me over my shoulder. "Easy peasy. You look so comfy and content there."

"I'm going to fidget," I grumble. "I can just tell."

"Don't trouble yourself about that. It'll be hidden by the table, and no one here is expecting anything but ruffian manners from you, anyway. I wouldn't even try for something different. You're a case more hopeless than the state of my love life."

I snort, glancing over my shoulder to retort back with something equally witty, but the words get stuck in the back of my throat – because although Tristan's expression is easy and his tone light, his eyes are such a deep, heavy blue. There's no mischief in them right now, just mourning and misery.

My own eyes sting viciously with tears. Thank the gods there aren't so many of us in the room this evening to see me struggling to hide them. There's no movement upstairs in the salóni either, suggesting the Irving girls are with their uncle, their young Guardian, and the tutor who's as nifty with a quill as he is a knife beyond Ioxthel's walls.

"Evening everyone," Sholto begins, clasping his hands together and placing them on the table right beside his kylix of wine. Wish I had one, too. Wish I had twelve. "Today's meeting discusses the oath Rose and myself just witnessed, and everyone leaving Io—"

"I'm going with Fjord," I blurt out, very prematurely. "Please. To Wivern. I'm going with him...please."

Sholto shuts his mouth, breathing out a sigh through his nose. He's obviously unimpressed by the interruption, but chooses not to chide me, maybe because the rueful expression on my face is undoubtedly earnest.

"You'll be pleased to know we're both to go with Fjord to Wivern, Skye. Though there is much to life back in Elysium that needs tending to, particularly in the political sphere, it will have to wait. It would seem the biggest clue we have about the whereabouts of Prometheus's Torch is your journey with Melody following your departure from Elysium, all those years ago. As my father said, 'The trail, the tracks you seek to follow, start with your very own footprints...and who knows where you'll take yourself'. I take that to mean we must retrace your footsteps through the past you don't remember. We know from Zelos that upon leaving Elysium you and Melody travelled to Wivern's most westerly mountain foothills, seeking The Hesperides...so it's a stroke of good luck that Fjord's duties also take him to The Cold Kingdom." Sholto nods with esteem to him. "You've done good work over the past few months finding your way into Ruby's trusted circle. You should be commended."

"Thank you, but the job isn't finished yet."

Sholto observes him down the bridge of his nose. "Mind how you go, Fjord. It would be a disaster if you blew cover now or forgot your priorities."

"We won't."

"Mind you don't. You should know Zelos was in an unhelpful mood on the hilltop. He goaded Skye by telling her he knew much of her parents and her lost past, but revealed little of either to her. Then he goaded me in trivial matters...and eventually told us the barest bits of information on the Torch."

Fjord leans forwards, placing his elbows on the table, and now it's his turn to look at Sholto with a very measured gaze – and it's only because I know that *he* knows there was much more to the hilltop meeting than Sholto is letting on that I see it's just a bit *too* measured.

"What of The Hesperides? Do you know much about them?"

"Nymphs of the West. Beings of evening light, who dwell in the foothills of Wivern's furthermost mountains...the same mountains where their father is rumoured to hold up the skies and the world is rumoured to end."

"Their father is Atlas?"

"Yes. The inglorious titan holds the heavens asunder from the earth in a never-ending test of endurance set by Zeus eons ago. As you know, Atlas was his main rival during the Titanomachy, the ten year battle that eventually won Zeus his throne on Olympus, and his mastery of the universe. Atlas was sentenced by him to hold the heaviest burden on earth astride his shoulders for all eternity – to bear the weight of the celestial heavens. It is he who swivels the stars on their axis, spinning the hearts of astronomers with it. He who is Prometheus's..."

"Brother," Fjord finishes slowly.

"Yes."

The two of them share a considered look, one I think I understand. That's a mighty coincidence, isn't it? Melody and me heading for the region near where Atlas, Prometheus's brother, dwells.

"So...how is Skye a guide to the Torch?" Fjord eventually asks, turning with intrigue to me. "How're you a guide to it, Skye?"

"Don't know," I mumble. "I understanding nothing, and remember even less, so don't look here."

"The prophecy, perhaps?" Rose suggests.

"Yes," Sholto nods. "The prophecy details Skye *holding and healing a broken and inglorious world*. After hearing Zelos talk of The Hesperides, I cannot help but think the vision has something to do with their father, Atlas, holding the heavens on his shoulders. And perhaps also with Skye's mother. I know very little of her time spent as a huntress to Artemis, but I've no doubt Saffron embroiled herself in trouble beyond Elysium's borders. She had a thirst for it..." He spares me a brief glance that clearly says, *Just like you have, Skye.*

I feel my lips split into a huge grin, something so giddy I fear I might giggle as euphorically as Ember...only thankfully I don't.

Time and a place, and all that.

"I suppose we won't know anything for sure until we journey through the destiny The Fates have woven for Skye," Sholto goes on. "Which thankfully is *soon*. We leave in four days for Wivern. We must hasten to organise ourselves. Time, it seems, is shorter than we thought. Now, moving on to the second oath Rose and myself witnessed tonight—"

"Wait," I interject quickly, wiggling excitedly in my seat. "Can we just talk about Saffron for a moment, Sholto? My mum? Zelos thought I'd stolen my bow from Artemis, didn't he? That's something else that happened on the hilltop. He *took* my bow from me and shot an arrow that literally disappeared into the heavens, and then he said it was a weapon befit for a goddess. He said it belongs to The Huntress, as in *The* one, *The* main show, *The* big deal..." I turn eagerly to first Fjord and then Tristan behind me, not even caring how prideful my tone sounds. Two hands immediately land on my shoulders, warming me through my shirt...urging me to go on. "*The* weapon of a goddess, right? I knew it was special, the bow, but you said it was my mother's, Sholto. So what did your dad mean by that? By saying *The* Huntress?"

His expression is very suddenly stern. "I do not condone the use of the term *dad* for my father, Skye. Nor would he. I told you this before."

"Oh..." *Whoops.* "Sorry. Zelos, then. What did Zelos mean by that? Saying it was the weapon of *The* Huntress?"

"He was toying with you. I still believe your bow belonged to your mother."

"Really?"

"Yes," he says, starting to sound frustrated. "*Really*, Skye. My biggest advice is never to get your hopes up in my father's presence, and never to trust a word he says. Your bow washed up on my doorstep in Elysium on the very same day I had a visitation from the Oracle. I take it as a sure sign the bow was Saffron's, and that she is no longer with us...for if you remember, I told you a huntress never loses her bow unless she falls herself."

"But Zelos said—"

"But *nothing,* Skye! We'd do well not to waste time tonight, for we are undoubtedly short of it with just days left in the city. Let us focus on more pressing things and discuss the oath, please."

He fixes me with an even sterner look, and it tells me he's thinking of our walk to the Temple of Thetis and all he said on it – the whole spiel about "This is bigger than you, Skye." As you might imagine, it takes me *enormous* willpower to bite my tongue...but I do.

"Rosie and I witnessed another oath being fulfilled tonight in the Temple of Poseidon. It was that of Sergeant Yasmine Hajjar. She met the same fate as her colleague, Lieutenant Jensen, bleeding from her orifices having drunk ichor from a large golden goblet. Just as was the case during his oath, Yasmine's body appeared to be a temporary vessel for the summoning of a spirit, until she fell and it escaped into the air, soon after captured by Ruby in her incense holder." He turns to his former student resting against the stove. "Unlike last time, Rosie and I were able to acquire some pivotal pieces to the puzzle. Tell the others what we saw, Rosie."

"Sagittarius," she states, pushing her shirt sleeve up to reveal her right wrist. It's slender but sinewy, like she's fought, and fought *hard,* for her entire life. She points to the delicate skin on its inside, just above her spidery network of purple veins, "The symbol of Sagittarius was branded here on Yasmine Hajjar's wrist, seemingly from a hot poker some time ago...and I noticed how the rest of the zodiac signs were embossed around the edges of the large goblet she drank ichor from. It's my belief they're directly connected to the ritual the Council was performing."

Sagittarius?

I think back to the last meeting here; to my stargazing episode when I'd begged the goddesses to sort out my messy muddled mind and noticed Sagittarius – the centaur, Kheiron, who gave up his

346

immortality for Prometheus upon the titan's release from Zeus's eternal torture of liver pecking eagles – shining brightest in the heavens. It's his month of the year, isn't it?

Then there's that day I stopped avoiding Enye and had breakfast with her, and saw part of a little mark on Yasmine's wrist outside the Guild's meeting rooms. It was something that, although half hidden by her leather fencing glove, looked just like the tip of a spear or an arrow.

Something perhaps just like the symbol of Sagittarius.

"My theory is that each Council member is marked by a different zodiac sign," Rose goes on. "For there are twelve members, and twelve signs. Twelve months with a full moon, twelve oaths, and thus...probably twelve rituals."

"You think their markings correspond to the month of the year they take part in the ritual, and fulfil their oath?" Sholto considers this, and nods. "Sound logic, Rosie. It would seem we have some semblance of a rhyme and reason to explain the Council's activities."

"The question is, how do they relate to the zodiac signs? Summoning that spirit? We'll have to observe further rituals, further summonings, to know that."

"How can we?" Fjord speaks up, running a weary hand down his jaw. "We're leaving in four days."

"Indeed," Sholto spares him a glance. "This is a problem I've thought on at length, and tonight, without my even trying it's been solved. Such is the way with grave problems – their solution usually appears when one least expects it to, and usually it's been right in front of you the entire time. I'm grateful we have a surprise guest here with us..." Sholto looks beyond me. "Hello, Tristan."

"Sholto."

"How're you?"

"Been better. Won't lie."

"Yes," Sholto looks understanding. "I have a request to ask of you in our absence."

"Speak it. I'll think on it."

"I would have you continue to watch Ruby, and mind her actions with the Council especially during each months' full moon. Find out if our suspicions are correct about each member having a mark that corresponds to a section of the zodiac wheel. I believe you have a young ruffian girl who might be fit for the job?"

Meaning Akira.

"Sure," Tristan responds in a level voice. "The ruffians will watch The Queen, especially during the full moon. We'll watch over Yasmine's brother too, the healer Vishnu Hajjar. Skye saw a small mark on his wrist, and believes he's also part of the Council." His hands squeeze my shoulders briefly, as if to say, *And Enye. I'll keep watching over her, too.* "I can't promise we won't do more than that, though. Can't promise the people's fires of rebellion and protest won't be stoked whilst you're gone. I have a hankering for causing a little trouble for our beautiful queen with intentions redder than her name..."

"Intriguing," Sholto says, offering him an accommodating smile. Somehow, it lacks depth. "I'll look forward to hearing of it when we next see one another."

"Upon your return?"

"Upon our next seeing one another, Tristan. I cannot say where that will be. Our business, at present, does not lead us back to Ioxthel."

The hands on my shoulders grow very still and *very* heavy. I can tell Tristan is staring hard at Sholto, and then perhaps Fjord, from the way he shifts to open himself to conversation. My best friend doesn't end up speaking, though. He's waiting for someone else to break the tension...and it surely isn't going to be me, because my eyes are wide, breath bated. This is the first time I've heard that. First time I've thought that leaving Ioxthel might mean something permanent. Life is never going to be the same again, is it? I can't go back to being a regular guilder or even a ruffian...

The stone in my belly is pure ice. I'm suddenly filled with the worst kind of dread. I have just *four days* left on these streets with my friends, maybe for the last time ever.

"What are the logistics for the day of leaving for Wivern?" Rose pipes up from the stove, and even though the question is a kick in the teeth, to her credit I think she does it in kindness. She's watching Tristan and I through her lashes, plainly seeing us both struggle not to succumb to distress.

Sholto turns to her. "You leave for The Cold Kingdom *never*, Rosie. I wish the Elysium folk to return home."

"Why?"

"The journey and our endeavours throughout it will be dangerous. Unsuitable for at least four of the six of you. To have you tag al—"

"I don't tag along," Rose interrupts indignantly. "That's not my style, Sholto, and you know that. I would ask to stay with you. To help you *just* like I did tonight."

"You'd ask to stay, and forgo your fealty to Yusuf in doing so?" Sholto *tsks*, but it has no real reprimand in it. If anything, it's full of fond exasperation. "Rosie..."

"I wouldn't be foregoing my loyalty! He wishes to travel with you! Jay wishes to be with the boys...and he *is* meant to be here, so you cannot deny him of that. Ember, Wren and Idris undoubtedly wish to follow the tutor around like pups..." She gives Sholto a firm look.

"It makes perfect sense, not least because we'd probably be in *more* danger travelling through The Nether back to Elysium without your company."

"You did so on the way here."

"In great peril, and with help!"

Sholto pauses in thought. "Levi?"

"Yes. He returned to Elysium to aid Jay in crossing the wastelands, and that, of course, included *us* given how the girls followed their tutor...something that would still astound me if they were less determined to meddle in adult life like they were *born* for it."

Sholto lets slip a fleeting, wry smile. "They're certainly curious creatures."

"*Young,* curious creatures," Rose emphasises. "Who would do best in the company of three other good, strong fighters when wading waist high through wastelands riddled with wraiths."

"Rosi—"

"Don't *Rosie* me," she says tartly, sounding *much* angrier than I'd expect. "Just listen to me, Sholto. We wish to be with you, to travel to Wivern. To help. To *fight.* Let us fight for what is right."

Sholto's sigh is long, and frustrated. He rubs his forehead for several moments as if he has a sudden, severe headache, muttering something, before twisting to address Levi by the door. "Your input in discussing Wivern is desired. You were there upon leaving Elysium just over a year ago. What were your findings?"

The Guardian straightens, standing to attention. "The kingdom suffers from the same troubles Elysium is increasingly struggling with. The same troubles native to The Nether. Wraiths and daímōns, mostly of ill intent, are breaching their borders, and there are casualties for it."

"Hence why you told Fjord months ago you believed Wivern would agree to Ruby's warmongering if she offered to aid them in fighting the demons from The Nether?"

Levi nods.

"What's the verdict, then? Just how bad is it in The Cold Kingdom?"

"It's not as bad as in the wastelands themselves. Wivern have a force of hunters working to protect their people from harm, much like The Guardians of Elysium. They're good at what they do."

"I take it that was your identity when dwelling there last year?"

"No, I was a stable boy."

Sholto's brows lift, "Oh? Hankering for a solitary life, still? How interesting." He offers Levi a tight smile. "Would you say it would be more dangerous for Rosie and the Irvings to cross back alone through The Nether without us, then, than to accompany us to Wivern?"

"If...we're simply talking of the threat from wraiths and daímōns then I would say yes," Levi replies, words suddenly very stilted. "Coming to Wivern with us is the safer option. I wouldn't like to think of Rose tackling The Nether as the sole fully qualified Guardian in their group."

"I see."

Sholto looks down into his kylix of wine. He moves it jerkily over the tabletop a few times, a mannerism filled with nothing but agitation, before he swills it and takes a long draught. Perhaps he's worried that the others might be coming with us to Wivern, troubled by the thought of the little Irving girls in danger...frustrated working through the difficulties intrinsic to having more bodies to care for. Whatever it is, a change settles over him – his temper shortening to something I have little experience with, excepting perhaps the time we met with his father. Excepting, perhaps, those times when he told me this was for my own good, and not to make *him* force *me* to leave...

"That wasn't so difficult for you was it?"

This Goodbye Isn't Forever

It takes everyone a moment to understand who Sholto is addressing, and as soon as Levi realises it's still him, he straightens again from the door and bows his head in deference...presumably for prematurely removing himself from the conversation. I'm starting to see that's how Levi is. Entirely respectful and humble, usually obliging others selflessly and silently...and then he's shamed for it.

First by me.

Now, Sholto.

"Forgive me," he says. "What do you mean?"

"Speaking for yourself and giving your opinion. It wasn't so bad, was it?"

Fjord immediately clears his throat gruffly from the other side of the table, "Please abide by the request I made of you months ago and refrain from mentioning this, Sholto."

"Silence isn't as hard to break as honour, Levi," Sholto says, totally ignoring him. "I find myself astonished you of all people would forget it given your reputation, and your history. This is the first time you've spoken to me during your visit to Ioxthel besides assuring me it was *your* wrongdoing that Skye was late for the last meeting here, is it not? A poor display of respect to a Mentor."

"Sholto," Fjord objects, with more emphasis. "Intimating broken honour when there is none is a deep insult. I'd ask you to apologise."

"If your Guardian has a problem I'd urge him to speak up and defend himself? He is, after all, a master at doing so for others..."

He waits expectantly, and receives nothing. Levi is utterly still, and silent. A faint pink blush might have bloomed on his cheeks, but I've a feeling that's the only response he'll give...and it's not like it's a voluntary one, is it? I try to watch him without appearing to do so, another cold stone settling in my belly...something of feeling for him. No one enjoys being embarrassed, especially when that embarrassment is solicited spitefully by someone else. And I realise I'm one to talk given what I said on that bad day many weeks ago, but we know I wholly regret saying it and have since apologised – would probably still apologise, if he'd let me.

"I'd ask *you* not to forget your age, or bare it to me in foolish light," Sholto now says to Fjord, his voice firming up. "The ancient son of a sentinel expresses remorse only when he thinks it's needed, and never when it's requested so callously of him. And he *never* expresses it to someone fallen from grace."

"Levi hasn't fallen from grace," Fjord refutes, looking shocked. "I know you don't believe that, Sholto. You're...you're letting stress get to you over this issue, which is understandable given what's at risk, but please would you apologise. Mentor or not, I won't have you slight my Guardian."

"Letting stress get to me? At four hundred years old?" Sholto *tsks*. "No, Fjord, I am not. And I'll tell you now that I think you *do* forget your priorities with your plans for the next few days. I know your endeavours will be futile. There is no escape for the damned in life or death. This is a truth that can't be battled. I find myself highly disapproving of the risk you take in trying."

There's a fraught pause. "Why would you say that, Sholto? How could you?"

"Easily, Fjord, because it's the truth. He's wasting your *time* by persuading you there's any remedy to the situation."

"Levi isn't persuading me," Fjord responds, voice becoming incredibly tight and heated, bringing more feeling with it than I've perhaps ever heard from him. He sounds...close to tears, actually. "He doesn't think there's a remedy, Sholto. He doesn't even have hope. I'm the one pushing for this."

"Then stop. We have bigger issues at hand, immeasurable problems to solve that far exceed your pointless endeavours to reclaim one boy's broken honour. If the Irvings really are to travel to Wivern with us we have lots to organise in the coming days...identities to hide, ruses to dream up, and it will be *your* job to make sure they stick with the other guilders."

"Suffering is suffering," Fjord objects, either choosing to ignore Sholto's last points or not hearing them. "No matter how many people you're talking about, suffering is suffering. You should never sit by and let that happen, least of all because it's not just honour. You know it's not. It's everything. His life, his freedom, his health..."

"You think he deserves those things after everything with your brother? I don't, and given how she disowned him nor did Nike. Don't you think she'd have stepped in if she deemed the punishment inappropriate? If she deemed it anything other than necessary?"

At this, Fjord pushes his elbow off the table so vigorously it scoots forwards a few inches, and stands up in protest, too. His entire frame is suddenly wrought with tension, expression something of outrage, chest rising and falling rapidly...humble, homely eyes pinned furiously on Sholto. My own gaze bounces over the room's other occupants with frenzied speed, spotting Rose unfolding her arms as if wary of something explosive to follow. Tristan's hands feel possessive on my shoulders, like he's also prepared for something to happen and is readying himself to whisk me from my chair, but Levi himself...Levi is suddenly staring at nothing on the stairs, looking shockingly lifeless. His grey eyes are totally deadened, dull like a tarnished mirror long left to ruin, expression just...gone. More than I've ever seen it go before, and that's saying something, isn't it?

What on *earth* is happening? What does Sholto mean, talking of the damned and Nike, one of Zeus's sentinels who Zelos himself said was his sister and Xavier Archer's mum? How mistaken have I been about the dynamic of this group? Clearly there's much more to Sholto's ancient character than I've previously borne witness to. Have you ever seen him be spiteful like that, shaming Levi for being quiet *just* like I did on that bad day? And how does age or heritage excuse you from needing to give an apology?

It doesn't.

My brain is *going* now, flicking fast through the pages of our tale...the ones where I was so immersed in the whirlwind of my own thoughts and anger, I wasn't really looking out. Wasn't listening or seeing things.

Now, with hindsight, I do see things.

I see how besides little Ember playing her strange game of *Hello's* and *Good evening's* during the last meeting here, and besides, very sparingly, Jay...I've never seen any of the Elysium folk properly address Levi. Sholto never bows to him upon greeting, but he did to Jay that time in Fjord's office. I've never even seen anyone stand *close* to him. He's never part of their conversation; always separate, quiet and alone. By the door. Or, in the Medical Syndicate back when I first saw him, all the way over by the courtyard walls.

Silent.

Shunned.

Something seems to fall into place, and *just* like the night recently when I said sorry to him and realised he looked sad, realised the weary grey of his eyes looked full of grief, I suddenly think I've unearthed another page in Levi's story. I suddenly think that the large moon looming over Ioxthel tonight is just *so* large, *so* luminous, that it couldn't possibly have done anything but unveil more about him to me.

Does this all have something to do with him being so quiet and guarded, or the other way round? Does broken honour mean something other, something more, than I think it does? What about falling from grace? And perhaps most importantly...do I believe it, when Sholto says something like that about him?

I look back to the table, to where Fjord and he are in a tough staring match. The age-old Guardian has a cruel expression of victory on his face, like he knows he's shamed someone and bested their defendant and is enjoying it...perhaps *just* as his father, the embodiment of rivalry, would.

It looks strange on him.

It also suits him.

Fjord is breathing hard, really *really* angry in a way I've never seen before. I open my mouth to fill the silence, then realise...I don't know what I'll say. I've *never* known Fjord and Sholto to have even the slightest disagreement with one another, and I'm at a loss of how vocal I should be during it...how vocal I should be about siding with Fjord, because obviously I *do* side with him. We're family. We fight for one another and trust in one another, which means I don't think I *do* believe what Sholto just said about Levi. And thankfully I don't have to make any of this favouritism obvious today, because Tristan beats me to it.

"We done here?" he asks, his heavy, dozing hands waking up on my shoulders and squeezing them. "Skye and I have things to do in the harbours."

It takes Sholto a moment to turn to him, but when he does his expression is mild, perhaps even wistful – and just how quickly he slips on that mask of composure troubles me.

"Does that mean stealing, Tristan?"

"Yes. Stealing our final moments together, because this is happening horribly fast, isn't it?" Tristan's voice isn't wistful – it's maybe the further thing from. He turns to Fjord abruptly, "I would ask you to step out with us, please."

Fjord immediately deserts the table. His profile is taut, and I can tell he's totally distracted by the way he doesn't push his chair in, and doesn't offer for Tristan and I to leave the room first. He barely even offers Rose a bow as he passes by the stove, before stiffly and ungraciously unbolting the kitchen's wooden doors and shoving through them, taking his Guardian with him. Tristan and I watch him go, I think both of us at a loss of what to make of all this.

We leave the others sharing a long, weighted look. Rose is observing her past mentor uneasily, perhaps even a little sternly, and Sholto himself now appears fatigued, like he really *does* think he should apologise for what he said?

The two boys are already some distance away in the middle of the moonlit courtyard, locked in dialogue...or rather it's just Fjord talking fast in Ancient Nereid. He stops to wait for a response, shaking Levi a little in encouragement, and receives nothing but the barest of reluctant nods. It's not enough for Fjord. He says something further with feeling and tries to run a hand through his Guardian's hair, the gesture just like it was the other week after our meeting before the trip to the Temple of Thetis – reassuring, nurturing, full of intense friendship and love. Only this time, Levi doesn't tolerate it. He shies away from Fjord like a little boy embarrassed by his mother's attention, turning jerkily to examine his surroundings as if there's someone or something he urgently needs to respond to.

Except, there isn't.

"Be right back, Wolf," Tristan mutters, shoving his hands deep into his pantaloon pockets and drifting forwards.

I watch him approach Fjord in confusion, telling myself to focus on the two of them and *not* to stare at Levi's stiff back. With a final, frustrated look his Guardian's way, Fjord moves to greet him, rubbing a hand down his jaw and seemingly expecting something like this.

"Might be interrupting something here," Tristan begins. "Yet, I'm too worried to feel bad about it. I have a request to make of you, Fjord."

"I thought you might."

Tristan nods slowly. "It isn't ok, what's happening. Even though I understand it, I *hate* that Skye and I are parting ways. Hate it. Hate that I don't know when I'll next see her, or *where.* I'm terrified of not having her in my sights..." He clears his throat suddenly. "You need to give me your truest word you'll look after her. Protect her through everything, even if it means forfeiting your own life to save hers..."

My mouth drops open in shock. "Hey, Tristan! Don't ask that!"

"You have my word and my honour," Fjord responds to him gravely, before I can stop him. "Every second of every day, I will endeavour to protect Skye. I love her just as much as you, Tristan. She'll never befall harm before either of us do ourselves."

"Either of you?" Tristan queries, then looks over Fjord's shoulder, to where Levi has turned to face them. His features are once again settled into something impressively inexpressive...like nothing ever happened. "Say it then."

"Tristan," I breathe, swanning forwards and tugging *hard* on the crook of his elbow. "Don't you d—"

"Be quiet, Wolf," he snaps waspishly, pushing me off him with enough force to have me stumbling away. "You're not involved in this. Please give me your word, Levi."

"I give you my word, Tristan," the Guardian vows, to my dismay. "My word and my honour. I'll protect Skye until I'm no longer able to."

"You'd step before her, without hesitation? Forfeit yourself if you needed to?"

"*Tristan!*" I shriek in horror. "Don't you dare!"

He ignores me. "Levi?"

"Yes, I would step before Skye."

"Swear. On your life?"

"You have my word and my honour, Tristan. Those are worth much more than my life."

My best friend watches him closely for several long moment. He starts turning to me, only to immediately twist back with a low hum, "Some people talk bullshit, Levi, and Sholto is usually one of them. I see nothing broken in front of me, and I'm King of The Streets here. My word goes like Zeus's. Remember it."

"King of The Streets my ass!" I exclaim, planting myself resolutely in his path. "I'm Queen of these streets, Tristan, and I say you can't go round *doing* that! I didn't want you to *do* that! I'm the demigod here, so I'm the one who needs to protect everyone else. The one who gives *her* word and honour that she'll fi—"

"Be quiet, Wolf. There's no way in all of Hades' underworld I'll let you protect *them*. Look at you. You barely reach my waist, and you can't even string a sentence together properly."

"I *will* protect them."

"Be quiet."

"No! I won't be quiet, Tristan! You shouldn't do something like that, just because you're the...the...the *stupid* King of The Streets here! I didn't want you to do that..."

My protests fizzle out as he finally looks down at me, meeting my gaze with his lips and jaw pressed into a firm line...and yet the rest of his expression doesn't match that frustration. His eyes are rimmed with red, deep blue irises like ocean waves of woe and despair, and I can tell he's really struggling not to let those feelings out. My own lips start trembling, throat tightening to something painful as my face screws up in an effort to keep myself together, too. I fight hard. Fight to prevent the sudden *total* collapse of dignity...and simply lose it, bursting into tears.

"I *can't* leave," I sob, throwing myself at him. "I can't leave you. I can't be without you. I'll die!"

"You won't," Tristan says hoarsely. "I've just had two people swear they won't let that happen."

"I w..will, because I can't be w..without you, Tristan. You're my everything!"

"You're *more* than my everything," he mumbles, arms coming to rest around my shoulders, but he doesn't hug me like I think he will. "Let's go to the harbours, Wolf. I'm about to lose it, and I don't want to do that here."

"Too late for me," I sniffle thickly. "I knew I was going to be the one to l..lose it f..first."

"Yeah, I'm embarrassed for you."

I cough out a laugh that's really just a huge, gut wrenching sob, and turn to Fjord, "We're going to the harbours, unless you need to sp..speak with us more?"

"No, we're finished here."

My attention drifts to Levi. I can barely see him at this distance through my bleary eyes. "Is it ok with you? For us to go to the harbours?"

"Yes."

"You s..sure?"

"Yes."

"I'll be returning to the Guild, Skye," Fjord says, moving forwards to embrace me. "The only person I still need to speak with tonight is Fin."

My heart skips. "About what?"

"About him and his sister meeting for drinks with Xavier, and how he shouldn't do that. To let him know I'm leading the reciprocal entourage to Wivern, and that you'll be one of the soldiers chosen to accompany me. To offer him a place in our ranks, too."

My eyes widen. "Fin is...coming with us? Is that for me?"

"As much as it is to have a good soldier in the force?" Fjord nods. "Yes, it is. I see that you two are close and what you have might be going somewhere. I see that he's important to you...that you're important to him."

"You do?!"

My eyes widen further, heart starting to patter fast. Then, for some reason, I peek at Levi. He's not watching us, because he's watching Tristan...taking the length of green fabric my best friend is offering to him with hushed words.

It's his ruffian attire.

Tristan is, really oddly, giving Levi his scarf.

"Skye?" Fjord's arms tighten around me to solicit my attention. "The offer is also made in the hopes that maybe the truth *is* best told to those you trust, sooner rather than later."

It takes me a moment to get what he's suggesting. "Do you mean telling Fin everything? About...everything? Soon?"

"Perhaps when we're settled in Wivern."

My lips start trembling again, gratitude and some other form of insensible emotion swelling inside me. "Thank you, Fjord," I whisper.

"Thank *you* for forgiving me," he responds with a sigh. "I don't know what I would've done if you hadn't."

* * *

I don't remember much of the journey through the streets after that. My dignity is once again disintegrating, tears never drying on my cheeks despite the wind lapping at our skin. Tristan and I all but fall from the rooftops when we reach the harbours, feet foundering their way through the forgotten bay littered with pebbles and crab shells and broken boats and just so many heartfelt memories.

So many beautiful memories.

"I'll miss you more than everything," he murmurs into my ear as we embrace, huddling together against one of the rickety overturned boats. "More than everything, Skye, but it's not forever. This goodbye isn't really a goodbye. I *swear* to you. I'll see you soon, so soon you won't believe it...and in the meantime, I'll be *with* you. Here." He moves a hand between us, palm resting gently on my sternum. "In your heart. I'll be right here with you. We're parting ways, but I'll never leave you."

"I'm with you, too," I whimper. "I'm not leaving you. I'll...I'll..."

"Think of me, every single second of every single day? Me too, Wolf. I'll never stop thinking of you."

He gathers me impossibly close. His breathing is getting faster, chest rising and falling rapidly through his own tears, but he's better at getting the words out. Always has been.

"I just *love* you," I sob. "I love you more than infinity."

"I love you too, Skye. Beyond everything."

I lean back and meet his gaze. I can't see him through my tears, but I don't need to, because I've had these honest eyes memorised from the moment he let me nestle with him in this harbour, both so small we didn't know what to do with ourselves...living on instinct, stale bread, and the one surety of each other's warm, dusty skin when the sun went down.

"We'll be together again so soon," he vows. "I swear to you. Say it with me. We'll be together soon."

"We'll be together soon," I echo thickly.

"This goodbye isn't forever."

"This goodbye isn't forever."

"Never forever."

"N..never forever."

"I'm with you, every second of every day."

"I'm with you every s..sec..."

My voice gives out on me. I press my lips together, trying to hold it in, but the terrible bleak sound still slips out, the whimper of a little wolf whining beneath the moonlight for her lost brethren – something of deep pain, and deep misery. I fling myself into Tristan's arms, entire body shaking as the tears fall so fast I can't breathe, sobs wretched and violent and soul shattering. Tristan holds onto to me just as desperately, and then he also loses the fight for dignity.

We stay that way for the entire night, spilling our souls through salt water *into* salt water, tethering ourselves to the spark of determination, the fire of hope, that this goodbye isn't forever.

It *won't* be forever.

Never forever.

Revelry

Midnight. Two days until we're expected to depart from Ioxthel and I'm expected to leave the better half of myself behind. My senses are wick ready to be lit, my shadow the mere echo of my form, a slip of darkness you'll never be able to see. Tonight, I'm living in the name of the hustle and the heist, bathing in moonlight and wind and reckless endeavour. Ghosting, perhaps for the last time in a *long* time, which means I need to make it a good one.

The *best* one.

My cheeks feel tight with salt, proof of how deeply, how irreversibly, the tears of two nights ago in the forgotten harbour stained them. With deep pain and misery, however, comes resolve to fight. To fight so *hard* there's no possibility I won't see Tristan soon. Or sooner than soon.

That's partly why I'm doing this tonight. To start fighting. To start being the heroine the world needs, living in destiny's name. The *other* reason is to keep the cold unknown at bay by pestering people for questions...or more precisely, pestering the *moon* for questions.

For secrets.

Stories.

I'm on Ioxthel's rooftops stopped in the shadows, listening to a pair of quiet, familiar voices filter up from the streets below – their conversation inaudible to most people, just like I surely hope my presence is to them. I don't think I've ever before been so obsessive about maintaining my silence whilst ghosting, clutching my bow in a fervent prayer to Artemis that Levi, the excellent listener, won't hear me.

And yes, you heard me right.

Levi.

I followed him and Fjord from the Guild to here where they quickly parted ways - Fjord disappearing inside Alcázar for his last night of revelry, and Levi staying to loiter in the shadowy streets adjacent to the fortress walls, waiting for Jay. To say I'm a little surprised to find myself ghosting on my new pack tonight would be an understatement. To say I'm not *very* excited that's what I'm doing would also be an understatement. I can't *wait* to see their faces when they realise I've been following them all night, dropping eaves.

"Good evening," Levi offers quietly to his companion when the tutor arrives, and I'm starting to think I'd recognise his voice anywhere. It's as hoarse and as weathered as the rust staining the rowlocks of the forgotten harbour's overturned boats, as earnest as sincerity itself.

"Evening, Levi," Jay responds, his own voice a hum of deep, lyrical baritone. "Good to see you. How goes it?"

"Well, thanks. And you?"

"Mm, I'm a little tired."

"The girls?"

"Yes. They're full on anywhere, but especially here. They're made of nothing but tireless intrigue, and thirst for meddling in matters well above their age bracket, especially Ember...though I suppose those are endeavours I commend them for, so I'm partly to blame."

"How're they feeling about the journey?"

"Excited. Apprehensive. Pleased we're leaving Ioxthel. It's too hot and dry for us here. And me. I miss trees, rain, windchill, snow..." He stops with a hum. "There's something in that look, Levi. What're you thinking?"

"I have noticed there isn't a day that goes by when you don't mention the weather."

"Maybe that's true. It's become my deepest passion, besides tutoring the girls and dabbling in alchemy. You disapprove? Do I need to watch myself?"

"No," Levi assures him solemnly. "I like hearing of it."

It sounds like Jay grins, like he knew Levi would respond that way to his teasing. "It's not going to change anytime soon, and there'll be far more for me to talk about when we get back to my preferred habitat, something the girls will bully me for no doubt, like the true diplomats their uncle wishes them to be."

He chuckles darkly to himself, then falls quiet – or at least, mostly quiet. For all their hushed undertones, Jay's foot is tapping out a vigorous beat, seemingly helpless to his body's infatuation with rhythm. The movement is scuffing softly down the street like the restless paws of a fox, which might be why Levi isn't stopping him. Or perhaps it doesn't matter if others hear or see them...which makes *me* want to see them, something I can't risk for fear of them noticing my presence.

And, in what I *very* much hope is a coincidence, Jay now asks, "I expected you to be with Fjord, Levi. He's not staying in the Guild with Skye after all, is he?"

"No, he's not. He's in the fortress already. He should be here to let us in shortly. Skye is with Sholto."

"He's watching over her?"

"I hope so."

Uh... I cast a frantic, furtive glance over the rooftops. *I hope he isn't?*

"I'm intrigued by her, you know," Jay admits. "So are the girls, despite never having properly spoken to her...which isn't surprising. Those two spot a spark miles away and beeline straight for it. Ember especially likes talking about her. She tells me she dreams about how breath-taking *The Sky* is most nights." He gives a fond, weary sigh.

"I see what Fjord means. He told me she was very similar to Kieran, and there's no doubt she is. Fiery and reckless, with a riotous set of feelings and a sweet tongue that has a habit of running away with itself. Yeah...I see it. I miss it. He used to wreak *havoc* in my classroom, the cheeky blighter, but he'd give me the most wonderful gifts for the winter solstice..." Jay sounds wistful, and sad, which is no surprise. Kieran is Fjord's dead brother, and I think I'm right in interpreting the tutor tutored them, when they were younger. "When did Fjord tell you of this, Levi? The prophecy? This whole situation?"

"Two years ago."

"When..."

"Yes."

There's movement, someone shifting themselves to ease their weight, and I've no doubt it's Jay. "He stayed with me for a time before he found you, you know. Told me of it all then. Told me he himself was only aware of the prophecy upon arriving in Ioxthel five years ago, because apparently Sholto summoned him here on the pretence he'd found Skye *and* Melody. Is that right?"

"Yes."

Jay makes a low noise. "I do not like to hear of that. Nor do I like the sound of what happened the other night in the safe house. Rose talked of it when she returned beyond Ioxthel's walls, and I'm sorry to say Yusuf was keen to listen, no doubt to report back to the gossip riddled burrows of the Sylvans." He sighs. "The Mentors are increasingly worrying me. I don't like how untouchable they're becoming in Elysium, especially compared to their students. Don't like how our kingdom has a ruling council of twelve houses, each representative of the different Nixen dynasties, but that they kowtow to the Mentors' bidding most of the time, with no incentive but that of fear. Diplomacy should be subservient only to the will of the people, not the old, powerful and deadly."

368

There's no verbal reply from Levi to this, and I become desperate to peer over the edge of the roof to see them in person. Something tells me this conversation about Elysium's politics is a *big* one, full of hidden histories and emotions, and I just wonder if this evening – this whole *thing* I'm spying on – relates to the warning Sholto gave Fjord in the safe house the other night, when he told him not to forget his priorities? Told him that his endeavours were futile...

I also wonder if this is what the three of them were discussing in Fjord's office, the day I returned from the Temple of Thetis and Fjord placed that parchment map on his desk. The map of a building that, in hindsight, looked a *lot* like my knowledge of Alcázar...

A strange feeling settles in my gut. What they're saying is that Fjord arrived in Ioxthel five years ago not knowing about the prophecy? That Sholto asked him to travel here from Elysium on the pretence that his mother was *here* with me. Melody, the lost lover of both Sholto and his father, shot by Eros with his magical arrows and maybe taken advantage of, now nowhere to be seen. Was her son also taken advantage of, in a very different way, by Sholto? What is Jay talking of with The Mentors? Does he mean the offspring of Zeus's sentinels, like Sholto himself, who train young Guardians back in Elysium – saying they're the ones who really rule Elysium, through fear?

"Hope it goes well, tonight," he says to Levi now, jolting me back to the present. "I have every faith it will, and when we're back in Elysium we'll start sorting this out. You'll have my full endeavour in helping you, in truly freeing you."

"You're helping now, Jay."

"Mm, yes, but you know what I mean. You'll have my *full* endeavour."

There's a long, hefty pause. "I would not ask that of you. Please don't trouble yourself with it."

"Too bad. Fjord already asked me and I said yes, hence why I'm *here*, Levi, in another kingdom I hate the weather of. I asked it of myself, too. Years ago, when I first started studying. First met the boys and you, and you all became my students, and my friends. I said *yes* then, because that's what fellowship is. You give each other full endeavour in whatever is needed, and you don't worry about the fallout." He clears his throat, voice turning a little dry. "It's been long years since I tutored the boys and occasionally you, my best student despite never formally being assigned as one, but we're still learning this?"

He waits for a reply.

Receives nothing.

"I would always have you voice your thoughts with me, Levi."

"I don't...have any."

"No?"

"No."

"That's a lie. You have thoughts on everything, and with them, the profound insight they probably aren't the only judgement to be had on any one matter. It's what makes you a good student, and a good Guardian. I'm asking you now to voice them regardless of their integrity. Regardless of how they sound out loud."

More silence.

It's painful to listen to.

"I do not..." Levi begins stiffly, then stops. Tries again. "I do not wish for you to do that, Jay. To give your full endeavour."

"Why?"

"It's a fallout I can't remedy, and a favour I can't return. Given your standing with the Irvings, and with the Sylvans, it's too much to ask."

"A favour you can't return, is it?" Jay sounds disbelieving. "So was the utter joy you brought me in actually *listening* to the lessons I tutored you in when you came back for the holidays...but you don't see me worrying about it, do you? Don't see me lamenting how to repay you for making my interests feel worthwhile. And regardless, friendship holds no debts. You have no need to feel guilty over my decision to help. I suppose all I'd ask is that you watch our backs in here? I won't be any use back home if I'm run through by an Ioxthelian blade, and no matter what Yusuf and the girls say, I'm not *that* nifty with a sword."

"You have my word and my honour no harm will come of you tonight, Jay. Or ever, whilst we still walk together."

The tutor chuckles. "Thus you've just disproved your fears, Levi. Safeguarding my life *for* life is a favour of a far greater magnitude compared to what I do here tonight, and again what I'll do back in Elysium for you, meddling with my potions and taking a few ego knocks. I most definitely cannot return it...so how about we call it even, for the sake of it? And why do you say *whilst we still walk together* as if there's a time limit to it? You don't think it will be sorted out despite what we're doing here tonight?" Jay's next hum of baritone is no longer smug or playful, or thoughtful. It's low and very unhappy. "Living without hope is a terrible curse to place upon yourself, Levi, and for what? Fear of having it dashed? I would have you change that, please. You must find hope. Myself and Fjord have, and so have your family. Find it and hold onto it tightly."

"Το έκανα, Jay," Levi mutters, in perhaps the hoarsest voice I've ever heard from him. "Το εχασα."

I did.

I lost it.

Out of nowhere, tears sting my eyes. I'm not sure why the reaction is so very immediate, and so very visceral, but...it is.

My counsel is also crying.

There's a very full stillness from below and then sudden movement. I think Jay is embracing Levi, but it's difficult to know without seeing them and although everything – literally *everything* – in me is begging me to risk leaning forwards to watch them, I don't.

My counsel's lesson way back on the streets haunts me without her even ushering it now; the lesson where she told me not to pry on someone's life story because it's theirs and theirs alone to tell in their own time. I'd forgone prying then, because I'd promised to spy on it. Promised to spy on Levi and the story left untold. Then I'd called him shy in spite.

Now I'm here dropping eaves, bearing witness to their secrets lifted by the breeze and doing what I always do...except I suddenly think it would be very wrong of me to lean forwards and actually *see* Jay and Levi together, sharing a moment that sounds incredibly heartfelt and personal, and full of a story I still don't understand, because it's still untold.

For the first time *ever* while ghosting, I don't press to witness what's not mine to see. Don't pry. I just stay very still on my rooftop as the two men fall quiet, this time for the last time before Fjord returns. The soft, dry scent of sleeping ash and fallen olives creates a peaceful ambience, at war with the flush of focus in my cheeks...because although my body is frozen, my mind is thinking up a storm. What was that entire conversation about? What is this entire *evening* about? Why am I so sad, hearing Levi say "*I did...I lost it,*" to Jay telling him to find hope and hold onto it. And just what did the tutor mean, when he said he'd help Levi stay free?

Free from what?

* * *

The rafters of the alcázarian courtroom smell of must and stale urine, quite like hemlock, a poison habitually slipped into the goblets of political opponents to sabotage their prospects, or used to lace guilder's arrows in battle. It's an unpleasant smell, souring my mood just as much as my stomach. I've been up here in the roof trusses for what must be two hours, perched on numbing tiptoes with dust tickling my nose and soft, sticky cobwebs snagging on the fibres of my cloak, surveying the scene below.

Alcázar's gaudy elite are introducing their Wivern guests to the joys of revelry for perhaps the fourth time this month, and the last. Dressed to impress, velvet and silk shimmer over their forms, billowing in huge swathes of beautifully rich ochres and sea-greens, violent reds and oranges, and magentas. Curved swords and sashes hang off the hips and shoulders of Guild veterans, always regarded as esteemed guests by those who have little experience of warfare, and there's a sheen of sweat coating most people's skin from the huge fire bowls lining the circular room, smudging the dark kohl rings around their eyes. It's either that, or the heavy perspiration too much alcohol can bring on.

Their Wivern counterparts appear comparably tame, the royal blue capes and silver jewellery they wear hinting at an uncomfortable level of sophistication and uprightness that hot, hectic Ioxthel will never wish to emulate. I suddenly wonder what the Elysium folk wear when in their home territory, then I wonder what *I* wore as a child there. Then I get a headache, trying to relive the past I don't remember.

The revelry room looks like it might be a place of meeting in the day, with a number of stone benches cut into the circular walls and a red quartz orchestra embedded into the marble floor. Large, evenly-spaced candles placed on the seats give the room a soft, flickering glow, and it's a wonder the tipsy revellers don't knock them over as they collapse there, drinks spilling over their hands...secrets spilling from their mouths. There's so much laughter in the room – laughter and drunkenness.

They're mocking me.

I'm sure of it.

I *really* hate hemlock, and yet here I am, still as the marble statues in the ludicrously luscious courtyards outside, tolerating the ghastly stench for the sake of spying on stupidity.

Three aulete players weave through the guests, blowing a frantic, reedy melody through their aulos pipes. The energy they create is infectious and heady, with some of the more intoxicated revellers breaking out into spontaneous stamping and twirling. They're drunk and look foolish, but I guess there's no embarrassment in being a fool amongst fools, and the stupid movements of a few soon entice more to join. Servers float through the room around them, refilling goblets until they overflow, waterfalls of sticky red wine falling to the floor. No one seems to mind the mess, the dancers least of all. They just laugh in delight as they slide here, there and everywhere, falling head first into the small groups socialising throughout the room.

One gathering has held my attention throughout the evening. They linger in a peripheral position amongst the guests, and become my sole focus when Fjord joins them. I've spotted him a few times moving through the room, dressed in his well-worn but immaculately polished leather chest armour and a red velvet cape tied over one broad shoulder. Now, I watch an alcázarian sentry lead him to where Raul, the Crown Prince of Wivern, and his sister, Princess Aoife, are talking to Ruby. Fjord is introduced and joins the conversation, bowing deeply to all three royals. He looks at ease, sipping wine in a relaxed, open stance, but as the minutes pass by I see him twice decline a server in pouring more for him.

I have no idea where Levi and Jay are. I lost them as soon as Fjord greeted the gate guards and ordered them to permit two further personnel into the fortress...and as soon as I scaled the wisteria-laden walls of Alcázar and crept through the forgotten water outlet beneath the battlement. I thought they might be here undercover amongst the revellers in order to provide reinforcements for Fjord, but they're not, and that leaves *me* to look after him doesn't it? The Little Ruffian Thief. The Renegade in the Roof Trusses. The Ghost with the Amber Eyes....who would do well to focus tonight, instead of dreaming up silly titles for herself and wondering what she wore in The Forbidden Kingdom she doesn't remember.

Ruby's gathering are leaving the room now, and I admit I'm relieved to see it. I jump into the shadows and follow them to the lower levels of Alcázar, where they start heading for the ocean. Torches slotted into iron brackets light the way, curved and ornate as is custom for all metalwork in Ioxthel, including our swords and daggers. The tiny fires illuminate divots in the stone walls and paving slabs; and as Ruby descends, crushing the crisp, expired brown petals of sea lavender underfoot, I see that her sandals are surprisingly well-worn for a woman with endless coin for new attire.

I ghost in the gloomy recesses of the stairs behind them, maintaining my distance. The sounds of revelry soon fade and the sandstone walls give way to exposed rock. The air grows cool and damp with a sea breeze, and at the last turn but one in their flight of steps, Ruby takes a right-hand fork, following a walkway skirting the cliffs. The bulk of Alcázar now lies over my right shoulder, with the ocean to my left glistening darkly in the moonlight. The water is deep and choppy tonight, submerging the shallows Sholto and I slunk over on our way to witness Lieutenant Jensen's death in the Temple of Poseidon.

The group enter a doorway built into the rough rock face. It opens into a generous underground room, lit by a few scant shafts of moonlight filtering through high, barred holes in the rock. Spying the perfect vantage point, I climb the slippery cliff until I reach one of them, clinging with difficulty to the jagged rocks. It smells of salt and war mongering...because that's what this group is doing tonight, isn't it?

Discussing the return journey to Wivern.

Negotiating *war* on Elysium.

The interior below is minimal, adorned with just one wolfskin rug, a silver pitcher of wine resting on a ledge cut into the rock, and a huge mosaic-topped round table. I squint, trying to distinguish its features in the dim light, and see a vast, elaborate map of The Realms. There's Wivern to the West, Astyros in the South, and Elysium in the North. A huge swathe of the painted glass tiles have been chipped or destroyed, revealing the bare stone slab beneath, my guess is to represent The Nether, the wastelands that lie between the two mortal kingdoms and Elysium.

I'm in no doubt about it now. This must be Ruby's strategy room, but its location in the depths of Alcázar surprises me. The area is poorly guarded, and the damp, depressing cavern is as far from opulent and ostentatiousness as it gets – as far from what one would expect from our queen, just like those well-worn sandals. I guess it *is* spectacularly private, well away from prying eyes and ears...excepting mine and Fjord's.

I watch everyone settle themselves in the room, and in particular Ruby. She looks serene but focused, as if she knows what she wants from this meeting and also how to get it. Her fingers play with a silver chain looped at her hip, and although it's impossible to see into the generous folds of her silk trousers and shirt, I bet it's part of the incense holder she favours carrying these days – the very same vessel she used to capture the summoned spirit in the Temple of Poseidon. Does Fjord think it is, too? It's hard to say, because unlike me his gaze isn't lingering garishly on Ruby. He doesn't have that option.

"Lieutenant Winters," Ruby addresses him first. "Have you had time to consider my request? Have you decided if you will accompany our Wivern guests back to their homeland?"

"I have decided, yes."

"And?"

"I would honour your request, without reserve and with pleasure."

Ruby's red lips tip up into something very suggestive, and she's so beautiful, so radiant, you'd never think she suffers from ill health like Vishnu said she did. Although, waging war on a kingdom for no reason? Searching for humankind's greatest weapon? Conducting fatal rituals in the Temple of Poseidon to summon parts of a malevolent spirit? Maybe she *is* sick, sick in mood and mind just like Enye queried the other week.

"You're saying you pledge yourself to my intentions, Lieutenant?" she verifies. "You pledge your loyalty to me?"

"I have already pledged my unwavering loyalty," Fjord responds, bowing his head in something of respect. It's only because I know him so well I think I can say the act is every bit as cordial as it is cautious. He didn't say *who* he'd pledged his unwavering loyalty to, did he? He didn't verify it was Ruby his honour served, and I think that's important. "I also pledge myself to your intentions with this, Queen Sabir. I will accompany Wivern's Prince and Princess back to their homeland, so that they might seek to be with their younger sister and tend to their own troubles. I would give my life in this endeavour."

"Your life?"

"Yes."

My unease grows.

So does Ruby's smile.

She glides over to the mantlepiece and fills a bronze goblet with liquid from the pitcher there, something that looks like red wine, and then gives it to Fjord reverently. "To celebrate."

Cold sweat prickles my skin, instantly dried as a vigorous gust of wind buffets the cliff face. Is it me, or does this remind you of her bestowing Lieutenant Jensen with that glowing, golden goblet in the Temple of Poseidon during his oath? The goblet whose contents contained ichor, the blood of the gods and goddesses, and killed him in a horrendous fashion because he was mortal? This is not the same vessel, but the way she hands it to Fjord is identical, and...good gods and goddesses, I think I might have a heart attack.

Don't drink it, Fjord! I think desperately. *Please don't drink it!*

My thoughts fall on deaf ears. Ruby is watching Fjord, and still standing right in front of him with that beautiful, mad smile. It seems if he wants to keep up this pretence he doesn't have a choice. I stop breathing as he brings the cup to his lips, every instinct of mine urging me to draw an arrow and shoot it from his hand even though that would be impossible to do without losing my grip and balance on the rocks.

Should I risk it?

What else can I do?

Nothing, except perhaps whistle like a ruffian. That would blow my cover, but...why is that a thought? Damn the consequences for myself. I should save him. I should whi—

Unfortunately, I've hesitated for too long, rambling in my mind like the *idiot* I am. Below, Fjord is tipping the cup to his lips with no more reserve. He's drinking, locked gazes with Ruby, playing his part perfectly...and nothing is happening.

I watch on with wide, terrified eyes, lungs filled with air yet to be unleashed in a sharp warning...and *still* nothing happens. There's just Fjord, finishing his goblet like he's drinking his favourite wine on his birthday in front of his friends, and Ruby smiling her glorious smile, fingers brushing his as she takes the empty vessel back.

"There we have it," she murmurs, turning to Raul and Aoife. "My friends, you will be in safe hands. I trust you're pleased with this outcome."

Aoife's expression is obliged, her eyes lingering on Fjord like Ruby's hands just did. "We are, yes. The journey here was long and arduous, and we're grateful for the company."

"Perhaps the three of you should get to know one another better throughout this journey, then?" Ruby suggests lightly. "Friendship, I find, is a very persuasive force for good. Friendship and...more. My Lieutenant might even stay a while in your kingdom, Raul, to help you mastermind a plan to battle the evils plaguing your borders from The Nether? I can offer you his services. Fjord is a very astute soldier, and I'm sure he's chosen his team wisely."

The Crown Prince clears his throat. "That is an appealing offer, although it is my sister you're best to address. She's our main strategist."

Ruby turns to the Princess. "You take after Athena?"

"I would hope I do," Aoife replies, standing a little taller at the mention of the Goddess of Strategy. "And you?"

"I am a strategist myself, yes. I enjoy planning leagues ahead so that I might always win. It seems we have that in common...but I hope we will share a great deal more than a clever, far-sighted mind given time? I hope that these similarities might even help form a firm alliance between us. A union of shared purpose."

"You mean...defeating Elysium?" Aoife's gaze turns considered, her fingers lifting to the fawn hair swept into a soft knot at the base of her neck. "I would say that the Nixen haven't harmed our kingdom for hundreds of years, Ruby. I'm wary of provoking their wrath for the sake of victory."

"More for the sake of demonstrating your piety to the *true* gods and goddesses, actually," Ruby amends with a gracious smile. "But victory is always a welcome outcome. You say Nixen haven't harmed your kingdom, Aoife, but what of the demons ripping through your lands like an ill-tempered typhoon? Are these attacks not orchestrated by the Elysium folk?"

"We couldn't say."

"Well, we're still in discussions about that actually, aren't we?" Raul interjects, throwing his sister a quick, meaningful glance. His slender eyebrows are drawn together, pinching his features. "I think what Aoife really means to say is that our forces are not in such a primed state as yours to battle an entire kingdom, Queen Sabir, especially given the troubles you speak of within our own borders. We would need assurance of victory, of minimal casualties, to agree on an alliance with you...and so perhaps you could tell us more of this weapon you seek to help your endeavours?"

Ruby's lips twitch, as if she expected him to request that. She takes a moment to head behind the round table adorned with the mosaic map of the four realms, leaning down and spreading her hands right over Elysium's lands. "With pleasure, Prince Wenslus. The weapon has served the mortal world before, and wields a power older, wiser and greater than that of the twelve Olympian gods and goddesses themselves. Your ancestors would remember it well, though it goes without saying they did not linger to witness its aftermath. Wivern forwent fighting by our side during the Impurity War, but...let me say, for the first and only time, I am willing to put that betrayal behind us for the sake of unity. The weapon I speak of is of course the Torch of Prometheus, found and lost by my ancestor, Scarlett Sabir, but very much still lit. *Very* much still powerful."

"The Torch of..."

Aoife trails off in shock, and maybe slight horror. She glances first to her brother, who looks surprised and...maybe impressed? Then she glances to their future companion, her formerly appreciative gaze for him now wary. I don't know how Fjord can sit so quietly with them discussing waging *war* on his people, though I suppose he is suddenly a little stiffer than he was before.

Not even just a little stiffer.

My eyes sharpen. Tension has leaked into his shoulders and thighs, speaking of stress and vigilance. He turns his head to the side, enough for me to see how hard his jawline is...but something tells me he's not thinking on the present state of war mongering in the room. I think his response is to do with something else – a danger he hears and heeds and I *don't*, because I'm foolish and distracted and much more worried for him than myself. I'm not paying attention to the reality that something might be a threat to me, that some *one* might be coming for me...until it's far too late.

Below, my counsel exclaims. *Below, Skye! Flee!*

My racing heart falters even before I look down and see the shock of blonde hair glaring beneath the moonlight; see the black cloak billowing in the wind like charred leaves and that predatory, obnoxious smirk thinning his lips...a smirk I've only seen once before, but have a feeling I'll remember for the rest of my life after tonight.

Goddesses, it's Xavier Archer.

It's The Rogue Guardian.

The Thief

I scarper up the cliff above Ruby's strategy room as fast as I dare, scratching my shins and elbows on the sharp rocks and disturbing a fleet of nesting gulls. Their forlorn cries of surprise echo mine, because I'm panicking.

I won't lie to you.

I'm *panicking*.

My fingers and toes search for their next grip so frantically they're definitely fumbling, cloak lifting behind me in a newfound breeze – and if only my limbs were so easily airborne to better defy gravity.

If only I were faster.

My brain whirls, thinking up a storm like always, but I'd do well *not* to get lost or distracted by this one because I need to escape...and I don't know how. I've only ever been in this part of Alcázar, so far round the Western Peninsula, when spying on the Council's oath with Sholto, and we were way down on the shoals below, not fleeing up this cliff face. When I reach the top...*if* I reach the top...I'm not sure what the quickest route back to the streets will be, because at least I know *that*. To the streets I must go. They're the only place I have any hope of losing Xavier.

I look below, hot adrenaline bursting through me when I see he's following and gaining ground...or cliff, rather. He's gaining cliff, and I'm panicking, jumping back in time to when Sholto first confirmed my use of the word "obnoxious" to describe the Guardian. Then I remember Fjord in the safe house, telling me of how dangerous Xavier was...urging Tristan that no word of what he'd told us was a lie, and that Xavier was *bad*. He'd stolen glances towards his Guardian as he did so; the silent, solitary, shunned sentinel who

Fjord swore was the only person he felt I'd be safe with from Xavier, and who is...not here.

Levi isn't here, is he?

Or *is* he?

He might still be in Alcázar with Jay, undercover amongst the revellers or doing something else...because I never saw them in the party room. Indecision enters the storm, muddling my mind...and was it ever unmuddled to start with? No. We know it wasn't, but I need to stop panicking and figure this out. Figure out which way is the fastest route back to the streets when I finish climbing the cliff. Should I head into the fortress to return the way I entered, through the old water outlet below the battlement? Or somehow skirt the Western Peninsula in the shadows of Alcázar's walls and hit the streets due north of here? Or *do* I try and find Levi somewhere in the fortress? Should I have stayed near Fjord, below me in the strategy room? Gods, he was just metres away, and he *knew* Xavier was on his way. I could have whistled like a ruffian to him...and ruined his plan by doing so.

Hades, does my route back to the streets even need to be the fastest...if I *am* going back to the streets, and not trying to find Levi in the fortress? What about the least obvious, the least predictable, route? What about cover from archers? Is Xavier carrying a bow? Do I risk foregoing my handholds to draw *my* bow and shoot at him below? Then I won't even have to escape, I'll just kill him. I've never done that before. Never killed someone. Not sure if I want to...

Skye! my counsel cries desperately. *Breathe, sweetheart. Focus.*

What do I do?!

What would Fjord do?

Fjord? He's below. I could have whistled to him. Would've blown his cover in doing so...

No. That's not what I meant. Calm down. What would Fjord do if he were in your position here on the cliff?

He'd...I suppose if he didn't know where Levi was, he'd probably skirt the Western Peninsula in the shadow of Alcázar's walls. Wouldn't risk travelling through the fortress to the water outlet because there are *so* many revellers, and subsequently so many sentries. And he wouldn't shoot Xavier, because Xavier...

I look down.

Fjord wouldn't shoot Xavier because he doesn't have a clear shot...which means *I* don't have a clear shot.

Good, she murmurs. *Now, stay present.*

I try, reaching the damp shadows at base of Alcázar's sandstone walls and heading north, mindful of the sentries on the battlements overlooking the sea. The sounds of revelry grow louder as I travel, but the guards don't, which means Xavier hasn't raised the alarm.

Which begs the question of...why?

I look behind me and then down, but he's nowhere to be seen. Unease spurs my little legs on. I make it to where cliff and fortress melt into Ioxthel's perimeter wall and the silent streets within. Sentries patrol the rampart in pairs, the section far narrower than where I stood overlooking the arrival of the Wivern entourage, but at least their attention is on the seas and lands *beyond* Ioxthel, and certainly not on Ruby's precious stronghold.

I barely have the patience to stop and wait for a lapse in patrollers I'm so pent up with worry – worry I didn't know was there, festering unseen in the shadowy recesses of my mind like cobwebs in a pantry, thickening with every day I spent forgiving Fjord and *trusting* him. Trusting his Guardian, too. Trusting what they told me about Xavier being the absolute worst of the worst. That's what Fjord said, during the second safe house meeting.

To Hades with waiting.

384

I leap recklessly from the rocks to the wall, and from the wall to the streets. Thankfully, none of the sentries see me; and I probably have thousands of nights of ghosting to thank for that...the lucky blessing experience bestows upon you in moments when you're not all there, because you're mad panicking. I'm running before my feet even touch the ground, tracking the moonlit path back to the Guild over the rooftops. I *need* to get up there. My terrain, and my hunting ground...

"Skye."

I startle violently at the sound of Xavier's hushed, humoured voice *singing* my name, my feet skidding to a haphazard halt. My head whips from side to side, trying to find him. There he is, watching me through the arched entrance of a narrow side-street just metres away. He's smirking, totally at leisure, as if he's been there for minutes. His gloved fingers toy idly with the leaves of a potted olive tree, reminding me of our first meeting in Alcázar when he'd trailed his hands over the pillars of the walkway. The gesture is just as playful, ominous and sadistic as it was then.

Something to be deeply feared.

I see that now.

His smirk grows. "How are we tonight, Skye? Weary and windswept? That storm breeze was really something. Pesky. I almost lost my grip climbing the cliffs a few times."

He starts stalking the slight incline to the main street. I back up, fingers spasming into fists at my side. I need to draw my bow, but I haven't been able to usher the insane speed I used up on the hilltop with Zelos since the event, and I'm worried it was a fluke. I'm worried Xavier is so close and the breadth of this street is too narrow...and I can't help thinking that's a deliberate, strategic move on his part. Or maybe not. And maybe I'm just too wired to commit to the intention to draw my bow. Maybe I *do* have time, and I *will* be as insanely fast as on that hilltop if only I believe I could be.

Or maybe not.

Maybe I'm not going to do well in this fight.

Skye, my counsel implores. *You're not a doubter. Don't start now.*

Not sure if she's ever been wrong about anything before, but I think she is with this. If I'm not a doubter, why do I suddenly feel nothing *but* doubt and dread? Why does the cold promise of violence and the certainty of his own supremacy glinting in Xavier's eyes scare me more than anything has ever scared me before?

"You're quite elusive when you want to be, Skye. It took me longer than I thought to find you dropping eaves tonight, mostly because I went to the Guild first." He laughs. "That was a waste of time. I should've known you'd follow that gracious Lieutenant you love to call a brother into the fortress tonight. It was nice to see him in the flesh again, if only fleetingly. And I will just ask, because this is now the *second* time in as many months I've seen you trespassing in Alcázar...you do know it's against the Ioxthelian law to spy on our Queen, Skye? You do know I'm now one of Ruby's personal bodyguards? Her favourite? Means you probably shouldn't get caught by me..."

I don't reply.

He's still advancing.

I still haven't drawn my bow.

He starts loosening one of his leather gauntlets, humming out another laugh. I keep my eyes fixed on him, waiting for the faintest tremor of a muscle that might betray his impending offence...might give me an edge in the ensuing fight. Seconds later, I learn my vigilance is a hopeless endeavour. I learn that *anything* would be a hopeless endeavour, and that's not doubt.

That's fact.

"I'll grant you, you're good," he praises, now removing his other glove. "You're good, and quiet, and I'm loathe to put it bluntly...except I'm not. I like the cold, hostile light of day and its ability to bare truths. To bare flaws. You're just not good *enough*, Skye. Nowhere near it. And you're going to suffer now."

I don't see him move. One moment the width of the narrow street lies between us, and the next my back is pressed into the cool, coarse wall of the taverna behind me, breath snatched by fear and surprise. Xavier already has me immobilised, his bare hands gripping my wrists and pinning them to my hips to prevent me drawing my daggers, his knees pressing firmly into my thighs, completely disabling my legs. Every muscle in my body locks up and then moves to explode, fighting to free myself from him, but I don't move.

Not even an inch.

He smells of red wine, a day's work, obnoxious confidence and power. I must smell of fear. Of panic. Of moonlight without endeavour, watching in horror as he dips his head, a lock of blonde hair falling into his eyes as they meet mine beneath the hood. His irises are a dark hazel, alight with mischief and menace and...something worse.

"By Zeus," he mutters. "I'm intrigued now. Very intrigued. If you're a phantom of retribution, why can I hear your heart *begging* you to run from me, as if it's beating and you're alive? Why can I taste the bitterness of your frenzied panic on my tongue? And how are we touching, if you're a phantom? A ghost?" He cocks his head to the side. "Unless you're not dead, Skye, because it's not just you...and I was right the first time. I *was* right, wasn't I?"

Phantom of retribution. Xavier is quoting the prophecy, isn't he? Except I didn't know he knew about it, didn't know anyone besides the Elysium folk here and my lost mothers knew about it.

When was the first time?

What was he right about?

He seems legitimately thoughtful as he pulls on my hand, drawing the dagger it forms a fist around. Air stirs my cheeks as, again, he moves faster than any of my senses can follow...and now both of my hands are clasped lightly in one of his, the edge of my own dagger pressed to my throat. My heart flips over heavily, blood a heady *whoosh* in my ears. This is not like our previous meeting, our first duel in Alcázar all those months ago. Xavier's speed and strength are inhuman tonight, in a way that leaves me in no doubt I'm totally, totally out of my depth, and that I should've whistled to Fjord.

Should've tried to find Levi.

Should've listened to them.

Xavier smiles absently as if he knows my thoughts. He's seemingly exerting very little effort in restraining me. As in...*no* effort. He's barely touching me, but whilst every muscle of mine should be trembling in the exertion of throwing him off, I literally don't move an inch. I don't even think I'm *blinking*.

"Interesting. You're not dead as I believed, Skye. I'll be thinking on that for a while, and I've something for you to think on, too. I've a new secret for you to hoard, and to tell the honourable Fjord Winters and his *ruined* Guardian, lonely little Levi Silverstone..." He lets out the barest puff of a laugh, breath stirring my eyelashes. The dagger is slowly making its way from my neck to the fringes of my hood, its tip snagging on the fabric like a hook. Cold panic swells inside me, because there's absolutely nothing I can do against him pinned to the wall like this – pinned by nothing but the barest brush of his skin against mine, it seems. He leans in further still, sharing my hood. He's smirking when he presses his lips to my ear, his voice full of twisted benevolence, as if my hearing it is a great honour...and I feel very, very scared. "That poor little heart of yours, telling you to

388

run fast and far from me is in for a disappointment, Skye. You'll never outrun me, and nor will they. I've got you all on puppeteer strings, all so *ready* to do my bidding, like servants to a god. Tell that to them, will you? Tell them history is on repeat, and they'll bow to me before the end...and I'll reign over them in glory."

"βάλλ' εἰς κόρακας," I growl shakily. "I'll tell them nothing you say, Xavier!"

The Ioxthelian curse tumbles from me before I can stop myself, its inflection alive with anger and fear. Gods, I hate him talking about Fjord like that. And Levi, too. He's so arrogant, and so overwhelmingly close to me...looking delighted. "She *does* speak! You make a curse sound sinful, Skye, but then you made me work for it like any good girl does. I wonder, is your face as rough as your tone? Or is it sweet? And have I seen it before, many years ago?"

He eats the distance between us, and I'd press into the wall with such vigour it would be a wonder I didn't melt through the stone...except I don't move.

I *can't* move.

The dagger twitches on the edge of my hood. A shaft of moonlight falls over my chin and down my neck as the fabric gapes, and I stop breathing. Stop feeling. Stop *everything*. Even though Xavier knows my name, if he sees the skin beneath this hood I've a feeling everything will fall apart. And...it does. With a flick of his wrist, my hood falls and my skin is bared, my scars revealed.

"Hello, Skye," he says in a low voice, eyes drifting...brows raising high when he sees the markings. "Oh gods, I was *not* expecting those. What in the heavens happened to you? I...do not remember this, visiting the Nereids. But then...what's it been? Fifteen years?"

He frowns, leaning in even closer. The dagger starts to trace my scars, inching over my cheek and jaw, down my neck, nudging my shirt aside to expose my shoulder.

"Don't touch me!" I spit. "Get off!"

"I've been touching you for a while, Skye," he remarks mildly, eyes flashing up to mine. "Surprised it took you so long to object to it...but I don't need a girl to tell me something twice, especially when she looks so scared."

The dagger leaves the side of my neck, moving down...and down. Without further warning, Xavier lifts my hands up between us, and he doesn't even need to force them – my limbs are limp, listless, flopping everywhere like they're tied to those puppeteer strings he was bragging about earlier. He pauses for the briefest moment, lips pressed together as if he's still thinking hard on something, before the blade falls to my hands and in one swift, startling motion he cuts my left palm open.

I hiss with pain, white-hot horror and fury instantly rising in me. Both are powerful and overwhelming. I struggle with renewed vigour, and this time I move a bit. A tingling starts in my knuckles, spreading to my elbows and shoulders, down my spine and lower back. Wind whips down the street, lashing at the overhead awnings and our capes as the edges of my vision starts shimmering in a strange amber glow, and then a guttural snarl rips from my chest...not consciously done but *very* welcome.

Something is happening in me.

Something triggered by Xavier violence that beckons for the wind...and that the wind *storms* for. Instinctually, I know it's me trying to ignite ichor, just like Sholto told me about on our way to meet with his father. I can feel the blood of the gods and goddesses in my veins heightening my senses, honing my abilities to fight – only I don't know how to use it.

"Don't be silly, Skye," Xavier says gently, patronisingly, like he's speaking to an infant. "You'll hurt yourself."

It's a horrible statement to make given what he's doing...and what he does next. In one of his hands he holds a small glass vial. He presses its fluted lip the edge of my palm, catching the blood bubbling there, but apparently it's not running fast enough for Xavier. Searing, stinging pain shoots through me as he places the knife back to the wound and slices it again. The power sparking in my tingling limbs and amber-hued vision heightens in response, buzzing with unspent energy...and then it slips from my grip, because I'm hurting and I don't know how to hold onto ichor, let alone how to use it.

I'm quickly losing focus. My breathing is harsh, struggles so violently *still*, mind beside itself with dread. Panic strikes again, only this time it's almost unbearable. Makes me feel light-headed, especially when Xavier squeezes the wound, urging blood to drip faster into the vial. I let out a whimper, the sound something of frustration and deep fear.

Of a wolf cub wounded, and losing will.

"Fjord!"

The low, hoarse voice cuts through the night air with the same ease as Xavier slicing open my palm...but I *know* it. My eyes widen when I realise he's just a street or two over, my lungs hauling in a sharp breath...

"Levi!"

Humming what could be a curse or a laugh, Xavier lifts a hand to my mouth to muffle the scream. He deftly slips the half-filled vial into his sleeve and drops my wrist, then hauls my listless body into the recesses of the taverna's doorway, pressing deep into the walls there to hide us from view. The shadows are cooler here, but he is so impossibly hot, so oppressive. My nostrils flare frantically to draw air around his hand...around my panic. I still feel utterly frozen, as unmoving as the despondent marble statues in the Guild's garden quads where Fin and I got it on.

Never have I been so incapacitated in my life. This isn't just Xavier's strength, is it? He's hardly restraining me, but it's as if there are hundreds of him here weighing every floppy limb down.

It's his will, my counsel grates out. *Break it, Skye. Ignite ichor and hail the others.*

I don't know how! I cry. *Sholto hasn't mentored me in this! What do I do?!*

Hail the goddesses, she urges. *Ignite!*

I don't know how!

Then...then fight back without ichor!

I don't know how! I can't move!

Her eyes lock with mine. They're *not* amber, but they're bright with terror for me. *You can fight, and you must, Skye. Xavier is making you* think *you can't move by willing you to be still, but you're stronger than him. Bend his will. Break it. Now!*

I try.

I try so *hard*, straining with every morsel of my muddled brain, and all Xavier does is laugh, the sound filled with quiet glee. Immediately from the next street over comes the sound of feet kissing the ground, as if someone is pivoting in a fast circle, searching for us. My heart leaps in hope at the next voice blessing the night air, because good gods do I ever know it.

Do I ever *love* it.

"Levi?" Fjord asks quietly, sounding unsure. "What is it? Why've we stopped?"

"You need to return to the Guild. Now, and without me."

"Wh..." Fjord trails off, his voice dropping *octaves* lower. "Where is he?"

"Nearby."

"Who?"

That's Jay. I'd bet you anything the three of them are on their way back from Alcázar, concluding their chapter of the story left untold. Footsteps scuff the streets again, followed by the sound of metal being drawn from its scabbard.

"Silver?" Fjord mutters. "Talk to me."

"Leave for the Guild."

"Without you? No way."

Something is said back in Ancient Nereid.

"No way."

"Yes."

"No w—"

"Yes, Fjord!" Levi interrupts in a firm voice. "You will leave me. Go back to the Guild. Check on Skye there. You too, Jay. Leave Ioxthel. Return to the others, and keep your guard up."

There's movement, more agitated speech in Ancient Nereid, this time from Fjord...and then hot, *obnoxious* breath right in my ear.

"Shall we play with him?" Xavier murmurs there. "Play with the great, glorious Guardian blessed by Styx herself? Get him riled up?"

His lips ghost lazily over my earlobe for a few passes before he chuckles. He manoeuvres us back into the street, and I *try*. I try so hard to do as my counsel wishes and break his hold by breaking his will, my muscles and mind straining to near breaking point. Sweat trickles down my spine, low tinnitus booms in my ears...

I get nowhere.

"Go *on*, Skye," Xavier goads quietly.

I hear myself grate out a scream of effort through gritted teeth, and he *lets* me. The hand over my mouth loosens enough to let slip the noise, because he wants his opponents to hear it.

He wants to play.

"Levi," he cajoles when it's over, his voice eerily smooth and clear in the night air. "Your friends might have disappeared, but I know you're still here. The silent hunter, set to ruin others just like he ruined himself all those years ago. Ha. Sometimes I almost feel sorry for you, but then I think of my mother and how she favoured you over her own son, and I don't feel sorry for you at all." He lets out a dark growl. "You should know I've already caught my prey for tonight. She's small and weak, with these weird scars and freaky amber eyes that make me think she's *burning* to fight back...but may Styx bless her like she blessed you, my will was never one to be bent."

Our surroundings are still.

Utterly silent.

"Don't miss out on the fun, will you?" Xavier calls, voice rising in taunt. "Stakes are always higher in a quick game, and this has been a *long* time coming has it not, Levi? Nearly eight years in the running. Stop hiding and *play* with me, Silverstone. Be the protector. Ruin yourself some more. Let's do this."

Stillness.

Silence.

Stress.

Then, the smallest wisp of smoke. The barest impression of solitude and steadiness, of hidden sentiment and raw, unimaginable power. Behind, on the rooftops.

Xavier feels it too. Pivoting us both around fast, we watch as a figure crests the roof's edge up ahead, his profile silhouetted by the moon behind, cloak billowing in the echo of wind I hailed and lost in my pitiful attempt to wield ichor. He stops and looks down at us, features shrouded in shadow...but of course it's him.

Borrowed Time

Levi jumps to the street with a soft thud, landing on the very tips of his toes in a deep crouch. Two daggers are held in his palms, both straight and not at all in the style of an Ioxthelian weapon. I *knew* he carried his Elysium blades on him somewhere. His eyes meet mine and linger before moving behind to Xavier. It's impossible to know what he's thinking, but his skin is pale beneath the stars and his features harsher than usual – focused, and oddly intimidating.

"Just the three of us, is it?" Xavier remarks lightly. "Sent little Fjord running back to the Guild? That's a turn of events, probably in your favour. He'd probably do something stupidly protective for Skye and hurt himself in the process...but I've a warning for *you* before we get down to business, Levi. Before you also do something stupid, like even *thinking* of using those daggers on me, or something even deadlier. If you move one step this way, I'll split Skye's soul. I have the means to do it now. I've the means to do a lot of things, so not one step this way."

He brandishes the stolen vial of blood from the folds of his sleeve, wiggling it beneath my chin. Levi clocks it, but gives no response to the threat...gives no visible sign he's even heard it.

"You're so quiet these days," Xavier muses darkly, deftly slipping the vial back into its hiding spot and pressing the dagger to my neck. His other hand is still over my mouth, stopping me from speaking. I can barely breathe around it. "But then you were always the listener, and he the talker, right? Loud, stubborn, prideful, reckless...Kieran was a handful. I'm delighted my new little plaything is *just* like him." He laughs under his breath, like a sadist about to get his fix. "You know what I used to say when he did as I asked, Levi? I'd say, *Kill the chief.* And he would. And so I'd say, *Good boy, Kieran.* Then

I'd say, *Kill your dog.* And he would. Killed it, and cooked the meat for me to eat. So I said, *Good boy, Kieran.* Then I told him, *Kill your brother and that precious Guardian of yours.* And...he failed at those, and more fool me for thinking I could best the great, almighty tether. To best his love for you." Another cruel laugh. "He was a good pet while he lasted, though. A good boy. I admit I miss him sometimes, and every time I wonder if you do, too. Do you? Do you miss him? Does his death haunt you?"

Still no reply from Levi, but I don't miss the way his fingers spasm around the hilts of his blades. He dips his head a little, tucking his chin to his chest and looking up through dark lashes.

The gaze is measured.

Full of intent.

"I wouldn't," Xavier says mildly, reading it. "I'll torture her, and that would be cruel and premature. Skye and I are only just getting to know each other, and we've got a long way to go yet." He presses his cheek to mine, as if feigning fondness. "You've also gone very quiet, Huntress. Don't tell me you're finally learning by example and taking after the silent, deadly Guardian who likes to shadow you these days? How boring. Or...in fact it's *my* fault you're quiet, isn't it?"

He lets up the hand over my mouth, wiggling his fingers to crack his knuckles, before slipping them to my shoulder. The hold is light, the dagger at my neck barely touching me...but I don't move an inch.

"Go on then, Skye. Let it out."

"βάλλ' εἰς κόρακας!" I hiss vehemently. "Throw yourself to the crows."

He snorts. "Perhaps I will, but know I'll throw you to them first. We'll go down together, Skye. Burning."

"Do it then, why don't you?! Throw me to the crows, Xavier. Let's go down together. Or do you need me? It sounds like you do, with your stupid vial of stolen blood and your freaky mind tricks.

396

Makes your words empty threats. Big bark but no real bite. Boring. I'm bored. No one likes a fraud."

"Mm," he sounds delighted. "You're bored are you, Skye?"

The blade at my neck starts moving slowly, pushing the folds of my cloak aside. The slightest shift in angle or pressure and he'd slice my flesh wide open...and then something else *does* nearly break skin. Something hot, wet and scraping at the juncture between my neck and shoulder. I try to writhe violently and get nowhere, then let out an involuntary, guttural noise of utter revulsion, because those are his *teeth*.

"My bite is worse than yours, Huntress. Don't tempt m—"

I gasp when my feet stumble over the hard, ash-laden street. Xavier is hauling us backwards...and Levi is suddenly just two metres in front of us, his daggers ringing with intent, cheeks flushed and weathered grey eyes *furious*.

"Don't do it, Silverstone," Xavier warns, his heartbeat lurching behind me, thudding down my spine with increasing force. "I'll hurt her."

"Let her go, Xavier."

"Who...Skye?"

Xavier says my name lightly, but the sound echoes for *miles* in my ears, deafening me...and when he next speaks, he's right there. Not behind me, as a warm physical force of violent violation, but somewhere worse.

Take the dagger, he murmurs inside my mind. *Hurt yourself.*

I feel my right hand reach up for the blade held against my throat. He drops it as soon as my fingers find purchase, and then *fast*, against my will, against every single fibre of my being, I start sliding it over my neck. I let out a noise of surprise as the sting of metal greets my flesh, as I heed what he's doing...what *I'm* doing...and how utterly powerless I am to stop it. My eyes flash to Levi as the blade starts

397

burrowing deeper, fear and pain rising. His features are tight with focus, gaze dark and raw like granite...and then he's right there. Not in my mind like Xavier, but just inches from us. Moving just as fast again, in a manner that reminds me of Zelos on the hilltop summit, he grips my wrist and mutters, "Παύση."

Stop.

Desist.

I do, much to Xavier's fury...and fear. From the way his heart is continuing to pick up pace behind me, I know he doesn't like Levi being this close to us, no matter how well his cruel mouth works to hide it.

"You never did need blood for that, did you? Yet unfortunately your hands are covered in it. Your soul, too. Permanently. Mummy couldn't save you from that, could she?" He snarls the words with pure hatred. "Back away now or I'll hurt her in a way you can't prevent."

"Let Skye go, Xavier. This isn't about her."

"Wrong. It's *entirely* about Skye, the great demigod in the prophecy. You're just a delightful bonus like the first time...and I was right, you know. Right about Kieran. Him being special, and not because he was so tightly tied to you...and not that you'd know anything about it, yet. You're *still* not backing away, Levi. It has me wanting to ask Skye if she knows what happens if a Guardian forgoes their honour? If she knows they're tortured by their own mind in a terrible debt entirely unique to our kind. Does she know how excruciating it is? Simply the worst pain imaginable."

The grip on my wrist loosens a notch. "Let her go, Xavier. Fight me."

"Fight you? No thanks, *Silver.*"

"Worried you'll lose?"

Xavier hums, but there's a *very* dark edge to it. "Yes, I'm worried I'll lose to you...but do you never learn? What did my mother, the great Nike herself, teach you most of all? What did she drill into you time and time again when she chose to train you over her own son?"

"Let Skye go, Xavier."

"'Hesitation doesn't suit a Guardian,'" he quotes, completely ignoring Levi, and instead leaning *into* me. Into my body, and my mind. "It doesn't suit them, Skye, because it never ends well for those they try to protect."

Fierce pain instantly splits my head in two, unlike anything I've ever felt before. It's overwhelming, unbearable...shattering. I sag in Xavier's arms, the dagger falling from limp fingertips with a clatter to the ground, head drooping like a wilting flower. A horrible, wretched groan seeps into the night air, seeps into my bones. It's coming from me, and it's endless.

"I won't stop, Levi," Xavier grates out. "Retreat. Before this becomes irreversible."

"Don't," I hear someone whisper as the hand on my wrist loosens more, then realise it's *me*. I'm speaking, but I sound different. Hoarse, and broken. "Don't retreat, Levi. You should go for him, because I'm f..fine"

"You're *fine,* did you say, Skye? *Really?*"

I let out another low, insensible gasp as the pain increases and the pulse in my temples gives a shockingly violent throb. Something bursts. Rust hits the back of my throat, stinging my nose...and then there's blood, dribbling from parched lips. I barely heed it. There are knives and knots, hands stabbing and twisting my mind into some warped, lost impression of what it should be. I'm on fire, or drenched in ice? Thrumming, so alive that more of me is about to explode...or am I dying?

I shudder, legs quaking and then giving out. Xavier arm around my shoulders and neck is the only thing holding me up, like a noose of flesh...and there's a grip on my wrist, too, something warm and gentle tethering me to a world beyond violent will. I think I might be sick, vomit the blood that's already burst its banks inside me...and maybe I am. I think Levi is saying my name, but I don't know. Not sure if I'm hot or cold, rife with too much energy or completely sapped of it...because all there is is pain.

Pain and fury.

"*Go* for him, Levi," I manage to get out, speech totally garbled. "Throw...h..him...t..to..."

"The crows?" Xavier finishes my pitiful stutter with a small laugh. The torture in my mind lets up slightly, the unbearable edge flaking away with each word spoken by him. "Unfortunately, Levi doing that would *really* hurt you right now, Skye. It's impossible to do something to me without also doing something to you, the fiery little hostage to my will. The puppet to my practised puppeteer hands. We're tied together at the moment, so I suppose you're my own special Guardian...and I should thank you for that, because Styx's great warrior would no doubt have ended my sorry ass minutes ago were you not shielding me..." His laugh is a snarl. "Too *bad*, Levi. In time, maybe you'll get your shot. In *time...*"

He halts, sniffing suddenly like a predator would upon first catching their prey's scent. Everything about him...stops. He stops torturing me, and he stops talking.

Stops *breathing.*

"In time time *time,*" Xavier mutters, voice dropping into a horribly low tone of disappointment. "Oh, *Levi.* That's not a good boy. What have you been up to tonight in the fortress? In my quarters?"

Gasping with effort, I manage to lift my head. The veil over Levi's expression is slipping, showing something of surprise. Something that tells me he didn't anticipate whatever Xavier is talking about. His eyes bounce between mine, searching for something...

Xavier is tutting slowly, "That's a *bad* boy, stealing from me. Did you think I wouldn't notice? Getting this close? *Big* mistake. I smell it on him, Skye. Borrowed time. The thief's way to freedom." He inhales deeply, right beneath my ear. "That is a *bad* boy, Levi. I'm not impressed, and you've just lost this game. Let her go and retreat. Right now."

To my shock and horror, Levi *does* retreat. As soon as his grip leaves me, I feel different.

I feel panic.

Xavier starts walking us backwards again, and his heart isn't quite so fast and fearful now. It's as if he suddenly knows the winning move, knows how to play his opponent; and from the way Levi isn't moving forwards, isn't pursuing us like he just was, I think he knows it too.

"Let's get onto the second message of tonight, shall we? Have a little reprieve from all this hurt. I need you to hold your tongues throughout your thrilling trip to The Cold Kingdom. Please. Hold them, and I'll refrain from doing the same to Skye as I did to stupid little Kieran. I'm leaving state life for a month or two, but I expect to return to my gracious duties as Ruby's protector when I return, and I expect *her* to be progressing well with that sweet little ritual she likes conducting in Poseidon's temple. Do you understand me? Hold your tongues on all of this, especially me, and I won't hurt Skye...and I *will* hurt her if you disobey me. I have a way of knowing everything. Messengers are *everywhere* these days, taking flight like a nightingale at dawn..." His hold on me shifts, both hands slipping to my shoulders and squeezing in a way that's almost fatherly...except it's not. It's just wrong. "No silence this time, Levi. I'll need verbal confirmation. Do you understand that if you keep your stupid mouths shut on your way to Wivern, I'll keep her sanity safe?"

"I understand," Levi says hoarsely. "So will Fjord."

"Well...that's better, isn't it? He's really a good boy...who does bad things occasionally."

"Don't talk about him like that," I spit out, lips sticky with blood. "Shut up. The moon is *furious* with you, so just shut up, Xavier."

He gives a low, bemused laugh. "What're you talking of, the moon being furious? You're a funny girl...a funny puppet. You look funny, too, and I find myself intrigued as to why. Maybe next time we'll chat about that?"

The curse I give him is too vulgar to tell you.

Xavier snorts at it, looking down the street. "I think you know my parting request, Levi. You almost had it, but it's now *time* to return what's mine. My trophy. Back up and throw it to her or I'll drop this one."

He lifts a hand and tugs something from around his neck, holding it out in front of us both. It's glasslike, on a leather cord...and very familiar. An empty hourglass? He swings it side to side like a pendulum, but it's the only thing that *does* move. I'm frozen, immobilised by the strength of his will despite doing everything in my feeble, fatigued power to strain away, and Levi is also so still. My eyes seek him out, watching him follow the hourglass's small ticking motion with a locked jaw...

"I said *now*, Levi!" Xavier barks. "Hesitation doesn't *suit* a Guardian, and it won't suit Skye, either. Not at all. Back away quickly....and throw it to her."

Both Levi's daggers are in one hand, and in the other is something small and glasslike? *Another* hourglass...though this one isn't the same as the one around his neck.

He looks at me carefully. "Don't drop it, Skye."

Xavier's hold lets up enough for me to snag the vessel from the air - and thank the gods I *do*. Glancing down, I see it's almost exactly like the ones the boys wear, only it isn't sand in this hourglass. It's something that looks like clear liquid beneath the moonlight.

Water?

"Very good," Xavier's murmurs from behind me. "That's a *very* good boy. Skye, turn around and put it on me."

Don't do it, my counsel urges, sounding absolutely horrified. *Fight him, Skye. You* must *fight him.*

I blink down at the pendant, so serene on the outside but screaming internally. With a terrible growl of struggle, I feel myself start to turn and lift it over Xavier's neck, submitting to his will. I hate that I do. I hate that I can't stop it...until I lift my gaze.

This time, it's not Levi's skin that breaks Xavier's order in my mind. It's just him. He's as still as a statue, muscles wrought with tension and lifeless eyes so bleak.

Ruined.

Maybe wet.

There's suddenly someone beside him, too. Someone who looks like Fjord, but younger and smaller. I blink rapidly, pulse spiking. Where on *earth* did he come from? And why is Levi standing there like he has no idea he's there?

The strangest feeling rises within me, something that exceeds the goosebumps prickling my skin from what my instincts *know* is the echo of a wayward soul. It's more than that, and it feels like recognition. Deep in my bones, I know that the awful expression on the boy's face is conveying everything Levi is refusing to show the world. Despair, horror, and pain of a horrendous magnitude that I've never experienced before, and never, ever will...

"Turn around and put it *on* me, Skye!"

I blink, twice. The strange figure disappears, but the wretched feelings remain, and so does my ability to fight.

Levi is so still.

So obliging and quiet.

"Now!" Xavier orders.

"No," I mutter.

"Yes."

"*No.*"

This time I say the word stubbornly and *hear* Xavier's lips pull back in an answering snarl. I resist his physical hold on me as much as I can, refusing to turn...refusing to do as he wills. My fist shakes with conviction around the tiny hourglass, but my grip on it is so gentle, because everything is telling me that this totem is very, very important. Everything in me is rising, like an ember in the ashes, to *fight* Xavier. To resist him. To deny him winning the pivotal scene in someone else's story.

Levi's story.

He snarls at me again. "If you don't do this, I will *destroy* everyone you've ever lo—"

"Levi...!"

I speak quickly and suddenly, and don't wait for a reply. I fling the pendant back down the street, thinking of nothing except to vaguely get it in his vicinity. The throw is awkward given Xavier's hold on me, but I watch with relief as he snags it easily from the air.

"I will torture you for that," Xavier growls in my ear.

"Get on with it, then," I breathe back. "I can take it. I can take anything."

Only I don't *let* him get on with it. Something in me snaps as I sense him moving to strike. Ichor, the blood of the gods and goddesses, surges through my veins once more, violent and volatile.

It happens too fast for me to even try to rein it in, or to think if I'll be strong enough to wield it.

Zeus is right with you, my counsel mutters. *Use him.*

I have no idea what she means by that, or if, in the heat of the moment, I imagine her voice. All I heed is the swelling sensation of power rising in me, and the deitous blood searing my skin, causing Xavier's hold to loosen suddenly. The blade at my neck twitches, the sting of metal greeting flesh...because he's striking.

He's retaliating.

But so am I.

Haunted

With my limbs propelled by the wind rioting down the street, I reach up impossibly fast and snatch Xavier by the forearm, pushing it away from my neck with borrowed, godlike strength. I dip and spin, popping up to face him in my favourite sparring move, and then I pull my fist back and punch him square in the jaw. Harder than I punched Fjord. Flesh splits and bones give, almost breaking, and I realise with cold pleasure I *could* break him.

I could shatter him.

Not a second later, air stirs my hair as Levi moves between us, heralding a soft puff of smoke and minerals. He backs me up several hurried metres, and yet I have the impression *he's* not retreating himself. The hourglass I threw back to him has disappeared, hidden somewhere safe in the folds of his shirt – just like I'm now tucked safely in his shadow.

Xavier's spits out a globule of blood to the street, either from a bitten tongue or torn gum. "Stand down, Levi, or I'll harm Skye again."

Levi doesn't, of course. The muscles down his spine ripple as he takes a single, intent-laden step forward, in the same moment that something visceral springs to life in me, a force that tugs the godlike blood faster and faster and *faster* through my veins. I realise it's him, igniting his own ichor, because I see it too. Just as with Zelos in the ruined hilltop temple, veins suddenly light up beneath Levi's skin, pulsing with every strong, steady beat of his heart – except where Zelos was magnificently golden, Levi is *silver*, his blood like liquid mercury.

Power.

Pure, glorious power is what I see before me. Instinctually, I know his ichor is thousands of times more potent than mine, infused with years upon years of deep, reverent understanding...the kind of understanding garnered only by a deity themselves, which later perplexes me. Awes me. Levi *can't* be a god, and yet he looks like one now, and I know down to my bones and soul that I'm blessed to witness this.

"I said stand down!" Xavier barks. His voice grows shrill when he sees Levi's silvery form, his knuckles blanching white around the hilt of his sword. He stumbles back several feet quickly. "Stand down now!"

Levi stalks forward, every step a stride closer to a sprint...a stride closer to striking his nemesis. The force of his footfalls sends shockwaves over the ground in the total inverse of his usual quiet, reserved self. My teeth rattle, blood heavy and swift in my veins...and I suddenly have an insane urge to hurry frantically forwards and bow before him. To give myself and the vigour of my own ichor to him in offering.

"Παύω!" Xavier shouts.

Stop!

Breath flees me in a sharp, shocked exhale, icy panic drenching my system as it senses something is suddenly horribly wrong. Xavier's order, his will, is on me and in me once more, squeezing my heart with bare, brutal intent...and the muscle is spasming.

Shuddering.

Stopping.

I fall from my lusty pedestal of power straight to my knees, gasping as something deeply torturous sparks inside me.

My heart is *stopping*.

"Stand down or I'll break her!" Xavier shouts madly, his voice fading as he flees down the street. "I will *break* her!"

I let out a horribly wet groan as the vice in my chest tightens. My mind is spinning but my heart is so *still.* My hands clutch at my sternum, fingers delving into the flesh there like they wish to rip the organ from me and prise his grip away. I taste blood idling on the back of my throat, feel it slipping over my tongue for the second time tonight, see nothing but singeing salt water...and hear the sound of thundering footsteps slow.

I don't hear a pulse in my ears.

"Follow me or run your mouths and her death will be on your hands! This isn't over. I *will* get that hourglass back, Levi, and I will *torture* her for robbing me of it today. Do you hear that, Huntress? I will break you."

I don't even have the wherewithal to lift my head. One of my palms lands clumsily on the ashy street as my body sags forwards. My breaths seem to be shrivelling in my lungs, the pain in my sternum so intense and sharp, but so *aching* everywhere else. My blood is too idle in my veins. There are footsteps. Two sets. One running toward me, the other away...but I can't look up to tell whose is whose, and it panics me. Then, just when everything grows unbearable and I'm teetering on the edge of something horribly irreversible, Xavier's hushed voice echoes in my mind again.

"Αρχίζω."

Start.

My heart judders to life, great swathes of blood rushing back into my system. My other hand lands on the street to stop me eating dirt, and I gulp down air as the beat inside me builds and builds and builds, until I'm not sure I can take it. It's never gone like this. Heavy, thick and so quick, thudding with utterly overwhelming force. I truly feel like my blood might burst its banks.

I think I might die.

"Skye."

Levi is crouching before me, steadying me by the shoulders. I try to look up at him and fail, head bowed by the weight of blood thumping through it like a battering ram, burrowing relentlessly through my veins.

"Μίλησέ μου, Skye."

"Fj..Fjord?" I groan.

"No, it's Levi. What's wrong?"

"I mean...is Fjord ok?"

"Yes. I had him return to the Guild when I knew what was happening."

"Jay?"

"He's fine, well beyond Ioxthel's walls by now."

"And you?" I gasp. "Are you ok, Levi?"

"Yes, I'm fine. W—"

"Xavier? Is he gone?"

One of Levi's hands presses to my cheek, helping me to look up. Eyes sharp with vigilance, vengeance and frustration search mine, then take inventory of the damage...or I think they do, but my vision is blurring and something thin and rusty is dripping from my nose and lips, disorienting me.

"Xavier is gone," he assures me. "You must tell me what's wrong. I don't know how to help. Where are you in pain? In your mind, like before?"

"No. In m..my heart. Xavier stopped it dead, but it's off now. So quick I think I might die."

Fingers immediately brush my neck, finding the erratic pulse there. It really is going mad, terrorising me. I feel bleary and heady and very seriously stressed. I don't know how to stop it. Don't know if I want to, if it was stopped before?

"I don't know how to stop it," I hear myself echo to Levi. "Don't know why it's so fast? Don't know if I *want* to stop it, if it stopped before? Don't know what's wrong?"

"Your system is in shock."

"Oh..."

"Sit down?"

I do, *hard* on my backside. "Do demigods go into shock? I don't think they do. That sounds st..stupid."

"It's not stupid."

"I think it is. Mad stupid, just like I'm mad p..panicking..." I haul in several shallow breaths, throat full of fast, stamping feet. "I'm just going to sit and rest, if that's ok with you? If you're here?"

"I'd have you do nothing else."

I bow my head again. "You should rest too, because it would..." *help me feel less embarrassed, please?*

I think I might actually mumble that last bit out loud, and I also think I might say something even worse after it. Something like, "Just because my head is down, it doesn't mean I'm struggling to breathe," or "Demigods don't go into shock, you know." Maybe even, "I've never had a heart attack before."

"Deep breaths, Skye," Levi coaches after what feels like hours. "Let yourself quieten."

"I'm not shocked, just stressed," I wheeze back. "Can't you tell? If I'm talking, I'm not in shock. Just stressed. I'm...I'm just..."

"Safe?"

I lift my head with difficulty, searching for eyes of granite. There they are, and though his response isn't what I was about to say, I realise it works. "I suppose I am safe here, with you? With someone who somehow glows silver?"

Levi nods. "Let yourself quieten."

This time I listen to him, and it turns out to be exactly what my body needs to hear and heed – for it to know I am safe, and there's no need to panic. No need for my system to wreak havoc on itself in shock and terror, because this is *me* going wild, and not something to do with Xavier's will. Long seconds pass before I manage to take several purposefully deep breaths, each one easier than the last. They ease my hunched shoulders and hazy, hectic mind – and as if Levi heeds his own words, the silvery, luminescent veins of ichor beneath his skin dim, fading to simple sun-blushed flesh blanched by moonlight. The unspent fury and missed opportunity splashed over his face give way to something steadier, something less intimidating that looks like a soft breath of relief.

"Good," he offers, listening to my pulse sort itself out into something vaguely normal. "Are you cold, Skye?"

"No," I sigh. "I think I'm boiling. But are you? Cold? Do you want my cloak? It's probably too small for you, but you can totally have it anyway. Here..."

I start fumbling with the clasp beneath my neck, watching him watch *me* through his lashes as he quickly strips himself of his own cloak and throws it over my shoulders, one hand briefly landing on mine to stop my clumsy endeavours in doing the same for him. His is blood red, and the breastplate revealed beneath it has detailing around its edges exactly like those the alcázarian sentries wear...and that makes me wonder why he's wearing it as a Guardian undercover in the Guild, and who exactly he was pretending to be tonight in the fortress with Jay. And that makes me think of the hourglass, and how he stole it from Xavier...and *why* he stole it from Xavier? Which is perhaps why it takes me longer than is normal to realise why Levi is looking at me like I'm odd after offering him my little cloak...because I'm shivering in shock, and he is not.

"I'm fine," I mumble randomly. "I'm fine, and I'm sorry, too. For getting caught by him. I didn't mean to. Not one bit."

"I know. Just rest now."

He focuses on settling his cloak around me. I watch him work, inhaling something of woodsmoke and minerals and rust. The last isn't him, but the others are, and they're oddly familiar. I suppose that's not surprising, given we've been patrolling together nearly every day for the past few months, but what *is* surprising is that my wolf senses haven't registered the smell as him before.

They surely have now, though.

They surely like it.

"Thank you for scaring him off," I hear myself say, and clearly *nothing* is enough to stop my mouth from running itself. "In the end. Thanks for doing that. I didn't know how to ignite ichor, so it took me a while to break his hold. His will. I find it quite terrible that he could order me to stand so still, and will me to feel so very bad in the head. Like he said happens when a Guardian's honour is lost? I don't think I've processed that yet, but I should've broken it sooner. His will. I'm a demigod, aren't I? Very poor show from me tonight, but next time I'll be better."

"Δεν θα υπάρξει επόμενη φορά."

There will be no next time.

Levi's eyes meet mine and stay there. I see anger in them, and also resolve. At a loss of how to respond, I nod. "Did...did you put it somewhere safe? The hourglass?"

"Yes."

"Is it ok?"

"Yes."

I think perhaps he means to say something more after that from the way he's still staring at me, unblinking...or maybe not. I just don't know. Never do with him, and especially right now. Something warm and sticky runs over my lips, disorienting me. It's blood. I give a horrible wet sniff, wiping the back of my arm over my mouth and nearly elbowing Levi in the face as I do. He dodges it expertly, weight still balanced perfectly on the balls of his feet – and he's even working to balance *me* too.

Gods, I'm a mess.

"Your hand," he mutters.

My shirt sleeve and the edge of his cloak are smeared bright red when I lower it from my face, but there's even more blood slicking my palm. The cut Xavier made is gaping open, and it hurts. My *right* hand is also sore, in a totally different way to the sting of a deep laceration. It feels tender and bruised, and probably will be for days, but you should know I feel more pride than pain looking down at it. That was the best punch I've ever given. It was so, *so* good that I want to do it again, and next time I *will* break Xavier's jaw. I'll shatter the obnoxious smirk right off his face, without regret.

I raise my hand to the moonlight and inspect the pink, mottled skin over my knuckles, bloody lips tipping into a grim, gruesome smile at the thought. Levi is busy doing something with the bottom of his shirt, shredding it with his daggers, but he glances over when he sees what I'm doing.

"How hard is it to make a fist?"

"Not hard," I say, without trying.

Turns out he's no fool. "Show me?"

I do...and expertly hide a wince. "Ok. It might hurt a bit, but it's fine. I'm fine. I just hope Xavier feels the hit tomorrow. Break me my κώλος! Next time I'll break *him*."

Levi takes my left wrist, inspecting the slash still bubbling blood on my palm. "He did this, too?"

"Yeah. Before you guys passed by. I think he sought me out for it tonight, because he told me he tried to find me in the Guild before he realised I wasn't there...realised I'd followed you to Alcázar."

"The vial of blood he held tonight was definitely yours?"

I nod, watching him closely. His nostrils are flaring, hiding something strained playing out behind the veil over his features. Something he doesn't share.

"This might hurt, Skye. I'm sorry if it does."

"That's ok."

He starts wrapping the strip of white fabric torn from the bottom of his shirt tightly around my palm, binding it. His touch is purposeful but so gentle, and that about sums Levi up doesn't it? Purposeful. Gentle. Godlike. Our gazes meet and hold for about the twelfth time tonight when he finishes, using my wrist to listen to my pulse. He's still sitting on words unspoken and sentiment unshared, and although that's not unusual at all for him, this time it's really worrying me.

"Are you ok?" I ask quietly.

"Yes."

"I'm sorry you didn't get to chase him. Or hit him. Sorry that was my fault."

"It wasn't your fault. Never say that again, please."

I swallow. "Are you ok, though?"

He shifts on the balls of his feet, adjusting his balance. After brief thought, he brushes the backs of his knuckles over my cheek. "Yes."

"You promise? We could go, if you wanted? I'm fine. My head doesn't hurt any more, and nor does my heart."

"I would have you rest longer, Skye."

"I don't need to, though. Not at all. Demigods *don't* go into shock – I've just figured that out."

No reply.

"Levi, I'm *fine.*"

414

No reply...but he does touch my cheek again, and tucks a strand of my hair behind my ear. Now I'm the one shifting restlessly, trying and failing to pretend to calm down, thoughts on how nice his skin feels against mine, and then on how twisted my priorities are.

"This is silly," I eventually mutter. "I'm wasting your time."

Now he chooses to say something back. "Given how much you just bought me, I shouldn't worry."

"What does that mean?"

No response! He just observes our surroundings as *I* observe him intently, infuriated...because what *does* that mean? That Levi still has the stolen hourglass? That borrowed time is the thief's way to freedom? That the damned are never pardoned? That...there's someone else once again in the street with us, and Levi is looking right at him and not seeing him?

"I miss you more than everything."

The words, the voice, are carried on the breeze. I squint as my vision blurs, but although there suddenly appear to be two people in front of me, it's not because I'm struggling to focus.

They're...distinct.

Two different beings.

It's Levi's shadow again. The same one that appeared right when he threw the hourglass to Xavier and I. His features are sharper and paler, like Fjord but younger. And then Fjord *is* suddenly there on the other side of Levi, looking startled and panicked, in a haze of exertion. I have no idea how I missed his footsteps approaching.

"What happened?" he demands breathlessly. "What happened, Silver?!"

"I told you to stay in the Guild," Levi says, turning to him and using a *very* stern voice. "I told you—"

"Shut up," Fjord snaps back. "You knew I was coming straight here when I realised she wasn't there. Gods, Skye. Sweetheart. You're bleeding everywhere?!"

Warm, slightly shaking hands find my cheeks, tilting my face up to inspect the damage. I feel Levi pull away but don't understand his reply. It's made in Ancient Nereid, and I'm not really paying attention anyway, because his shadow is crying. He's watching Levi speak with an expression torn by deep feeling, and with tears welling in his eyes.

"Levi, there's someone beside you," I whisper.

He breaks off, twisting around to survey the street. For a second time, he looks straight at the weeping shadow and doesn't see him. "There's no one there."

But there is. And with that white skin and those shockingly blue lips and dark hair, I'm not dizzy and I'm not seeing double, am I? I'm looking at a ghost. A crying ghost.

"He's like you," I breathe to Fjord. "Younger, but just like you, and he's right there."

His eyes turn bright with worry, "There's no one, Skye. No one anywhere nearby. I think you're in shock. Come here..."

I slip through his arms as he tries to gather me close. "Xavier didn't hurt me *that* much, Fjord. I'm ok. I just...I *see* you there."

I move to standing, wobbling only slightly. Their shadow, the ghost, blinks rapidly. He seems to realise with horror that I'm speaking to him and immediately turns away, wiping an arm roughly over his face just as I had minutes ago...only he's wiping away tears, not blood. I stumble towards him, ignoring Fjord's noise of indignation and the echo of an attempt Levi gives to stop me. I'm really not imagining this, am I? This isn't some scarred, orphaned enigma who wields a silver bow and tries for invisibility but never *quite* blends into the shadows.

This is a real ghost.

"Who are you?" I press, drifting closer. "Do I..." *Do I already know the answer to that, Kieran...?*

I lift a hand to grip his shoulder – but he turns and stumbles back on his haunches before I make contact, shocked to see me standing over him. His eyes dart beyond me, expression twisting once more into insurmountable grief...and then he vanishes into thin air.

Fjord is right there to replace him, looking very distressed and *very* similar in looks. He takes my hand still poised in mid-air, his grip gentle but highly possessive. "What's wrong, Skye?! Did you hit your head?!"

"No," I peer around him to search the empty street. "I'm fine. I'm not delirious, I just...I think I just saw a ghost."

He stares at me like I'm mad. "People don't *see* ghosts, Skye. Wraiths maybe, but not ghosts...and if it were a wraith Levi and I would've been able to see it. We would've had to fight it. There are never any in Ioxthel anyway. You're...you're definitely in shock. Come on, we need to get you to the infirmary."

"I'm not in shock. I'll have you know demigods don't go into shock. Levi and I have just been over that."

"Don't lie to me. You're still bleeding, and shaking, and you need to see a healer...doesn't she?"

He turns to Levi, appealing for backing from him. The Guardian is busy watching our surroundings through his lashes, and then me.

"I saw a ghost," I mutter to him. "Right beside you. He...he was right there. I swear it."

"Did you hit your head? Levi? Did she hit her head?"

"Not with me."

"Are you sure? Are you *sure* she didn't?!"

"I can't be sure what happened before I arrived, but..."

He goes on to say something further in Ancient Nereid, something that has Fjord immediately picking up my left hand. Even though the wound is hidden by Levi's shirt-tourniquet, his face blanches of all colour, until his skin is almost as white as the ghost of his brother's had been.

"No," he mutters, aghast.

"I'm ok," I tell him quickly, instinctually hating how horribly worried he sounds. "I'm fine, seriously!"

"Did he do this?! Xavier?!"

Warily, I nod. His features become impossibly deep with strife. He stares at me, shocked and unspeaking, then lets me go and puts his head in his hands. He lifts it almost immediately, looking to Levi with woeful eyes and increasingly sharp breaths, and then puts it right back down.

"This can't be happening," he mutters, then sucks the words right back in with a sharp inhale. "Silver, I don't...I *can't* do this again."

My eyes bounce to Levi. The Guardian is watching both of us with a locked jaw and a sudden, severe strain to his face, like he's struggling to hold his sentiments behind closed doors. He turns quickly, shoulders rising and falling rapidly, the muscles down his spine rippling as if to prepare themselves for battle...except there's no battle here.

Just the war to hide emotions.

"Something is wrong," I say in a small voice. "What is wrong, Fjord?"

"Xavier killed my brother."

"Wh..what?!"

"He stole Kieran's blood, and made him do terrible, terrible things that drove him to insanity. Then he forced his death. He's just done the same to you, Skye. Με πονάει, he's just done the same to you!"

His voice jolts as he starts speaking in Ancient Nereid, and I wouldn't be surprised if he's letting out an expletive – or several. He reclaims his hold on my wrist, fingers spasming. All I can do is stare up at him with wide eyes, my icy gut plummeting. *Everything* Xavier just said to Levi now makes sense.

He stole Kieran's blood.

Drove him insane.

Controlled him.

Killed him.

"Don't argue with me!" Fjord bursts out in our tongue, and I'm not sure what he thinks I'm about to say...because I'm not about to say anything. The only reason my mouth is slackening is shock, and dismay. "Don't argue, Skye! Just let me get you somewhere safe! I just...I need to figure this out! Find out what happened! I need to remedy this! You need to *stop* fighting me, and I..." His voice breaks, then crescendos. Over his shoulder, I see Levi turn around quickly. "I need to *stop* this. To get it back. Your blood. You need to *stop* fighting me, Skye. We need to return to the Guild, now. And...goddesses this can't be happening. Please tell me it's not. Please tell me—"

"Fjord."

"— I can't do this again. Not with you. It's my fault, isn't it? I didn't tell you about Kieran, and I didn't *tell* you what we were doing tonight in the fortress. Shit. I'm so —"

"*Fjord.*"

Levi's voice is quiet, but it somehow brings more force with it, more thunder, than if ten men had shouted Fjord's name. He's watching his friend with an expression that barely tames the wretched distress I think he's feeling, and he looks much younger than he usually does – a different being entirely to the glorious, godlike Guardian of just minutes before.

"We should return to the Guild," he urges. "Skye should rest. None of us should be out here on the streets. Not discussing...this. Let's go. Back to the Guild."

"I can't do this —"

"I know," Levi interrupts. "I know, Fjord. Please. Can we go?"

Please.

Can we go?

The words are said in a voice that's also younger than usual, and they seem to burst through Fjord's haze of horror. He looks to his Guardian, his next sharp inhale stuck in his lungs. "Gods, Silver...is this happening?"

"Ναί, είμαι."

Yes, it is.

Fjord looks back at me, the frenzy of fear in his eyes dimming to something utterly devastated.

"I'm so sorry," I whisper, and my lips are now trembling for both of them – for the terrible strife I know they're now feeling. "I just wanted to help. I followed you to Alcázar to keep you guys safe. To impress you."

Fjord's expression twists itself inside out. He ducks his head quickly, hiding it from me. Several breaths pass before he reaches up and gathers the edges of Levi's cloak together beneath my chin. His forehead drops to mine, gentle but heavy, like there's a terrible weight in his mind.

"Gods help us," he murmurs there. "Help me keep her safe."

The Story Left Untold

We return quickly to the Guild. There's a brittle haze loitering in my thoughts, something that feels frantic and urgent but at the same time hinders my ability to truly focus on anything. I think, or know, it's me coming out of shock. I lied earlier. I don't feel fine. I feel shaky, worried, fatigued and violated realising Xavier had been in my mind, controlling me, forcing me to do things I did *not* want to do.

He'd been right there.

Is...he still there?

I insist on showering before Fjord bundles me into my room, because now that *he* is coming down from the shock of finding me bleeding all over the street, he seems to think better of taking me straight to the infirmary with unexplainable injuries that will no doubt make their way to Fin's eager ears.

I don't see much of my skin as I lather sandalwood soap over my arms and stomach beneath the pipe of cold water, but from the way it hurts scrubbing them, I assume I'm doing a good job. When I finish, I move towards the eyelet mirror I always have to stand on tiptoes to see in, the one embossed with scenes of Eros around its edges...and that I swear I don't look in very often.

It isn't kind to me.

My amber eyes are bright and wild, cheeks flushed but skin everywhere else several shades too pale, and that means the scars of lightning over my face, shoulders and torso seem more visible than they've ever been before.

For the first time in a *long* time, my throat closes up at the sight. The markings are extensive, now definitely reaching my left buttock, and just like Xavier intimated earlier they're angry and loud, different and unexplainable. I find nothing remotely good about them in this moment. I don't like them, or the way I still feel dirty for what's happened – and not just because there's blood leaking from my left palm, thinned by water and staining Levi's torn shirt.

Levi.

Just who have I been walking beside for the past few months? The silent, shunned Guardian who glows with rivers of silver when he summons the powers of the gods and goddesses, and who Xavier clearly hates and fears...and who I wanted to *bow* to? The Guardian who I think is haunted?

We did see someone else on the street. Someone who looked like a younger Fjord, watching Levi speak with tears of impossibly deep strife, deep feeling, in his eyes.

I stare at my own weird, frenzied amber gaze in the mirror, blinking slowly but thinking so quickly; burrowing down rabbit holes, surfing storm cloud after storm cloud, realising I want to speak with...

You there?

I'm here, my counsel responds immediately. *I'm always here, sweetheart. Are you ok?*

Yeah. How're you?

Worried for you.

I'm sorry. I panicked so much, and couldn't ignite ichor like you wished me to. Sholto hasn't taught me how to do that yet, so I'm not sure what hailing the goddesses actually means?

Don't be sorry.

I have a question about the ghost.

Yes?

Was he...Fjord's brother?

What does your gut tell you?

I swallow tightly. *That it was him, Kieran.*

She nods.

Should I tell Fjord, and Levi?

You already did.

Yeah...but they thought I was in shock, or mad, because of what Xavier did in stealing my blood and forcing my will. Fjord said he did the same to his brother and it drove him insane. So is this...is this me, already going insane? Is that why I still feel dirty, even though I've washed?

My counsel's expression turns pained. *No, sweetheart. This isn't you going insane. I won't let that happen. We'll figure this out, and keep you safe. Together.*

I like the sound of that. Of together.

Me too.

She smiles and I smile back, because I'm not insane. I'm just smiling to an imaginary voice in a mind that feels breached and a heart that *stopped* earlier. *So...should I tell them again? About Kieran?*

My guidance would be to wait, Skye. Ghosts who haunt the shadows of those they love walk in their footsteps until the end of time itself, and Kieran loved those two. So much. He'll mind the passages of both his brother and his Guardian throughout their lives. Why don't you wait until you see him again to say something further to them. Or indeed, to him.

To him?

Talking to Kieran, the *real* ghost. That's what I'm thinking about when I push open the door to my room and spy Fjord standing by my window. He's staring down at the dark, moonlit quads below, expression one of stress and feeling and his shoulders incredibly tense beneath the velvet of his Lieutenant cloak.

"Hey," I say quietly.

"How're you feeling?"

"Fine," I lie. "Totally fine."

I look up as he stops before me. He holds out a hand for my left palm to examine the slash I've just rewrapped, this time with my own shredded shirt. Levi did a much better job with his tourniquet, so it's probably a good thing he's not here to see this one.

Part of me wishes he was.

"Do you know where Sholto is?" Fjord asks after he's checked me over. "He was supposed to be looking after you tonight."

"I don't think he's in. He definitely didn't follow me through the streets to Alcázar. I'm so sorry, Fjord. For not listening to you enough about Xavier. For getting caught."

He shakes his head. "It is I who must apologise to you for not telling you everything sooner, Skye. Let's sit. You should rest, and I need to talk." He guides us to the bed and busies himself pouring me a cup from my bedside pitcher. Then he goes *straight* for it. "Kieran died eight years ago, just two years before I left for Ioxthel. He took his own life, having fallen prey to Xavier's manipulation for several months...though this was unbeknownst to both Levi and myself at the time. We had no idea what was going on. Kieran was loud and full of life, and that meant he always put on a good show. Outwardly, he was fine for the most part...and I think at first he didn't *remember* the terrible things Xavier was forcing him to do, but then he did, and it ruined him. He pushed Levi and I away. Fell into something of drink and turmoil and trouble, and then one day he showed up in our family kitchen with this terribly torn expression on his face, something of hatred and murder, and pain, and...he went for me."

Fjord swallows hard. His eyes are holding mine, their muddy hue deepening with feeling and unhappiness, and memory. He seems to muster strength of the kind I don't have experience with to say what he does next, his voice like gravel. I want to look away, to give him space to tell me this, but I can't. I'm already frozen, snared by the story.

The tragedy.

"Levi stopped him of course. Easily. But we were both in shock. We didn't know this was Xavier manipulating my brother's mind. Both of us were trying to figure out what on earth was happening, trying to subdue someone struggling *not* to do something he didn't have control over. Kieran was...beside himself. Manic and...and just not himself, in a very overwhelming, scary way. And in our confusion and desperation to understand what was happening, to help him and prevent him from going for either of us again, Kieran took his own life. I'm sure he did it to stop himself fulfilling Xavier's order to kill us, but...he still took his own life, Skye, right in front of our eyes, and I lost my brother."

Hot, horrified tears spring to life in me, immediately spilling from my eyes. "Fjord. I am...so sorry."

He nods, jaw so hard you could sharpen a sword on it. I can tell he's holding back tears, too, but he forces himself to go on. "Levi and my brother were tethered, Skye. United upon birth by the eternal tie. It's a rare infallible bond that sometimes forms between a Guardian and their ward. Kieran was a brother to me, and I loved him so dearly, but for Levi his loss was just unfathomable. They were the very truest and deepest of friends, anchored to one another in a way that's impossible to understand unless you've experienced what it is to be tied to someone else physically, spiritually and mentally. I believe it breaks something in you, losing someone you're tied to and maybe especially with this. The circumstances of Kieran's death were unspeakably bad. Losing someone like that is just...there are no words, Skye. I would wish it on no one, ever. And it was made so much worse because they *blamed* him for it. They blamed Levi for Kieran's death, as if he didn't already feel something beyond guilt for losing the boy he loved...losing the boy he would have given his own life, a thousand times over, to protect. Gods, it was wrong. Blaming him like that and then punishing him...it breaks my heart to think of it every single time. And it's so hard for both of us to talk of, hence why I haven't before now. I should have done. I'm so sorry for it. I feel like this evening is my fault, because if I'd just *told* you of what Xavier had done to my brother maybe you wouldn't have risked following us. You'd have realised what we were doing in Alcázar and stayed *safe—*"

He breaks off, his voice giving out on him, and I watch helplessly as he puts his head in his hands, shoulders slumping in on themselves. I want to reassure him, want to hold him so tightly to try to take away the pain...but my tongue is heavy, my limbs weighed down by my own remorse. It's now blindingly obvious how wrong I was to act like I did on that bad day, when I called Levi shy and interrogated him on his history. I remember being so short asking him about the tether, because I thought he was being unhelpful in not responding to me. I was wrong, we know I was wrong, but it's no wonder he was so very quiet. No wonder he later told me he found the topic of conversation difficult, and that his weathered grey eyes are so full of grief. Weighed down by it the entire time.

"I'm so sorry, Fjord," I manage to get out when he lifts his head. My gut swoops at the terrible, grief-stricken expression on his face, enough to having me tipping forwards on the bed to embrace him. The cup of water he poured for me spills over my covers, but I don't heed it...couldn't care less about it. "I'm so, *so* sorry."

"I'll kill him," he says hoarsely into me. "I'll kill Xavier, or Levi will. I swear to you, one day we'll end this. And I just...I'm terrified he's going to do something terrible to you, Skye. With your blood, he has the means to do terrible things. To spite us. To...I don't even know what."

"Why does he hate you guys so much? He *hates* Levi, doesn't he?"

"Xavier is the son of Nike, one of Zeus's sentinels. He's young, so not ancient like Sholto even though he's technically his cousin...but he's still powerful, and bitter. His mother chose to train Levi over himself, and he's never forgiven him for it...as if Levi or any Guardian can choose who they receive mentoring from. They can't. Guardians have very few luxuries in life. Very few freedoms. But...I can't help thinking that Xavier hates us for more than just jealousy over his mother training Levi, especially because he seems to be targeting *my* family, doesn't he? First, Kieran. Then maybe my mother. Now, stealing your blood and terrorising your streets..."

I think on that. "What does stealing someone's blood even do? What does it have to do with forcing them to do your will?"

"The control is a form of manipulation that Styx's offspring, Zeus's four sentinels, have. It's no real surprise their own children also share the ability to control others, but they're not as powerful as their parents. Unlike the sentinels, who need no aid to help them bend your mind, their children need something material, something physical, to tie you to them. This can be skin or most potently, blood."

"Levi can do it, can't he?" I guess. "He can bend people's will? He stopped Xavier from controlling me on the streets by touching me."

"Yes. With skin contact, Levi can will others to do his bidding...but he wouldn't, Skye. Unless it was to help him do something like he did tonight, to *reverse* Xavier's manipulation of you, he doesn't believe in doing it. Nor do I. It's totally violating bending someone's mind. And...after everything with Kieran..."

He doesn't finish the sentence, because he doesn't need to. I squeeze him again, then pull back and meet his gaze. It's weary, unhappy, tormented...and I just want to lean right back in and free him of it all, as if I *could.*

"Is Levi the son of one of Zeus's sentinels if he can do that?"

Fjord shakes his head. "No, Levi's parents are regular Guardians. They actually served my parents for a time. They're good, honest people, remarkable in their faith and integrity and loyalty. So is Levi, but he's also somehow enormously powerful with it."

"Yeah," I say weakly, thinking back to everything on the streets. "He glowed tonight, Fjord. He glowed with rivers of silver, and his feet *shook* the earth. It was like he was a god."

Fjord hums. "I'm not surprised. Facing Xavier, Levi will have been very primed to fight."

Right. He was *so* primed...except he didn't do it, did he? He forwent his attack on Xavier, forwent seeking revenge on his nemesis, because of what the other Guardian was doing to me.

"Xavier mentioned something about Levi being blessed by Styx?" I query. "Is that why he's so powerful?"

Fjord's weary brows lift. "I'm sorry?"

I repeat what happened on the streets to him. "When he was goading Levi, Xavier called him, 'The great Guardian, blessed by Styx herself.'"

"Oh," Fjord's brows rise higher. "That's interesting."

"Does it mean something to you?"

He seems distracted. "There are tales about individuals blessed by the mother of Zeus's sentinels, the Guardian's greatest ancestor, Styx. We thought Levi's powers had something to do with him being tethered to Kieran, because it's so rare to be bonded together like that. So rare. I'll admit a part of me has always thought there was more of a reason to it, though, and so has Levi..." He trails off, blinking rapidly. "Thanks, Skye. I'm going to look into that. Discuss it with him."

Don't thank me. Thank your nemesis, the evil Guardian who killed your brother and whose jaw I'm due to break.

428

"I love you," I mumble, at a loss of what else to say. "Lots. And lots."

"I love you too, Skye. I'm worried. I can't help thinking there's more to what happened tonight, that Xavier stole your blood for reasons other than spiting us. Maybe to do with you somehow being a guide to the Torch, or being the demigod in the prophecy. He seems to know of that, though only the gods know how. Whatever that ulterior motive is, we can expect it to be bad."

My throat is thick with fear and guilt. "I really am so sorry for getting caught by him. I panicked, and then didn't know how to ignite ichor..."

"Please don't apologise," he ushers, sounding just as soft and pained as my counsel earlier...quite remarkably similar, actually. "It's not your fault, and I won't *ever* have you excuse Xavier of his sins. We just need to work through this. Remedy it and make sure you're safe, and that Xavier can't hurt you or others. And whilst we do, I have a huge favour to ask of you."

"What is it?"

"Please would you conceal what happened on the streets tonight from Sholto?"

I blink in surprise. "Can I tell Tristan?"

"Of course," Fjord says immediately. "I would only ask that you tell him the same...to request he keep from mentioning this to Sholto."

"He won't, and I won't either. But...can I ask why?"

Fjord's exhale is faint, but highly troubled. "Yes. It seems both of us are sitting on big truths. Him for reasons I don't trust, and me because I *just* want to keep you safe, Skye. I want to keep Levi from harm, and the only way to do that is to keep our cards close to our chest. To keep them amongst people we trust until our dying breath and no one else."

I nod. "I won't tell him ever until you say so. The same goes for the stuff about your mother and what happened on the summit with Zelos. It's all safely secret with me, locked up in my busy house of a mind...and my heart."

Fjord lifts a hand, smoothing back my hair. Then he leans in and kisses my temple, "Thank you. I'm grateful, and so very sorry we weren't at the Guild tonight. I'm sorry Sholto didn't do his part and look after you, but we had to go to Alcázar. Me, to ensure myself a place in Ruby's inner circle, and Levi..."

"For the hourglass?"

He nods.

I open my mouth and close it several times, telling myself to understand the gravity of the situation and *not* to say the wrong thing. Not to blurt out something without thinking about it. "Has Levi been mistreated, Fjord?" I ask, very quietly. "When everything happened eight years ago, did they mistreat him?"

"Yes."

"Is he still? By people like Sholto?"

Immediately, Fjord's expression darkens. I know he's thinking about the remarks made in the safe house the other night. "The only person with broken honour in that moment was Sholto, Skye. What he said was out of line, Mentor or not. He knew it. And he didn't even believe what he said. I'm still furious at him."

"Why did he say it, then?" I ask. "I didn't like that he did, Fjord. It didn't sound like Sholto."

"My experience is that unexplainable power either garners unfounded reverence or unfounded reserve, Skye. Sholto wasn't around much when we were growing up, and nor was Levi for a time – too busy training to be a Guardian in Mount Olympus, of all places – but when they both crossed paths Sholto was always tough on him. I *don't* think he meant what he said in the safe house, at least not in its entirety, but I suppose no one is immune to following the herd, especially in times of stress. Even someone that old. Regardless of what he said, Sholto was unsettled during our meeting by the thought of the Elysium folk coming with us to Wivern. Just like when they first arrived in Ioxthel and we didn't bank on having to look after them, it makes things much more difficult for us travelling there, keeping up pretences as guilders and *not* Nixen. I'm confessedly very stressed about it, too. Those girls are young and vulnerable, and it worries me thinking of what it will take to keep them safe and their true identities hidden. Sholto without a doubt also feels those stresses, but he went too far that night, jumping on the side of everyone else in Elysium in renouncing Levi, in the name of letting out his frustration. It's...a flaw in humans, I think. To *need* to have someone or something to blame, especially in moments of intense pressure. To scapegoat, and lash out in spite."

Goddesses.

Don't I ever know that myself, now.

"So Levi is shunned in Elysium?"

"Yes," Fjord hauls in his deepest breath yet. "It pains me, Skye. You see, being tethered is so very rare, and my family were not inconsequential in Elysium. We had eminence with the Nereids, and when it became clear the two boys were united by this incredibly special, unique force, everyone had their eyes on them. And *all* of those eyes seemed to think that by observing something it meant they understood it, and had the right to *judge* it. Had the right to determine that Levi failed his guardianship of Kieran, neglected his duty when my brother fell prey to Xavier and took his own life. They seemed to think it was right for them to deem his punishment to be something eternal, and something that entails impossible cruelty..."

Fjord's voice lowers in turmoil. He turns to stare out of my window, his profile one of anger and pain just like it had been in the safe house...or worse. I watch him, a terrible feeling settling in my belly at what he's implying, and wondering if I should go on to say what I do next. But then I think, if tonight is proof of *anything*, it's the dangers of not sharing things with those you trust.

"I overheard Jay and Levi talking tonight before you let them into Alcázar," I begin hesitantly. "I was up on the rooftops in the shadows, and they were talking about Levi not being free, and about you, not knowing of the prophecy until you came here. They said that the only reason you *did* come here was that Sholto told you your mum was here with me?"

Fjord stills. "What...you heard is true," he says after several long moments, turning from the window to face me again. "It was the first sign I should be cautious in what I tell to Sholto. His summons here were a manipulation, one I don't entirely regret believing," he adds quickly, obviously realising what I might think to that. "I don't regret coming to Ioxthcl, Skye, even though Melody isn't here. I am beyond grateful I did because we are now a family again, and that is so important. But...at first it was a manipulation, a ploy to draw me from very pressing troubles at home. You see...Levi was imprisoned in Elysium following Kieran's death, and in coming here two years after it happened I deserted my endeavours to free him. Sholto *knew* that. It's why he summoned me here the way he did. He knew one of the only reasons I'd ever leave someone that important to me in something of such wretched ill treatment was to find my mum."

My gut hollows. "He...he made you—"

"Sholto didn't make me," Fjord interjects tiredly. "I must take ownership of the decision to come here myself, and Levi would have had it no other way, even though...I wasn't exactly seeing him, then."

He hauls in another pained breath, and I was wrong before because *this* is his deepest one yet. His eyes brighten with tears...and the pit of my tummy hollows further. I just know deep in my bones that what he's about to say is so bad.

"They kept him in solitary confinement for almost seven years, Skye. For *years*, Levi was imprisoned to something of impossible cruelty. No human should ever go through it, let alone someone struggling to deal with the loss of someone they loved more than everyone and everything...a loss he was then told was his *fault*. It meant he was kept somewhere with nothing in his room except a bed, a wash basin and toilet, and some poor excuse for a window. There was no seeing other people, and no talking except when he was interrogated in the early days. He was just in a room of nothing, literally *nothing* but the walls, alone and forsaken, wholly dependent on them for food...unable to leave except when they tried to force him to tell them the truth of Kieran's death..."

He stops with a noise of disgust, expression something of irrevocable remorse. I am *lost* to feeling, so shocked I know my mouth is hanging open, horrified.

Fjord isn't even finished yet.

"If you remember, I left Ioxthel on Guild duties for several months a few years ago. Except, I wasn't doing that. I suddenly knew how to fix things, at least for a time...woke up from a dream when I remembered Kieran, Levi and myself stealing my mother's hourglasses, filling them with sand and water from the Nereid beaches and swearing we'd protect each other. They always included me, even though the two of them were tied together by something I'll never understand. They always acted like I was part of it, too...and so one day, when Levi was back for the holidays, we all swore to protect one another. Kieran and I obviously meant what we said, but a Guardian's honour is binding, Skye. It's what makes them such valuable fighters to Nixen, and so easy to strip of their rights...and it's why sworn fealty really does mean unwavering loyalty. They're literally bound to serve those they swear it to, and that's exactly what Levi's word did on that day. He bound himself to me. I returned to Elysium immediately after the dream and took the case to the Elders, the ruling council you yourself will sit on to represent the Aeolus Dynasty. I told them *they* were breaking the law if they denied me of the fealty Levi had already promised to me. I showed them the hourglass. Told them to bring it before the gods and goddesses, if they didn't believe me. They eventually agreed I was right and that Levi should be free to be with me and to guard me...but only with conditions. We have until our hourglasses run out of time, or until I can find a suitable Guardian to replace him...as if Levi Silverstone could *ever* be replaced?" Fjord makes that angry, frustrated noise in the back of his throat again, cheeks flushing a deep, dangerous pink. "Tonight was about making more time, Skye, in order to right wrongs and figure out how to make the impossible possible, in order to truly free Levi from his life sentence. To pardon him, because I won't have him live with a reputation of ruin once he's out for good. He deserves so much more than that. *So* much more."

I've never been so at a loss of what to say. Even learning the shocking news of my past life in Elysium two months ago – learning of me being the demigod prophesied to save the world with a dad who's a god and a mum who served Artemis – doesn't compare to this. At least in those stories there was no real strife. No harrowing tale of loss and injustice, and torment.

Everything, or at least a lot of things, start to make sense in my mind. Levi's reservedness and silence, the relentless veil hiding his expression, the tiredness and grief, the obliging nature, the hoarse voice and rough mannerisms, both of which are rusty from disuse.

From seven years of *misuse.*

"Why didn't he escape?" I whisper. "Is he not powerful enough to escape where they kept him?"

Fjord looks so sad at this. "When utterly submerged in the grief of losing his best friend to something so tragic in front of his very eyes? Losing the other half of his soul? Beaten raw by his own guilt for not preventing it as Kieran's Guardian, and then beaten by the cruel hand of those who think penance should include impossibly deep loneliness and torture? Those who don't know when to stop, even when flogging a fifteen year old boy? He'd just turned *fifteen*, Skye, and they took him straight from the kitchen. Straight from holding onto my brother's body..." He shudders, his eyes swiftly filling with too many memories to keep at bay. "I don't think anyone is strong or powerful then, Skye. And I think if you spend years somewhere so cold and so forlorn, with *no* one there to tell you to hold onto hope, to offer you even a single look of reassurance, let alone an embrace, I think you start to believe that maybe they are right, and that it *was* your fault, and that...you deserve what you're given."

I suck in a sharp inhale, amber eyes blurring as Fjord's own tears spill from their home, tracking down his cheeks. He bows his head in defeat, sniffling down at the hands hung limply between his knees.

"He didn't speak to me for weeks," he whispers, then lets out a desperate, lost noise that reminds me of me, just days ago in Tristan's arms, totally unable to hold in my misery. "He *still* doesn't really speak to me, but I think in those early days he thought it wasn't real. Thought that maybe he'd passed out or...or passed *on* from their punishments."

My voice is less than a breath. "Like what Xavier did to me tonight? The mental pain?"

"Gods," Fjord swallows thickly. "No. Luckily that isn't judged by just anyone. When a Guardian forgoes their honour, it's only their own mind or those they've sworn fealty to who have the power to inflict that pain upon them. It's a twisted assurance of their loyalty, and I'm so sorry you suffered something similar at the hands of Xavier. I should have asked if you were ok?"

"I'm ok," I say immediately, then watch him staring heartbrokenly down at his hands. It's physical punishment he's talking of, isn't it? He's talking of Levi being physically punished for doing nothing wrong, for *years*. "How did it happen, Fjord?" I ask, appalled. "How did he end up there?"

"Through Elysium's twisted system of power and politics. Guardians might be prized back home, but they hold no power and they don't have a voice. Their service is valued only for the protection it brings, and never the sacrifice it entails. They give up their lives to protect others and receive nothing for it...or at least that's the case in the majority of households." He presses his lips together, and I know he's thinking of his own family. I know, without a doubt, that it isn't included in who he's talking of. *"*All of Elysium's power is skewed in the hands of the wealthy, the leaders of the Nixen dynasties, who in turn have *their* hands tied by the Mentors. By people like Sholto...offspring to Zeus's sentinels who train Guardians. They are the real rulers of our kingdom, and they are not all good people, Skye. Sholto *is*. Even if he lies, and even if he's someone unto himself given his age, who I'm struggling to forgive given what he said to Levi in the safe house...despite those things, I believe he's fundamentally good, and his presence has been missing from Elysium whilst he's been here with you. Amongst his peers his balance and prestige is greatly needed. Levi was sentenced unfairly by Elysium's ruling council, but what that really means is that it was the Mentors who prompted the decision...and I expect it was entirely driven by those who saw his power as threatening. He's just *so* powerful, Skye. What you saw tonight would've been the echo of a spark before his potential to ignite. He's more powerful than Sholto, maybe even as powerful as Zeus's sentinels themselves hence why he was trained by one...trained by Xavier's mother, Nike, on Mount Olympus. And to see someone so good, so strong and honest and true and with such enormous potential to fight utterly destroyed of life's spark, utterly defeated by what they put him through there...it breaks my heart, Skye. It shatters it. He mustn't go back. We *have* to make sure he never goes back. I'll die before I give up."

Lost.

I'm so *lost* to feeling.

"How...much time do you have, Fjord? In the hourglasses?"

He shakes his head. "We don't know, because they're not normal. They were my mother's, and they seem to be very long-lived, lasting for years and years. Some days it seems like time isn't ticking in them at all...others the sand is slipping through the funnel fast. We just don't know, and that's why we've been searching for this hourglass – the one we just stole *back* from Xavier. It was Kieran's from that day, and it's filled with seawater from the Nereids' coastline. We're hoping we can somehow suspend the sand in ours with the water in order to freeze time indefinitely. That's why we need Jay. He's good with things like that. With alchemy, logic...magic."

"But your two could run out at any moment?" I verify. "The ones you and Levi wear around your necks, they could run out and he could go back?"

Fjord nods heavily. My gut and heart twist into something of violent fear. Fear for them both, but especially for Levi, because that is a *horrible* uncertainty to live with. It's not just grief he's weighed down by, is it? It's seemingly the worst burden imaginable, something just as heavy as I envisage the world feels like on Atlas's shoulders...something *I* might feel, if the prophecy comes true. That's the weight of never knowing when you'll suddenly have your freedom ripped from you. Never knowing when you'll go back to something of deep loneliness and despair, and torture, without friends or hope or fresh air. The impossibly awful weight of waiting for lost liberty.

"I'm in," I breathe. "So in."

Fjord lifts his bleary gaze to look at me, brows pulling together in puzzlement. "You're...in?"

"Yeah," I say earnestly. "I'll help free Levi. If you needed a demigod thief to steal another hourglass? You guys just let me know and I'll be right there. Faster than lightning. And I'll shoot anyone who tries to imprison him again, too. Find some silver arrows for my silver bow and protect you all. Fiercely. No reserve here, just resolve in the name of freedom. I've decided that's what demigods are for, aren't they? Freeing people. And guarding Guardians. It doesn't seem right they don't have someone protecting their interests and voices back in Elysium, does it? No, not right. Guardians should be guarded too, so that's definitely my job. Guarding them all, and especially Levi. I'm *in*, Fjord. On instinct, with heart and honour, like you guys always say. I'm totally in."

He stares at me, his wretched expression slowly transforming into something utterly bewildered, and fond. He reaches out without a word and hauls me into his chest, wrapping his arms tightly around me and dropping his mouth to my hair, resting it there for long seconds. His breath is warm, wetter than it usually is from his tears...or maybe it's that my hair is still damp from the shower.

"There's no one like you, Skye," he eventually shares, voice tight with emotion. "We're so lucky to have you. The *world* is lucky to have you as it's heroine."

"I mean it," I mumble into his shirt, shuffling closer...heart swelling at his words. "I'm in. I'm *there* for you guys. I'll keep you all safe and happy."

"It would seem we need to find you some silver arrows for your silver bow, then."

"Where from?"

"Artemis, perhaps."

I freeze in his arms. "You think it's hers, Fjord?! My bow?!"

"I think there's every possibility Zelos was telling the truth up on that hilltop summit," he replies, in a way that makes it clear he's thought a lot about this. "I think he might well have lots more to tell us of your parents...and mine."

"Yeah," I respond immediately. "I think he does. I think he was telling the truth about your mum. He was really heartbroken talking of her, and obviously cared for her a lot...and you. He liked hearing of you."

Fjord looks as if that news is very welcome. Neither of us says much after it, and I'm helpless to the excitement that buzzes through me thinking on how my bow really might belong to *The* Huntress. The warm, effervescent emotion is a very strange companion to house alongside the horror and deep remorse I'm feeling – and will probably always feel – having listened to the story of Fjord and Levi's strife, but I'm a demigod and a ghost, a ruffian and a Guardian to Guardians, and I'm no longer lost to pointless ire and rebellion...so you should know I have space for all the emotions in my messy, muddled mind.

With them comes an unwavering resolve to fight.

To fight so hard there's no possibility these battles won't be won and destiny won't be ours. Seeing Tristan sooner than soon, freeing Levi forever, holding and healing the entire inglorious world on my shoulders as I fight against the gods, when all is ablaze with fire and wrongs are chosen for the right reasons.

Yes, I'm ready now.

The world's heroine is finally awake.

Somebody's For The Night

Dinner, the night after the night of revelry...and one day before we leave Ioxthel. Enye and I are eating together in the Guild's busy mess hall. I'm stuffing food that tastes like ash down my throat but barely tasting it, and she's ripping her bread and fish apart like they did something *bad* to her, looking incredibly morose. It reminds me of the day I stopped trying to avoid her and we started having breakfast together again. The day I learnt she had a suitor – no longer, you should know – and I saw a little emblem on Yasmine's wrist that first hinted she might be a member of Ruby's Council.

Enye is now *Sergeant* Tsitak, Yasmine's successor, and she's not entirely happy about it – she has to stay in Ioxthel instead of signing up for the Wivern entourage with her brother and me.

"I can't believe both of you are going," she says now, throwing down her bread in a very pointed protest. "I just can't believe it. I'm so jealous. What am I going to do without you both? Lie around getting fat and sunburnt, and depressed?"

"Maybe manage an entire platoon of soldiers?"

"That's child's play compared to the toil of missing you both...and anyway, I can't believe Yasmine has really disappeared. Can't believe I've already replaced her. Do you think foul play is behind this?"

Yes. "Don't know. Have you spoken to Vishnu about it?"

Her lips twist down. "No. I feel bad, because I know he's upset, but we're not really, you know, pursuing things anymore." She plucks up a piece of her fish and eats it, chewing without enthusiasm. "I hope he's ok, though. Him and Yasmine were close."

"Any other suitors on the horizon?"

"Not really."

"Not really?"

"No," she sighs once, then twice. "Goddesses, I just can't *believe* you're going, Skye. I'm going to miss you so damn much. I'm going to be heartbroken."

Our eyes meet over the table, and something lumpier than soggy bread forms in my throat. It's called emotion that has nowhere to go. Enye's own plump lips quiver, her fingers dropping to her plate to start dismembering the bread there. Both of us are holding back tears.

"I'll miss you too," I say hoarsely. "But Fin and I will be back soon, Enye. *Sooner* than soon. And that reminds me...I have a friend, someone who I've known for my entire life, and who I'm also coming back for sooner than soon. He's normally in this little forgotten bay just south of The Eastern Harbours with a few of the city's stragglers, but they're good people. The best. If you need anything you just need to whistle to him. Wolf whistle, that is. He'll hear you, and help you. He's called Tristan and he is simple the best."

"Tristan?" Enye looks puzzled, and a little intrigued. "Why have I never heard of him before?"

A mighty good question, and one I can't answer right now. "I don't know, but if you need help he'll be there for you. I've already told him about you loads of times. All good things, obviously. He's there for you."

She still looks a little perplexed, but eventually nods. "Ok. I'll remember that, thank you."

We try to smile at one another, but both are watery and they slide off our faces very quickly. Enye goes back to picking at her bread as I stuff some more food into my mouth. I've no idea what it is. I just slopped something onto my plate, too busy trying *not* to realise this is my penultimate dinner in Ioxthel to notice what that dinner actually is.

"Honestly, I don't know how I'm going to survive without you two here," Enye repeats after a while. "You're like my only friends, and Fin isn't even my friend because he's my *brother.* Maybe I'll visit my parents more, chill with our family dogs on the vineyard. That's a great idea. If I extend my social life to include canines, do you think Dionysus will take pity on me?"

Dionysus, God of Wine and Ecstasy. "Who cares about him? He's mad. Your dogs will like it, and so will your parents." *Not that I've met them, and if I did...gods, I'd be so nervous. Would probably pee myself because of everything with your brother.* "Also, remember that you'll have a lot on your plate here, Enye. As new Staff Sergeant to Delta, you're queen bee. *And* as a young single woman in want of heaven's fortune...you'll be so busy batting away future prospects, and the countless suitors pursuing you, that you won't be able to miss us. Right? You'll have lots on your plate, so much so that you won't have room for torn little pieces of bread or chewy fish. No room whatsoever. Full house, here. No space for bread or tears or missing Fin and I."

I try for another watery grin and watch Enye's expression twist into the *opposite* – her features falling into something of wretched misery and lost dignity. You and I both know I have recent experience of that. Jumping up from my bench like I have ants in my pants, I bustle over to hers, shove her along to make room for myself and then fling my arms tightly around her.

"Don't do it, Enye. Don't go there. I'll start crying too, and I feel like I've only just stopped. Then it'll be so embarrassing, because it's busy here tonight. Think of all the suitors you'll turn away with snot dripping from your nose! So gross. More gross than the fish on your plate right now."

She snorts thickly, frame shuddering with a hefty sigh. Her arms snake around my waist, head falling to my shoulder. "You say the

442

stupidest stuff, Skye. I'm going to miss everything about you, but I think I'll miss *that* most of all. The stupid stuff you say."

I think quickly on that. "I can try and write down a few sayings for you if you want, to keep in your pocket? Tristan makes these little origami swans for..." *stealing*. "For stuff. I could get a few from him and write you stupid things on them? Love letters for you to hand out to your suitors. Even rejections. Or maybe I'll write fortunes for you?" I pause in yet more thought. "Mind you, my handwriting is so appalling you'll need heaven's luck just to read it. Can't spell, either."

"Fortunes, love letters..." Enye's hum of humour is sniffly. "That all sounds fun. Maybe I'll just have lots of boyfriends to keep me occupied whilst you're away."

"Great idea. They're just a means to an end after all, aren't they? No replacement for sisterhood. I'll do the same."

"Don't," she says immediately, lifting her head. "You'll break my brother's heart, Skye. Besides, you're going to The Cold Kingdom. You won't have time for boys. You'll be so busy seeing exciting things, *doing* exciting things. Every time I think about it I get jealous. Then I think *again*, how will I survive without you both here? I'll just cry, and eat too many peach pastries and then have to put *two* extra notches in my dagger belt."

"Sounds ok to me," I squeeze her. "Could be worse. And don't forget, it won't be *you* putting the notches in your belt now that you're Sergeant Tsitak. Ask some of those scrawny new recruits to do it. They'll fawn over you. Work so hard on punching that little hole through the leather it'll be the *best* new belt notch you've ever had..." I reach up and grip the forearm hung over my shoulder, shaking it a little in encouragement. "Besides, if I can do my things in The Cold Kingdom or wherever..." *Maybe in Elysium, saving the world and finding the Torch of Prometheus. Guarding every Guardian, leading a Nixen dynasty, freeing Levi Silverstone forever...* "If I can do my things, you can do your things here. You can do this. *We* can do this."

Enye squeezes me back. "Yeah...we can do this. We *will* do this. I'll see you guys soon, won't I?"

My voice leaves no room for doubt. "Sooner than soon."

* * *

Midnight. It's still, if you're not into semantics, the night after the night of revelry...and still one day before we leave Ioxthel indefinitely. I'm in the Guild's shoddy library, browsing its shelves of scrolls and tomes for something readable to give to Levi; the grieving, guarded Guardian who must have endured endless suffering throughout his imprisonment. An inhumane punishment that should never have happened. He should have received the *opposite* following the death of his best friend. Should have been held so tightly and tenderly, surrounded by dear ones reassuring him it wasn't his fault and that it's ok, not to be ok. Should have been loved, instead of sentenced to something impossibly lonely and forlorn. Something that would drive me, and I think anyone on earth, insane.

I've thought about him a lot over the past few days. Thought about him, and about *me* being a Guardian to Guardians. I meant what I told Fjord, in *meaning* what I said about fighting for them. My words might usually come across as silly and young, and there might usually be quite a lot of them for no reason, but they're never empty. I don't like the sound of things back in Elysium at all; the skew of power there, and the supposed treatment of Guardians as slaves with no voice. I don't like how Levi was treated, and is still sometimes treated.

I'm not sure what fighting to better these things will entail, but thinking on them only firms my resolve to help – and it's made me realise that this, the first endeavour of tonight, is really important.

Finding Levi a book.

That's what I'm doing here in the Guild's shoddy library. I'm finding him a book because Fjord said he *loved* to read, and I've decided I need to properly say thank you to him for following me around Ioxthel these past few months. It's going to be a gift, something that will hopefully impart my gratitude and brighten his day enough to lighten those weary, weathered eyes.

Hopefully.

But honestly?

I'm struggling a bit with it, because it's all very well Fjord telling me that Levi *reads books like no one else*, but just what kind of books are they? Those based on fact, or entirely on fiction? Something light-hearted or thought-provoking? What genre? What length? What *language?*

I mosey down yet another random aisle, feet busy and mind fretting. So far, I've coming across nothing I like the look of, and I've been here for hours...

Perhaps that's because you haven't really looked at one yet, Skye, my counsel pipes up, not unkindly. *You've picked out several books and stared at them...unseeingly.*

Yeah. I don't even try to refute it. *But that's not entirely my fault. You know I find reading difficult.*

I do know, sweetheart. Keep searching. You'll find something soon.

Her gaze is so precious on mine, so unique, like it was made for me or me for her. Just like the other day on the streets with Xavier, it's not amber. It's green and wisened...and I *swear* to you I'm not insane imagining the voice in my head has eyes.

I do as she says and keep searching...for what seems like more hours. Growing impatient, I stop down my current aisle, close my eyes and fling a hand out, grabbing the first book I touch. Letting it fall open, I tell myself *not* to stare unseeingly at the pages and instead to really browse it; to really try to see if it'll be suitable for Levi. Hot frustration rises when the words tumble over themselves on the pages, jumbling until they're barely legible to me...and it's not just the terrible lighting in here tonight that makes it difficult to reorder them, or my hopeless patience. I'm just not the best reader. Never have been, not least because I only remember learning when Sholto picked me up off the streets, aged eleven.

Try the one to it's left, Skye, my counsel suggests.

I discard the first book somewhere behind me, then search for the space I made by pulling it out...the space I really should've put it back into, thinking about it. Rolling my eyes, I pull the one to its left down. I'm greeted by a rumble tumble *jumble* of letters, except two words – two names, in fact – finally piece themselves back together and jump out at me, like hands grabbing my attention.

Metis & Zeus, I read internally, brows raising at the latter. *Zeus is someone interesting, isn't he? Very impressive, being King of the Gods. Levi might like this if it's about him. He's also impressive. Handsome, too.*

What of Metis?

Yeah. Well...her too. She's cool.

My counsel sounds very slightly humoured. *Good to hear. Go for it, Skye. You'll be here all evening if you don't pick one soon, and don't you have other plans? Other endeavours for tonight?*

My throat dries up. *Yeah. I do...to say sorry to Fin. To see him, and make up after the other night...somehow.*

I stuff the book up my shirt and start hurrying out of the library, only to immediately double back on myself and pick up the first book I discarded. I nestle it back where it belongs on the bookshelves – upside down, but who cares – then leg it to my room and drop Levi's gift off.

The quads are mostly deserted when I bounce back down the stairs and hang right, heading for Beta barracks where the Captains and experienced guilders like Sholto have their rooms. The air is still warm even at this hour, because Ioxthel never *really* cools down, and I know I'll miss that when we leave. I'll miss a lot. The smell of dry earth and ash, the sand in my food from its fickle gusts of wind, the sweet scent of wisteria and stringent smell of spices. The bouzouki strummed soulfully from someone's private courtyard, the sail like awnings of the rooftops, the fishy Eastern Harbour full to the brim with memories...

I'm really going to miss it.

My heart is mad by the time I reach Fin's door, springy feet tripping over themselves in my haste and nervousness. I knock softly, wondering where he'll be if he isn't in his room at this hour, and wondering if he *is* in there...will he have someone with him? I should have asked Enye that at dinner, shouldn't I? Should have made *sure* I knew Fin didn't have plans tonight, maybe with that plump, beautiful girl from the ta—

The door opens.

"Hey," I blurt out hoarsely, and *far* too loudly. "Please can I come in? If you're not busy and...you don't have guests? Or...if you do...I can come back later? If that's better? Or maybe not later. Maybe tomorrow, because it's quite late now..."

To my immense relief, Fin steps aside and holds the door wide. He doesn't say anything as he does so, and he doesn't give me much of an expression, just something cool and reserved. I patter past, feeling hot and worried and hopeful, but grateful that he *is* in here alone.

He shuts the door and faces me, folding his arms...and I start staring dumbly. He's so gorgeous to me, with his light brown hair and those sea-green eyes – those expressive lips that are made for whispering something sweet and then sinful...and then doing those things. Strong shoulders. Tall but not *so* tall, which is really good for me, being so small.

My heart picks up speed, as if it wasn't already terrorising me; and in a very stark moment of clarity I realise Fin is totally out of my league, and I'm totally out of my depth.

I realise I could lose myself in him.

And he wouldn't offer to find me.

"I heard you're part of the entourage going to Wivern," I eventually squeak out to the silence, because we need to say something, and he's not going to be the first to do it. "So am I. That's what Fjord wanted to speak to me about the other night when he interrupted us."

"I know."

"Yeah," I nod vigorously. "You do, because he talked to you after me, didn't he? I'm...really happy you're coming, but I also don't want you to be in danger. Ever. You shouldn't be in danger."

Fin lets slip a wry laugh. "Yeah? Well, that feeling is mutual, Skye, hence why I agreed to sign up."

My heart flips. "For...me?"

He doesn't respond, just drifts further into the room. His arms are still folded, his expression still severe.

I look up at him, feeling so hot and flighty, just like my heart. "I meant to visit you sooner, Fin. Much sooner..." *It just took me a while to get over what happened last night.* "I was nervous, because last time you left...angry."

448

"Not at you."

It felt like it, and you still look it. "Fjord isn't my suitor," I entreat cautiously. "He's literally the opposite. I think of him as a friend and a brother, but *not* anything else. I don't have one either. No other suitor. I'm nobody's. There's just you. Or not even, because I know you're not really *my* suitor. You're too out of my league to be that, and this is casual and temporary but...I'm nobody else's, Fin. You need to know that. You need to believe me. There's no one else, not like there is for you."

"I don't really have someone else either," Fin says, frustration creeping into his voice.

"But...the other night...?"

"The girl in the tavern is great, but she isn't you."

"Oh..."

His lips press together. "Yeah."

What does that mean? "So we're...ok? You still...want to do this? With me?"

"Yes."

"Yeah?"

"Yes, Skye. That's what yes means."

I move forwards one step, two steps, then lunge the rest of the distance and fling myself at him. Peppery warmth surrounds me, the feel of him so firm and familiar, and yet still just as exhilarating as it was on that first night five years ago, when Enye's handsome older brother hugged me for dancing with her at her birthday celebrations because the other boys wouldn't. Boys can be stupid, can't they? They don't know a star even when they have one tucked neatly away in their pocket.

"I don't like arguing with you," I mumble into his shirt. "I'm so sorry for deserting you the other night. I know that wasn't nice."

Fin's chest rises and falls in a sigh. "I wouldn't call what happened between us an argument, Skye."

"But it felt like it. It felt...bad. I've been thinking about it a lot, tossing and turning. Worrying it might be the first of many."

I tip my head back, eyes and expression woeful. Recklessness and something else that's strong, warm and good rises in me when our eyes meet – and I'm helpless to it. Reaching for the collar of his shirt, I stretch up and kiss him.

Fin follows my lead, but he's half-hearted and restrained. Tens of seconds pass before his sigh washes over me, maybe one given in resignation. His shoulders loosen and two strong hands drop to my waist to tug me closer, hot breath brushing against my teeth and tongue as our mouths open. Both of us stop for a moment, breathing in the other.

It feels magnificent.

We start again. His hands slip lower as he walks us towards the bed, sitting down just as we had when he stole the book on Eros; only this time there don't seem to be any pretences or games or hoaxes. There's just me, breathless and earnest and kicking furiously to stay afloat in deep waters, and Fin totally the opposite, softly tugging the tie from my hair and letting it fall over the backs of his hands.

I pull back, breathing heavily and shifting restlessly in a lap that tells me he's restless, too. That...undoes me, a little bit. I stare at him, eyes wide and glazed and lips trembling with feeling, then duck my head, pressing my cheek to the little nodules of bone at the base of his throat. I feel embarrassingly emotional, but try hard to get myself together as his arms slip behind me, embracing me.

"I have a question for you," Fin says gruffly to the silence. "You mentioned you were nobody's, just now."

Oh, dear. "Did I?"

"Yes."

"Sometimes I just say things, Fin. Just blurt out words and don't remember what they are, especially when I'm nervous. So, if I *did* say I'm nobody's—"

"You did. It sounded lonely."

"Lonely..." I swallow. "Or liberating?"

He hums, but it's lacking lightness. "My question to you, Skye, is instead of being nobody's, would you be somebody's?"

"Somebody's?"

"For...the night."

"For the night?"

"Yes."

"Whose?"

"Do you really need me to say it?"

My mouth opens...shuts. Fin's expression is a mystery to me, but the wings of his cheekbones are blossoming with a light pink flush like he's recently rubbed them with his hands...except I know he *hasn't*, because they're still nestled in the small of my back, holding me close. There's also that watchfulness to his gaze, a wariness that makes me think this question is serious.

"I'll be yours," I hear myself say, trying to hide the excitement and emotion from my voice, but my next words still come out sounding breathless. "I'll be yours for the night, Fin. For *this* night, if you want. Maybe you could ask me the question again next time, too? On the road? Or in the ocean? Somewhere deep? Out of my depth?"

"Why don't you ask *me* next time, Skye. On the road or in the ocean...out of my depth?"

"Maybe...I will."

"Maybe you should."

I stare at him and nod, even though I don't exactly know what I'm agreeing to. Leaning in, I seek his mouth again, and end up straining forwards in his lap – because unlike last time Fin doesn't meet me and follow my lead. He just keeps *evading* me. My fingers tighten on his shoulders but I soon give up, pressing my cheek to the side of his neck.

His pulse is thrumming *fast.*

"What're you waiting for?" I whisper.

"I don't know," he replies, sounding frustrated. "I've no idea, Skye."

"We...we don't have to, if you're...tired..."

"I'm not tired," he replies immediately. He shifts, arms tightening behind me to bring us together in a very exhilarating area. "Thought you might have felt that for the entirety of the time you've been here."

The words are light and so is their meaning, but the tone is still unsettled. I lift my head, looking at him searchingly. "Are you ok?"

"Better than."

"Are you sure?"

He finally leans in and brushes his lips against mine. "Yes. Just do one thing for me, please."

"What?"

"Swear that there'll be a next time to ask about everything. To be in deep waters together."

That isn't what I expected him to say. Isn't it *my* fear he's voicing? That there won't be a next time for us...and that this, whatever this is, might end before it even starts?

"I swear there'll be a next time, Fin."

"More tonights?"

I nod a little, sitting on words that sting my nerves...and then I stop doing that and just *say* them, because Jay was right on that fateful night of revelry.

What is life without hope?

Without risk?

"I don't want this to end, Fin. Don't want to lose you, because I've fancied you *forever* and I just...like you. I don't want to lose you."

"Nor I you."

My heart *sings* at that. "Maybe...make me yours now. I would like for you to do that. A lot. Would you, please?"

One hand slides to my hip, the other behind my neck. Leaning in, he kisses me deeply. The evening melts to moonlight and more, but we don't talk again. Don't say a word, even when we wake up to a dove grey dawn the next morning, for once *together* in the afterglow, and he goes to organise himself for the entourage to Wivern...to sign up to ventures in dealing war. And I go to meet with his enemy.

The Start

My last evening in Ioxthel is spent at the safe house with the Elysium folk and Tristan. I think the two of us are both grateful Sholto requested we stay here tonight instead of allowing us to be in the harbours, because there's a very big chance that if we were there, we'd run away together. I'm presently in the kitchen with Ember, Idris, Sholto and Yusuf, waiting for my best friend to arrive; although from the faint chorus of ruffian whistles sounding from the surrounding streets I can tell he's nearby already. Jay and Wren are upstairs tutoring, and Rose is out in Ioxthel collecting a few things for the Irvings' travels, commencing with us tomorrow.

She's not alone. Fjord *and* Akira have gone with her to mind her steps through the streets...because my people are Tristan's people, now. That's how best friendship works.

There's a gentle, surprisingly cool breeze toying with the ends of my hair as I sit fidgeting at the kitchen table. You know, the strands that never manage to stay in their braid? They're tickling me, driving me to distraction...mostly because the wind is filtering through one of the kitchen's two wooden doors, giving me a glimpse of the mostly deserted courtyard beyond. I say mostly deserted because there's a guarded Guardian standing in the fading sunlight there, leaning against one of its sandy stone walls. He's a portrait of solitude. Of stillness, silence and sadness...and I suddenly decide I've every reason to join him and disrupt that.

Gathering the few belongings I'll need for the night, I stand from my seat and slip out through the door. Sholto is too immersed in discussion with Yusuf to really heed me leaving, and Ember is sweeping up a pot of smoked almonds she knocked off the table earlier, overlooked by a very amused Idris. There's little danger of

454

her following me out. She's started doing that, along with the imitations and funny games of greetings, and like everything with her...it's annoyingly sweet.

Levi looks over as I step outside and start beelining for him; feet busy, mind busier. I briefly debate joining him in leaning against the wall to oversee the courtyard's non-existent happenings, but quickly realise I'd prefer to hover here in front of him. I want to see his expression...or not even that, because there's usually very little I can read from it. I suppose I just want to see Levi's eyes – weathered grey irises that I go on about all the time, and that I once thought were dull but are really just full of grief and suffering, and make it their business to miss nothing, and hide *everything*.

He straightens to his full height as I stop before him. I'm starting to think that's Levi's way of greeting people without speaking or giving the rusty little bows he has a habit of bestowing upon me. I'm starting to think I'm getting better at reading the silent language of others, too, because with him I *have* to, and in doing so I'm being patient. That's an utter novelty to me – but if you think about it, probably a lesson well learnt. Well taught, too, because Levi ushered it with no words, and no intent.

I smile at him sheepishly. "Hello."

"Good evening, Skye."

"I thought I'd join you out here without invitation. You were looking lonely."

He blinks. "Oh?"

"I'm joking..." *Sort of.* "I'm waiting for Tristan, but I'm not going to do that inside any longer. Ember has a habit of imitating me, which is sweet, but..." *I think I see myself in her, a child many, many years my junior, way too much for comfort.* "But I guess I needed fresh air, too. He's spending the night here with us, did you know? Tristan. Or, not *here* here. We'll be on the roof, but what I'm saying is there's no need to go to the harbours with us tonight. Except you knew that already, didn't you, because I think I told you of it earlier?"

"Yes, you did."

I say stupid things in front of you. "Tristan is here. I can hear him a few streets over, as I'm sure you can...being the excellent listener that you are. I bet you he's stealing some kind of parchment. He always leaves little origami swans in the wagons he lifts from...folds them himself every night for the next day. Not sure if you noticed that, watching over us?" I hum fondly. "And I hope he's stealing food. I'm so hungry."

"I believe there's bread and wine in the kitchen."

"Mm..." *But it's not the same.* "Yeah, I know. I'll get you some if you want? Or you can share whatever Tristan steals?"

"I'm fine. Thank you."

"You sure?"

"Yes."

I examine him, wondering if that's an honest response. There's a long pause, only slightly stilted, before Levi goes back to resting against the wall, slouching a bit. Very rarely have I ever seen him sitting down, but I've noticed he does this quite often – rests against something whenever he can, as if he's fatigued or bone-weary from burden. The weight of grief? Or suffering injury from cruel hands who don't know when to stop, even when flogging a fifteen year old boy? Goddesses, both reasons make my heart ache so much for him.

"How're you feeling, Skye?" he asks to the silence.

"Good as the silver I stole last month," I lie brightly. "You?"

"I'm well, thank you."

What about *that* response? Do you believe it? I don't. Not after what was revealed the other night...and I'm not sure Levi believed mine, either. Those grey eyes are taking inventory of me, lingering on where my hands are holding their bundle of cloak. The knuckles of my right hand are still bruised, but the cut Xavier made is itchy and unbound, which means it's almost healed. That's weird, given how deep it was. Must be some sort of fun demigod power...but anyway, Levi is taking inventory of me, I think deciding for himself if I *am* good as silver instead of taking my words for truth.

That means he might doubt what I say.

Might realise I fib, quite often.

The lie just now was probably pointless, to be honest. Tomorrow, I'll be leaving my best friend indefinitely. I'll be losing my lifeline and my tether, the saving grace to my whirlwind of stormy thoughts and emotions, the steady shoulders I share *everything* with. I'll be leaving Tristan, and breaking my heart when I do...and I think Levi knows that.

I feel myself growing hot under his scrutiny and regret my decision to stand in front of him, because it goes both ways, doesn't it? He's reading me just as much as I am him, but I *lose* the game because I'm utterly hopeless at hiding anything from the world, least of all deep sentiment, and *he* is the best reader I'll ever know.

Which is the reason I came out here, isn't it?

I reach into the folds of my cloak and extract the book I stole from the library yesterday – the one on Metis and Zeus. I all but shove it at him, pushing it ungraciously into his stomach, mostly because I'm so *hot* under his studied gaze. He takes it, eyes bouncing questioningly between the tome and myself.

"Fjord mentioned you liked reading," I explain. "Said you read lots and lots of books."

Levi sounds and looks surprised. "Yes, I do like reading."

I nod, pleased. "This is a thank you, then. To you. For following me around Ioxthel for these past few months. I hope you don't mind it's stolen, although only from the Guild so it's not *really* stealing, and if you were against that kind of thing maybe that makes it better? It's still a gift, though. To say thank you. To you. And...I know it's small, compared to what you did, but it's quite good. Or, I *think* it is. I saw it was about Zeus and Metis, and I thought that would be good because Zeus is quite impressive, isn't he? Very mighty. So is Metis, I guess..." *Admittedly I don't know so much about her.* "I hope you enjoy it. Hope it's good. Thank you for everything, Levi. I'm really grateful."

I watch him flip the book over and examine the blank leather covers briefly, before he lets it fall open. I won't lie to you. I'm intrigued by what I see, because he's scouring the pages fast like he can't get enough of it already. Levi is something else, I'm quickly realising. Something else good and godly, gentle and grieving...and when his gaze finally lifts back to mine, it's less hollow than I've seen it before. Brighter and lighter, like his day *is* better for this – just liked I'd hoped back in the library.

"There was no need, Skye."

"I think given my behaviour early on there *was*, actually," I reply, and then I grin. Goofily. "*Or* maybe this is a ploy, and I'm buying your loyalty, like you said happens in Elysium? Maybe I'm bidding for your services. Except I know you've already sworn yourself to Fjord, and something tells me Guardians and their fealty are worth a bit more than just one stolen book. You told me the highest bidder usually wins the Guardian because you're so prized back home...so fealty is definitely worth more than one or even *two* stolen books. Especially yours."

"I...wouldn't be so sure."

"Really?"

He just stares at me.

"Well," I fidget a bit. "I hope you enjoy it."

"I've every belief I will."

"Honestly? I've no idea if it will be good, because I tried to read a few pages to check and..." *struggled.* "Well, I suddenly got *really* busy, you know? Had to just grab it from the library. Stuffed it up my shirt, too. So what I'm saying is if it's bad or boring please don't hold it against me. It's not my fault. It's the book's. Or the author's, or authoress's..."

Levi's eyes drop back to the open pages below. "I'm sure I won't find it bad or boring, Skye. Every book is worth the read."

"Yeah..." *I wouldn't know, because I never persevere long enough with them, but if you wanted to tell me your story, Levi, I'd listen. I'd wait to listen for it, because I think you're teaching me how to be patient.* "Can I ask you something?" I pipe up, trying to tame my voice into something calm. "Please?"

His gaze lifts. "Yes."

"Fjord told me some stuff the other night about..." *his brother, and the two of you being tethered, and the terrible things that happened to you for years because of it* "...how you're a very impressive Guardian. *Really* powerful. And weeks ago on the hilltop where Thetis's temple is ruined, I saw Zelos do the same as you did on the streets the other night. He glowed. Lit up. It was like he was made from rivers of gold, except yours were *silver.* I just wondered...if that's why Fjord calls you Silver? Why your eyes are grey, too?"

Levi's brow furrows, I think in bewilderment. "Well, I su—"

"Except those weren't the questions I meant to ask. I meant to ask you *why* you glowed, and what it is you do when you're like that, because I felt my own ichor responding to you, hailing you. I felt like bowing to you, to tell you the truth, because you were quite godlike. Very godlike. But...why were you silver and Zelos gold? *Those* are what I really wanted to ask. The other questions about your name and eyes were just extras. Sometimes I say the second ones first because my mind is weird like that, so I suppose you can pick what to answer, if you like? If you wanted to answer any, that is..." I heave a shallow breath, looking up at him very ruefully. "I'm sorry, Levi. I was trying to be really patient and measured when I started talking, but that didn't happen. I didn't mean to bombard you with *quite* so many questions. I just...sometimes I just talk. Rabbit on, because my mind is full of rabbit holes. We've been over that. How I talk for two, and more. This time I didn't mean to...and I'm sorry for it."

"Don't be sorry, Skye," he replies, a little distractedly. He takes a moment to gather his thoughts, and goddesses, you can't blame him after that spiel. "I don't know why I'm so powerful. It started when Fjord's brother was born, a few years after myself. He was the first to call me Silver, I suppose initially because of my surname, and then it stuck because of how I am when I summon my powers and request to use the strength of the gods and goddesses." He pauses to observe me, gaze pensive. "I'm not sure why you'd also have felt a summons in your ichor, or why you felt like bowing to me. I would never request that of you."

"No, I didn't *think* you would," I say quickly. "Ever. It was just strange, you know...?"

Levi looks like he doesn't quite know. He's still studying me closely, thinking on something I doubt he'll ever reveal.

"Uh...and your eyes?" I press hopefully. "Are they to do with you being silver when you ignite ichor?"

"I don't believe so. They run in my family, and I share them with my father, and younger brother."

"You have a brother?"

"Yes."

"What's he called?"

"William."

"Oh," I smile. "I like that name. Very handsome. Like you. Does he go by it? Or Will? I like Will, too. Maybe even more than William..."

"I believe he goes by Will these days."

I hum in interest. "I have one too, you know. I have a brother, but he's older and he's not called William. Or Will."

"Have...I met him? Your brother?"

"Yes. I think so. Quite a long time ago."

"I thought I might've done."

"Really?"

"Mm."

Levi's expression has softened. I realise he's playing along...except it's not really playing, not really a joke at all, and my heart feels quite full. My freaky amber eyes bounce frantically, happily, between his, and then I say *very* stupidly, "It's Fjord, Levi. I'm talking about Fjord being my brother, if you didn't know."

"I did know."

"Oh."

A beat passes, and then his lips also soften, lifting at the corners in a small smile. My eyes widen, because good goddesses, does that ever look utterly charming on him. Exquisite. I suddenly have an obsessive urge to hunt more of it down, to summon it fully into the world. It's quite obvious Levi doesn't smile often. I'm about to try when Tristan whistles from the roof of the safe house, hailing me up there. I look over quickly and wave, and immediately receive a very short, restless whistle in return...as if *he's* the one who's been waiting here for hours and not me.

"I'll see you tomorrow?" I ask, turning to Levi.

The smile is gone, if it was ever there to start with. He looks a little sombre when I move to leave, actually, and I've barely made it two steps before he calls my name with unusual suddenness.

"Skye?"

"Yes?"

I twist back *very* fast to face him, and the sight there just stops me. Would stop me forever. Levi offers little expression, but I somehow see every suggestion of him feeling something simply overwhelming.

"Thank you for not doing as Xavier wished with the hourglass the other night," he says. "For throwing it back to me. I am eternally grateful, and have been meaning to say so since the event."

"Oh...please don't *thank* me, Levi. If he hadn't got his hands on me you wouldn't have been forced to give it over in the first place. He'd never have known you stole it from him that night."

He shakes his head. "I do need to thank you, Skye. You risked your life in giving it back to me. I'm entirely indebted to you."

"I just...did it because it seemed important."

We stare at one another. I think he knows that Fjord told me some of his story the other night. Indeed, I think he must have authorised it, because no matter how grave the situation I doubt Fjord would've shared something so deeply personal without clearing it with Levi first. Still, neither of us has referenced it yet...

"I would do it again, Levi, if Xavier comes back for the hourglass. I won't let him have it. I'll help you with whatever troubles you need help with. Literally. You just need to tell me if you need it, then I'll give it to you. I swear on my life. I mean, if there's a fourth hourglass you need, I can steal that one too? No problem. No questions asked." *Lie.* "I'm really good at stealing, so if you need help I'm here waiting. I told Fjord that, and now I'm telling you...for about the fifth time. I'll be here waiting to help if you need it. I'm a very hopeful person too, Levi. There's lots of hope here, because I'm just...a ruffian full of hopes. Glass hopes in a glass heart that sometimes I'm worried I'll drop, but then I remember that unlike with everything else, I'm actually quite good at keeping them safe. And I'm good at finding them, too. Good at finding hopes, maybe especially for other people? So if you needed that, I can find you hope and bring it to you. Just...so you know. I'm your ruffian."

Incredibly, I could go on and on...but I force myself not to. Levi's mouth is slightly parted. I think he's struggling to know what to say back to my ridiculous spiel, and eventually he ends up ignoring the offers – or that's what he does outwardly, and verbally. *Physically* he reaches up and touches my cheek, then slips his fingers beneath my chin and tips it up so that our gazes meet.

I'm no longer breathing.

No longer thinking of glass hopes.

No longer even a little bit chilled out.

"You have my word and my honour that Xavier will never touch you again, Skye," he vows. "Please don't trouble yourself in thinking he might, or in thinking you'll ever be put in the same situation as a few nights ago. Ok?"

Dumbly, I nod.

He glances over my shoulder. "I won't delay you further. Your presence is requested elsewhere."

"It is?"

"Tristan."

Oh. Get it together! "Yeah. Tristan. Need to go to him."

He nods a little and drops his hand, but I don't move to leave. *Still* don't move to leave. Something unspoken is settling between us. It feels like respect, and understanding; a gratitude for our mutual friendship with Fjord, along with everything that springs from it, like the resolve to risk the wrath and violence of another by throwing back an hourglass in the pivotal scene of someone else's story, or like spending months forgoing the person you really wish to serve in order to walk beside a wilful, stubborn, insolent girl...a scarred wolf cub who happens to be prophesied to save the world, and haunts the secrets of the night under the silent guile of moonlight, thinking herself quite superior for it...even more so now she can see *real* ghosts. Or I guess it's just the one ghost I've seen, just the one time.

"See you tomorrow?" I suggest, to stop myself blurting this all out to him. And then, as if he'd damn well forget, "Remember? For the journey to The Cold Kingdom with Fjord and his team of guilders. Are you looking forward to it, Levi? I'm not. Not really. Don't want to leave Tristan. But are you? Looking forward to it? Goddesses, I bet you I'll fall."

Levi looks puzzled. "Fall for?"

"No. Off."

"Oh. Fall off...your horse?"

"Yep, probably on the first day. I've never ridden one seriously before. A horse. Never ridden one. I'll tell you now it's *not* because I'm scared of them. Not that."

"No?"

"Nope," I hum out a self-important sound. "I'm a demigod. We don't get scared, and we don't go into shock, either. Only fools think we do. Fools, horses...and silvery Guardians who like reading."

Just like earlier, when I was talking of his brother, I think Levi might look a little endeared by me. He's not smiling, and he's not offering me a very easy expression to decipher, *and* he probably doesn't think anything of that night on the streets with Xavier, when I was definitely in shock, is funny. Still, his eyes are lighter than usual – like clouds only half-inclined to snow. Like he finds me a *teeny* bit entertaining, or sweet. Not that I want to appear sweet in front of him, and not that I'd know what that image really looks like – clouds half-inclined to snow – having lived in Ioxthel for the entire life I remember. I've only ever known heat and drought, and the sun, although that's about to change, isn't it? We're travelling to Wivern, which will be cold, frosty and snowy. Admittedly, *some* of me is looking forward to experiencing that, but I just wish Tristan could be by my side.

"I should go, Levi. Be with Tristan. I'll see you tomorrow for the journey."

"You will, yes."

"Yes. I will."

Eloquence at its finest...and I'm *still* just standing here. Levi examines me, the ruffian king on the roof behind, then me again. Eventually, when I don't move and it becomes clear I'm not going to, he steps away from the wall and bows in farewell. "Good evening, Skye. Call for me if you need me throughout the night."

"You too."

"Me too..?"

"Yeah. If you need me, just whistle like a ruffian and I'll come running in and protect you. Guardian to Guardians and all that."

His eyes dip fleetingly, taking in all my tiny, overly-energetic glory. Slowly, his mouth tips up on one side. "Thanks."

"You're welcome."

I'm such an idiot. As if he needs protecting!

"And for the book, too," he adds, raising it a little. "Thank you."

"You're welcome, Levi. More than."

"Good evening."

"I'll see you."

I watch him walk back inside, utterly caught up on that small, charming smile, and wondering how *he's* the one leaving first when it's my best friend waiting on me; and when the entirety of my being is desperate to be in Tristan's arms to maximise the time we have left together.

There's just something about Levi, isn't there? Something about the guarded Guardian with weathered grey eyes and a story left untold, standing in humble prowess and silent honour and deep, unshakeable grief. Standing, more often than not these days, beside Fjord and I. And I should probably tell you, or you should probably already know by now, that this is just the start of it all. Of the stories, the journeys, the half-smiles, the glass hearts...the endeavours in finding hope.

This is just the start.

Acknowledgements

Thank you...

To you the reader, for embarking on Skye's journey with me. To Francesco for producing the portraits, cover art and mapwork (coming soon) for this book. I am so grateful for your time and talents, and really enjoy working with you. Thank you for your patience in helping bring this world and my imagination to life. Thank you also to Farjana for the book cover's lettering. You are so radiant, and kind. Finally, to my Tristans, Fjords, Sholtos and Melodies...my friends and family. You mean everything to me, and I love you.

About the Author

Alice Bamber, London. Lover of running, Golden Retrievers, cheese, wine, chickpeas and a good story. May or may not also befriend and surprise readers in very stupid but adorable ways.

https://www.alicebamber.com
https://www.instagram.com/alicebamber/

Printed in Great Britain
by Amazon

68593151R00281